BEDLAM

BEDLAM

Greg Hollingshead

THOMAS DUNNE BOOKS

St. Martin's Press ✠ *New York*

THOMAS DUNNE BOOKS.
An imprint of St. Martin's Press.

www.thomasdunnebooks.com
www.stmartins.com

Library of Congress Cataloging-in-Publication Data

Hollingshead, Greg, 1947–
Bedlam / Greg Hollingshead.—1st ed.
p. cm.
ISBN-13: 978-0-312-35474-9
ISBN-10: 0-312-35474-6
1. Bethlem Royal Hospital (London, England)—Fiction.   2. Psychiatric hospitals—Fiction.
3. London (England)—18th century—Fiction.   I. Title.

PR9199.3.H549B43 2006
813'.54—dc22
2006044416

First published in Canada by Harper*Perennial,* an imprint of HarperCollins Publishers Ltd

First U.S. Edition: September 2006

10 9 8 7 6 5 4 3 2 1

For R.S. and D.B.H.

Love is merely a madness; and I tell you,
deserves as well a dark house and a whip
as madmen do; and the reason why they
are not so punished and cured is, that the
lunacy is so ordinary that the whippers
are in love too.

—William Shakespeare, *As You Like It*

I'll tell it, cried Smelfungus, to the world. You
had better tell it, said I, to your physician.

—Laurence Sterne, *A Sentimental Journey*

MARGARET MATTHEWS

1797

ESCAPE

What woke me I don't know. His ragged breathing perhaps.

My first sight: two blood-encrusted hands outstretched above me, as in bene-diction, obscuring the face though not the nakedness. Yet I knew those hands as I knew the nakedness, or would have, except that above them gleamed a moonlit curve of shaved scalp.

My first thought: *Who does this tonsured priest think he'd exonerate before he climbs on?* But it was no priest, it was my own husband James, ascertaining my mental health by the magnetic condition of my head.

"Jamie! What happened to your clothes?"

"Sir Archy sold them."

"Who's he?"

"A monster of depravity. You're stripped on admission for delousing then tossed a blanket-gown to shiver in. Mine caught on the wall as I jumped down. I pelted it here naked—Mags?" He was finished his diagnosis of my head. "The signs aren't good. I never saw anybody so wide open for habitation." He rose from his crouch. "It's a good thing I'm out. I can take you back."

"To Bethlem?"

"Best madhouse in the kingdom. And Thomas Monro the best mad-doctor who ever lived." The pride he spoke this with seemed to offer testimony to how bad things had been for him there.

"Monro of Bethlem," I said.

"Physician in charge. Like his father and his father before him. And son af-ter, I'll wager."

"But Bethlem's not a private hospital, surely, to be run dynastically?"

When Jamie said no, it was not, and began a detailed account of the history and governance of Bethlem Hospital, I was too distressed to listen. Even when not in his right mind he was not one to miss a meaning. It was another sign how far Bethlem had pushed him. I was out of bed, lighting the lamp, the taper shaking in my hand. What to dress him in? It was February. He was blue-lipped, shivering so hard he could scarcely sound words. Who says the mad don't feel the cold? The problem was, the one outfit of trousers, shirt, and coat he'd not lost in France he'd had stolen in Bethlem.

"—though I never met him myself."

"Never met who?" I cried.

"Monro."

"They've kept you a month and you've not yet met the physician?"

"Not so much as his satchel."

He too now seemed struck by the admission. He rubbed at his neck. He was leaner by a good stone than I ever knew him, and in the lamplight I saw to my dismay that much of what I'd assumed to be smeared dirt was gashes and fresh blood studded with cinders. This would be from tumbles and scrapes on the way, though some of it might have happened inside, there was no way to know. Every day for the past three weeks I had been to the gates, but they wouldn't let me in, saying he refused to see me and blamed me for his incarceration. And yet for the first week after he was admitted I had no idea of his whereabouts, and even began to fear he'd gone to France, for a fifth time. It was not until I received a letter from the clerk of Bethlem Hospital, a Mr. Poynder, saying my husband was now their patient at the expense of Camberwell Parish, that I knew where he was.

"It's only the apothecary sees me," Jamie said.

"The apothecary? Isn't he just a nostrum-seller?"

"Not this one. He doses us all right, but he also runs the place. John Haslam. I call him Jack the Schoolmaster, because he's inhabited. He's new there, only eighteen months, very capable, yet there's something about him. His vault to Apothecary of Bethlem has made him king, but is it only of a dunghill? And what of all these responsibilities dumped on him when he has no say in treatment and no authority to discipline the keepers? Yet why should he have? Who but a low-born, impoverished, uncredentialed medical man would choose the profession of mad-doctor? Though he's undergone training aplenty—at St. Bartholomew's, Edinburgh, Uppsala, and Cambridge—he's come away with no medical degree. This in itself is no mystery when you realize he couldn't afford one and, if he could, lacks the advantages of breeding necessary to assemble a lucrative practice. Why pay for what won't? He's one of those who speaks his mind, if only you could tell what he was thinking as he did it. He's an article of clothing you're drawn to in the shop, but you can't be sure if it's in the best taste or the worst. All you know is how struck you are by it and, if you ever wore it in public, you'd create a wonderful stir, but you have no idea what kind of stir it would be."

As Jamie talked, it was articles of clothing I was piling in his arms. He sniffed at them.

"Please put them on," I said and crossed to the wardrobe, to dress myself.

When I looked over at him, I saw the black-bloody footprints he'd tracked from the bedside, and clearer than before, because he'd shuffled round to watch me and was now full-lit by the lamp, I saw the grim state of his wounds. "Dear God, Jamie! You've butchered your feet! And your knees and arms too—they're bleeding pulps!"

He set the clothes on the bed and cautiously lifted one elbow, then the other, peering at them. "From coming over the Bethlem wall," he explained. "Did you know pineapples once adorned it? A few yet remain, I'll show you. It's because you need to be a monkey to climb up, and then it's such a long fall you think you'll never land, you think you've been excused, you think, *Flight! Am I bird now?* and that's when you're smashed by such a terrific force of gravel and frozen earth you think you'll never rise again."

I took the clothes from my poor madman to help him dress.

He refused to lift his arms.

"Jamie, what is it?"

"This is my old friend Robert Dunbar's shirt. I know the stripe."

"Jamie, we've talked about this. You understand what happened. I've never betrayed you, you know that."

"It won't fit," he said, not listening. "The pants less."

"We'll roll the cuffs."

"And roll with them too, right, Mags?"

"But the boots won't fit you."

"Nor mine ever Robert Dunbar."

RETURN

Did you ever notice, dear Reader, the readiness with which people will fall in love with a variation upon the one thing (whether they know it or not) they're unhappiest with in themselves? And so they match noses. Or he's been feeling the slide of discipline from his life, when along comes a female sergeant-major. Or desperate to feel herself as virtuous as she might compared to the vilest scoundrel in the room, does she resist his advances? People say, How can she be with him, they're night and day? But night and day make twenty-four hours. Day pines for shade and night for definition. Each completed by the other becomes more assuredly what it is. Human love is a symptom not that we are imperfect but how wretched we are to know it. Those who don't know it or can't face that misery will pour their love on a horse, lapdog, or parakeet, saying, *Polly won't leave me,* when they themselves departed long ago.

Does this then make me, who love my mad husband, one who needs to know she is sane? We were married six years before his brilliance first tipped to delusion. Now that it has, I would say the reason my love for him has not fled but grown is not that his illness was what I was looking for all along but because sane he's always showed himself a man of surpassing sympathy and loved me constantly, and now that he sometimes raves I love him as a helpless child does a parent or a helpless parent a child: either way stunned by the emotion of that inadequacy.

After Jamie's return from his three years' detention in France, we lived for ten months, if it was possible, happier than we did for the seven years before the project of saving his country first took him to Paris. Happy as people grateful to have again what they'd feared forever lost. The only thing we needed now was a family, and for ten months we did everything a man and woman can do to become parents. Meanwhile, we were happy as any loving couple who by dint of hard steady work have achieved a middle station in life and must work ever harder to keep it.

In Jamie's three years' absence, though I could blend and package tea with the best of them, I didn't, being a woman, get far at the East India Company auctions and so could do nothing to stop the eventual collapse of our wholesale business. In desperation, and with assistance from Jamie's old friend Robert Dunbar, I took it retail, not knowing how little breathing space under the ice the East India Company monopoly would allow for the little shop in tea. So Jamie's first task back was to carve us out something again on the wholesale side, to afford us the luxury of selling to customers off the street.

Though Jamie's schooling in Camberwell finished at age ten when his father—in summer a digger of graves and ditches and in winter a cutter of pond ice—died of the cholera and his mother moved to Spitalfields for labour in the silk-works, he's a talker to everybody and a reader of everything, with a mind so nakedly attuned to every facet of life that the risk is overstimulation unto mania. One day his understanding's so sensitive he could be reading your thoughts, the next he's off chasing a will-o'-the-wisp. If I hoped to see my husband returned safe to Bethlem Hospital while he raved I must join him in the fantasy he was the one taking me there. But my feet in their winter shoes felt they had lead weights strapped to them as, wrapped tight in my quilt coat against the cold, I trailed behind, him striding in his unshod, butchered feet up St. Mary Axe and so along Wormwood Street in the hour before dawn, the moon a medallion time-worn imperfect and streaming high before us, the air præternatural in its clarity, the streets empty, the city stones dew-burnished and glowing paler in the quickening dawn.

How I love London when the meanest street has such a blessing of first light upon it that it might be a broad pavement in newest, grandest, westernmost Mayfair; when the old woman collecting dog dung for the tanners is not a gin-blasted hag but a white-haired grandmother plucking mushrooms in a flag-stone meadow; when the tattered heap in the doorway is not a desolated ruin of humanity but rags for the dustman, who'll be along directly; when the fetid smoke of the grease lamp that lights the oyster barrow, in the first confused instant it reaches your nostrils, might be incense from the Orient, and the monger is not a half-naked urchin shivering with cold and disease but a flashing-eyed Gipsy youth with a life before him.

But he's not and it's not, and my husband is not always sane, as I'd known by his increasing erratic conduct since '89, when the Paris mob stormed the Bastille, affecting the sensitive balance of his mind, for he began to think there was something he could do for England, though *what* kept changing as Revolution went from freedom for the French people to the guillotine and blood in the streets, to the execution of their King and war with us. And now in order to get him out of Bethlem soon, I needed to know the particulars of the circumstance that had got him in. While I had long understood there was nothing I could do to stop my husband's mania when it grew full-blown, I also knew his welfare at such times was nobody's first concern but my own.

"Did you try to see Mr. Pitt, the Prime Minister?" I asked him. "This isn't about France again, is it?"

"No, that would be politics. This is truth, which Pitt, who is now politics through and through, can no longer hear. Four years ago he'd see me anytime, but last month his office denied me. So did his cousin Lord Grenville, the foreign secretary, though his man on the door treated me with such humanity I embraced the dry bundle of his bones in his shabby greatcoat, which amazed him. He stood and watched me go. But once I put the corner between us, it was anchors aweigh to Hertford Street."

"What's there?" I asked. I was not humouring him. He was capable of anything.

"Home of The Dark Lanthorn."

"Who's that?"

"Lord Liverpool. They call him The Dark Lanthorn because he gives off no light."

"But who is he? I never heard of him."

"You will. He's Baron Hawkesbury, lately honorificked by Pitt. As Hawkesbury he once listened, remember? Five years ago, when I was our government's chief secret liaison with France? I imagined as Lord Liverpool he might listen again. Oh, he *listened*."

"Was it him called the authorities?"

"I think not. But he tried to set the coal-man against me, for it was his cellar stairs I was obliged to enter by. Except, it turned out the coal-man was a secret republican and concluded I must be another after he heard me assure his Lordship I was at open war with him and his apostles in treason and swear I would see his head on a pike above Temple Bar."

"No! I thought Hawkesbury was somebody you admired!"

"Not since the truth he's a traitor has dawned, and I told him as much."

"Oh Jamie, you can't say these things to their faces!"

"The coal-man seemed to like what he heard. He carried a pistol in his black sack and wanted me to come to a meeting to plot attacks on the King. I didn't go."

"That's something."

"You forget, Mags, my true cause has always been the brotherhood of man. I never sought harm to the King. It was only in the early days, when I still had hopes of The Dark Lanthorn and my hero was the republican David Williams, that peaceable Revolution seemed to offer a way forward. It had a future look about it, and had perhaps only come a little premature in America and France."

David Williams I knew from six and seven years before, when he used to come to the house to tutor Jamie in radical politics. I remembered his shining blond hair, which he wore fastened behind with a neat ribbon in black or grey, the sombreness a sop, I suppose, to suspicions of vanity. As he'd slip past me on his way to the parlour (where Jamie waited with his notebook and a thousand questions), I was put in mind of a cat in a gold hairpiece. The stealthy *froideur* I ascribed to the perils to which the high-minded must be constantly exposed. Though genteel and peaceable, as author of the anti-denominational *Liturgy on the Universal Principles of Religion and Morality* for the use of re-publicans, Williams had as many enemies among clerics as among the powerful in government. Given his enlightened principles, not to mention Jamie's awe and love of him, he had to be more sympathetic than he seemed, or perhaps would have been were he not preoccupied by grave international concerns that precluded acknowledging the simpering wife of a tea-broker he tutored two hours a week because he needed the money.

At that time, war with France was not yet declared. Then late in November 1792 French gunboats weighed anchor in the River Scheldt and headed for Antwerp to seize that city in the name of the French people. As Prime Minister, Pitt responded by descending hard here at home, declaring a state of emergency that allowed him to recall Parliament early, mobilize the militia, visit severities on aliens, prosecute republican works, find Tom Paine guilty *in absentia* of sedition, etc. In the midst of these hammer-blows by a government fearful of radicals, Jamie slipped away to Paris, where Williams had gone the week before to help his friend Brissot and the Girondin faction of the French government draft a new French constitution, on solid republican principles.

My husband's goal, somewhat different from his teacher's, was to prevent the chaos uncorked in France from foaming across the Channel and destroying English liberty. This he'd achieve by offering himself as negotiator representing Lord Liverpool—at that time still Baron Hawkesbury—and others in government to stop the outbreak of war by an honourable peace. But to his grief and amazement, though he took care to book himself at the same Paris hotel, Williams declined to introduce him to any French authorities, or for that matter even to meet with him—though the fact Jamie wasn't invited along in the first place might have told him his mentor had doubts about his readiness for work in the field.

"But how," I asked, "did you come against the authorities in such a way as to get you in Bethlem?"

For some minutes a dray had been approaching behind us, and now came the squeak of its axles and the deafening cobblestone clatter of its iron tyres. Jamie held his answer until the racket diminished. Meanwhile he watched the horse, which turned its blinkered head as it passed to watch him.

"From Hertford Street," Jamie said, "I hastened direct to the public gallery of the House. There the gang (by a method I haven't yet discovered) stifled Lord Erskine for the Opposition. After declaring we'd been seduced into war by the Monarchy, Erskine opened his mouth, evidently to utter the entire heinous truth of what the Ministry had been up to—"

Was this gang who stifled Erskine the same one Jamie had talked about before, when he was raving? "Jamie, what heinous truth?"

"No, Mags. The burden of it would be too great for you at this precarious juncture in your affairs."

"Jamie, tell me. You know I'm like you: I must know what's what."

He only held up his hand and continued. "However the gang did it, Erskine fell back in his seat too thunderstruck to go on. This required Fox, as Leader of the Opposition, to take over, which he did, all impromptu scruff and bluster, lamenting the rashness and injustice of his Majesty's ministers and calling our war with France a war of passion and prejudice, not policy and self-defence— but in this saying nothing everybody didn't already know.

"I slouched home dejected. Was this all the truth the nation could bear?

"But the next time Liverpool spoke in the House, which was January, I made sure I was back to hear him drone on, saying (while scarcely taking his eyes off me) the French never desired peace and never showed any interest in negotiation, rhetorically asking why, if they were dissatisfied with our proposals, didn't they bring forward some counter-proposal of their own? By such lies I was filled to bursting with the traitorous venality of him and monsters like him—"

"Why? What did they do? Are there French counter-proposals you've learned of that they ignored?"

"When I was centre-stage in the game there were—"

"But that was four years ago and more! Four years of war! Why do you say Liverpool was lying?"

"Because he lied then and is lying now—"

"How do you know?"

"Don't doubt me, Mags. Last month, believe me, he was covering tracks so vile I was left no choice but to leap from my seat shouting over and over, *Treason*!"

"Jamie, no! You'll be hanged!"

"Not yet. But they did want me out of there. When I resisted, a scuffle ensued. The next time I opened my eyes I was in a workhouse at Tothill Fields. After a week as a guest of that rigour, I was hauled before the Privy Council, which for the first fifteen minutes was three men and a clerk coughing and shuffling papers in an ill-lit room somewhere in that rabbit-warren disgrace to our nation, Parliament House. The Duke of Portland entering made four. Four against one. As the playwright Nat Lee once said of his own case, *They called me mad and I called them mad, and damn them, they outvoted me.* In their wisdom, the Privy Council predicted the figuration of my thinking better served by Bethlem than Tothill Fields. So it has been, but it's turned out only a visit. Did I tell you my counsel's Lord Erskine himself, as a noted former defender of madmen and republicans? He'll see the Government pays me for my services.

"Meanwhile, Mags, it's you they want in, for your sympathies, and believe me, the opportunity won't soon come again. Did you know they'll give you straw to sleep on only if you grow so dirty or senseless as not to be fit to make use of a proper bed? And did you know it's a strict rule with the keepers they'll beat you only upon absolute necessity for your better government? I tell you, the William Batties and other mad-doctor critics of it can say what they like, there's no place on earth like Bethlem Hospital."

By this time we were coming west along London Wall, approaching a stretch where you can look up and see the windows of the cells on Bethlem's second and attic stories. Somebody's blanket-gown hung from the bars of a window, and that enigmatic thing glowed blush-pink against the bricks in the predawn. God knows what some poor soul was sleeping in. A sad and sloven place, Bethlem, and no less that morning for being in a state of eerie quiet. Once the day starts up, the wails and cries of the inmates arise in answer to the mounting bedlam of the city: a chorus of lunacy that makes a fitting commentary on our modern age. But Bethlem in silence is even more terrible, like a house when the witch has stopped dancing.

Though our route should have taken us north up Broker Row along the eastern reach of the Bethlem buildings, Jamie led me past that junction to indicate three Bethlem doors opening directly into London Wall. The nearest, reached by stone steps, was, he told me, the main entrance to the house of the apothecary Haslam, the one he calls Jack the Schoolmaster, who so intrigues him. A short distance along was the door to Haslam's office, and next to that was the gate to the Bethlem vaults. For some reason, these nondescript portals were of surpassing interest to my husband, and as I stood and waited, he devoted scrupulous attention to each. All were shut and featureless; the two at street level had a greasy band at hip level from a century of idlers.

Having fully examined the three doors, Jamie pointed to a row of houses immediately across the road: dreary, sealed-up affairs, martyrs to the government tax on windows. I wondered what he wanted me to see.

"A gang of seven has headquarters in a cellar over there," he said. "I only wish I knew which house."

The gang again. "What kind of gang? Pickpockets?"

My question was met with a remote, cautioning look, as you'd give a child who has no idea what she's just said. "Nothing so humdrum, Mags. Nasty pluckskulls is more like it. The cellar connects to an ancient subterranean route out of the city under London Wall. In the last century, when this, the new Bethlem, was under construction, the workers being infiltrated by them—"

"By who?"

"The gang—connected Bethlem's cellars to this one. That's why today their Air Loom influence extends into every part of the building." He paused, as for questions.

"Air Loom," I said. It was a contraption he'd mentioned before. Though he once told me an account of it is to be found in Dr. Rees' 1783 edition of *Chambers' Dictionary* under "Loom," and an engraved plate of it under "Pneumatics," I didn't see it there the one time I looked. From what he says, it resembles a great desk with drawers and is powered by magnetized vapours (that is, what men of science now call *gases*) from putrefaction constantly underway in hooped barrels. It has whirligig windmills, tubes, keys, levers, and other attachments above (some very indistinct), and a hidden chamber below, which Jamie complains he can't see into.

"A terrible device," he affirmed. "In the *Annual Register* for October '91, Mags, there's an interesting account of the Clyde River in Scotland overflowing its banks, water soon filling the cellars of adjacent houses. As soon as it reached the basement of the Town's Hospital, in Glasgow, the raving fell quiet and so revealed the true secret of these places: the rising water forced the gang working that madhouse to abandon their subterranean Air Loom post. During their absence, the lunatics, being temporarily unassailed, grew calm and composed. Became, in other words, themselves again."

"Jamie—"

"There's one of the gang, Mags, I have a particular interest in. Her name is Charlotte."

"What kind of interest?"

"Not that kind. She's a filthy creature but with a knack of probing my vitals. She speaks French, but in a queer English idiom. Though prone to call a spade a bloody shovel, and kept naked and chained by Sir Archy, she's an excellent recorder of everything they do. In all, a steady, persevering sort of one. How much a slave to Sir Archy she is is open to question. She knows what she's doing and will only say she can't help herself. Which pretty much sums up her case. As for Sir Archy, a thorough molly he may or may not be, but one thing's clear: he don't like women."

"Would this be Sir Archy, the monster of depravity?"

"It would. Known to others as Alavoine, the steward. As with Jack the Schoolmaster, who inhabits Haslam, I don't as yet have the whole story on him, Charlotte, and the rest, but I will."

"Haslam the apothecary is part of the gang?"

"You could put it that way. But how much he knows is a good question.

They're a singular stripe of villain. In their nasty way, far more insinuating than Clyde water, I assure you."

His smile as he said this resembled a fanatic's. At the same time, it shook me to see how much in his friend Robert Dunbar's too-big clothes he resembled a child playing at grown-up, and along with these likenesses came the horror of where we were and what we were about to do.

What had I been thinking? How could I for one second consider returning my husband to such a place? "Jamie," I whispered, and stopped, trembling, in my tracks. "We must not come here. We must go back home, now."

He stared at me. "Why would we do that, Mags? After trudging all this distance?"

"It's a terrible destination!"

"No more than what's on the way. The residents of Bethlem are the most human people on earth. It's a college where the scholars arrive already broken. They make the best kind." He was stretching out his hand. "We'll still have our visits. If you do everything they say and slip Sir Archy something for his trouble, he'll leave us alone now and then a half-hour in the visiting room, where we can be as lewd as we please. You'll be let out as soon as you're showing."

"Oh Jamie—!"

Though I moved to embrace him, he stepped back out of reach, tilting his head to regard me. "You must be mad, Mags," he said quietly, "to love a madman like me."

"You're not so!" I cried. "Not at heart! Only sometimes! They do this to you!"

"What do they do?"

"Chase you down! Put you in this place!"

"Not this time. This time it was me chased them down. For nonpayment of services rendered, among uglier crimes. And now I've chased you down. Please, Mags. The company of my like can't be good for your health. Especially if you intend to be a mother—"

Did he know, then? It would be just like him to know—

"You see, Mags," he continued gravely, "the time has come again for me to ensure the survival of two nations. But operations have now switched to the realm of the mental, and you, as a woman of too refined intelligence for such horrors, require the security of a madhouse."

"Jamie, my home's with you!"

He shook his head. "Only lately again, and didn't these past ten months slip away on us pretty quick?"

He brushed past me and started back toward Broker Row. Over his shoulder he said, "It's better this way, but nothing's certain. The rule is, you must be mad less than one year before you go in, and if they can't cure you, it's out again after a year. Unless, of course, you qualify for the incurable wing, in which case they keep you for good. It's not just anybody's admitted, and fewer still are allowed to stay. I'm saying we can't count on anything. There are stories of people fighting twenty years to get a loved one in here."

When he stopped and turned, I was perhaps ten feet behind, following with the greatest reluctance. I didn't know what to do for my poor husband and never did in the six or seven years he'd been suffering these episodes. All I'd learned was, if excessive energy of mind exacts a toll on the man himself, those who dwell in its borrowed light pay too.

"Is this Saturday?" he asked, waiting for me to catch up.

I had to think. "Yes—" and then remembered and said silently, *Justina, pray open the shop. Please don't let us lose the business of a Saturday.* Reluctant to expose Jamie's confusion to our maidservant, I had let her sleep through his return. But what if she didn't open the shop?

"Good." He was walking again, me following, up Broker Row. "The committee of four or five governors meets Saturday mornings to view all applicants—"

"Did they view you?"

He stopped again and looked around at me, surprised. "No—"

"Why not?"

"The keepers did it all. I was roughly used."

"Where were the governors?"

"Maybe it wasn't a Saturday."

"Maybe it wasn't a lawful incarceration."

Jamie nodded at this, though he seemed doubtful. He resumed walking. "As I was saying, those they consider a fit object they sign in on the spot. In your case, I'll be there in person to give bond, to whit, if you're released alive I'll come and get you. If dead, I'll take charge of your burial. That would be after Jack the Schoolmaster opens your head to examine the cause of your madness."

"Jamie," I asked, "why are you in at the expense of Camberwell Parish? Why would so poor a parish enter into a hundred-pound bond to put you here?"

He looked over his shoulder at me, seeming surprised at this information. "You mean it wasn't you paying?" Again he stopped to think. "Camberwell could mean the Ministry intended me for a longer stay." He started walking again. "Why would they change their mind?"

"They didn't! You escaped!"

He made no sign he heard.

I hastened to catch up. "Jamie, why did you refuse to see me?"

"Did it come to refuse?" He was still walking, not looking at me.

"I was there every day! The porter wouldn't let me in!"

"Alf Bulteel? Did you give him a penny?"

"He took everything I gave him! Sometimes he said it was not visiting hours and sometimes he said you refused to see me!"

"Visiting hours is ten to twelve of the morning, Monday and Wednesday. Did he tell you that?"

"I found it out myself. It didn't help."

"He should have wrote you out a ticket. Never mind. He'll write one for me when I visit you."

Now we were coming into the Common Passage, which runs between the front wall of Bethlem and the open ground of Moorfields, or I should say what's left of it, after the squalid creep of houses and shops. As we rounded the corner, Jamie gestured upward, and sure enough, at the top of a wall-post, a stone pineapple. Also of note about that front wall: set in it every fifth panel is a barred section, so passers-by might gaze upon the building it otherwise obscures. Gaze and tremble. I glanced through the bars of one section as we passed it but was too distraught to see what I looked at. Up ahead, Jamie pointed out what appeared to be a threadbare sheet with a great rend in it, snagged high on the wall. "That's where I came over," he said. "To land naked as from my mother's loom."

"Womb," I corrected him.

He wasn't listening.

Soon we arrived at the right-hand everyday entrance by the main gates. At this hour its iron door was locked shut. Here for the past three weeks I had been daily told by the porter Bulteel—a scrofulous animal done up in a sky-coloured gown and gripping his great silver-tipped staff as a bully holds his truncheon—that Mr. Matthews wanted no visitors. This morning the beast was nowhere in evidence, but Jamie soon changed that by stepping up to the main gates and directing through the bars several stentorian *Hallos* and *Rouse up theres,* and suddenly everything was happening very fast. A door of the hospital to the right of the main ones, not more than forty feet from where we stood, flung open and the beast itself emerged stumbling unhatted, one arm caught in the sleeve of its coat, trousers undone, to weave and stagger cursing across the pavement toward us.

I tugged at Jamie's arm. When he turned to me, his expression was not, as I expected, stubborn calm—the beast's eruption only what he'd been after—but incredulous terror. "That's not Alf Bulteel," he whispered. "It's a French agent, disguised as him."

"Jamie, we don't need to be here—" I was struggling to extract his fingers from the gate.

But the beast had sent up a roar, another ruffian in blue was cannonading out that same door, and Jamie was peering to see who that one was. Tremulously, not looking at me, gripping the bars with whitened knuckles, he whispered, "This other's a French agent too. He only seems like the one they call Rodbird, though he's really The Middleman, by a clever impersonation of the gendarme who did me violence in '95, who it happens Rodbird bears a resemblance to—"

Now came the true nightmare part, for such moments of crisis are apt to ignite Jamie's wildest delusions. As I struggled to unhook his fingers, his head swivelled from the advancing brutes to me, except it wasn't me he saw but more French agency. *Lâche-moi, Charlotte! Salope française!* he gasped, starting back. In doing so, he let go of the bars, and I was able to yank him away across the gravel into the sheep-stubble of Moorfields, the snowdrops (I remember this so clearly) just beginning to pierce the cold earth, past the pond in the direction of Field Lane, thinking if I could get us safely lost in that shambles of tents and goods-stands. But with Jamie's butchered feet on the uneven ground and his reluctance to go anywhere with a French whore, and him hobbled as well by Dunbar's unrolling cuffs, our progress was stumbling. The men in pursuit of us, though hardly specimens of physical health, once they got through the gate were soon upon us. The one who'd come second out of the building threw himself at Jamie and brought him down hard, while I spun round to aim kicks at his kidneys as he pinned my husband making grabs at my legs until the old porter came panting up to dance lumbering between us, using his staff for a barrier. Not long after, the other muttered in a voice of sullen resignation, "Give us your stick, Alf." As the porter reached it back to him, I tried to go round on the other side, but his arm hooked me and drew me close. It was with my face pressed against his stinking gown that I heard the sickening blow, and another, and another.

"Devil bastards!" I moaned, "Sweepings of Hell!" and coarser epithets—sailor coarse—while the porter continued to muffle me to him, as he heaved for breath.

"I beg your pardon, madam," he managed, once he'd retrieved his stick and let me go, advising, "Stay clear now—"

And so we were set marching, as the one called Rodbird, a grim-beaked facetious individual, in a nasal tang befitting his hawk countenance, addressed poor Jamie (who tottered before him, head streaming with blood, dazed and lost), calling him his *Little Fly-Coop* and his *Wee Darling Home Pigeon,* and other grimly jesting endearments, as he pulled him to his feet and pushed him in the direction of the gates. And when Jamie stumbled and would fall, Rodbird clutched the back of his shirt—Robert Dunbar's shirt—and half-carried, half-marched him before him, and when I angrily demanded to know what right they had to seize and beat my husband, "By his right to be where he belongs," Rodbird advised over his shoulder. "Straight back up his own arsehole."

Too soon we arrived at the gates, which stood open. The porter, who until now had not let go of my arms, rotated me away and gave me a shove, and the gates clanked and were locked even as I threw myself against them. And so it was now my turn to shout through the barrier as they supported him one at each shoulder in the fashion of soldiers a dazed and stumbling prisoner as they escort him to his execution.

HASLAM

For some good time after Jamie was taken into the building and the doors slammed shut, I called out that I was his next of kin and had given no consent for his confinement and must speak to someone in charge. I shouted until I was hoarse, and still no one came back out and no life stirred in the hundred and more windows I could see as far east and west as the building stretched. Black pits, all, except for the ones on the ground floor nearest the gate, which had been boarded up, as if to prevent direct communication of visitors with those within. At last, my voice ravaged, I sank down in bitter abjection, my back against the bars. It was then I saw my commotion had attracted a coterie of the sort as might indicate not all Bethlem's lunatics, once discharged, wander far.

A snag-toothed young woman who leaned on a crutch informed me without preliminaries, "Saturdays Bulteel don't take up his post till past nine-thirty."

"What time is it now?" I asked.

"Not nine," someone offered.

"Not nine," a child with the haggard look of a dying sweep put in, "on account of it ain't eight."

I nodded and several nodded back.

In the quiet you could hear the dawn hubbub of London Wall and from across the way in Field Lane the clamour of the shopkeepers as they opened for trade.

"When does the committee arrive that sees to Saturday admissions?" I next inquired of my on-lookers.

I might as well have asked them the best means to determine the longitude at sea, for they only continued to look at me. But not for long. Soon a head among them bound in greasy rags, of a sort more often seen washed up on the banks of Fleet Ditch, revolved toward a scarlet rim of light along the eastern rooftops. Now we were all looking, for the sun rises faster than you can ever believe, and so it did, a ball of molten scarlet adhering a moment to that rickety horizon before lifting clear. We were still looking when footsteps sounded at my back. Twisting where I sat, I saw a man in a snuff-coloured coat crossing the forecourt toward me.

No more than Jamie had I ever set eyes on the famous Dr. Monro, or any picture of him. Yet, imagining this must be him, I scrambled up, watching him as best I could with a green sun bouncing before my eyes. Still coming on, he held up a key to mean he'd let himself out and we'd talk. When I nodded, he offered a guarded smile before his eyes returned to the pavement in front of him. I stood up and brushed myself off.

In John Haslam—for that's who this was, not Monro, physician of the place, but Haslam, the apothecary—there was something right away familiar to me, though I could not at first tell what it was. The man I watched approach was of middle age, somewhat stout but not heavily so. I don't think it was the cut of his frock coat that gave him the look of one whose spine contained an extra vertebra, with the consequence his legs appeared shorter than they were. In fact, Haslam stood well above the middle height, but that hint of top-heaviness made him seem not yet fully grown. There was also an exuberance of energy, like that of one who's received an unexpected boon, or of a boy still inside his bubble of perfection's hope, in the way he came striding out to me, though the closer he came, the more that hope seemed fraught with an adult perplexity bordering on outrage, mysterious amidst so much innocence or vitality or vanity of life.

In all this, as I say, he reminded me of something, or somebody.

By now he'd passed out of view and stood in shadow on the other side of the right-hand iron door. He then fumbled so long with the lock I thought he must have picked up the wrong key. When he first reached the door, I walked over to wait directly the other side of it, but when the fumbling grew interminable I was reluctant to discountenance him further by waiting so immediately upon the site of his embarrassment. So I walked back to where I had been, wondering if you need to be a woman to be squeamish about the feelings of a stranger it would appear you have every reason to hate.

At last he got the lock to turn and came wincing into the full blast of the rising sun, shutting the door behind him. I made a step toward him, but my ragged crew crowded past me. With a glance of apology at me he paused to shake their hands and listen to their complaints, now and then offering solace in a manner amiably gruff. For their part, they were gratified by his attention and pleased to apprise him of their continuing afflictions.

The apothecary's face was common in a memorable way. It was the sort a skilled painter would situate in a crowd scene just so, to galvanize his canvas. The hair was brown with auburn lights, fine and thick, receding at the temples and lying disordered against the skull. It was unpowdered, but you don't see much powder nowadays, and lack of it certainly no longer signifies your monarchy-loathing republican. The side whiskers, not in good trim, were long and large, the nose a lordly flute of a proboscis, or would have been lordly on a face that, though evidently shaved once this morning, was not already sordid with black shadows.

But a stronger feature still than the nose, and one that militated against this being mistaken for the face of a nab, I mean well born, was the mouth, which had too much expression about it for a gentleman's. A droll mouth, yet one capable, you immediately knew, of forming and saying hard things.

Abruptly he broke from his suppliants, telling them he was sorry, he must excuse himself, he had business with that woman over there.

Which was me. We made our introductions. "Your humble obedient servant, madam—"

"Mr. Haslam, your bullies have no right to seize and beat my husband."

"Did they? Was he trying to escape?"

"Yes, because he doesn't want to be here."

"He didn't go far—"

"He came home to me! Leadenhall Street! That's pretty far!"

"Then returned and hung on the gate?"

I hesitated. The truth was too mad. "He wanted me to see where he was prisoned."

"A consideration that has got him in again, and the problem now is, any release of patients must be sanctioned by the governors' subcommittee—"

"That meets today."

"I'm afraid they won't get to your husband today—"

"They? I thought you sat on that committee—"

"From time to time. Would this be the Matthews who insists on the *Tilly?* James Tilly Matthews? Tilly, what is that? Huguenot? So he's French on one side? His mother a Spitalfields silkweaver?"

"Yes—"

"And Welsh father? Interesting. Good. Well. Now we've got that far, why's he with us?"

I was stunned. "You don't know?"

"Nobody's told me, and he refuses. All I know is his trade, which is teabroker, and a story of how he's preventing French chaos here by doing battle with a gang of French magnetic fluid-workers responsible for all madness in this hospital. Ever since he discovered the existence of this gang and others, his energy has gone into opposing what he calls their *event-working.* Their response has been to have him labelled insane and so rendered harmless, for in here, he says, every word he speaks against them is chalked as another symptom—"

"He told me he's in by an order of the Privy Council. He also mentioned Lord Portland—"

"Your husband's never spoke of Lord Portland to me, and the only kind of privy he's mentioned is the close-stool kind, how the stinking condition of ours is an insult to the nostrils of a gentleman, and how a dusty vapour he calls Egyptian snuff overcomes him, conveyed by the gang from Nile marshes in August heat, when stagnant pools emit their nauseous stench. Mind you, it's also such vapours as Egyptian snuff; effluvia of arsenic, sulphur, and dogs; gas from the anuses of horses; and vapours of human seminal fluids, both male and female, all harnessed in barrels, that power his Air Loom—"

"Mrs. Matthews, we don't exactly comb the streets. Most people can bellow at the gates as much as they like. This is not a private madhouse that must solicit patients of paying families. As to your husband, I would say he's a republican—"

"He's not!" *At least, no longer—*

"—in a condition of nervous collapse. Unable to vent his politics for risk of being hanged, he talks nonsense. Whatever the particulars of his initial admission, he's hied himself back to safety inside the finest madhouse in the world. He's a lunatic who knows exactly what he's doing, and while he goes about it, your duty as his concerned spouse is to ensure your visits have a calming effect."

"I've tried to visit him ever since I found out he was in here! The porter won't let me pass!"

This appearing to contradict my claim Jamie had brought me to see where he was kept, Haslam just looked at me. Then he said, "He's willing to see you?"

"The porter says not. I say he's lying!"

"Why would he lie? You know, it often happens the patient feels betrayed by those that put him in here—"

"I didn't put him in here!"

"Is your husband clearer about that than I am?"

"I want him out."

"No more than do I. If it was up to me, all but the dangerous ones would be out today. Back to the attic, the stake in the yard, or the hole in the floor with the crib over it. Harmless ones lacking homes to go to could be Tom o' Bedlam again, with his metal armclip licence to beg. But who can wind back the clock? Nowadays, once the mad exhaust the tender mercies of their families, they come, if they're lucky, here to Bethlem Hospital, where for a little while we treat their suffering, before we push them out again, cured or uncured, because we need the bed."

"Mr. Haslam, please open this gate so I can see to my husband."

"Mrs. Matthews, I can't. First, because it's not a visiting day. Second, because the rule here is, disobedience so extreme as an attempt at escape is met by a temporary suspension of all privileges."

"But he returned!"

"To do that, he first had to escape."

"This is insufferable!"

"I can see that. But if you come back Wednesday morning at ten, we'll go

over the details of your husband's admission. Afterward I'll take you along to
his private room, where with your own eyes you'll see how we do the best possible in circumstances constrained by a ruinous shortage of funds. The sad fact
is, the recent upswell of public solicitude for lunatics that's been a consequence
of madness striking down our mighty monarch King George hasn't translated
into an injection of hard currency for our oldest and finest public hospital devoted to the care of unhinged minds. But I promise you, Wednesday you'll go
away from here assured I'm as steadfast in my intention as you—only mine is
for the real benefit of three hundred patients and not the hoped-for benefit of
one."

I looked at Haslam then, attending to what was still visible in his eyes, that
eloquent opaqueness of emotion. For a moment neither of us spoke, until, saying only, "Wednesday," I stepped around him and walked away. It was do this
or burst into tears and so enact the seal of his power upon me.

But before I reached Broker Row, I glanced back to see, I think, if my
ragged crew had been there the while, because the first thing I noticed was they
were gone. It was now only John Haslam standing before the iron door he'd
come through, the image of a man who'd locked himself out. Except, even as I
looked round, he turned from the door with an odd little wave and made a pantomime with the key to show me he could not get it to work and found this
amusing and seemed to think I would too. Yet considering his treatment of me
just now, this was strange. Besides, I was too flustered to be caught looking
back to indulge that collusion, and turned away, so abruptly I nearly twisted an
ankle.

But that odd little wave stayed in my mind, and there, as I walked on, it was
joined by another, by which I realized what Haslam reminded me of. It was
something I once saw when I was a girl of seven or eight and have never forgot.

I was with my mother in Southwark High Street. (O Dearest Parent, though
a poor widowed schoolmistress with barely means to dress and feed thy
Daughter, Thou gavest her something of infinitely greater worth than fine food
and fine clothes: experience of what genuine love is, and love of reading and
good books, so as a Woman she might not only by the common superiority of
female virtue but also by an uncommon strength of female intellect be truly
worthy to love a good and intelligent Man!) She and I were on our way to the
fair in the last year of its operation—and if you know when they closed down
Southwark Fair for good, you will know my age to the year. As we went, we
were passed in the street by a chair carrying an English seaman who'd survived
shipwreck in the South Seas by crawling out of the surf to spend two years in
solitude on a tropic island. When I saw him he was just off the ship that rescued him, then at Wapping Docks. Having contracted a fever on the voyage
home, he was being carried to St. Thomas's Hospital. He was bundled up in
blankets, helpless as an infant, and he was waving at the passing scene with a
slow, kingly wave, his mouth formed in a little smile like a digestive grimace.

Maybe it was his eyes that made that smile appear so uncanny, for they seemed to gaze at me from out of that haggard young-man's face as from ten thousand miles away, but there was something more in them than distance. My mother and I were not at the fair, only on our way to it, and yet the sight of him gave me a confused idea he was somehow of the company of those we would see when we got there. I mean the tumbling posturemaker lad and the midget lady and the Scotsman who broke glasses by shouting at them. It was that same look in the eyes.

In those days, crowds were not so well-behaved as now, and when an un-usual figure passed, they seldom failed to let him know their feelings. If he met their approval they might offer up a hip-hip-hooray. If not, they were as likely to pelt him with offal. Or if there was something about him peculiarly incensing—if, say, he had the look of an Italian—then they might spill him out of his chair and set upon him with kicks and cudgels. But in the case of the sea-man it was as if he carried along with him through the streets so commanding a space of silence and unease that the entire scene blanched and faltered before him as he went. Many averted their eyes. Others hesitated, or stepped aside, hardly seeming to know what they did, like automata, or animals suffering a premonition. And it was not just because he had the look of a sick man, or a dy-ing person, though he had both, it was something else.

The sailor did die, not long after. By that time a story was abroad that he'd survived those first days on the island by eating the flesh of his drowned ship-mates. How anyone could learn this without the man himself confessing it, I don't know. Perhaps it came out in a final delirium. For my own part, I have al-ways doubted whether the cannibalism was the cause of the look or only the story that those who knew nothing had fabulated to explain it. As I remember it, the look was that of a man in a condition of triumph, who even now was coming heroically through, and yet at some unfathomable cost. It was the look of one who'd always understood that if he ever made it back alive, his exile would be over, yet here it was, only beginning, and all his triumph one long farewell to human regard. This was why it was a look at the same time and in equal measure proud and abashed.

But there was something else in it—or so I thought at the time. Something especially for me, or that it asked of me. But what?

Perhaps I've made too much of one thing or another I saw in John Haslam on my very first encounter with him. And maybe it's true I didn't see much that first time, and memory has enriched itself since, like a crude sketch grown un-accountably to a Dutch portrait. Perhaps it's this habit of writing things down. When Jamie first disappeared into France, I learned that without him to talk to, if I would keep hold of my life as I actually lived and knew it (as knowing Jamie had taught me I did live and did know it), then I must talk to paper. After the travails and loneliness of the day I must retreat to my corner window at the turn of the stairs and scribble into the night while the nonscribblers of the dark city dream the dreams that nourish them another way. I am not a dreamer but a gatherer-in. My fear is of the daily vanishing of all experience down the drain of Time. In this age of cataclysm, storm, and madness, with monarchy, nobility, and Church seeking to destroy the heroes of equality—the David Williamses and the Tom Paines and my dear husband and the French male population on the march in a dream of freedom—I struggle to hold on to what matters, and at the end of the day and in the small hours, what to me matters has little to do with rank or no-rank or who has more power and who has less but with the things that won't change when everybody has the same. I mean how people are with each other and what each suffers and why.

I was taught these things by the way my mother was with me. She knew childhood is a dangerous illness you must be nursed through by love. Without love you die a child, not knowing life, not knowing death, not knowing the first thing that matters. Without love your guide will be every bully and fool in the playground.

As for Haslam, a purpose may be served in setting down these reflections about him now, if only to indicate what kind of man I seem to be up against. Not a cannibal, of course, but one for whom, from certain angles, all seems more than possible, glory is more than achievable: achieved. Except the matter keeps turning.

As I rounded the corner, John Haslam's odd wave still visible in my mind, I could hear the man himself—as Jamie had done earlier, and me after him, and many others over the centuries I am sure—shouting forlornly through the bars of that asylum, *For God's sake, somebody open this door and let me in!*

JUSTINA

Home before ten o'clock, I was relieved to find our servant Justina had opened the shop for business. Though cool in her manner toward me, she'd cleared the counter, dusted the shelves, swept the floor, and put the sign out, forgetting only some of the lights. Jamie had been in Bethlem but a month, yet for lack of his daily efforts the wholesale trade he'd patched together over the previous ten was already unravelling. We needed every customer who wandered in. In the note I'd left Justina, I wrote JAMES large, underscoring it. Beauty, not reading, being her strong suit, I hoped she'd recognize the name and gather where I was. When not flouncing by in a sulk she loved nothing more than to please me, and being popular with our customers and knowing it, why would she not open the shop? Because, while she professed to pray as fervently as I did to have Jamie back with us, she was sunnier when it was just us two. But yes, she did open the shop, yet her look, when I thanked her for it, too much resembled those I used to receive from her when Jamie's old friend from his Camberwell days, Robert Dunbar, was often on the premises with Jamie away on the Continent. It was a look that said, Why must *he* be here?

I sometimes think I have too much hope of people always to admit to myself the danger they pose. Justina Latimer, now that was danger—yet how far would she need to go before I recognized what it was I harboured, and acted?

Robert Dunbar had been danger too, I suppose, but was too transparent and compliant to seem so—and necessary. It was he who helped me when I took the business retail. An eager, practical man adept with hammer and saw, he appeared at my door a year after Jamie disappeared into France. It was he who built for me, his labour *gratis,* the counter and dividing walls necessary to turn the office into a shop. That job finished, he stayed on to help me open the books. By the time he was competing with Justina to be first to greet the customer when the bell jingled, it was evident (if I would only give him a sign, the one he was getting from everybody else telling him his old friend wasn't coming back) he'd next be exercising his ingenuity in my bed, his own by then a mat on a treadle we kept under the counter he'd built. With Robert Dunbar's muscle and penetration I might have clawed my way back to wholesale. But my experience has been that while pride, desire, and the compromises of security are quiet enough temptations when met with singly, in concert they make a noise on the conscience. Finally I could not betray my husband, even if he was mad and missing in war time on the wrong side of the Channel.

It was some while before Robert Dunbar was able to grasp my fidelity for the plain dull thing it was, convinced as he was (and so like a man) my reluctance had something to do with him and therefore, if only I would tell him what it was, could be fixed. When at last, by saying it in as good as so many words, I got him to understand the difficulty did not extend even so far as his existence, the shine for Robert went off the do-gooding life. One mopish day, before he would take up his treadle and walk away, he made a fumbling, I suppose despairing, attempt upon the virtue of Justina, who welcomed his advances long enough to eviscerate one, and make an energetic start on the other, of his testicles with the razor I thought he knew she always carried.

Hardly was our poor crippled Lothario packed off to Guy's Hospital and Justina's tears dried than her mood, which had been in eclipse for a year, rebounded as cheerful as it was in the interval between Jamie's first disappearance and Dunbar's first showing his face. That's how it stayed until the morning last March when the shop door jingled, and Jamie, back from three years imprisoned in France, staggered in like a buyer for the dead. I was too concerned for my husband's health, not to say overjoyed to have him with me, to take overmuch notice when Justina's mood passed again into eclipse. But in the ten months Jamie was back with us, I would sometimes catch on her face an expression of disgust with me that I should sink to being a *dirty puzzle* in my own bed with my own husband. This I ascribed to youth's queasiness at the animal, as well as to the callous violations of a child-bride by her late husband Latimer (mysteriously stabbed to death in his bed when she was out of the house not ten minutes for bread for his morning tea, as she explained to the police).

But I never saw Justina's mood so black as that morning I arrived home from returning Jamie to Bethlem. Mistaking it at first for sympathetic concern, I was amazed when, after I thanked her for opening the shop, she turned from me and coldly asked "what Mr. Matthews wanted in showing his face again" and said "she hoped this time they'd keep him—" She then stole a glance round and, seeing me angry, quickly added, "So he'd have benefit of treatment from expert practitioners—"

This was insolence from a maidservant with a politic coda, and I can only plead it was the first time I ever heard anything like it voiced so brazenly by this one. Gazing at her in my shock, I thought, *As a child, Justina, you were illtreated by a homicidal parent and when not much older by a savage husband, yet have turned out decent enough, if moody, in many ways intelligent, with good impulses, only slow to know what they are and not much skilled in the articulation of them. This reticence has left you hostile to men and what you call their* performing snails. *But perhaps forgiveness by me this morning, and one day heartfelt love by a good man, might assuage the bitterness of so much cruelty and loss in your life—*

This was as far as I had got in my earnest delusion when the shop bell jingled, and I watched a girl as relieved to be saved by it as I was to watch her trip away.

On Monday I tried to see Lord Erskine, a mad-eyed republican Scot famous for his unsuccessful defence of the second part of Tom Paine's *Rights of Man.* Though Jamie'd told me Erskine had agreed to act as his counsel, I soon learned either this was fantasy or Erskine had changed his mind. I couldn't get past the man's secretary, who said his Lordship was no longer taking criminal cases, and when I mentioned Bethlem, added nastily, "—and never did charity for lunatics."

The small hours of Tuesday and Wednesday I spent tossing and turning in a struggle to believe I had delivered Jamie back into the best medical hands in the kingdom, which would soon enough return him to me. It was true what Jamie had said: If Bethlem hasn't cured them after a year and deems them a danger to no one, they're released, whether the family likes it or not. So there was no reason to believe I faced more than eleven months' wait, in which case our child (if we were so blessed) had a chance of growing up secure in a loving household of London tea dealers, whose head was only at times of exceptional distress prone to pluck a privet-leaf and call it Orange Pekoe.

As, however, to the mysterious circumstances of Jamie's admission to Bethlem: What if this was no ordinary lunatic case but a political one, meaning he'd be held as long as who-knew-who wanted him held? But how to set about finding who wanted what, when I had no idea what Jamie had done (if it was more than crying *"Treason"* in the House) or was thought to have? For that matter, was it for new transgressions or old?

Meanwhile, life must carry on. The staff in the shop now just us two, those were desperate days. Nauseated by worry, exhaustion, and perhaps something else, I had no reserves of patience with Justina, who at times behaved with such sullen insolence I must dismiss her, but then where would I be? My fear was any increase in demand on my energy and time and I would crack. Alert to my fragile condition, Justina chose a thousand small ways to punish me for the crime of wanting my husband back. So she would linger two or three seconds longer at a task before moving to greet a customer, or silently wipe away tears that were somehow my doing, or when she burned the pudding apologize so vaguely as to imply it was only to be expected given all she now had to do.

These little needling things reminded me, if I didn't already know it, how self-ish what some call love can be.

Wednesday dawned warm (for February) and foul. Leaving Justina pacing crackly as a cat, I made the walk that by now I knew pretty well, this time carry-ing a basket of goods I imagined Jamie would appreciate: warm stockings, clean linen, a half-dozen oranges, a block of chocolate, a plate and knife, a toothbrush. My basket also contained two books, the first the second part of Mr. Paine's *Rights of Man,* which (Lord Erskine being unsuccessful defending) was rare, having been burned. "The flames," I can remember Jamie once re-marking, "is where the English consign the Rousseau of British democracy." I didn't think he'd read the second part, but I knew well his enthusiastic opinion of certain sentiments in the first, as well as those in Paine's pamphlet *Common Sense,* written against our King and nobility. The second book in my basket was Jamie's hero the republican David Williams' *Letters on Political Liberty,* which I did know he'd read but thought he might like to have by him, as Williams (a Welshman like Jamie's father) had once been instrumental in his first mission to Paris.

At the gate, as I half anticipated, the animal Bulteel made a great show of knowing nothing of my visit and would see me off, but you could tell his heart wasn't in it. Well before I could make a scene, he turned away and wrote me out a ticket, instructing me to wait inside the gate for my guide, the hospital steward, Mr. Alavoine, who—whether by arrangement or chance was not clear—was standing only a few feet away, in conversation through the bars with a dissolute lascar. This Alavoine I knew was the monster of depravity known to Jamie as Sir Archy, and I must say, with his greasy ginger-yellow locks and his ginger-white grizzle and his tiered black hat pushed back high on his degraded brow and his dirty red coat and his breeches buttoning between the legs, he showed himself as unwholesome a human figure as I ever met with in my life. When at last the horrible fascination he exerted on me palled to mere disgust, my attention reverted to the situation I found myself in.

BETHLEM

How strange to be at last inside Bethlem's gates. If you've seen them, you'll know they're adorned left and right on top by the sculptor Cibber's giant reclining statues of Melancholy and Raving Madness. Directly behind and above where I waited, it was Raving Madness, naked and head-shaved and shackled forever. Forever about to draw breath and bellow forth his rage. As I looked up at him and at Melancholy, all drooping and woebegone, verses about them from a poem I once read sprang into my head. "That seems to whine, and this to roar," something, something, then,

> Ingenious toil that could devise
> One foaming fury, one as cool as ice.

A Jew at the gate the week before told me Raving Madness was modelled on Oliver Cromwell's porter Daniel, a giant who went insane and was lodged at Bethlem and used to preach from the window using a Bible given him by the actress and mistress of Charles II, Nell Gwyn.

And here in front of me, no bars intervening, was the building itself: a stately edifice vanishing left and right into the dingy fog. At the invisible far ends, beyond the east and west pavilions and beyond them the newer, incurable wings, are grass plats where the patients are said to walk in fair weather. Being high-walled, these cannot be seen from the forecourt, and on that day I could not even see the walls. But straight ahead the central pavilion was only a little enshrouded in murk. Above the main doors of it are set pilasters worthy of the architect Wren, and in the pediment over them I could just make out the royal arms, enwreathed with carved flowers. A-top this rises an octagonal turret with a three-dialled clock, the whole thing crowned by a handsome cupola.

The structure is noble enough, or was once, but dismal, and it wasn't only the bars and boards on the windows. The Jew also told me this is not the original Bethlem, which stood four hundred years just east of Moorfields, outside Bishopsgate, but rather the one that took its place, hardly more than a century ago. Unfortunately, Moorfields was always a fen, and the builders, after they filled in the garbage dump the City ditch had become along there, rejected any effort at proper foundations, setting the bricks a mere few inches beneath the floor of a basement sunk only three feet into the rubbishy soft ground. Imagine the Tuileries Palace thrown up on a levelled trash pile, and you have a pretty good picture of Bethlem at Moorfields.

From the rear, which is to say from London Wall, on the other side, you see the effects of a century of sinkage: the gaping fissures running from ground to eaves. But from inside the front gate that morning there was nothing visible to account for so strong an impression of decay. The whole fabric was black with soot, but in London anything is soon that. With Bethlem, it's more a case of what's audible: the clanking, screaming, roaring, and wailing that emanates— or suddenly falls silent—within. But why should it be surprising when associations of sound contaminate those of sight, or human misery have power to inflect iron windows and make a horror of stone?

At last the obscene banter between my guide and the lascar grew desultory, yet still they lingered, though they knew I waited, because I heard them joke about it. Finally, with a look of impatience, such that you'd think he was the one kept waiting by me, the steward turned in my direction, and that was when it struck me how bizarre it was to see breeches that buttoned between the legs. It was something I had never seen before in my life and don't expect to see again soon, and it so rattled me that when, in an accent I never heard before, he said something like, "You have got your ticket, have you?" I was in a state approaching mental deafness. He could have been a citizen of Nova Zembla, addressing me in Zemblan. *Yho hahv g-haht hyohr t-hehk-haht, hahv yho?* He, meanwhile, not looking to see whether I had my ticket or no, or indeed caring whether I understood him or if understanding knew that I was meant to follow, went sloping away across the forecourt.

From my first glance at him at the gates, the judgment *low-minded blackguard* had fixed itself in my brain, and ten minutes' eavesdropping on the mélange of smut and jibes that passed for conversation between him and his friend had done nothing to dislodge it. Here was a being that I did not want to know had power over any creature on earth, let alone the one I loved more than life itself. Yet he might have information I needed, so I picked up my basket and made haste, and coming abreast of him I asked, "Why was my husband admitted here?"

At first he pretended not to hear. I was about to put the question again, when the head began a slow rotation. As it came, it dragged behind it a gaze so recalcitrant it was not until several seconds after the arrival of the face that I felt the scorn of its scrutiny. At last, in that uncouth accent, he said, "Why, because he's mad."

"But who put him in here?"

"You are mistaken if you think I am the one to ask that of," was the eventual reply, spoken in such a slow, queer way—*yho hahr mihz-tuh-heykhahn hehv yho t-hinkh*—with provincial affectation so outlandish, that its primary purpose seemed to be to treat as an imbecile anyone who'd expect anything of a response uttered in so grotesque a fashion.

"Who should I ask? Dr. Monro?"

This query issued in a spasm of mirthless amusement before he said something like, *Yahz, yho hahzk hem, lahz. Dho theht.*

Now we were at the door, not the main one but the penny gate the porter and his colleague had come reeling out of. Here in niches left and right stood ancient wood figures of young beggars, male and female, life size, holding great black jars with slots for money and above them the inscription, *Pray remember the poor Lunatics and put your Charity into the Box with your own hand.* The figures were painted and shellacked, the paint rubbed away by the strokings of visitors at their noses, nipples, and crotches.

And then it was down a miserable narrow passage and up a few stone stairs into a large hall with several doors leading off it, streaky windows, and cherub-festooned tablets listing benefactors. Here it smelled like a refrigerated lavatory, with an understink of greasy cooking. Here the dirty daylight scarcely intruded, and the squalls and jinglings of the inmates resounded less muffled than they did outside.

"Haslam you're to see, is it?" the steward ascertained over his shoulder, adding, "Because I have no bloody idea where he is."

"We have an appointment," I piped, the ninny with her basket, tripping after.

"He ain't in there," he volunteered, dismissing with a flick of his hand a door on his left as we passed down the hall.

Here were iron gates on both sides. Beyond, a winding staircase, which we climbed to a landing on the first floor. It too had iron gates on both sides. The one on the west, as I knew, led to the women's wing, which had exposure to the warmest and most salubrious winds. The men were eastward, being better able to endure the bleaker air.

Spying a horseshoe set in the floor on the west side, before the women's gate, I asked my guide what it was for.

"To guard against witchcraft," he replied. "Or keep it in. They're all witches through there."

As I looked about me, I could see that though by its façade Bethlem might pass for a palace, on the inside it was genuinely a madhouse, and I don't just mean the bars and malodorous damp and dull interior clamour (now seeming to issue mostly from the back of the building, below us, though also through the iron gates). I mean the fractured walls and the short-timbered, gaping floors. I mean how every surface was out of true, how there was nothing here sound, upright, or level; no bonds, no ties, no securement between the parts. I mean how you could see daylight around the window frames and glimpse the main floor through fissures in the boards of the first. This was not just an old building settling into the ground, it was a building that was never built right in the first place. One of those just thrown up, as if it didn't matter, they were only lunatics, and now it was falling down and mattered less.

"Should we look in the court room?" the steward asked me in his inimitable fashion.

Not knowing what an assent to this question would mean and thinking confusedly the court room was where the Bethlem subcommittee would be meeting (though it wasn't Saturday), I said we could, but not wanting to interrupt anything added, if he liked he might also take me direct to my husband, I could see Haslam later.

This suggestion meeting with no acknowledgment, I next found myself standing behind the steward as he tried a door at the back of the hall, but it was locked, and so he knocked, and this producing nothing, he sorted through the keys he kept on a ring inside his jacket. Why he would think if Haslam was in a locked room he would want it unlocked when he didn't answer a knock, I don't know. In any event we went in, and it was a clean bare space under an ornamental plaster ceiling, with a large table and many wood chairs scattered here and there as if by a gust of wind. As my eyes grew accustomed to the dim light, I saw over one of the two empty fireplaces a three-quarters portrait of Henry VIII, all bejewelled, with the fat-arse, purse-mouth cat look he always wears. Otherwise, arms and portraits I didn't know.

"Haslam must be where he's usually at," the steward said, giving me a knowing look.

"Where is that?"

"In't Dead House, opening heads."

"Please," I said. "Take me direct to my husband."

"And who would that be?" *Hehn whoh whohd theht bhay?*

I told him. He seemed to wait. I gave him sixpence. He left the room. I followed.

We next passed through one of the iron gates, the east, as I determined (unless I'd got turned around), by a small door set in the bars, with a sill you had to step over, and then I was following my escort down a long gallery lit on one side—the north, Moorfields side—by windows set too high to see out of, while the south side was all doors, one after the other, some open, most closed, each with a barred aperture and overhead louvre, so light came from that side too, though today not much. It was not cold in the gallery, but it was colder than outside. You glimpsed your breath only faintly. At the far end of the gallery, which was perhaps two hundred feet long, were more iron bars, floor to ceiling, and still the building continued beyond. What most struck me, besides the length and draftiness of the space, was how subdued the commotion immediately inside it was, much of the noise seeming to come from elsewhere, mainly below. It was so subdued, in fact—and in the grey light—I didn't at first see how many patients were out of their cells, moping along the walls.

But our arrival was having an effect, and as we made our way down the gallery, faces were looking to us and various soliloquies seemed to rise in volume. There was a general shuffle closer, as of a battalion of invalids and beggars, and something my mother used to say chimed in my brain: *If you can't earn a living, it's only another way of starving.* Though many were dressed in shirt and breeches and had shoes on their feet, others wore coarse, ill-fitting blanket-gowns, with shaved heads and no shoes. I could not take my eyes off their feet: black and chilblained, most of them, though here and there some were wrapped in flannel. I was put in mind of an army in rout. But it wasn't rout, it was debility, and those who approached, whatever they said, were only begging to be given back what they had lost, and those that didn't approach seemed only to have given up begging, having lost all they ever had or could have. But whether they approached or not, they were all of them equally poor. Poorer than beggars. Poor as the dead.

"What news of London?" one old gentleman in jacket and waistcoat enquired of me quietly, laying a hand on my arm. "How does the King?"

Another asked me what he should do about the weakness in his knees.

Another assured me several times he had "jumped to save a fall," and truly, he kept telling me, "there was nothing for it." He then tried to sell me a canary, saying, had he only been it, he'd have flown, and if I listened I could hear it— and indeed I could, singing its heart out in a near-by cell. I told him I had no money to spend on a canary. Incredulous, he was demanding to know why, when a squirrel ran across the boards at my feet. Thinking it a rat, I let out a cry.

The steward halted. "Major Capstick!" he called sharply to an old man in a ragged military tunic who stood by, a piece of dirty string dangling from one wrist, his terrified rheumy eyes following the squirrel's zigzag dash. "I want that animal on its leash by sundown or Mr. Hester's up here first thing tomorrow to bite its head off!"

Major Capstick went shuffling and moaning after the creature.

This was a gallery for the male sex, not just adults. A boy of eleven or twelve blocked my way. "Are you come for me?" he asked, lightning-quick, and right away I regretted meeting his eyes. He was a desperate, cunning creature with a pilfered look, and I had nothing for him. "Are you come to operate Dr. Monro's electrical machine?" he asked me, touching the basket with one hand, my stomach with the other. "Have you a generator inside?"

I stepped back. "No, it's things for my husband."

"Not from him?"

"Madam," Mr. Alavoine said wearily, waiting for me.

When I tried once more to by-pass the boy, he moved in again, whispering, "Listen close. Irish Maximus died last Friday. The basketmen haven't noticed yet. Me and Percy's obtaining his meat. Tomorrow's mutton. We're holding out for a second Sunday: beef. You're a woman—pray slip us a little perfume to fight the rising stench."

Here he was yanked away from me and sent reeling by the steward, who muttered, "Leave her be, Jo. She's no need of your consultations."

And so we were walking again.

Now I became aware my presence was being made known to the entire population of the hospital, for the patients communicated with one another from the top of the house to the bottom and from one end to the other. For the most part, the exchanges were unintelligible to me because either muffled or conducted in arcane jargons or private languages. What I did understand was so obscene as to be either comical or breathtaking, depending on the ratio of wit to hostility. I won't outrage sensibility by recording any of it here but only observe everybody's primary concern: what most ingeniously splitting use might be found for my arsehole, mouth, and cunny—in that order. No wonder women imagine themselves all lightness and vacancy, when the world would have us so porous. But what most struck me about the tumult of opinion that boiled up in my wake was how many women joined in, and how aggrieved they were at the thought of a rival set of orifices loose on the premises.

We were nearly to the bars at the end of the gallery when Alavoine stopped at one of the closed doors and peered through the peep-hole. "Presentable, are ye, Tilly-Fally Fiddlestick?" he said and opened the door, which was not locked. He stood back for me to enter. As I attempted to do so, he placed a hand on my basket.

"It's for my husband," I said, tightening my grip.

"All baskets are to be inspected by the keeper on duty."

"And where is he?"

"On't women's side. I must take it to him—"

"If he's engaged, inspect it yourself. There's nothing—"

This proposal was a blow against his honour. "Am I a basketman?" he asked, looking shocked.

"No, you're an ignoramus!" I cried. "Or think I am! Keepers aren't called basketmen because they're inspectors of baskets!"

"So why are they?"

"I don't know!"

"Then an ignoramus is what you are."

"Margaret—" I heard, and there in the gloom of the cell was my husband in a blanket-gown, sitting on the edge of a bed, looking at me.

Suddenly I had no time to argue about a basket. "I want it back," I muttered, letting it go to fly to him. The door clicked shut behind me.

THE PATIENT

Now as I rocked my dear husband in my arms, with the noise from the gallery Pandemonium, I knew by his passive response he was no longer maniacal.

"Jamie," I whispered, letting him go and and sitting back. "Where are your clothes?"

"You mean Robert Dunbar's?" he asked, touching his fingers to the blanket-gown.

"I mean why have they dressed you like a beggar?"

"Perhaps because I'm in as a lunatic vagrant."

"You're neither. I'm getting you out of here."

He smiled. As he did, his eyes fell to something on the bed between us, a penny notebook I now saw I was half sitting on. He must have been writing when I arrived. He still held the pencil. I extracted the notebook from under me and handed it to him, wondering how I could have forgot to bring him paper and something to write with. Did I think I was the only one of us in need of such life-savers now?

When Jamie took the notebook from me he did it with his right hand, which also held the pencil, and yet he was left-handed. I looked to that hand, where it lay on the bed. Around the wrist was an iron shackle attached to a chain bolted to the wall.

"Jamie, they've chained you!"

He lifted the hand and gazed at it. "Where would I go?"

His cell was a space perhaps twelve foot deep and a little more than half as wide, with rough board floors and a broken-glazed, barred window above the bed. There looked to be closable shutters, except then you would lose the light. Aside from the bed—a mattress in a wood trough—was a small seat, also wood, and that's all there was. The wainscotting on the three interior walls was dark with age, every inch of it inscribed, the way you see in old schoolhouses. So was the plaster above, to the height a tall man might reach.

"You could walk up and down the gallery." My voice seemed to issue from under water.

"I could, so," Jamie replied, without conviction, his eyes on his notebook.

I'd forgot what we were talking about.

"Why are they so noisy?" I said.

"You've roused them."

"I was supposed to meet with Haslam," I said next, weighing the chain. "The steward didn't know where he was."

Jamie shook his head as if marvelling but made no reply.

"Oh, Jamie! Do they treat you well?"

In answer he held up the pencil and notebook. "Jack the Schoolmaster give me these." He meant Haslam. "There are some," he continued, "who live shut up in the gaol of a set character, witnessing and comprehending more than they can acknowledge or act on, and when you glimpse them, what you see is eyes of alarm in a mask of consternation. A sane man imprisoned in a madhouse. This is John Haslam in the grip of The Schoolmaster."

"Does he teach you?"

"Yes, though nothing he intends."

"Why do you call him The Schoolmaster?"

"Because the gang do. He's their recorder and, like Charlotte, though in a biased way, keeps notes on us all, which they consult at their leisure."

"Has anybody told you why you're in?"

"Nobody has to. It's because I know who the gang is and labour daily to destroy them before they destroy me. So far what's saved me is the intimacy prevailing between us. I stave off the worst effects of their brain-workings not by shutting my mind against them (which only hardens their resolve) but by cultivating attention to the cast and tenor of my own thoughts. By spotting an untoward reflection as it crops up, I remain alert to their alien incursions. Who can hope to meet the force of the Air Loom who makes himself deaf and blind to it? I count myself fortunate to be imprisoned in a building where one such as I can hardly miss it. Of course, it would be the same at St. Luke's or Bridewell. It would be the same if my affairs took me daily inside Parliament or the Admiralty, though they're places of work a man can walk away from at the end of the day. Or imagines he can. Every hour I spend in here convinces me more that attention to the ways of the gang is the best antidote for living and working in the kind of place that the better you know it the sicker you become."

"Did Haslam say when they're letting you out?"

"It's not his decision."

"He's on the subcommittee—"

"Just one voice—"

"The only medical one—"

At this, Jamie looked at me sharp, perhaps because he knew I didn't know this for certain. What he said was, "What's his secret?"

"That a man with three hundred lives in his charge can have no heart?"

"Listen. The Glove Woman, who inhabits Matron White, wants none of us up on meat days, plus one other. That means everybody abed four days in seven. She and Haslam are at war. He believes reclining does raving no good."

"And not-raving—" I lifted the chain—"it benefits?"

Jamie's reply was in the considered way I have often heard him discuss politics in Europe. "Going over the wall has set back my case. Haslam will let me up as soon as he can trust me. The terms between us are pretty clear, if he ain't."

"Jamie, you were always a fighter for truth and justice."

"I am still. Only, the arena's shifted to the modern age, where truth answers to no human voice and must be dived for, every diver for himself. Now all talk is pretense and meaning suspect."

"But not our talk, Jamie—?" At that moment I was so desperate to tell him my news, I almost believed I had some and it was not simply the ups and downs of the past month, for I was too old, and if I wasn't and miscarried (as had happened twice before) then why raise his hopes?

Or did he already know, and I should be asking him?

"Your talk and mine?" he said. "That too."

"Jamie, no!"

"Like The Schoolmaster, I'm of the old order but unlike him know it, and working day and night to fathom the new."

"What truth to be discovered?"

"Any."

"What enemy?"

"The ones just under the skin."

"Oh, Jamie—"

"I know."

He was in my arms once more. Unresisting. Outside, the commotion raged on. Sitting back again and looking at him, I said, "Have you seen Monro yet?"

"No, but only because he ain't been through."

"Still not? Will Alavoine return the basket?"

He shook his head.

"How will I get it back?"

"You won't. They're called basketmen because once upon a time they brought round the medicine in baskets."

"But visitors are allowed to—"

"They'll sell what they don't eat."

"They can't do that!"

"But they will. Next time slip him sixpence."

"I did!"

"For the basket, or to be brought direct to me when you couldn't find Haslam?"

With his shaved head and watchful eyes, he seemed to have grown still younger. I never saw him so subdued and feared his doubts of me had travelled deeper. "Are you all right, Husband?" I whispered.

"As well as might be. Who's asking?"

"Jamie, you don't blame me for putting you in here—?"

This amazed him. "You admit it?"

"No!" I cried. "I don't! I didn't!"

"That's what I thought your position was. Don't forget I survived three years of French gaols."

"As you'll survive this place because you shouldn't be here either."

His eyes had gone to his notebook. "France was the grave," he said, and smiled. "This is Hell."

"Next time I'll bring you pen and ink," I promised. "And a fresh book. Look! This one's fat already!"

He didn't answer, only hefted the notebook, turning it this way and that.

I told him I'd tried to see Lord Erskine, to help him with his case.

At this news he grew almost animated. "The gang's had Erskine tied up for years. Even as he assured me he'd represent me, I could feel them quickening the fluid inside my brain, to let me know he wouldn't. Already by their Air Loom warp they had him stagnated in the Commons, as I told you before. Pitt sat poised to take notes on Erskine's first speech against the Government but soon tossed down his pen with a laugh. Had I not been there as witness, the gang had killed Erskine afterwards for an example. Last year he saved a dog from a mob in the street, assuring them it was mad. He cares about the dog, but I who saved his life may sleep in the stable."

As Jamie raved, I silently resolved to keep on at Lord Erskine. When Jamie finished, having nothing to answer I said, "Speaking of a defender of Tom Paine—" and told him about the Paine and Williams books I'd brought for him.

Now he set down the notebook with care, looking where he put it. When his face came up, it was drained of colour.

"What, Jamie? What is it? Will they sell them?" I asked, thinking this was the problem.

"And have you as whore to make copies!" he cried. "So they can file evidence world-wide that I know the pure form of everything you all pretend to!"

"Pretend to, Jamie? Pretend to what?"

"Equality and brotherhood, to disguise a senseless game of power whose goal is the ruin of two nations and my destruction, that's what!"

"Jamie, I pretend to nothing!"

"Nothing? And I suppose Sir Archy can't read?"

"Him again?"

"And again and again, with the magnet he commits unspeakable crimes with!"

"Magnet?" I cried, struggling to take him in my arms once more, babbling anything to keep him talking. "What can a man—"

"Sir Archy's no *man*!" he screamed and would have sprung from my touch, except the iron chain preventing this, he grew furious and yanked at it as if he would pull it out of the wall or rip his hand off in the attempt. To lessen the damage, I threw myself on that arm, but in his fury he was superhumanly strong, and I could only hang on. This is how we were when the door slammed open, the room filling with the roar from the gallery, and John Haslam rushed in, blasting Jamie with so ferocious a glare his body seemed to freeze in the air then flop down limp on the bed.

"Mrs. Matthews!" Haslam cried. "What the God-almighty did you do out there? And what's this—?"

"I did nothing!" I wailed. "I was brought here when you couldn't be found!"

"Forgive me, an emergency—our surgeon suffered a blow. Come, before you cause more chaos." He returned to the door.

"I'm not leaving him like this!" I cried.

He looked at me a moment and then came back to the bed. "Very well. We'll talk here. Mr. Matthews, please tell your wife why you're in."

But this, though kindly enough asked, was cruel. When Jamie, half insensible, attempted to answer, his tongue fused in his jaw, and the torment caused him by the struggle against that restriction was dreadful to witness. In all the years of his illness I never saw him so overcome, and in my mind two ideas arose in grim contradiction: *If he's this ill, Bethlem is doing it* and *If he's this ill, Bethlem is where he belongs.*

"Your answer, madam," Haslam informed me, before he strode out into the din of the gallery shouting, "Mr. Alavoine! Mr. Hester!"

When I tried to stroke Jamie's brow, his head jerked from my touch as from an electric charge. His eyes fluttered back in his head, his body lifting and twisting in a slow convulsion. I was hovering dumbstruck over this awful process when suddenly I was in flight from the room, spirited as if by thieves—it was Alavoine and another—who allowed me no time to shout or resist. We sped amongst gargoyle faces falling away lamenting and foaming, through an iron gate, down a staircase and outside, to whisk along a rubbish-strewn passageway that reeked of stewing laundry. Haslam must have followed close, for when we halted at a scarred door, he stepped around us and (after fiddling with the key) unlocked it and entered before us. I was carried in and set in a chair. As soon as my Hell dogs released me, I leapt up. They were moving in to push me down again when Haslam dismissed them with a look. As they slunk out, I saw the other besides Alavoine, the one called Hester, was a doughy massive Albino with a cherry-pit-and-porridge complexion and the look about him of an egg-sucking hound.

It was a large, deep-bookcased office smelling of mildew and embalmments and lit by a dirty skylight. I was standing before a desk stacked with books and papers looking down at Haslam, who sat not looking at me, rubbing his temples. I took my seat again and worked at breathing as deep as I could.

"Mrs. Matthews—" he began.

"Why is my husband in here?"

He sighed. "Insanity."

"What kind?"

"Are there kinds?"

"Tell me he'll be out after eleven more months like any other harmless madman."

"He should be out at least by then, but I can't absolutely make you that promise."

"You have no idea why he's in, do you?"

"No, I don't. Not the formal reason."

"Was it not the Privy Council that admitted my husband?"

"Mrs. Matthews, the fact a lunatic's talk is full of politics don't necessarily mean he's a victim of them. One result of the recent bloodbath of republican fraternity in France is that every second Englishman now construes himself his own master, which would be well and good except in most cases he's already got one. So a fellow happy and secure in his station one day, the next is a-boil with confusion and ingratitude. One in three admissions to Bethlem is a pretender to the throne, and believe me a pretender to the throne is ten times the trouble of a lunatic who's merely convinced he's visiting from a distant star or filled with frogs. One thing can be counted on from a convinced Monarch of the Realm: he won't take calmly to being ruled."

"Why have you chained him?"

"Because strait-waistcoats are itchy and hot."

"Mr. Haslam, you know what I mean. Why anything? Why can't he be up and about like the rest of them?"

"Like the rest of them that are allowed to be up and about? Because he escaped."

"Why have you taken his clothes?"

"No one's taken his clothes. They'll be at the laundry, if he hasn't tore them to ribbons in a fit. I seem to recall he doubted they were his."

"How long do you threaten to chain him?"

"Excuse me, Mrs. Matthews, I don't threaten, I execute, for as long as it takes. Now that he's in our care he must, for his own good, be governed by our rules."

"Your rules are enforced by animals."

"Animals can be trained. Does one man complete the reformation of a four-hundred-year-old hospital in eighteen months?"

"A reformer, Mr. Haslam? I wouldn't have guessed."

"That's because you imagine I'm your enemy."

"If you weren't, you'd take me back to my husband."

"Visiting hours end at noon. There's no use traipsing up there now."

"Who received him when he first arrived?"

"That would be the steward, Mr. Alavoine, who was just here. Whether Dr. Monro advised him I can't say because I don't know."

"Pray let me speak to Mr. Alavoine."

"I can't do that, because it's not his business, which is only to assign the patient the degree of care and confinement the case requires. All Alavoine will tell you is he was advised by the physician, whether he was or not, because that is the rule."

"May I speak to Dr. Monro?"

"Of course. As soon as you have found him."

"He's not here?"

"No."

"Is he expected?"

"He is always expected, he does not always arrive. When he does arrive he seldom stays long. He has Brooke House, his private madhouse in the sunny pastures of Hackney, to see to, and it tends to consume what energy his easel don't. You see, our physician's an enthusiast of the paintbrush. And since he don't believe in records, I won't know why your husband's in until I talk to him, except I haven't seen Monro in a fortnight and only assured you I'd tell you today because he needed to be here Monday morning without fail, and I thought to myself, if he misses Monday he'll be in later Tuesday or first thing Wednesday at the outside. Except here it is Wednesday noon and no sign of him. So there it is. But tell me this. When you saw your husband just now, did you notice a new reserve in his manner?"

"Why? Have you poisoned him against me?"

"Yesterday I asked him if he wants to be in here, and he said he does, he wants to be part of what I'm trying to achieve. It appeals, I think, to his republican inclinations."

"He's not a republican."

"Isn't he? Of course, who nowadays could afford to admit it? He's not *that* mad, but he is a lunatic, and before you devote any more energy to his premature release, you should ask yourself if this in any way resembles an involuntary confinement, and if it don't, whether it deserves to be complicated by a lot of hysterical agitation that won't have your husband home any sooner than if you did nothing but your spousal duty, which is to impart the special consolation afforded by present views of future happiness and comfort."

This advice he was pouring into my ear as he ushered me down a narrow, crooked, unlit corridor. Unlocking the door at the end of it, he said, "Mrs. Matthews, finally it don't matter who put your husband in here, or why. Obviously somebody has, and obviously, it so happens, this is where, for now, he needs, and wants, to be. Not only for his health but in these days—I won't

mince it—for his safety. If he's not a republican he certainly does at times manage to sound like one. And perhaps if you're honest with yourself, you'll recognize the reason you're so keen to know who put him in is not so you can better
get him out, because you can't, and won't, but so you won't have to accept that
in your heart you want him here as much as he wants to be here."

"Which is not at all."

"No, I think you do understand me."

"But I don't, Mr. Haslam. I don't understand you at all."

I believe he took my meaning, because he looked at me a moment before he
said, "Mrs. Matthews, if there's an injustice here, it's that in all likelihood we'll
have your husband too short a time to do him any lasting good before his bed
goes to one worse off. I know this temporary separation must be hard, but try
to see the larger view."

"The larger view, Mr. Haslam, is I don't want my husband in here."

"I understand that, Mrs. Matthews." He was taking out his watch. "But now
I'm afraid I must go see if our surgeon's regained his senses, such as they are.
When a patient pushed him at breakfast, he fell down a flight of stairs." As he
spoke, Haslam pushed the door open on London Wall. Looking out, I saw the
boarded-up houses from one of whose cellars Jamie had assured me a gang of
French magnetic agents had dug a secret passageway to insinuate confusion
into the minds of Bethlem's inmates. "I apologize, madam," Haslam was saying, "for bringing you onto these premises for information I don't have to give
you. In the meantime, I can assure you that from my own exchanges with your
husband he's a danger to no one and will be home in due course."

"Mr. Haslam," I said as I stepped out, "I am taking this higher."

"We're in England, Mrs. Matthews. You have every right to take it as high as
you can—" He hesitated.

"*Crawl,* Mr. Haslam? Is that not the word you want to say?"

If this struck a hit, he didn't show it. "No, Mrs. Matthews, not *crawl: manage.* As in such difficult circumstances as these are we all must—"

And softly he closed the door against me.

DAVID WILLIAMS

In the calm rational fury that engulfed me after my second interview with John Haslam I wrote two letters, one to Jamie's good friend and mentor, the republican David Williams, and one to the subcommittee of the governors of Bethlem Hospital. In both I begged interviews to discuss my husband's incarceration. On Monday of the next week, no flow yet, Justina alternately loving and difficult, me still awaiting answers to my letters, I arrived at the Bethlem gates at ten in the morning with another basket, no books this time, only shirt, waistcoat, breeches, stockings, linen, shoes, pen, ink, paper. Bulteel, however (saying my admission Wednesday, which he pretended to be vague ever happened, must have been an error if it did), refused to let me in. The next Wednesday the same again. But Friday of that week (still no flow, Justina still erratic) I received an answer from the Bethlem clerk, Mr. Poynder, which set us on a fortnight's dance by post that resulted in an invitation to address the governors' subcommittee on Saturday, March 19th. By now I'd decided that with the tumult of Jamie's disappearance and imprisonment, I had missed a month and must remain calm until my next regular date. There then followed a mysterious confusion of communication with David Williams. He seemed either not to remember my husband or, with the Government still opening private correspondence to discover traitors, to remember him too well to say so in writing. At last he agreed to receive me at his home in Dean Street, by Soho Square, on the 15th, which was the Tuesday before the Saturday I was to meet with the Bethlem subcommittee. The 15th was also, it happened, the day my menses were next due.

Though principally I remembered David Williams as a cat in a gold hairpiece tied in back by a drab little ribbon, I hoped his professed beliefs, such as that we're all equal in the eyes of our Benevolent Parent, would inspire him to help my husband. I was also curious to know how things went for him living in a country at war with republican France.

Like himself, his house, which stood recessed several feet from those on either side, was conspicuous in its refusal of ostentation. The plain door was
opened by his wife, a hard-favoured, high-principled spouse, the choice of a
man who, though he may abjure women's charms, has need of their services.
With a look at me of mingled censure and distaste, she led me into a small cold
parlour where her husband sat at a spindly walnut writing table, looking old. It
doesn't always take long for the male prime to phase into something pretty
gristly, for the fine thrum to dwindle to tinny and plunking. A ruin of middle
age that's neither illness nor senescence. The thick gold hair was now a hollow
puff, the cheeks each with a little pit of shadow. The bony body swaddled inside thick stiff fabric.

As she led me in, he rose alongside his table to indicate a wood bench I
could sit on. Once I did that, and Hatchet Face left, he sat back down and
looked at me with his attention fixed somewhere just above my head, upon the
general idea I represented: "petitioner"; "wife of former protégé, latterly a lunatic"; "interruption"; "trouble"; "danger"; it didn't matter.

I described Jamie's situation.

My host was beginning to shift in his seat like a man on the brink of saying
something at once reassuring and self-exculpatory, when Hatchet Face returned with our tea. He hung back until she left and we had taken our first sips.
Mediocre Congou. "Alas, madam," he then said, assuming an air of lugubrious
regret, "you find in me no friend of Bethlem Hospital."

"Who could be?"

"What I mean— You need someone acquainted with a governor."

"I need someone who loves my husband."

These words set off a vibration of his left eyelid. "You do understand, don't
you," he said, assuming an air of instruction, as for a slow student, "this could
be politics. Your husband was in very deep. How mad is he?"

"Unaggravated he's the coolest I've seen him since he returned from
France." *Coolest to me.*

"And if aggravated?"

"On my one visit he suffered a seizure, but it was Haslam's doing—"

"Whose?"

"The apothecary."

"I never heard of him."

"Even he's not claiming my husband's dangerous—"

To this Williams made no response. Were it not for that eyelid, he might
have just died.

"Do you think he is?" I said.

With a shrug identical to one Jamie used to give—did they learn it together
in Paris?—he answered, "If someone's decided so—"

"Can it be that easy? What do we do?"

He shook his head.

I took a breath. "Mr. Williams, like my husband, you were always a battler against injustice—"

This, however, he heard not as a statement of what he didn't appear willing to be now but as a compliment to his life's work, which had been a failure. "Madam," he said, shifting his thin hams to alleviate a fresh surge of discomfort, "we did as much as the times had it in them to accommodate."

"Will you visit him?"

This at once ended the shifting and caused so buzzing-lidded a disclaimer of a smile you'd think he'd been asked to post himself in the next cell. To rescue him, I suppose, from his own awkwardness, I sprang to my feet. Limber with consolation, he was up too, and by these automatic actions the interview assumed a concluding momentum. Before I knew it I was descending front steps.

Had Williams been strong in the days when Jamie loved him but was now broken by a government with a policy of destroying republicans, or had he always been this weak?

Still asking myself such questions, I arrived home to be confronted by Justina demanding to know where I had been.

"I told you," I answered, taken aback, I assure you, at an inquisition from my own servant. "Speaking to David Williams, the republican—"

"Is it him you're pregnant by?"

"No," I said, too flabbergasted not to say more. "It's James my husband I'm pregnant by!"

"Mr. Matthews is in Bethlem Hospital."

"Yes, he is. Six weeks now, and I'm over two months—"

"He came back a year ago. If it was him, what took you so long?"

"What?" And I looked at her close, to see if she was serious. She was. "Justina, it's not a human decision."

Now the tears rained down. Between sobs she begged me for God's sake don't dismiss her, she'd die if I dismissed her, she loved me so dearly, and swore she wanted nothing more than to be my dutiful servant, cleaning and cooking and serving in the house and shop, and guardian-to-the-death of my little child, and she hoped and prayed for all our sakes Mr. Matthews would be back with us soon, so we could be a complete family again, as she knew God wanted us to be.

Reader, what would you have done? If your answer is *Forgiven her*, then either I lack your compassion or maternity, even in prospect, exhorts severer judgments. No mother deserving the name will risk the life of her child, and Justina's solicitude, impertinence, and garter-belt razor now made too appalling a conjunction. I dismissed her then and there, with a fortnight's wage, and even as I spoke the words I knew I should have spoke them the day she said Bethlem should keep my husband or the day the year before when she half undid poor Robert Dunbar.

Dismissal confounded her. Seeming at a loss what to do, she fell to her knees and clutched wailing at my skirts. When I made to disengage myself, she recoiled from my touch, springing to her feet, and with dead eyes on me sulked away to her room. That night I slept, or tried to, a table wedged against my door. Shortly before daylight she let herself out. When I went down to lock the door, the hush in the house was less of relief than reprieve. It told me I had not heard the last from my devoted maid.

And I only wished I could say the same of David Williams.

PETITIONER

My meeting with the governors' subcommittee took place four days later, in the Bethlem court-room I had first entered with the steward Alavoine on our futile search for Haslam. Now that it was full of men, it was warm and well lit, both fireplaces ablaze. The individuals I faced were eight or nine kindly enough looking businessmen in ordinary business coats, sitting round the far end of a long table. John Haslam not being among them, I recognized no one except Alavoine. You know you're in foreign waters when that's your familiar face. My words to them were simple and few. Nervousness took the volume out of my voice, but I think they all heard me.

"I am wife to Mr. Matthews and demand to know by what authority my husband is detained."

In response, Mr. Poynder, Clerk of Bethlem, with whom I'd been in correspondence, a rangy, quiet-spoken fellow in a bag wig, with crooked teeth somewhat furred, as if his regular practice was to dip them in a solution of mouse-coloured velvet, stood up and after looking at me softly, read out in the sonorous style of a barrister-at-law the terms by which James Tilly Matthews had been admitted.

These, however, telling me nothing new, only that Jamie had indeed been admitted, when (the 28th of January), and at whose expense (Camberwell Parish's), which bare facts I already knew, I demanded to know further why he could not be discharged today and allowed to return home with me, his lawful wife, who hereby swore to take entire responsibility for his care and future conduct.

They then asked me to withdraw, and I did not need to wait long before Alavoine fetched me back in, so Mr. Poynder could read me a motion they'd just unanimously passed, saying they would not comply with my request. But by a second motion, they ordered Mr. Poynder to forward a copy of the day's proceedings to Mr. Fasson, a Camberwell churchwarden, to request that he and Mr. Clark, overseer of the poor of that parish, attend the committee at its next Saturday meeting.

And so the following week (after two more fruitless attempts to get past Bulteel), the shop temporarily closed, there being no one now but myself to run it, I waited once more on the bench outside the court-room, this time in the company of Mr. Fasson and Mr. Clark, and these gentlemen, calm Mr. Lean and nervous Mr. Fat, confessed they were as much in the dark as myself concerning the reasons for Jamie's admission. All they knew was, a certain government authority had required their parish to pay for the incarceration of a former parishioner.

"What kind of government authority?" I asked.

They supposed it would be the Board of Green Cloth. "And you thought that was only a billiard table!" Mr. Lean said, winking at me. But no, he explained, it was the Privy Council acting as a court with the power to imprison anyone deemed a threat to the Crown in an area twelve miles around the King's household, wherever it may be: St. James, Windsor, etc. Lean and Fat together explained the Green Cloth goes into effect every once in a while, which is fair enough, but if relied on too often can prove, as Mr. Fat expressed it, "a mighty drain on the old coffers." At £3 4s payable on admission for bedding and £1.11.6 per week thereafter, a patient can fast eat up parish funds, especially when you consider the political ones are often kept much longer than the usual year for incurables—those incurables, that is, who aren't locked up for good as a danger to themselves or the public.

Mr. Lean then mentioned the case of Peg Nicholson, whose cell it happened was not a hundred feet from where we sat, she having been a resident of the women's wing nearly twelve years.

Of course I had heard of Peg Nicholson. Whenever Bethlem comes up in conversation, she's the inmate everybody agrees they'd most like to shake the hand of. Peg was an upper servant in a good family who misconducted herself with a valet and was let go and reduced to needlework in a room over a stationer's in Wigmore Street. From there she first sent the King a petition intimating he was a tyrant and usurper. But real fame came only when, at age fifty-two, she made a public attempt on his Majesty's life, using some say a rusty, some say an ivory-handled, some say a worn-to-razor-sharpness, dessert knife—though by her own account she was only trying to deliver a second petition and in her nervousness happened to draw the knife from her pocket along with the paper. Accounts of the incident vary, but the one I know has the King, who was in the midst of receiving the petition with a noble condescension, avoiding the sudden knife at his breast by stepping back. Peg then making a second thrust (or perhaps only, as she said, once again encouraging him to take hold of the petition), the King's footman wrenched the weapon from her hand, at which his Majesty declared with the greatest equanimity and fortitude, "I am not hurt. Take care of the poor woman. She must certainly be mad."

And things might have gone well for her had she not at her Privy Council hearing insisted she wanted nothing but her due, which was the Crown of England, and if she wasn't given it, the nation would be drowned in blood for a thousand generations. And so, by the King's express direction, for the past dozen years she's resided in Bethlem, where by all reports she does nicely, though daily expecting a visit from His Majesty that never comes.

"Now, Peg would be a Green Cloth case," Mr. Fat leaned over to remind Mr. Lean.

"Aye," Mr. Lean agreed. "And Monro and his father together were the doctors consulted. Once Peg was in here, old Monro used to play at cards with her. It's him who said it's possible to be insane and still take a hand at whist."

"Is your husband a threat to the Crown?" Mr. Lean now politely asked me, as if enquiring after Jamie's taste in pocket handkerchiefs.

"My husband," I assured him, "wouldn't harm a flea."

"I know," said Mr. Fat warmly. "He don't have to. Not in these perilous times. Do you remember that missile from an air-gun that broke the window of the King's carriage and passed out the other side, about two years ago—?"

"And how the mob," Mr. Lean taking up the story, "once the coach reached St. James, flipped it on its side and half destroyed it? Of course by that time his Majesty was home safe in the palace—"

"Yes," I said. "I do remember something—"

"These days you can't look sideways at the lowliest fart-catcher," Mr. Fat continued, "but they'll toss you in here and throw away the key. It's all this revolution in the air. The nabs is quaking in their boots, and when they quake they come down hard on the poor and unsuspecting. They come down very hard indeed."

As he said the last of this he looked at me smiling, not grimly, I don't think, at the thought of coming down hard on the poor and unsuspecting, but to let me know he was pleased to believe with me my husband wouldn't harm a flea.

And then the court-room door opened and the steward Alavoine emerged to summon the two of them in, and I was left alone to wonder, yet again, what it was Jamie had done to get himself in a place like this. Told Lord Liverpool he'd live to see his head on a pike at Temple Bar? Created a curfuffle in the public gallery of the House? Are these offences of the sort likely to get you locked up in a madhouse? Perhaps Lean and Fat were right: In times like these they could be. But why would Haslam, whether or not he knew why my husband was in, act so sceptical when I mentioned the Privy Council? Even new to the job, he'd know about the Board of Green Cloth, through the case of Peg Nicholson, if no way else. Or has he listened to too much political fantasy from too many lunatics to believe Jamie could have had dealings with the leaders of Britain and

France and so got into actual hot water? If so, for all he's found out about him, he doesn't yet know my husband or what he's capable of.

My vigil on the bench continuing, my thoughts moved next to Haslam's assertion that this committee saw all patients on their admittance and discharge. Well, they hadn't seen Jamie. And neither this week nor last while waiting on this bench had I seen anyone enter or leave that room who resembled a patient, either pending or dischargeable. In a population of three hundred, were so few admitted and sent away each week, there'd be no one to pass before this committee two weeks running? Then again, how would Haslam know whether the committee saw them or not, if he came to the meetings only once in a while?

Now the door opened, and without Lean and Fat emerging, Mr. Alavoine indicated with a haughty look it was my turn. And so inside once more, and everything was the same as the week before except every face but Alavoine's and Poynder's was different. Again no Haslam. This time I was not invited to say anything but only made to listen to a resolution read out by Mr. Poynder that Mr. Matthews continuing to be insane—

"Upon whose judgment?" I said.

This interruption was ignored, unless you counted Mr. Poynder's patiently repeating, *Mr. Matthews continuing to be insane* the committee had reconsidered my application with great attention and unanimously concluded they could not, consistent with their duty, discharge my husband, unless so directed by a higher authority.

"And who would that be, Almighty God?" was my next question, also ignored. A possible twitch about the lips of one or two was assurance of nothing more than a little surreptitious amusement.

The members were, however (Mr. Poynder continued), desirous to acquaint me that I might easily apply for a writ of habeas corpus to bring my husband before a judge, who would determine on the propriety of his detention. It's long been the right of every British citizen, I was reminded, to live free of arbitrary imprisonment.

At this information I nodded and said nothing, wondering if this was their way to signal that some among them had sympathy for my case or only to shift the responsibility elsewhere while *easily* increasing the difficulty and expense for me. Probably all three at once, as well as others invisible, in undiscoverable proportions.

Next, Lean and Fat were asked if they approved the answer of the committee. Craning round, I spotted them at last, seated along the back wall. They bleated out their approval. A further statement read out by Mr. Poynder informed them they'd be apprised should the committee receive any further application from Mrs. Matthews—who was me, standing right there, by every appearance voice-deprived, and rights too, if these stranglers had their way.

"On whose judgment," I said again, louder, "is my husband insane?"

The time for this question must have arrived, for all eyes now went to a certain member of the committee, a man perhaps forty, with a head in the shape of an egg, the smaller, top end adorned with cornsilk hair indented in a ring just above the ears, and with a long nose and keyhole mouth high up under its drooping tip. This individual, who for some reason had been making a great show of being engrossed in sketching with pencil on an overlarge sheet of paper in front of him, next to his hat, now glanced up and, seeing all eyes on him, though I think he knew the whole time what was going on and only feigning this ridiculous insouciance, tilted his head toward the man beside him—more play-acting, because the man only looked at him blankly—and then, as if he'd just had something crucial cleared up, rose to his feet to address me as from a considerable height.

"Madam, I am Dr. Monro, physician here. I know we'll have met upon the day or thereabouts of your husband's admission—"

"No, I never saw you before. My husband is not here by my consent, and I was not informed of his admission until a week after it was effected."

This information seemed a source of shock to several on the committee. A murmur went round it.

Monro, meanwhile, at my ungrateful behaviour, glanced pointedly about the room with a look that said, *Do you see what I mean? Do you see?* before he turned smiling hard-eyed to me. "However that may be, Mrs. Matthews, it is my unhappy duty to assure you your husband is completely mad. But this don't mean his condition won't change with isolation, rest, and care of the sort we've long known how to provide here at Bethlem Hospital. Madam, I know what great temptation it must be to believe a loved one well when he's not—"

"Well or not," I said, "my husband's not dangerous. I want him home with me, as the law requires, and if I can't have him, I want to know who wants him in here. If it's you or Mr. Haslam, then tell me. If it's not, I want to know what higher power of government this committee is awaiting direction from. If it's the Privy Council then tell me, so I know the charge and what I can do about it."

"Madam—"

"You might also while you're at it tell me how you can assure me my husband's mad when after four weeks in here he never saw you."

"Why, that's entirely—"

"What colour's his hair?"

"I attend this hospital—"

"What colour is my husband's hair?"

"Madam, you can't expect—"

"Admit, sir, you're just pronouncing on him what the apothecary's told you to pronounce."

"I'm doing nothing of the kind! I have been here, regularly, and yes, I have conferred, as usual, with Mr. Haslam—"

"If Haslam's a member of this committee, where is he? And where was he last week?"

"—and I've seen your husband too, as a matter of fact, and do pronounce him totally mad, and that's all I have to say!" Monro sat down.

Now I was in a fury. "Who admitted my husband if not you as physician of this hospital?"

Once more all eyes went to Monro, who, without rising from his chair, and not looking at me, for he was well aware he was not answering the question, in a trembling voice said, "Madam, I assure you Mr. Haslam's in perfect agreement with me when I say your husband's a most insane and deranged lunatic, and this court don't need to call in a mere apothecary to announce the same thing all over again."

At this I flew into a tirade but was not so beside myself I didn't see Monro tip Alavoine the wink, and the next thing I knew strong fingers were gripping my arm and that clown accent was in my ear. "Come along, Mrs. Nuisance—"

And so, still crying, "Who admitted my husband?" "Why can't I see him?" "What higher authority of government?" and "Where's Haslam?" I was carried squirming from the room.

Thus ended my second interview with the governors' subcommittee of Bethlem Hospital.

Later, walking home, my mind running the event over and over, as it will do, never quite sure whether for tips to better conduct next time or for proof the course of action it came up with was a model for future behaviour, I remembered a glimpse I had when being led out, of Mr. Lean and Mr. Fat, sitting in chairs along the back wall, both with eyes closed and heads bowed, though whether seeking divine assistance for my husband or in the ostrich way of more modern mortals, my escort allowed me no leisure to determine.

Next, to the continuing detriment of the shop, I turned my energies to making my case in writing before the full Court of Governors of Bridewell and Bethlem, the two institutions—house of correction and hospital—at that level being jointly administered (which tells you something). This fact I discovered from my conversation with Lean and Fat, the Bethlem subcommittee comprising a small group of these governors serving in rotation, whereas the Court of Governors of both institutions meets not even monthly.

And so, while I waited for an answer to my petition from the larger, slower-moving assembly, I spent another six weeks being stopped at the gate by my Cerberus, Bulteel.

One warm spring morning, after being turned away as usual, meaning that in the more than three months of Jamie's incarceration I had seen him only once, and with as yet no answer or even acknowledgment to my petition to the

Court of Governors, I was walking back home down Broker Row, at the east perimeter of Bethlem, when it struck me the commotion issuing from inside was louder and more anguished than I ever heard it. First I tried to convince myself it must be my own imagination, but I didn't think so. And it wasn't my being downwind, for there was no breeze and the din had been no less loud at the front gate. Some dire celestial alignment? The only kind I ever knew to affect them was the moon—they're not called lunatics for nothing—but the full was weeks away. And yet this morning the noise was extraordinary, the wailing and howling of Banshees, for just as infants before language has harnessed their brain utter sounds they never will again, so lunatics make noises unavailable to sanity.

Reaching London Wall, I looked along there, and seeing the door to Haslam's house that Jamie had showed me the morning he brought me to Bethlem, I climbed the steps and hammered away until a maid, a blithe little thing with a pretty face, opened the door a crack to tell me Mr. Haslam was where he usually was, in the Dead House.

Pressing a coin into her hand, I said, "Sixpence to take me there. I have urgent business with him."

As she peered at the money I asked her why the patients were so noisy today.

"First week of May it's warm enough," she murmured.

"For what?"

"Why," she said, extricating her gaze from the coin to look at me as if I might be a lunatic myself not to know, "to be bled."

"Who? Not all of them—?"

She nodded. "All strong enough, who ain't incurable. It's policy. Next, vomits once a week for four weeks. Then purges, to the end of September." She smiled. "After that, the cold weather is medicine enough."

Looking cunning, or pretending to, she told me to wait.

"If it's not while you bring me Mr. Haslam," I said, "you owe me sixpence."

Laughing, she pushed the coin back at me and was gone.

Now I peered into the hallway, which was not the one Haslam had led me down from his office but the one to his own residence. But there was more light on the stoop than inside, and all I could see was rattan carpeting and bare walls, which seemed fresh-painted, in a cheerful plum.

Eventually a handsome woman, though pale and frightening thin, came to the door with a girl perhaps five years old clutching her skirts. She wore her straight black hair cut short and was sombrely dressed in a plain charcoal gown. Her left hand, when not covering her mouth as she coughed, she kept lightly at the back of the girl's head. The girl was sturdy and fair-haired: what her mother was not. She gazed at me saucily, but when I smiled at her, she grew abashed and hid her face in her mother's skirts.

Though Jamie had told me this was Haslam's house, it never occurred to me he'd have a family, but why wouldn't he? Wasn't this the better part of him I didn't want to know, so my enmity could remain unalloyed?

Mrs. Haslam's impatience to be brought to the door by a stranger was communicated by a glance at my basket, as if I had something to hawk. But her maid must have told her what I wanted, for without inquiring anything of me she said her husband would be somewhere in the main building, she didn't know where.

"The Dead House," I said. "I was to meet him there."

"Then I'm afraid you've come to the wrong door. This is his residence."

"Yes, but the porter had no—"

"I'm sorry, you must make another appointment—" She was already stepping back to close the door. Before it reached the eyes of the little girl I cast her a glum look, which she answered with a grin as her foot shot out to help the door along, so it slammed in my face. Immediately it opened again upon the sight of her mother extricating her from her skirts, so she could apologize to me, which, once she was facing me and knew she must, she readily did. As she lisped the formula, her mother looked at me apologetic, and I liked them both. Then her mother bowed her head and stepped back. Once more the door closed, and that time it stayed that way.

A week later I received a letter from Mr. Poynder informing me of two developments. First, by a legal process he failed to specify, on May 2nd, 1797, my husband had been brought before Lord Kenyon, as Lord Chief Justice of the Court of the King's Bench, in his house in Lincoln's Inn Fields. After conversing with him, Lord Kenyon was satisfied my husband was a maniac. Second, on May 6th the Bethlem subcommittee passed a motion ordering that until their further instruction, the wife of Mr. Matthews not be permitted any visit to Bethlem Hospital, the patient's disorder being manifestly exacerbated in consequence of her company.

This letter I could only stare at, saying *Haslam*.

JOHN HASLAM

1798

MONRO

"So, Haslam," Monro said to me two months after my book went on sale, "you never told me you're a scribbler. Let's see this great work of yours that's set the medical world a-buzz."

"A trifle, Dr. Monro, I assure you. My book has been held in greater esteem than its intrinsic merits could justify."

"No, no! Don't play humble, man. Fetch us a copy!"

His muddy boots were up on his desk, a magazine open in his lap. This was in March, one of Monro's rare days in from Hackney. For two or three hours I'd taken him round to those patients most in need of him. Excluded from their number were the several who'd died in need of him since he was last here, in January. Now he'd summoned me for a nominal consultation, or so I thought. For once I was grateful he had, because sometimes he was gone before I knew it, and I wanted to ask him why he'd given instructions for the removal to the incurable wing of so harmless a lunatic as James Matthews, for on the face of it this would mean we were keeping him forever. But upon entering Monro's office and being called a scribbler by a man whose father had written a good book but who himself, having no mind, never would and so hated all writers, I suddenly regretted my recent good luck in becoming a celebrated English author.

Still breathing hard from my dash, I handed him his copy.

"You're going to have to inscribe this, you know," he warned me.

"Yes, I was intending—"

"'Observations on Insanity.' Now there's a title. 'By John Haslam. Late of Pembroke Hall, Cambridge.' Why, I never knew you were at Cambridge, John. But no degree, eh? Too bad—'Member of the Corporation of Surgeons.' A surgeon as well? A man of many talents, evidently. 'And Apothecary to Bethlem Hospital.' Now, that I did know."

Next he read the dedication, frowning, for it makes no mention of the physician. After determining it didn't continue overleaf, he directed a bleak look at me and then fell to skimming. " 'Gentleness of manner and kindness of treatment . . .' Yes, that's our policy here all right. 'Knowledge of the recesses of a lunatic's mind is beyond the limits of our attainment . . .' Hear, hear . . . What's this?" His eyes came up from the page. " 'Lunatics should never be deceived'?"

"Your father John believed the same," I assured him, too quickly. "Not if we'd obtain their confidence and esteem—"

"What happened to obedience?" He was back reading. "Hmm. I didn't know we were wrapping bare feet now. In flannel, no less. What next? Night-caps?"

"Only the worst cases. They—"

"We'll take it out of your salary." This was humour with dead eyes. "You know, Haslam, it's a queer thing to be sitting here gleaning, from a book I didn't even know was being written, information I never knew about a hospital I happen to be physician of—"

"Yes, I can appreciate—but the opportunity so rarely befalls men busy as ourselves to sit down and—"

He was tapping the cover with a paint-stained fingernail. "So what exactly's your god-damn point? What's your conclusion from your year 'observing insanity' around here? Jesus Christ. I never knew we had somebody knocking about the place so mad for attention. I suppose the King's madness has everybody ready to listen to mad-doctors, whoever they might be. You know what Dad used to say, and his dad before him? 'Madness is a distemper there's no use to say anything of to anybody.' "

"It's been two and a half."

"What?"

"I've been here two and a half years."

"Two and a half, eh? Do you know how many years Monros have been 'observing insanity' at Bethlem?"

"Seventy."

"Is it that long? I guess you know people call us 'the other Georges,' eh? Like the kings? Only, none of us is named George, and ours ever was the Kingdom of the Mad. Ha! ha! It's been forty years since Dad answered William Battie's mistaken optimism when the bastard attacked us in his *Treatise on Madness*—"

" 'Like a man whose every word communicates resentment of its instigation.' "

"What?"

"Someone said that of your father's answer, which was a brilliant one." It was a relief to be able to say this without dissemblance. Old Monro's *Remarks on Dr. Battie's Treatise* was bloody good. Old Monro might have been *a quacking madman* (as someone once called him), but he had a nice sense of the refractoriness of the condition.

"It's always been a mystery to me," Monro was saying, "how a man like Battie ever got himself taken seriously. Oh, I suppose he helped found St. Luke's Hospital, but to hear him ramble on about curing madness you'd think he was taking a piss on the wrong side of the hedge when the brains was passed out—"

" 'From Punch's forehead wrings the dirty bays.' "

"What?"

"From a poem on him."

"Ah. He deserved poetry all right, the cunt." He was fumbling for my book. He held it up. "So what's your stand, Haslam? What's your theory?"

I shrugged. "You'll get no metaphysics from me, Dr. Monro. In my view, theories about madness are another form of it, parasites dining on a tumour. I disentangle myself as quick from their theories of madness as I do from theories of the mad. Most books on the subject are romances, hooks baited for the emolument of the author. Grinning advertisements for private madhouses, mumbo-jumbo catalogues for their hotbed nurseries that never produce a human crop fit to be transplanted into society."

"That's my boy! Ho ho ho!" But this outburst came across less hearty than intended. While the eyes lingered on me with ostensible approval, the face registered a slow succession of thoughts that grew by turns more gloomy and tormented until the little mouth burst out with, "But what d'you actually *say,* man? There must be thousands of words between these bloody boards! Goddamn! Excellent things about us, by the Jesus!"

"Oh yes," I said quickly. "That's why it's dedicated to the governors—"

"Yes, yes, very politic. You're referring, of course—" he went flipping back to the dedication—"to those 'vigilant and humane Guardians of an Institution which performs much good to Society, by diminishing the severest among human calamities.' Hear! hear! I say again." Now the disappointment in his eyes was pathetic to see.

"You might also want to glance at page 136."

"What?" He was already on his way. "Let's see. 'Dr. Monro, the present celebrated and judicious physician to Bethlem Hospital, (to whom I gratefully acknowledge many and serious obligations) . . .' " By the look he gave me then, this almost pleased him. I had worried the barefaced fiction of it would annoy him. It certainly annoyed me, who heard in it a slave grovelling before a nincompoop. But what rankled for him was its appearance so late in the volume. "Let's hope your reader lasts this far," he said, with a mean little smile.

"Let's hope he does," I replied, bland and world-weary as a seasoned author.

He was reading down the page. "So you don't think much of vomiting them—?"

"No, I never found any good from it. Bleeding, on the other hand—"

"In all your months here."

I just smiled.

"Me neither," he admitted, continuing to flip. "But considering we still do it—" he looked at me—"I wonder if we should announce it in print—" He returned to reading. "My God, blisters neither? What *do* you believe in?"

"I only say no blisters of the head—"

"A funny thing, but Dad never saw value in blistering of any kind. That never stopped him, of course. He always said, 'If she works, Tom, do 'er,' but the damned thing is, he never told me how I'm supposed to know what works and what don't. Between you and me, Haslam, when it came to treatment of lunatics, the old man was as much in the dark as we are."

"Dr. Monro, my book's simply a series of accounts of my own unmediated encounters with the insane. Each portrayal of a lunatic character I follow up with a description of their brain after they died."

"Who did your autopsies? Crowther—? How's his head, by the by? Kicked by a patient, was he, and fell down the stairs?"

"The kick was a nudge. Crowther was drunk at breakfast. His head's mended. I do my own autopsies; he does his."

"And your conclusion?"

"While as yet there's no definite correlation between lunatic symptoms and brain state at death, that don't mean we won't find one, once medicine better understands the brain. In the meantime, recovery from insanity sometimes occurs, but the affliction remains intractable to cure."

"But I say, Haslam, what use to us is a book that admits nothing we do does any good?"

"Only to keep in view the truth. Some nowadays—and I fear our colleague Mr. Crowther's among their number—are inclined to pretend madness is a disorder of ideas, or mind alone. How something by definition incorporeal can be diseased they don't say."

"Crowther too? I'd have expected better from him. What are these people thinking of?"

"Money."

"Why didn't you say so? What are we waiting for? Ideas it is! Ha ha!" He'd turned vexedly back to my book and was fanning the pages. There was something else he wanted to ask. "Speaking of brains, Haslam, you didn't by chance examine anybody I tried the electrical machine on—?"

"Possibly. You never told me who they were."

"Well, there was Rophy and Crawley, and Blackburn—who killed Crawley, didn't he? Last summer? Did you do Crawley?"

"I couldn't do Crawley. The skull was crushed."

"And there was that fellow who used to take off people's hats with his toes and destroy his food bowl with his teeth, to sharpen them, he'd say, for his next meal—"

"Brody. I did him—"

"Any splinters? Ha! ha!"

"No splinters, but a milky fluid on one of the posterior cerebrum lobes, like a boil, with a corresponding depression in the convolutions, which was so marked they looked like the intestines of a child. But nothing to suggest an electrical current."

"No charring? No burns?"

"Nothing like that."

"Because he was an extreme one. I used to give him ten minutes at fourteen cells, and he didn't like it at all. Four keepers we needed to buckle the straps on him. And when they took them off he was more annoyed than ever."

"So far, Dr. Monro, I assure you I've seen nothing to indicate effects traceable to an electrical current."

"That's good. So no harm's been done. But I guess you know I've given up on it. Another Continental gimmick, if you ask me. Bloody Italians. Nobody here seemed to like it, and the staff was never keen. But did I tell you last month the committee approved my application for a shower-bath?"

"Yes, I attended that meeting expressly to support it." And initiated and wrote the application.

"Now, that will be a good thing."

"A very good thing."

"Improvements, eh, Haslam? Always looking for ways to improve the place, aren't we?"

"Yes, we are."

"My shower-bath, this 'mouth-key' I hear you're at work on—no, don't tell me about it now, show me when it's ready—this little book of yours. We're pioneers, you and me, and Crowther—"

"Especially Crowther."

He looked at me close a moment and then laughed. "Who can say," he continued, wiping his eyes, "that one day the mad won't recover faster by the help of medicine than without it. Ain't this what all this 'observing' and scribbling comes down to? Breaking ground, aren't you, Haslam, just like a Monro? One day you'll call me to the Dead House and say, 'Look here, Monro, d'you see this inflammation on this lobe here? It always accompanies a general paralysis. I wonder what that tells us.' And I'll say, 'Well, Haslam, why don't we spread a little salve along there, a smear of clove perhaps, or maybe powders'll do the trick,' and the next thing we know another fellow's up to an honest day's work. Isn't this the message about us your little book here's intended to send out into the world?"

"Something like that," I said, as confused as he was if he thought we'd soon be dissecting living brains. "Though your version," I added, "perhaps has more life and colour in it."

He beamed at this. "Why, that's because I'm a painter. I work with colour all the time!"

My chance. "Matthews—" I said.

"What?"

"James Tilly Matthews—"

"He's in your book? He ain't dead yet, is he?"

"Alavoine tells me you've ordered him to the incurable wing."

"That's right. Hasn't it been a year?"

"He's not dangerous."

"Lord Liverpool thinks so."

"So it *is* politics."

"Smells like it to me, but Jesus Christ, the bugger's a lunatic."

"Did Liverpool put him in?"

"I wouldn't know."

"What's his crime?"

"Another republican, I suppose. You'll have to ask his Lordship if you want details."

"How long do we keep him?"

"Long enough, I should think, so you can examine the boils on his convolutions."

"He was doing very well until he heard where he's going."

"That's because he's lucid enough to know what it means. Did you ever notice a funny thing: they're all insane, but only the idiots are fools? Which isn't to say everybody except the melancholics don't live in hope they've no right to, even as they object to any sort of change. Listen. If Matthews' path of resistance is to sink and perish, it'll be the sooner Camberwell's relieved of the expense of him and the sooner his brain repays what he owes society for the useless bastard it's made of him."

"His wife—"

"Ah, yes. A pretty thing, and then she opens her mouth. What about her?"

"She wants to visit."

"We settled that."

"Yes, but too long a solitary confinement in a dreary place can itself—"

"Where else are we supposed to confine 'em? He *is* a madman by your definition, ain't he? You're not saying he's not mad—?"

Can there be anything more infuriating than a weak and doltish authority when it springs an inflexible *No*? "I'm only saying, Dr. Monro, in this instance, periodic visits from his wife might—"

"Damn *might*. Let sleeping dogs lie."

"This one's not asleep."

"Neither lately have we had the bitch yapping in our faces. The one thing we're in a position to offer here, Haslam, the one thing that's been any proven use at all, is quiet. Not silence—I'm not deaf. I mean removal from the unremitting din they've made of their lives. You let even a little of the old noise pursue them in here and nine times in ten the only worthwhile thing we have to offer flies straight out the window. She's old enough to know a barred door when she comes to one. For God's sake, she married a lunatic. What does she expect?"

"Humanity."

"What?"

"She expects us to treat her husband and herself with humanity."

"Which is exactly what we do, as you say so well in your little book here, and there's an end on it!" Saying this, he pressed his watch, which sounding four o'clock amazed him. He threw the book across the desk at me and swung his boots to the floor. "Haslam, be a capital fellow and sign this squib of yours to me, as the physician of the place you do your precious 'observing' in. And this time don't spare those sentiments of glitterary admiration you're so dab a hand at—but quickly, like a good man? I needed to be out of here an hour ago—"

EXALTATION

The next morning, I invited the steward Peter Alavoine, my Bethlem eyes and ears, to my office to give me word of Matthews. It was *raving*.

"He tells me," Alavoine said, speaking not in the register of aggrievement that his queer unplaceable dialect was perfectly suited to convey but with a quality in it of enjoyment that surprised me so much I glanced up. It was the Alavoine I knew, a grizzled stick in tiered hat and filthy red jacket but at this moment with a tamped smile about the sunk cheeks. "I must now address him," he told me, "as James, Absolute Sole and Supreme Sacred Omni Imperias Grand Arch Emperor of the Universe."

The delusions of lunatics, however fantastical or comic, did not normally win our steward's indulgence. There was something in this one he relished. I am tempted to say *already loved*. It's not every lunatic he makes sure is properly dressed when nobody's paid him to do it—or can prove he's paid him.

"Does he approve his new quarters?" I asked.

"No, he does not." As he said this, a gleam in those gummy eyes lent the degenerate old face the look of a schoolboy's. A toothless hoary schoolboy's. "He considers them insulting even to the most unassuming of Absolute Rulers."

"Does he like the wood chair I found him, with the arms? Does he like the arms?"

"His Omni Imperias Throne, you mean? I think he does. He sits in it doing ledgers of rewards he intends for the execution of would-be usurpers of his power: £300,000 for the death of the King of Portugal, a million for the Emperor of Persia—"

"And of England?"

"The Infamous Usurping Murderer George Guelph (as he calls him) he includes in a special package with his Majesty's family and government—"

"I thought he loved the King. I thought he was an unconfessed republican driven mad because he loves the King. Or claims he does."

"Not today. Today the King's his mortal rival. Also included in the package for execution are the Lord Mayor of London and Council; all police officers and secretaries of state; you, me, Alf Bulteel (whom he particularly condemns for obstructing lawful intercourse in families), and all other employees of this place; everybody responsible for putting him in here; the directors of the Bank of England; all courtiers, etc. For everybody, four million pounds. Though he regrets the number who must die, he says it's not half those murdered annually by event-working gangs. Today he revealed the gangs themselves prefer to speak of *working feats of arms,* since their main assaults are against individuals who claim heraldic bearings."

"In here they must work with lowered sights. Tell him I'll drop by when I can." Saying this, I bowed my head to the letter I was writing to Lord Liverpool, but I was thinking of Matthews, for this was painful news. Lunatic or not, he knew what the incurable wing meant and knew as well as I did he didn't belong there. We should not have added to his suffering by putting him through that, even if it was only until I could return him to his wife.

Hearing a cough, I glanced up. Alavoine was still before me, extending a fist.

"Something, sir—" the fist opening to deposit on my palm something crumbly and reddish—"you might be interested to see."

I looked at it. "Pieces of brick, Peter? No. Not interested—"

"With your permission, sir—"

In my thirty months at Bethlem, one member of staff I had learned to listen to (aside from our clerk, Mr. Poynder, whose strengths were policy and precedent, and so rather different) was Peter Alavoine. I said he was my eyes and ears. He was also my nose, tongue, and whiskers: his cat to my old woman. When work kept me shut up in my office or the Dead House, who patrolled my world but Alavoine. Yet this feline had jackdaw blood in him, for he was ever spiriting things away. An inveterate thief. That was the hitch. I was not one of those who discover too late that what they'd thought was an employee's love was embezzlement. I knew from the start Alavoine was crooked as walnut meat. His corruption was a cancer on a body already sick enough, and if I could have rid Bethlem of him I would have. But I couldn't. Officially he answered not to me but to Monro, who though he rarely saw him wouldn't hear a word spoke against anyone good enough to have worked for his father.

After I finished my letter to Liverpool, I followed Alavoine to the basement, where some of the incontinents—what we called our dirty or straw patients— had lately been demoted, for lack of space. In one of the cells he indicated a gap in the ceiling arch. The brick could have struck and even killed the patient, who seemed frail. Mercifully she was locked by the arm to the wall, her only comment, "How can I catch larks when the sky's falling?"

"You can't," I told her.

The brick landed in the centre of her cell where it broke in a dozen pieces, being like all the bricks of this place, of inferior and unseasoned composition.

Alavoine's point to me was not the badness of the brick or the uselessness of the mortarwork, nor was it the danger to the patient, but the larger consideration that no one who lived and worked in the building was safe.

Walking ahead with a lanthorn, he led me past more straw-patient cells into an entire other world, the last you'd expect to find down here: the section of our basement we lease to the mighty East India Company, a treasure-trove of pallets and shelves stacked with sacks and baskets emitting every fragrance of spice, and with crates of pepper, tobacco, tea, fruit—all the way to where the shelves ended and the floor fell away to clammier air and different darkness.

"What's this?" I said. "Where are we?"

"Under the east wing."

"But this space—?"

"Fresh dug."

Fresh but with a sour reek of rotten metal from the ancient city dump Bethlem was built on. My first, shameful thought: How many straw patients we could fit down here! To Alavoine I said, "Who did it? Matthews' magnetic villains, to set up their Air Loom for more precise beaming of mayhem into patients' skulls?"

"No," he replied, not amused by raillery at Matthews' expense. "By diggers hired by the East India governors." And I followed him down a springing ramp of boards to witness how, out of greed for more space, they'd widened doorways, compromised exterior walls, and undermined piers intended to uphold the structure rising three storeys above us. I was shown leaning uprights, sagging joists, and universal dry rot, until it seemed at any moment a thousand tons of bricks, timbers, and lunatics would come raining down on our heads. In my nervous glances upward and repeated moppings of perspiration from my brow, Alavoine discovered dramatic affirmation of his point. I would characterize his expression while lighting my hurried steps out of there as severe tending to grim, yet with a certain satisfaction about the mouth that betokened consciousness of a hand well played.

Before reaching daylight, I resolved to argue again before the Saturday subcommittee the imperative of calling in a surveyor to tell us how or if the walls could be underpinned. If my words failed to convince them, I'd lead a delegation down there and let their own cold sweat do it. But I knew this time would be different: Even as I made the argument, I would understand it was too late.

Let me explain. When at age thirty-one I had first took up this post, the fever of renown burning in my veins told me Bethlem and I would rise together. Monro thought Bethlem was his; I knew it wasn't. He would ride in once a month; I would live on the premises. He would see patients now and then; I would visit them daily. I was the one who would make of Bethlem a masterpiece that would say to the world, *Here is how you order a hospital for lunatics.*

But then one of various series of experiments I undertook on arrival issued very naturally in a small book. Though nothing new, this little opus was the thing of mine that got cried up as the masterpiece—which, by catapulting me to fame as an author on madness, demoted mighty Bethlem to my materials only. At the same time, it promoted my thoughts from her low, intractable galleries to a struggle more hygienic and winnable: the selection and arrangement of words on a page. Except, the more I grew used to rarer elevations, the more I wondered how I had ever been pleased to imagine nothing more for myself than a life spent shoring so dreadful a place against its final ruin.

Such pride I wish to God was never mine. But it was, and now, if I am to grasp how my fortunes came to take the nightmare course they did, my only hope is naked candour, or as much as I can muster.

As for Matthews, though his condition drastically worsened once he learned of his transfer to the incurable wing, that was only the crowning blow after a year of no visits from his wife. For this he blamed me and Monro, as the medical officers, and our porter Bulteel. (Why on earth, if she was so keen on his rescue, didn't she at least write him? Did she think the quicker he sank, the stronger her case? Or was her life too crisis-filled to afford the luxury of uncut losses? I didn't think that was it. Something about this one told me we were still under siege—invisibly only because she couldn't get over the wall.) As for me, like Alavoine but in my own way, Matthews affected me more each day. My fear now was he had come to us an addled republican in a state of nervous collapse and would leave a barking lunatic. A lunatic who when first he knew me was intrigued and now he knew me better was revolted.

I was coming along the front hall, still blinking from the basement, when our clerk, Mr. Poynder, accosted me in a state of wordless excitement. After fumbling a letter into my hands, he fell back to view my reaction. Poynder is an odd fish and since the first day I met him has had an odd effect on me. Sometimes, talking to him I feel it would take very little for everything suddenly to shift and the two of us to start communicating in an altogether different capacity— though what it would be I can't imagine. When my reaction to the letter was blushing incomprehension, he stepped to my side to help me decipher the French. After that I was excited as he was and set out to tell my wife, Sarah, but my route taking me through the incurable wing (which for the men is at the far east end of the building, suspended over our fresh-dug Black Hole of Calcutta) I first paid a visit to Matthews, who was crouched quietly on his bed, writing or drawing on a sheet of paper, his Omni Imperias Throne standing empty.

"James," I said, rustling the letter at his ear, "here's something to interest you. The celebrated Philippe Pinel is coming to visit us."

No response. Matthews is a small, fair-haired man with the sharp, handsome features of an intelligent clerk, an impression compounded that day by his neat grey shirt and snug-fitting waistcoat. Hunched over his work, he seemed sharper and smaller than ever. A specimen of a lunatic patient so exemplary he didn't look like a lunatic at all.

"He's writing a book on the management of lunatics," I continued, "and eager to see first hand how we do things here. He wants to meet everybody, inmates included. He even mentions by name two of our more famous: Peg Nicholson and James Tilly Matthews. Peg I assume because she tried to kill the King, and you because he approves whatever you did to advance republicanism in France—"

"Who told you that?"

"—or whatever it was you did there."

"Why do you persist in calling me a republican, Jack? Are you so ardent a monarchist?"

"Ain't England a monarchy and I an Englishman?"

"And if it was a republic?"

"Then it would be perfectly unimaginable to me."

"No longer England, you think?"

"I think I should not know where I was—"

"Or who? And do you now?"

"Not when I find myself once again in debate with you."

At this he only looked at me disgusted and turned away.

"Forget politics, James, you're to meet the great Pinel."

"Who is he?"

"Most recently, director of the Salpêtrière Hospital for female lunatics, in Paris. A genuine revolutionary: you'll have much to talk about. In '93, when he was put in charge of the insane at another Paris hospital, the Bicêtre, his first act was to strike the chains off the patients. Most were immediately afterward strapped into strait-waistcoats, but in a legend of Revolution what's that but a detail? Pinel's one of only two or three Frenchmen capable of appreciating the difficulties of management in a place like this, and he approves what he's heard."

"About you."

"In part about me. He read my book—"

"This is flattery to insinuate themselves. Next they'll have their Air Loom set up in the stove room. If this Pinel's not their instrument, he'll be one of them, sent out as him. The only question is, Why a Frenchman? A perverse and vicious taunt, I suppose."

Thinking that if Matthews was in a state to talk to Pinel, he'd talk to him, and if he wasn't, then Peg Nicholson could tell him about the avenging dolphins slicing through the Thames to offer her the throne, I was leaning over Matthews' shoulder to see whose death he was ordering this morning. It seemed to be a printed page he was writing on.

"Who tore that out, James?" When he made no answer, I leaned closer and was astonished to see him shaping the next letter himself, as he'd apparently done the entire page, freehand, and yet it was perfect, every character upright and level as if typeset, the latest still glistening wet. And all done with a chain on his wrist.

"James, what kind of talent is this?"

No reply.

"What does it say?"

"It recounts atrocities committed in this place."

When I leaned closer to read, he put his other hand over it and looked round at me. There was a puff-paste quality to his features, and I wondered if water had been discharged from his brain, and that's why he was calmer. It frightens me sometimes how little we know.

"A perfect lettering of everything," he said, and returned to his work.

"Everything?"

"Everything. You'll be thrown to the wolves."

"Why? Don't Anne Gibbons and Jane Taylor, who murdered their husbands, though whether their own or each other's has never been—"

"Each other's."

"Good. That's settled. Don't the darlings both separately and together write me *billets doux*? Am I not well-loved here?"

"Yes, like a favourite uncle who invisibly works machinery so cruel that any little favour he brings is seen as a godsend. The patients think, *Well, the keepers may be vicious bullies, but at least the man in charge is good and kind. So good and kind it's no surprise he's an easy dupe of monsters so evil.* And of course, like the King's, your scarceness makes you even more beloved. 'What a treat it is,' the patients say, 'to have the doctor about again!' But Jack, you know what goes on here as well as I do. As you grow more famous and spend more time writing, you see less, but still in general you do know what goes on."

"I do. And work daily to alleviate all suffering that I can, considering I have next to no authority, labour under an absent superior, and have three hundred patients to see to. What time do I have to know about these wolves I'm to be thrown to?"

"You can't know about 'em as long as their identities remain in flux. With the Ministry undermined every other day, a patriot Monday is a ravening traitor come Friday. Who can predict who'll be who in the wolf pack the day I'm out?"

Saying this, he fixed me with a cold stare. "And if I'm still in when the wolves come for you, I'll scatter my pages in the forecourt to ensure they squeeze through the gates."

"Wolves have no interest in print, James."

"These will be fascinated."

"Tell me this. If you could change one thing about the place, what would it be?"

"My presence. My awful susceptibility to its every abuse originates in the one."

"What single abuse otherwise?"

"The fact there's more humanity in the victim than in the persecutor."

"Isn't this just your natural sympathy for your fellow patients?"

"No. What in here is called treatment, outside is called what it is: punishment."

"James, I understand it must look at times—"

"You need to be mad, Jack, for it to look any other way."

What was I thinking? Only a fool engages with a lunatic when he's raving. As Pinel himself has said, he's too acute. To which I'd add, unconvincible of anything except his own fixed obsessions. The duty of medicine is not to puzzle what madness says. With language already mostly metaphor, the only question is, How committed is the patient to these wild pronouncements? Is there some way to lessen the grip of these proud views and even bring about remorse or abjuration? What other goal could justify provoking delusions into the light?

"I'll have Alavoine give you more ink and paper," I said.

"Sir Archy, you mean. Alavoine will give me clothes and ink and paper, but Sir Archy will pretend it's all a favour I don't deserve and make me pay for every piece of fabric, every drop of ink. I'd rather dip a brush in my own blood and write on the walls than go through that again."

"What does he do? Pay how?"

"Why, Jack, must I keep explaining it? You've stopped listening, and what you once knew you've forgot. Your theme is gentle kindness. But all nature's creatures listen, you don't."

"Tell me how Alavoine forces you to pay."

"I told you: not Alavoine. Sir Archy. By making me his talisman. Did I mention Charlotte's in chains as his tribade, for he's secretly a woman? And so accomplished at brain-saying, most victims don't even know it's happening. But I do. Anything from Sir Archy is remarkable for its depravity, and easy to spy as ragweed in clover. What's harder is rooting it out, for it grips the mind with a tenacity that belies its degenerate source."

I must say I preferred Matthews close-mouthed and sullen. The raving only stirred in me an unavailing dismay. "I'll give you ink and paper myself," I said.

"Do you mean it? Be the instrument of your own arraignment?"

"Yes, out of kindness to its author." Now that he was talking, there was information I needed if I would be more than his stationer. Cautiously, I sat down on the bed. After allowing him several minutes to grow accustomed to me so close as he worked, I said quietly, "James, tell me why exactly Lord Liverpool wants you in here."

"Liverpool wants nothing exactly. Try sharpening a blade once it's rotten."

"But why has he picked you? Because you interrupted his speech in the House?"

"No, because I know what he is."

"Which is what?"

"Nothing."

"Did you offer a threat against his life?"

"Not in so many words, but here's a better idea, Jack, and more how you like to think of yourself: Skip the threat and straight to the execution."

"James, listen. To secure your release I need to be clear why you're in."

"Why don't you ask Monro? He knows less than nothing."

"And Liverpool?"

"Liverpool you'll find treacherous in the approach. Like Jefferson and Washington, he has the smell on him of the blood of slaves. Did you know the reason I refuse sugar in my tea is slavery in the sugar trade? In Grosvenor Square, in the days Liverpool was still Baron Hawkesbury, I once caught a glimpse of his first wife, Lady Hawkesbury, in the company of her mother, a Hindoo. Her father was a Clive man who cheated his way to a Bengal fortune. Lady Hawkesbury's name was Amelia, a dusky beauty, only seventeen when I saw her. At nineteen she was sent down to the house at Hawkesbury, which had sat empty for a century owing to a curse after the first baronet's sister, prevented by her father from marrying a Papist, fell from an upper window. The beautiful Amelia was sent down for convalescence of a fever after the birth of a son but arrived dead. When the coachman unlatched the door of the cab, out she tumbled. They buried her across the road and gave over all thought of reclaiming the house, now doubly cursed. They say on windless days there hangs about the ruins a smell of the blood of slaves."

"Does any of this have to do with why you're in?"

"Only the part about the smell of the blood of slaves. Liverpool's ultimate purpose is to disenfranchise the nation."

"How will he do that?"

"He's done and is doing it. Most lately by keeping up the conflict with France in hopes of causing the assassination of both nations and the destruction of my existence."

"By what means? Because Liverpool's anti-republican views since the fall of the Bastille are well known?"

"No, because he's a liar, cheat, and destroyer, activated by the gang."

"But aren't we all activated by the gang, according to you?"

"Not all. The honest, decided, unwitting ones they ignore."

"And the honest, decided, witting ones?"

"There's only one of them in this place: me, who daily suffer bodily and mental torments. Separated from my beloved Margaret, the other half of who I am, and she from me, we're both murdered daily. But I tell you this, Jack: I'm not afraid of all the gangs put together."

"James, what evidence for these charges?"

"Fluidical."

"Ah yes, of course. Fluidical."

"You may patronize me, Jack. Don't condescend."

I stood up. "Speaking of fluidical, James, you'll have your ink by tomorrow noon, and with it a dozen sheets of good-quality paper."

With this promise I took my leave, which his gratitude, if he felt any, was insufficient to rouse him to acknowledge.

Now I was eager for Sarah to know of Pinel's letter. With praise for my book now arriving from the Continent, I felt in need of perspective, lest like Matthews for anything good he gets from Alavoine (or Sir Archy, as he calls him) I must pay another way. As an Ancient once wrote, *The man whom praise greatly pleases, censure must greatly pain.* As I say, *Better a man's wife whisper him the truth in private today than he reveal himself an idiot in public tomorrow.* In this too I was like Matthews: My wife worked hard to keep me sensible—a constant struggle. Like him I was fortunate to have married one whose judgment I could rely on and have sometimes thought, *If only he had listened to his more, he wouldn't be in here and we wouldn't be shutting her out.*

As I hurried home, I was nagged by a fear Pinel would find little to admire in Bethlem as she was. Didn't I write my book while I still wore rose-tinted spectacles, being half in love with the place I would one day make it? Thinking this, I thought again of Matthews, which reflection led me to marvel at his talent for black lettering, and then I had an idea. In my auxiliary capacity as overseer of the artsmasters at Bridewell Hospital I'd recently engaged a Mr. Logan to teach the delinquents there engraving. Well, why not have Logan stop in at Bethlem once a week and teach it to Matthews? Surely Poynder could scrape up a little something for supplies. Engraving might serve to counterbalance Matthews' raving, allay the tedium of his hours, and once I secured his release, provide him with a useful hobby, or even new trade. Meanwhile, the generosity of my initiative, even if it wasn't enough to mend relations between us, would at least let him know I was kindly disposed.

Calm, Matthews was the most discerning of our inmates and of them all the one who seemed to speak direct to my understanding. How otherwise could he roil my blood so? There was far more to him than some unhuman fantasy, and I had no trouble grasping his popularity with our visitors or the fact his renown had spread in France. Alavoine's devotion to him spoke volumes. People don't want to know that true fame begins with those daily familiar with the person, who yet persist in their admiration. What are stories of public paragon, private monster, but sedatives for envy? And while they're at it, cautionary tales. Why trouble to aspire, lest you become a monster too? But true fame's not like that, it's the splash of a small, rare drop that has rippled steadily outward.

As to Matthews' affliction, I would say it needed to be as dreadful as it was to overcome a man so quick, honourable, and intelligent, so his intellect was ever at the mercy of a hurry and confusion of thinking that swept him along on its tide. Many in Bethlem had an air of predisposing weakness, crime, or tendency to backslide. Not this one. This was a tragedy, the undoing of a fine, good man. If his condition ever eased, his mind would be good again, and morally sound. Better and sounder, in fact, than most men's I ever knew. Seeing such a one in the manifest grip of the disease was truly terrible and, whatever else its effect on me, left me too sensible of the uselessness of all we were doing and of my own impotence before so much suffering to do any lasting good at all.

My engraving initiative would mean that any work Matthews produced between now and June would be evidence Pinel could hold in his own hands and see with his own eyes that when it came to actual care, we were no less enlightened than my book had him imagining. For good measure I'd slip the chains off Matthews before he saw him, so our visitor could walk away knowing that when we unshackled 'em at Bethlem we didn't immediately cinch 'em into a strait-waistcoat—or *camisole anglais,* as Pinel would call it when among his cronies. And with my mouth-key ready to show, not to mention our new shower-bath, he'd see how progressive we are. Who knew but the great man wouldn't be so dazzled he'd out-do himself with praise for us in his next book. *They order this matter better in France,* indeed.

At home, our maid Jenny was nowhere in sight. Young John was braced in front of the parlour door wearing his Beefeater toy-hat of Canadian beaver pelt and pointing his toy musket at me.

"Ahoy, lad—"

Wrong militia. I tried again. "All quiet, yeoman?"

"All quiet, sir." He lowered the musket.

"Where's Jenny—?"

The yeoman headshake.

"Mum—? Sis—?"

He indicated the parlour door. I held it for him; he presented arms.

"Sarah—" I said, sweeping up Hetty from the rug, where she was stacking letter-blocks. "Sarah, news—"

From her cocoon of blankets by the fire, my lovely wife lowered her book and turned to us smiling. With the heat and the reddish light from the coals, her cheeks framed by her dark hair seemed almost rosy. Hetty meanwhile, as if she knew what my news was, had slipped Pinel's letter from my pocket and was testing its fabric. Needing two hands, I set her back down and extracted it from her grasp. The double bereavement stunned her. She looked uncertain whether to scream or flail. "Resume play with your letter blocks," I instructed her, "as our sober philosopher *cum* pedagogue Mr. Locke would have you improve yourself by doing." Ignoring my Swahili, she flung a look at her mother, who lifted an arm. She scrambled to her. I blurted my news.

When I had finished, Sarah, after a tactful pause, set about my instruction. "You don't think, John, Pinel won't be mainly coming to enhance himself at your expense—?"

"He doesn't need to do that. He already has preeminence in the field—"

"Preeminence in the field is very often first won by luck or subterfuge, then by riding the shoulders of successive contenders. Besides, what Frenchman—" she coughed—"unless he had something to gain by it, ever acknowledged another did anything right?"

"Reflected glory's a gain," I tried. "By all appearance he approves very well how we do things at Bethlem and like an honest scout will take back word to the rest."

"After five minutes' conversation with Watercolours Monro he'll have nothing to take back but ridicule."

"Watercolours don't often come to town for these things—" I was beginning to see the larger picture.

"He will if he finds out in time you forgot again to inform him of an important visitor."

"I won't forget—" I said, by now distinctly uneasy, not having decided if I would tell Monro or not. The problem was, he preferred not to know. That way he could avoid the nuisance of making an appearance. Yet if he found out he'd missed something, his pride was doubly hurt, first that he wasn't invited and second that he'd lost a chance to strut about and act the third-generation Monro. But this kind of hurt he could always drown in rage at me, whereas the inconvenience of coming all the way to town to have his inadequacies scrutinized he couldn't do anything about at all.

"When," Sarah asked, "is this meeting of the greatest mad-doctors of England and France set to occur?"

"He visits England late June."

"In any event?"

"Why should we be his only stop?"

"Why indeed?"

She smiled, and I smiled back, at this woman for whom my love had grown in proportion to my respect for her unblinking intellect, compounded by my terror of losing her to her illness. What joy I had known in casting my life at the feet of one so steely minded, in every aspect so contained, and yet, when she had strength, so passionate and so loving.

"Did I ever tell you, Sarah, how much I love you?"

"Daily. More often will look like you have something to hide."

"Rationed, am I? All right then, who are you reading?"

"John Wesley."

That old humbug. "Sarah, did you ever notice how many great authors are named John?"

This drew another smile, before a cough. "Oh yes, and now a fresh one to their ranks. But you say John Wesley was nothing but an old actor."

"I do not. I only mentioned the reason he was banned from sermonizing at Bethlem was his religious system is a wretched calamity rivetted to the mind by terror and despair—" I broke off before adding, *And so turns fools to madmen and madmen to foaming dogs,* because one thing Sarah never was was a fool. But her illness had given her of late a morbid taste for things Methodist. If her illness was a constant reminder that my paragon of wisdom and beauty was, after all, human, so was this.

"You don't think, Author John, when life's predicated on death," she was saying, "there's no place for terror and despair?"

"Yes, and also for frustrated love, disappointment, and grief. Which five conditions of mind account for ninety percent of our admissions here, one-third of whom are doomed republicans and one-third Methodically mad."

"Now you contradict yourself. You always say madness is owing to brain disease."

"It is. The affliction's physical. Methodism, like frustration, like a reversal of fortune, exacerbates a root disorder. A cracked tooth feels fine, until you bite on it or sugar gets in. The problem with talk of mental cures, you open the sluice-gates and in pour the Wesleys with their religious opiates and ghostly therapeutics. But religion has too much madness in it to qualify as its cure."

"And mad-doctoring too much ignorance."

"Which is why treatment here is palliative when it's anything." Now was my chance to tell her my idea for having Matthews taught engraving, and so I did. I wanted her to say this was only for myself, so I could reply that in order to be for myself it first had to be for a patient I care about.

But she surprised me with a new tack. "You actually believe you can get your madman out, don't you, John?"

"If," I replied cautiously, "I take responsibility for his actions, then yes, I think I can. I've wrote to Lord Liverpool and expect an answer."

"You assume they imagine him dangerous, but you know he's not. Dangerous how?"

"Alavoine's just told me he's offered four million pounds for the death of the King and sundry others. That's how. And how, somehow, not."

"I should think whoever wants him in here knows the danger he presents to them better than you do."

"What does that mean? You think he'll act?"

"I don't know if he'll act. I don't know him at all. I'm saying somebody thinks he'll act, and you don't know why or what they expect he'll do. All I know is what you've told me: He's been four times to Paris immediately before and after our declaration of war with France and has publicly charged the Ministry with treason."

"Which in these times," I said, "is all it would take to get him in here. Republicans are locked up on any excuse at all. But make a strong, simple case to the right party for freedom for a lunatic that your own, celebrated expertise can guarantee is harmless, his republicanism merely the going fantasy it is, and who'll object?"

"I'm only saying, John, somebody does seem to object to this one's being free. And it could just be that everybody—you, Bethlem, the government, and your madman—will be securer with him in than out. So don't be surprised when his release turns out more difficult to achieve than you imagine. Don't be surprised if the only way to get him out is something not for you but for his wife and friends to undertake, and their last resort—"

"What? A writ of habeas corpus? A legal challenge for us to say why he's in or else release him? But if we can't say, we could be damaged—"

"Not Bethlem so much perhaps as Author John's great good reputation. Of course, the writ could fail—"

"Or not. Which is why I must do everything I can before it ever comes to that—"

"For him, you hope, but mainly for you. Like your engraving initiative—"

"Ah, yes. Blinded by my self-interest to the creep of it, am I?"

"No more than the next lowly apothecary newly famous throughout Britain and Europe." She coughed. "Perhaps more accurate to say, in your newfound confidence a little over-sanguine in your hopes."

"What? Deficient in terror and despair, when I must daily stand by and watch you suffer?"

She smiled. "At least you have this place, where the inmates bear some of it for you, by bearing so much. I just hope all this fame, combined with your conviction a mad-doctor must impose his will on his patients while calling himself a model of civility, never causes you to lose sight of the miserable humanity he shares with them."

"But I *am* different from what they are," I said wearily. "They're lunatics."

Hetty had begun to squirm. Jenny would need to be sought out and discovered in a sweating clutch with the new assistant keeper. I swept up our daughter and left my beloved invalid to continue Methodizing her mind against all scheming and pride below.

LIVERPOOL

London nowadays is one great dark shop that grows more sprawling, crowded, and foul-aired by the hour. The hackney cab I rode in that Wednesday morning to the home of Lord Liverpool carried me down the centre aisle—Cheapside, Ludgate, Fleet, Strand, Cockspur, Haymarket, Piccadilly—with glimpses left and right of bejewelled showcases of goods, while on the pavement everybody was all mixed up together, shopper and hawker alike. What democratic zeal a hunger for lamps, wine, gloves, gold, maps, cheese, soap, hats, knives, toys, fans, tea, bread, and silk brings out in people—or a hunger to grow rich by selling them. Such daily public commotion! Such hotch-potch surgings of colour in the fog! There must have been ten thousand lamps ablaze out there, and this was nine-thirty in the morning. Thanks to the King's carriage stopped for some reason in Holywell Street, it took us an hour to pass through the City gates into The Strand. But it's always like this, whether the King's abroad or no. Who would guess last year's harvest was stubble? Who if they never saw a newspaper would know this was a country at war?

Who for that matter would have predicted, now that Christianity's grown too enfeebled to inspire yet another century of mass slaughter, that a mere political idea could set armies marching? But how *mere* really is republican *égalité,* that has every French soldier convinced his country belongs to him and the only reason he's marching against other countries is to hand them over to their own people? Could this deluded wretch in his motley strength be a harbinger of what's to come in Britain, as it has in America and France? Was what I viewed from my carriage that morning human order and confidence in its new, prevailing incarnation, or was it sheer outright confusion confounded, the rush before closing time?

You travel from desperate Moorfields to gracious Mayfair with its splendid squares (Hanover, Berkeley, Grosvenor), or cross the slough of the Tyburn Road to new-built Marylebone, to Cavendish Square, or Portman, and it's a voyage east to west, old to new, low to high, poverty and lunacy to wealth and privilege. The farther west you go, the fewer the hawkers and beggars and the quieter the streets, until by the time you reach St. James Square you have left the shop. Out here, the stables and amenities are close by but hid, and the stately silence of gentle lives conducted inside homes and private gardens leaks through stone walls and spreads along the broad streets. Here the air is breathable. Here death is unlikely and when it happens, seemly. Here is where you move your family when your stake in the shop has paid off. Here is where everybody wants to be.

Lord Liverpool lived in a house that came with his second wife. It was a handsome four-story structure designed by Robert Adam, faced in Bath stone, in Hertford Street at Hyde Park. Liverpool's granting by next-day's post my request for an interview on the subject of Matthews I took for a positive sign. The matter must have weighed a long time on his Lordship's mind, I reflected, and how grateful he must be for a chance to lift it off. When he answered his door in person, things seemed more propitious still—though strange. A roll-necked morning-gown hung askew on his clumsy frame, the sash half untied and sleeves rolled back. An ebony cane shook under his hand.

"Mr. Haslam," he said, his breath very bad, for he leaned heavily forward on the cane as the dull rays of his eyes passed through me, scanning the street as if for one of Matthews' assassins. "A pleasure— No end of respect for the work you're doing— Come in, come in—"

So I did, and found myself in a hallway floored in black marble and with walls oak-panelled to twice my height. Some distance ahead, a staircase went up, with railings in Chinese fret. To the side of that, a door, through which I was directed, opened into the deeper glooms of a study, my host hobbling after.

"You must excuse the wretched state you find me in, Haslam— A rheumatism of the knees—"

He was a tall man, old and ugly, heavy-torsoed, with long, unsteady legs. He was one of those who carry about with them their own prickly climate, by which they transform entire rooms to worlds of unease. High-born, that's all, in the old style, but in this day and age too clumsy and irascible not to *seem* as illbred as his visitor must have struck him.

I apologized if my visit had him on his feet when he shouldn't be.

"Were you not invited—?" he wondered abstractedly, indicating a settee I should sit on, as with difficulty he lowered himself into an easy chair and groped for a bell set a-top a book on a little ormolu table. We then sat in virtual darkness while he spoke gravely of his days as war minister and the long nuisance of our colonies in America. I must say I sympathized with his Stoic acceptance of a career spent mostly carrying out his superiors' orders with no more say than concurrence. Silently I vowed to bear my Monro yoke with a dignity as seemly. He then castigated the French and the disaster of republicanism there. Like his friendship with the King, these views he was well known for, ever since things went horribly wrong across the Channel. It was an impressive note of moral indignation he struck, marred only by an unfortunate lapse now and then into a vacant grin. But when he fumbled for the book on the ormolu table and held it up and said, "It's genius, Haslam. I never read anything so fascinating on the subject of insanity," I knew this was a true-blue gentleman, the kind it behooves a man not born one to learn from. "I swear I don't know what to admire more," he declared, "your compassion for those wretched sufferers or your devotion to improvement of their care."

"Thank you, my Lord," I said, my face ablaze. "I do my best."

"I know you do. This nation is in your debt."

Now a Negro dwarf entered carrying a tea-tray, which he set on a mahogany tea-stand that he wheeled between us.

His cup rattling noisily as he returned it to its saucer, Liverpool said, "But enough of you and me. What news of our madman?"

"Simply this, my Lord—" As I started to speak, I noticed I sat forward on my seat, elbows planted on knees, hands framing air. It was an attitude intended apparently to convey that I would come direct to the point and not waste his Lordship's time with distracting details, such as our madman's frequently professed eagerness to murder him as a diabolical traitor. "Matthews is a lunatic but hardly dangerous. Normally by the time they've been in a year, we return ones like him to their family and friends."

"You have many like him—?"

"As harmless, yes. Few so acute of intellect. None for so long, unless—"

"Acute of intellect, yes, go on—"

"In this case too, his wife's made it clear she wants him back and will undertake full responsibility for his actions—as, for that matter, will I. So it does seem a needless expense for Camberwell and for us, and certainly a most painful detention for his family."

"Painful, perhaps. But not needless— By no account needless."

I nodded, waiting to be enlightened.

Instead he said, "And—?"

"My Lord?"

"Continue."

"I confess I have no more to say. My point is simply he's not the kind we usually keep."

"Well, Haslam, you surprise me. I was rather expecting you'd travel all the way from Moorfields only if you had some particular piece of intelligence from him to impart. Something—ah—telling, even useful—"

"No, nothing like that, your Lordship. The man's a lunatic."

"So he is," Liverpool murmured and seemed to reflect. Then he said, "Here's how things stand. There's what you have determined—or haven't—

about Mr. Matthews and what I have. And it's by reason of what I have that you've got him."

"Perhaps, my Lord, if you were to indicate, in general terms, what it is you have, it might assist us in our treatment—"

This irritated him too much to conceal it. "To the deuce with your treatment, sir. It's not your treatment you've come about, it's how to be rid of him. But allow me to tell you where this begins and ends: Your Matthews is a dangerous fellow. More dangerous than you can begin to conceive."

"Has he made a threat against your life, my Lord?"

"Nothing so trivial, I assure you. I'm not a coward, Haslam, if that's what you'd imply—"

"Not at all, my Lord—"

"Because a Hawkesbury shall not be shot like a dog, Mr. Haslam. A Hawkesbury laughs at death. And if you're thinking, what harm can a peaceable madman do, remember that the radical fever that has gripped this nation for nearly a decade now is itself a state of collective mental illness. Madness is not an extenuation, Haslam, it's the problem."

Before I could reply to this, he started pitching about in his seat. When I saw it was a struggle to stand, I sprang forward to help. He batted me off. "Now, if you'll excuse me—"

Something nudged at my hip. It was his little black man, to escort me out.

As I reached the study door, Liverpool said, "Haslam—?" He was standing in the half-light like a stricken wraith, one arm across his stomach as if that part pained him as much as his knees.

"Yes, my Lord?"

"If he says anything interesting, you'll let me know."

"It is mostly lunacy, my Lord. Delusions of greatness, counterfeit letters found on the ramparts at Lisle hinting plots against him, money owed him and never paid, agents on all sides. That sort of thing."

"Yes, of course— But you know what I mean."

"Not yet."

"What's bothering you, Haslam? The fact I'd expect sense from a man you've been asked to keep as a lunatic? Is that it?"

"Something like that, my Lord."

"Did you never hear of such a thing as a lucid interval?"

"I did. I consider it a medical fiction propagated by private mad-doctors to encourage spurious classification of the mad, to engender false hope in their families, for the purpose of extorting money to have them kept longer."

"Once mad, always mad, in your books, is that it?"

"Until recovery."

"So why argue a madman's convictions?"

"Lunatics are not unacute, my Lord—"

"You said that a few minutes ago about this one and have hammered the general point in your book. It's the same thing I'm saying to you. Matthews-a-harmless-lunatic don't pass muster with me, Haslam. I thought I'd made that clear."

Here I might have stammered out a response, but he doubled back. "I take it recovery's not also a fiction of your profession?"

"I see patients get better under our care, my Lord. In some months, nearly one in three. I don't know how or why."

"No, of course not—" Now, still in shadow, his back to the window, which was half shuttered, he said in a reflective tone, "These assertions, Haslam, coming from one in a position of public responsibility I confess I find astonishing. Tell me this. What if he does recover? What then?"

"Then we've got a Ministry that would keep a sane man locked up in a madhouse. But if you want him lucid, my Lord, you should know his recovery will be likelier out of Bethlem than in."

"Will it? In that case, sir—" and he started out in such a slow, quiet voice I thought, *At last, accession to my request. Birth will out. This gruffness has been my trial by fire, the resentment what any practised politician must feel at acceding to anything. It's only a facet of his strength. The plain fact is, if he wants to know what Matthews knows, he wants him lucid.*

Alas, I was mistaken. "I ask myself—" he continued, his voice rising steadily in volume and temper, "when patients are likelier to get better out of it than in—" shouting now—"if Bethlem should be a *public* hospital at all!"

In the silence that followed this outburst, he lurched sideways to wipe spittle from his chin with shaking fingers.

"If I might, my Lord, be permitted—"

I was not. A flick of his glistening hand and I was dismissed.

IN THE DEAD HOUSE

In the carriage back to Moorfields, still a-tremble, I fell into reflection. If this was a war of worlds, which side was I on? The one I was leaving or returning to? The noble or the lunatic? Bethlem was a hospital, not a gaol. Any approbation I had won from the right side of town I had won by knowing what was what on the wrong side. If Liverpool and the government had their priorities, I had mine. This was a case of differing professional judgments. The politicians only wanted the nation safe, I only wanted justice for my patient.

I was not on both sides but could see both.

Yet, what if Matthews was in all but name a Green Cloth case like Peg Nicholson, only happening to come into our care before that provision was formally in place? How did I know the government lacked excellent cause to believe he was a threat to the King? Why should I take offence that my expert opinion counted for nothing in the matter? What can a nobleman and politician be expected to understand of madness, even if he has read my little book? What Liverpool did seem to know was Matthews posed a danger, which would suggest, as Sarah warned me, he knew something I didn't. Matthews must have the equivalent of pulled a knife on the King. Who could blame Liverpool for thinking he might again?

The carriage stopping, I looked out to see if we were out of The Strand yet and was amazed to see my own door. Time passes quick when you're at a loss. Home again reminded me I had things to do: On top of three hundred other patients to worry about, a tour of the premises by Pinel was fast approaching. I had tried Liverpool; I'd remove Matthews' chains; I'd have him learn engraving if he would. What more I could do for him I didn't know, only that I had no more time to think on it now.

Young John was sitting crossed-legged in the middle of the front hallway, awaiting my return, his little bow and arrow across his knees.

"What's this, lad?" I greeted him. "Are you powwowing?"

"I made Hetty a paper canoe, but she crushed it. Did you see Lord Liverpool?"

"I did."

"Did he give off light?"

"Light?"

"You said they call him The Dark Lanthorn because he gives off no light."

"Ah, light. No. None." I was hanging up my coat.

"But you thought he would—"

"Yes, I did. I underestimated him."

"Did he mention America?"

"Yes, he spoke with grave eloquence on that subject."

"What did he say?"

"He said we should not have wasted the resources we did on the place."

"He said that? Does he think it was not worth the fight? How does he know? Has he been there?"

"Liverpool? No, I don't think he ever—"

"I'm going, Father. I'll be joining a hearty band of Indians and paddling down the Mississippi."

"Do you need to be an Indian to paddle down the Mississippi?"

"Pardon?"

He was following me to my office.

"Does an English boy become a Red Indian, just like that?"

"Well, he can live with them—they're not brutes, Father—and grow his hair long and wear buckskin and smear himself all over with bear grease and grow dusky in the sun—"

"Did you know, John, some say the Indians of North America are the Lost Tribes of Israel?"

Here he halted and clapped his forehead in a droll stagger of surprise. "Not red-skinned Hebrews!?"

"Aye. Why don't you convert, get snipped, and save a voyage—"

"But I want to paddle down the Mississippi—"

I sat at my desk. He climbed into the chair opposite.

"If you were a Jew," I said, "you could paddle down the Nile, in a bulrush ark— Mind you, some people say Moses was Egyptian."

He gripped his chair arms in a clench of astonishment. "Not Moses an Egyptian!? An Egyptian Jew, I hope!" Growing serious he added, "Father, I do want to paddle down the Mississippi."

"Yes, and a dozen other ippi's, -assi's, and -gumi's. Why not? But you must carry a life-buoy, write often, and solemnly promise to pay a visit now and then to your aged parents, who will be thinking of you every day."

He nodded, not listening. He was waiting for something. I looked at him. What a boy I had. "Father?"

"Yes, my intrepid voyager?"

"You said when you came back from seeing if The Dark Lanthorn gave off light you'd show me how you look inside a dead person's head."

But of course. This was why he'd waited and followed me so expectant.

Together we took the back way, through the Laundry House, past the maids with their arms plunged in steaming tubs, calling out endearments to their favourite, then down the side steps into the yard, his play ground, a strip of toy-littered lawn between the east wing and the Infirmary (the sod-ceiling part, now I think of it, of our Black Hole of Calcutta), and into the Dead House, which comprised on its main level the carpentry shop for coffin-making, etc., with downstairs the dissecting room, a usually-frigid half-cellar with open gratings for the longer preservation of the deceased, not the comfort of the anatomist. This was a Bethlem building John had never entered, and as we left the yard, he slipped his hand into mine, and as we descended the stairs, he squeezed hard at my fingers.

The dead person's head I had promised to show him was Mary Creed's, prepared by me that morning before I left to see Liverpool. Mary was a good-natured woman deserted by her husband after he defrauded her of a small inheritance. When her four children were took from her she went out of her senses, imagining herself a boy (Matron White dotingly called her *my beauty*) and would bow and scrape like a footman to everybody and took humble delight in offering assistance to all, cheerfully attending the sick and suffering with a benevolence that made her loved from one end of the women's wing to the other. Generally, the patients have a sympathetic compassion for their sick companions that the keepers can't or don't, but what Mary felt and did was exceptional. Yet she could never help others enough not to blame herself for losing her children and would tell you smiling she could hear the workmen under the window, erecting the scaffolding for her execution on the morrow. The day before her death she stole a patient's wooden leg and mounted it in an attempt to hatch it like an egg to a limb of flesh and blood, and when she failed to effect that miracle blamed it on the misery of her sex and hanged herself with a strip of her blanket-gown.

Now Mary lay on one of our slabs, that entire world of goodness contracted to what might have been a buckle in the fabric of a canvas sheet. Setting John on a stool by the head, I asked if he was sure about this and receiving a vigorous though wordless nod that he was, lifted away the canvas to reveal the shaved cranium I had already slit across the crown, from ear to ear. Now I wondered what I was doing. It wouldn't be the first time my boy's precociousness had me thinking he was older than he was. As I peeled down the skin of the forehead and folded it over the face far enough to expose the bone, my doubts did not diminish. But it was too late. All I could do now was act the man of science.

Saying, "Here you see, John, where earlier today I cut the skull—" I easily lifted out the segmented plates, having spent twenty minutes that morning scraping the pericranium and dura mater from the interior of the bone, not wanting him to sit through that.

Glancing at him, I saw his eyes directed where I indicated, but he was not leaning in for a better view. "And there it is—" I said.

He made no answer.

"The brain of Mary Creed," I added, and looked at it. "This depression you see here, John, is called the lateral ventrical. This is where fluid from the spine collects. I mention it because it's larger in maniacs. I found that out by spooning water into it—"

I looked at him; he looked at me. He seemed a little pale.

"Are you surprised the cerebrum's not pink?" I asked.

He shook his head.

"Alive it wouldn't look so pasty— There's copious blood, only no longer at the surface. Observe—" With my scalpel I sliced into the pia mater. The blood welled up like quality red port, as it next did from the medullary substance. "D'you see—?" Awaiting his response, I idly palpated the brain and was astonished how doughy it was. "John—?" I had never felt a brain so *impressionable*. Could doughiness, I half wondered, be the key to benevolence, to generosity, to goodness itself? Is it possible a person's nature is nothing other than their brain state metaphorized? "John, feel this—"

When there was still only silence, I glanced round. He was clutching the edge of his stool, swaying, eyes squeezed shut. I put down the scalpel and swept him into my arms. Immediately he threw his own around my neck and held on like a drowning boy. With my free hand I re-covered Mary Creed, and we climbed the stairs. Outside, I set him on the grass. He put out a foot for balance, gazing about at his toys as if they were contraptions fallen from the moon. Then he walked over and picked up a ball and looked at it and took a deep breath, and said, "Dad, will you play catch with me?"

Thank God I said yes, because he threw himself into seizing out of the air and returning my gentle lobs with such wild, earnest energy that I have never experienced love of any human being, no, not even of his own mother, as fierce as I loved my little man then.

CROWTHER

That night late I was back again in the Dead House carpentry shop at work on my mouth-key—to have it ready to show Pinel, so he could know that in England what we do for our patients is more than symbolical—when Bryan Crowther wandered through on his way to the basement dissecting room to start his day. He liked to have his post-mortem examinations out of the way earlier than the two or three hours before breakfast when he saw to *the living,* as he resignedly called them, as if the root of their afflictions was their reluctance to be dead. Once Crowther told me weepily of a brave eulogy for a lunatic spoke by the lunatic's daughter, a girl only eight or nine, mentioning her beautiful long *grey* hair when he meant *blonde,* and that macabre little slip summed him up pretty well.

Sarah used to tell me I only despised Crowther so much because he was what I lived in fear of becoming, were I ever to let down my guard. This was why I never gave him the chance he needed to do enough around the place to maintain his self-respect. I would say there was something in what she said. In light of how things turned out, there's not a day I don't regret how hard I was on him. Yet, at the time, I didn't know what to do about it, when I could hardly bring myself to look at him.

In appearance he resembled a slug that had staggered to its foot-pads after ten hours under a rock. Not so much fat as soft. Hair close-cropt, short almost as our inmates', short enough to show the scar that wound from behind his left ear to the top of his head where I sewed him up the year before when he tumbled down a flight of stairs after he was kicked in the head drunk by a patient. He was in every sense a creature of the place. Sunlight excruciated his eyes. In them you saw the same swollen, muzzy look as entered any keeper's after a few years of working and living in the galleries. It was the miserable, complacent gaze of a man the terms of whose employment allowed no life beyond the workplace except what could be guzzled from the beer tap. But Crowther lacked the

stolid menace of a keeper, having more in common with the patients. His phys-
iognomy betrayed the same twitching, beleaguered irresolution as theirs, his
body the same absence of definition. He wasn't mad though, Crowther, at least
not yet, and not a fool either. And totally incompetent only when he swilled like
a tinker, which was not every day.

Sober, our surgeon showed a pathetic eagerness to be part of things, and
that night he took an immediate interest in my mouth-key, though when he first
detoured from his usual path to the dissecting-room stairs to stand and watch
as I pondered a better shape for the handle, he had no idea what he was looking at. But soon as I explained the purpose of the key, which is simply to open
the patient's mouth, he understood, assuring me how painful he found it to
consider the number of teeth he'd seen smashed and mouths lacerated because
patients refused to eat or take their medicine. On this point we were in perfect
agreement. Too many of our patients, especially the female, and among them
the more interesting, left us to be restored to their friends without a front tooth
in either jaw. I don't suppose there had been a Bethlem keeper on the job more
than four years who hadn't lost a patient under his hand in the act of what
is called *spouting,* or force-feeding by knocking out the teeth. When Mrs.
Hodges, wife of the vestry clerk of St. Andrews, Holborn, had died that way
two years before, I made a personal vow to him I'd discover a way to avoid this
dreadful practice.

"What's your procedure with the key, then?" Crowther was curious to know.

I explained to him how, if a patient insisted on keeping her teeth shut, we re-
stricted her movements and blindfolded her, then squeezed her jaw, or used
snuff to make her sneeze, or tickled her nose with a feather. Anything to get the
teeth apart long enough to slip in the key. Then, the instrument consisting of an
ovoid of flattened metal with a wood handle, all you did was depress the patient's tongue, or with a turn of the wrist force her mouth open, for the insertion of food or physic as required.

It so happened (Crowther now told me) he'd himself for some time been
considering what material might be sufficiently flexible to make a hollow tube
that could be fed in through the nose and thereby a nourishing wine posset, say,
passed direct down the throat of patients who refused to unclench. Leather,
he'd been thinking, lubricated with olive oil. But to his credit he immediately
appreciated the genius of my key and right away was making suggestions for
improving the handle, on the model of a simple corkscrew, the principles being
similar: firmness of grip and ease of rotation.

As we worked together on a drawing, the two of us looking at the paper and
not at each other, we went on to talk, by way of the subject of forcing, about the
general lot of the keepers, and he readily agreed when I said they didn't have an
easy life, always needing to compel and coerce individuals who were not only
disposed to recalcitrance but capable within seconds of overwhelming vio-

lence. Combine this with daily exposure to madness on all sides, no life outside these walls, a steady diet of beer, the creeping infirmities of age, low pay, and no pension, and it was no surprise an observant patient like Matthews was kept busy recording daily abuses. What we ask of warders of lunatics is more than is expected of the most brutalized foot soldier, galley slave, or workgang convict, and nobody would think of putting tormented unfortunates at the mercy of them. You don't call in hardened killers to keep the peace.

But I went too far, frankly confessing I agreed with William Battie when he argued keepers ought to be properly trained, at least in order to acquaint them with certain elementary principles in the humane treatment of those in a condition of mental suffering. The instant these words were out of my mouth, I regretted them. Praising Battie with qualification to Monro's face in order to let him think he'd caught a true glimpse of the limits of my position was one thing. Concurring with Battie in the presence of an uncertain quantity like Crowther was quite another, and very likely to mean my view would reach Monro by a route that made it appear subversion. First a book, now this.

Right away, as if eager to confirm my worst fears, Crowther replied, with a knowing look, "Battie got more than that right."

And thinking, *There's candour, and then there's the naked intemperance of a Bryan Crowther,* I said, "What do you mean," in a flat tone intended to warn against any real answer.

At first he made no reply, and I thought he'd taken the hint. Then he said, "There's more to madness than was ever dreamt of in the Monro philosophy."

"I daresay," I muttered, and thought, *For God's sake, man, shut it now.*

But no, he pressed on. "What Reverend Willis did to cure the King of his insanity, whether you agree with his methods or not— The thing is, it looked to everybody like they worked."

"Not to me," I said flatly. "The King came round by himself and could relapse at any time. The nine-out-of-ten success rate Willis boasts of has made him the laughing-stock of the profession. Everybody knows the man is a mountebank."

"But so does everybody imagine the King has been cured. I'm saying Battie's optimism has not gone away. It's in the air we breathe."

"Somewhere out there somebody's curing madness? Is that what you think?"

"I don't know if they are or aren't," he replied. "I just know the time's ripe for different approaches. People now have it in their minds that if the King can go mad, anybody can, at any time, and they're asking themselves, How would I like to be treated if it happened to me?"

I knew what lay behind this. Though a decade older than me, and like Monro the son of his predecessor, Crowther was of the new breed of mad-doctor: a believer in mental illness as a disease of the mind. As our surgeon, he performed such incisions, extractions, and amputations as the bodies of our patients required. Also, like me, he was engaged in a study of the physical state of their brains at death. But the purpose of his research was explicitly to contradict mine: to establish that, except in cases of head injury, insanity need have nothing whatsoever to do with the physical brain.

"Have you a new treatment in particular to recommend?" I asked him now. "That we could try out here, perhaps?" Though I hated the facetious tone I took with him, relax with such a one and you quickly found yourself in a quagmire of dubious sentiment, and I don't think this was just my fear that at heart I was him. He had a mind, Crowther, but in his misguided humanity you constantly glimpsed symptoms of his laxity. I wouldn't have been surprised if in moments of alcoholic stupor he didn't also experience visions of universal brotherhood.

Of course he couldn't, to me, come right out and say *Mental illness is nothing but a confusion of ideas,* so instead he said, "Well, to start with, perhaps treating a lunatic as a rational being would show better results than treating him as a brute."

"Is that what you see us doing here? Because Monro would be surprised to hear it."

"Are you surprised?"

"To hear this coming from you, yes I am. I don't treat them like brutes—"

"I'm not saying you do. I've often heard you speak to Matthews, for one, when he's calm, as a rational being."

"Which don't mean I don't think he's an inveterate lunatic until he stops being one for reasons I won't understand. I treat none of them like brutes. I'm sure you don't. Monro's certainly kind enough with them, when he's here—"

"Exactly. Mostly it's the keepers with them."

"So we're back to the keepers. The red-nosed keepers, who must bear the brunt of the filth and violence of the insane. And what's to be done there, I wonder?"

"Proper training, as we've been saying. As Battie said nearly half a century ago. Define their work hours. Pay them a living wage, with a pension. Let them reside outside the walls, if they want to. And no more of this practice of hiring former inmates."

I sighed. "And the money?"

"The Government must come up with the money. What's government for if not to help those in need?"

"The Government help those in need?" I cried. "My God, man! What country are you living in? The Government, don't you know, would prefer the private interests took over. Private madhouses make money out of madness, the Government only loses it. The less money the Government pours into madness, the more quacks pop up to turn madness into money. What in this does the Government not approve? Not only are public funds not being spent but at the end of the day much more of it than was never spent is going into the economy of the Commonwealth, and what's good for the economy of the Commonwealth is good for everybody. As everybody knows. It's only a matter of time before we have some enterprising practitioner scrambling around on our ramparts, hollowing wild accusations up at us. Seeking to found a lunatic-Elysium on the rubble he intends to make of our good name. And when he does, the only losers will be medicine and the mad. And you stand there and tell me it's time we behaved more like quacks."

This time he didn't venture a reply, for he could see he'd annoyed me. He made an excuse and shifted back to work.

But my anger didn't slip away so easy. I was as angry at myself for risking candour with such a one as for the pitiless, crazy note I struck with him. But I was no less angry at him, a man incapable of the most elementary management of himself, that he should dare to tell me we treat our insane like brutes when he knows perfectly well I do all I can six days a week, just as he does when he's sober and Monro when he's here.

By now I was turning a longer piece of hickory on the lathe, for a handle with a better grip, but I was working mentally blind. My every cell and faculty registered the infection of Crowther, who seemed to me then the living shambles of Bethlem as it was and always had been, a type of what was coming in the larger world, when confidence of progress plus ignorance of human nature would force Truth deep down where Matthews said it already was: into the basement of things, for each man his own basement, a solitary fantasy.

And then—I don't know why, unless it was thinking of Matthews on the subject of Truth buried deep down and, who knows, a guilty sense our patients do live like brutes—my thoughts came round once more to our lunatic and his situation, and gazing at the mouth-key I now saw myself so servilely *making for Pinel,* I thought, But what *of* Pinel? What if he could get Matthews out? His interest in our lunatic could well have to do with why he was being held, which might mean a simple word in his ear could set off republican alarm bells. Perhaps if Matthews' detention was owing merely to some former embarrassment or annoyance he'd caused the Ministry in its relations with France, then Pinel could speak to the French authorities. He'd have the access; it was a scruffy crowd in charge over there, and the fact he could propose a trip to England in war time bespoke influence. He could sway the authorities, who would second my reassurances, and Matthews' release effected that way.

And then I thought, *My, how luxuriant have grown my ambitions since I graduated to words.* By talent and hard work a man throws off the shackles of his station, and the next thing you know he's dreaming republican collusion. Perhaps instead of assuring Margaret Matthews she could count on me to do the best for her husband, I should have taken from one who loved him a lesson in alarm. Because however reasonable a plan can seem in candlelight, there's always the grey dawn as type and figure of old habits and old doubts returning and new doubts cropping up all the way to the moment of action—or paralysis.

Meanwhile, my thoughts continued to proliferate so feverish, conflicting, and unaccountable I feared next I'd be joining the ranks of the insane, so I quit the lathe and went to bed. There I lay saucer-eyed next to Sarah, whose every breath was an effort, and as I imagined a hundred versions of what I'd say to Pinel and what he'd say back to me, with my mind I caressed Sarah's suffering lungs, from the apical to the posterior basal lobe, until the starlings under the eaves started up their dirty racket and it was time to rise dizzy and bilious and head out into another day in the place Matthews in his witting way called simply Old Corruption.

One look at a keeper after he'd been with us two years and you knew Bethlem made people mad. Thank God I had a loving family about me at home, and when I went out, friends I could go unbuttoned amongst and so ease the strain of modelling behaviour in a madhouse. Jerdan, Kemble, Incledon, and Braham: these were my boon companions. Once a week we gathered at the home of the sixth of our party, the eminently lovable Dr. William Kitchiner.

Like me, Kitchiner's of common stock, but, unlike mine, his father rose from wharf-porter to well-to-do coal merchant and Justice of the Peace for Westminster. Kitchiner attended Eton and later Glasgow University to study medicine. Like me he never sat for his examinations, though unlike me he could afford to and with two thousand pounds *per annum* from his father could also afford not to practise. Instead, convinced that few circumstances impair British health like the dreadful quality and preparation of British food, he threw himself into writing a compendious cookbook, to be called *The Cook's Oracle*. As Jerdan put it, "Kitchiner's medicating is cookbook-making and his cookbook-making is medicating." To this end, we were all invited to dinner on Sunday nights, to pronounce upon the dishes served. With the assistance of Henry Osborne, who had time on his hands, being London cook to the tireless explorer Sir Joseph Banks, Kitchiner's goal was to prepare and test six hundred recipes. At three per week with subsequent variations for fine-tuning, we had our work cut out.

Kitchiner's a narrow, stooped, bespectacled fellow my own age. Though married once and with a natural son by another woman, that part of his life was long over by the time I speak of. The man was a born bachelor, too fussy to live with. Fortunately, his friends didn't need to, only to obey the rigorous rules of his culinary *converzationes*, viz., though we five enjoyed a standing invitation, we could not just show up but must indicate in writing the previous Wednesday an intention to be there—punctually—on the Sunday, heading swiftly into the dining room as soon as the dinner bell sounded, and before the doors were locked. Looming on the mantelpiece above us as we moved to our stations was a card declaring, "Come at Seven; go at Eleven." Those who'd applied in writing on the Wednesday and on the Sunday entered the dining room on time constituted that week's Committee of Taste, to assist which in the centre of the table stood Kitchiner's Magazine of Taste, a swivelling teak cabinet with shelves displaying bottles of sauces and flavourings and with drawers underneath containing assorted implements: a mortar and pestle, a nutmeg grater, a corkscrew, measuring spoons, graduated cylinders, scales and weights, etc. These last-mentioned items indicated what was revolutionary about Kitchiner's recipes: exact proportions. It was time, he believed, science retrieved the lost art of British cookery. His motto: *No proper taste without measurement.*

A typical Kitchiner menu included an appetizer of soup, Mulaga-tawny, say (his secret: cut up and fry the chicken after it's half boiled and put it in last). For the second course, calf's head with sage and onion sauce was a dish he was particularly good at, the brains ranged round the tongue on a separate platter, dressed with lemon juice, mushroom ketchup, and cayenne. Roast potatoes. A boiled salad of baked Portugal onions, baked beetroot, boiled cauliflower, boiled celery, and boiled French beans, all tossed together with a sauce made from the yolks of two eggs rubbed through a sieve with a wood spoon and mixed with double cream, melted butter, salt, mustard, and tarragon vinegar (the tarragon gathered just before it flowers, dried at the fire, steeped fourteen days, strained through a flannel jelly bag, then corked). Served with a sprinkle of raw burnet. For dessert, he would offer a batter pudding drizzled with four-year-old curaçao ketchup (take half a pint of curaçao, a pint of sherry, an ounce of lemon peel, a half-ounce of mace; steep fourteen days, strain, and combine with a quarter-pint of capillaire; mix with melted butter).

The serious business of pronouncing upon such *wonders of science* concluded, our Sunday evenings turned into voyages of loving Tom-Fools. Someone (I think it was me) had inked "to it" between "go" and "at Eleven," and it was true we rarely cleared out as punctually as we entered in, not after four hours of the best food, wine, music, and conversation in London. Between courses, Kitchiner would scoot over to the piano and vary proceedings with a splash of Handel or a composition from his own hand. Sometimes he'd accompany Incledon, Braham, or the two together as they sang a pretty or facetious air (often composed by Kitchiner himself) that they'd all rehearsed together in secret. As well as gastronome and musician, Kitchiner's an astronomer and hoarder of telescopes. On clear nights we'd stump upstairs to peer at the heavens through the dozen instruments he has set up in what he calls his Crow's Nest, an observatory that consumes the entire top floor of his house.

How good it is to be free of care for an evening! Crouched at the eyepiece of a Kitchiner telescope, smoky Mars jiggling in my sights, the majesty of the universe aweing us all to an embarrassed hush, I knew Bethlem was only a gloomier vale amongst many such here below, and each of us was a miniature firefly Newton, emitting now and then a few glimmerings in our respective narrow spheres. It's a sanity of proportion such moments of drunken poise can offer, and these together with the love of my family and hope of rescue by my pen were enough to render supportable a life spent six and three-quarter days a week inside Hell. Then, before we'd know it, we were back downstairs and had reentered the bright ring of fellowship of the Captain's Table, and hauling down with us those larger views, we'd set about reminding each other of them in our lives.

Braham, a stout tenor, in those days a great success in Drury Lane, would tell a story on himself, how once in the festival at Hereford he was singing "The Bay of Biscay," and at the line in the last verse, "A sail! A sail!" he went down as usual on one knee, except across the front of the stage the organizers had erected a low barrier, behind which he disappeared entirely from the sight of the audience, who, thinking he'd fallen through a trap door, leapt to their feet as one, shouting with laughter to see him there on one knee, still singing away.

Incledon was a tenor too but like Kitchiner and me had a medical connexion, being the son of a Cornish surgeon. At age eight, he was sent from home to sing in the Exeter Cathedral choir, but after a few years he ran off to sea, where the officers noticing the beauty of his voice, wrote him letters of recommendation to musical promoters up and down the country. Soon he was a regular at Covent Garden. Between acts of operas, he'd come out in nautical gear and sing sea-shanties. In farces he had a gimmick of throwing out his arms as he sang. Each time he did it they grew longer. You never saw anything more comical. He was an affable, witty, restless fellow who wore seven cheap rings on his hairy hands.

Incledon was a fine singer, especially of tender ballads, but his inability to remember lines made him a poor actor, whereas our friend Charles Kemble was universally acknowledged as one of the true greats of the age. Though as corpulent and ungainly as Incledon, Kemble stood taller, had a handsome head, and by his carriage made the most of what he'd been given. As an actor, his range was as broad as Garrick's, or so we told him, but I would say he showed himself most original in comedy. Amongst company he affected such a world-weary, indolent manner you asked yourself why if he was this exhausted he'd bothered to crawl out of bed on his day off. But the ostensible fatigue had no effect on the spontaneity and quality of his drolleries, the manner of delivering which varied depending on the character he'd been playing that week. The effect was of a heavy, discarded puppet now and then rebounding to charmed life.

And then there was Jerdan, the philosopher of our crew, and the one I knew best and keep in closest touch with to this day. A newspaperman, he has a first-rate writer's way of placing faith in no system of ideas, and yet by a miracle of character he's not in the least cynical or jaded. Though serious in outlook, he's ever on the watch for human absurdity, which being copious affords him plentiful amusement. By his face he might be a pop-eyed bumpkin just arrived in the city, but he's shrewder than he appears, and his good humour runs deeper than ordinary country equanimity.

Often in those last days of the century our *converzationes* revolved on what the nineteenth held in store. The fact the demarcation's a calendar fiction didn't mean a fantasy of new beginnings could fail to operate on every mind. The only question was, With what effect?

In Jerdan's view, the newest thing about the new age would be its fascination with its own newness, which it would view as a worthy quality in itself, as if everything was now mysteriously growing better, so all a thing would need to be to win enthusiastic approbation was the very latest.

"An uncritical faith in the new," Jerdan declares, "is daily replenished."

"And will infantilize us all," I mutter, thinking of Crowther.

"And if ultimately there's nothing in it?" Braham wants to know.

"The only thing *in it*," Jerdan replies, "is this unaccountable phoenix of hope. The bloody bird is not even hope, it's the *assurance* of hope. It's like the monarchy. There's nothing in it, but it works. The less in it, the better it works. And won't easily be toppled, not here. Here there's too little in it."

Some of us (I mean Kitchiner, Jerdan, and myself) believed one order of business would—or must—be the abolition of our trade in slaves, if not the granting of freedom to the poor wretches. Surely this was one respect in which the fantasy of human brotherhood needed to take effect. The fact seven years ago the French had freed all slaves on French soil (though not in their colonies) should not stop us from at least getting out of the trade.

Incledon and Braham are not convinced. In the midst of one such debate, the former turns drolly to the latter. "I'm surprised at *you*, John. With your kinked locks and sizable *Schnauz'* you're a good way down that road yourself—"

"Aye, but not so far as in chains," Braham replies equably, "and somehow that makes all the difference—"

Speaking of chains, there was also the question of Catholic Emancipation. Once we joined with Ireland, Jerdan argued, it would be only a matter of time before Catholics were elected to public office.

None of the rest of us could see it. "And what of the Protestant religion, sir?" Incledon demands to know.

"Finished," Jerdan informs him. "Dead and gone. Empty churches. The reason you haven't noticed is you never go. What do you think Methodist tents say about Anglican cathedrals? The Catholics will have their emancipation for the simple reason Christianity will continue to pitch camp farther and farther out from the centre of things. This is no temporary truancy, it's a popinjay disappearing over the horizon never to return. The soul of the coming century, gentlemen, will not be found in the parish church but *in the town itself,* in the ashes of our phoenix hopes, daily reborn in these streets, squares, arcades, gardens, markets, parks, fairs, factories, racetracks, taverns—"

"Brothels—" Incledon mutters.

"Hospitals, should Fortune happen to smile—" I put in.

"Oh my, yes," Kitchiner agrees, "and her gaols and asylums, and plenty more of them, certainly—"

"London's too great a city," Jerdan declares, "not already to provide—or at least to promise—what the French are still fighting for: pleasure, freedom, and wealth. All an Englishman needs to do is find work in London, and he can profit himself enough to buy all the pleasure and freedom he wants. Or at least in London he can hope he can, for he will daily see and hear of so many others' success he'll blame only himself if it turns out his own pleasure and freedom begins and ends in the alehouse—where he'll have plenty of good company to console him. How can life be more modern than that?"

"And the war, *O Vates?*" Incledon wants to know. "When's it over?"

"Soon," Braham announces.

But the one everybody looks to is Jerdan, who grimly shakes his head. "In an age of banks, credit, and the mechanized production of weaponry, in an age when, as Mr. Paine has said, there are men who get their living by armed conflict and make it their business to keep up the quarrels of nations, war will be simply the normal state of things."

"I wouldn't speak that name aloud, William," Incledon mutters, "unless you want us all disembowelled and hanged."

"You don't need to be a republican," Jerdan calmly replies, "to know Paine's right about that much."

In his more playful moods, Jerdan likes to have fun with my hopes of Philippe Pinel.

"So, Haslam," he says. "Could you tell us once again, *slowly,* how you reckon Pinel's visit is going to help you free this raving lunatic Matthews, whom word has it you enjoy a natural affinity with?"

In reply—silently cursing I ever confided my inchoate plans to my good friend and now knowing I only did so out of a guilty fear it was more selfish pride than concern for my patient that would have me working against the wisdom of Liverpool and the British Government—I say I hope to alert Pinel to the dubious circumstances of Matthews' incarceration.

"Tell me, sir, if I have got this straight," Jerdan says, with the same amused detachment he showed as when I first told him. "You're looking to a Frenchman on a tour to help you extract a mad Welshman from an English madhouse run by yourself."

"That's it!"

"Sir, on behalf of those who love you, let me wish you every success in this remarkable international-flavoured endeavour."

A favourite topic with Jerdan was how the administration of Bethlem actually worked, when Monro had all the power while I had all the responsibility and when the steward and matron, who were in charge of the keepers and gallery maids, answered to Monro, who was never there, and when the clerk was a sphinx who answered to who-knew-who and the surgeon a drunk who took his orders solely from Mr. Chivas and Mr. Haig. "No wonder they call it Bedlam!"

"Only in the street," I reply. "Inside, everybody knows the administration is John Haslam and John Haslam is the administration. For inside those walls Haslam is God and produces law and order from his own mouth."

"Pen, don't you mean!" Braham exclaims.

"Ha ha!" cries Incledon. "God Himself now lays hold of His own instrument to ejaculate how passing fine His world is!"

"On paper tablets," rejoins Braham, "that reveal neither *pre*scription nor *pro*scription but cock-and-bull *in*scription. The Ten *Commend*ments!"

"I don't know how this can be so," trills Kitchiner in his sweet sing-song, "for I see it all so clearly: Apothecary Haslam seated at a table with Surgeon Crowther, Steward Alavoine, and Matron White, the four of them gathered together to discuss treatment of cases and argue intricacies of physic, while Physician Monro sits over by the fire, for the light, introjecting sage counsel as he sketches away—"

"The truth is," I glumly confess, "we all labour despairing and alone in dire circumstances, and it's the patients who pay."

"But if Bethlem don't work, John," Jerdan puts to me, "why are you so dead against private madhouses?"

The mock solicitude of this is a call for one of my speeches, which goes like this:

"I hate private madhouses because they're advertised to suffering families by drapes flung open to show a docile lunatic in the window, chatting with his keeper over tea. I hate them as harbingers of the smiling future that's coming, when the nasty parts will be hid away. I hate them because as soon as that lunatic shows himself unable to take his tea without first whipping out his cock and pissing in the cup, it's a crust and water belowstairs for him. Out of mind, out of sight. Better he were on the street. At least when he's there we know our true condition. Better any day honest grey uncertainty everywhere than this merchandising checkerboard of dazzling public proof and private darkness."

"Hear! hear!"

I'm just getting started.

"You'd think if unmedical practitioners set out to do the work of doctors, they'd learn from them something more than mystery, silence, and mumbo-jumbo. But how can a lunatic-trade expert-for-hire make a fine living if he advertises what he actually does? Spins lunatics in chairs until they pass out with blood gushing from their noses, plunges them in surprise baths of icewater or electric eels, or does nothing at all, only immerses them in a treacle of loving-kindness. The first law of advertising is you don't sell them what it is, you sell them what it can do for them. And since here the buyer is not the lunatic but his family, what your magical nit-comb of publicly kind incarceration can do for them is comb a troublesome nit out of their hair without by the same act depositing him on their conscience. All they must do in exchange for this deceptively simple (for a reason) service is give you enough money so you can grow rich enough to open another house, and another, and that way build your empire, until all the spare lunatic nits in the kingdom have been combed out of the hair of every family genteel enough to afford their removal. That way you can retire to your estate and never have your peace disturbed by another madman until age, conscience, and isolation from the common run of mankind have worked their chemistry and made one of you."

Now in comes Jerdan, as Devil's Advocate. "Nobody's getting rich off The Retreat, that William Tuke's opened at York."

"The Retreat's just getting started. Give Tuke time. Quakers always end up wealthy, one way or another."

"But this is where Tuke's money's going."

"Tuke's no better than the next self-praising pedlar. The only difference about Tuke is he's had no medical training at all. He uncovers appalling conditions at the York hospital and so founds his Retreat on the ruined reputation of a public asylum."

"And didn't the York hospital deserve it?" wonders Braham.

"John, believe me. Tuke's another Willis, a reverend fraud. Unless Quaking now qualifies a man to treat the insane. Unless what we're really talking about here is that easy-as-kiss-my-arse alternative to sanity, religious conversion."

"From what I hear," Jerdan puts in, "when the patient first arrives, Tuke tells him, 'If you want the peace and benefits of a Christian household, then you'll behave like a gentleman. If you don't behave, you'll miss out.' His method, you see, is to make the patient want to be good—"

"The moral pharmacopia might work with children. If Tuke says it works in one single case of genuine insanity, I assure you, gentlemen, he's a liar, idiot, madman, or all three!"

"Hear! hear!" they all cry again. "To your great good health, Mr. Haslam! May things go as well for you as things can go in living Hell-holes!"

Now there's no stopping me.

"You see, Gentlemen, even when they have the best intentions, Tuke and his followers are no less charlatans than those thousand and one hucksters out hawking nerve tonics, dancing lessons, and water cures. What are these myriad purveyors of what-you-want doing but wrapping people's wishes and anxieties in decorous packages and selling them back to them? 'I sum up half mankind,' observes our poet Mr. Cowper (who did the mental suffering to authorize his tally),

> And add two-thirds of the remaining half
> And find the total of their hopes and fears
> Dreams, empty dreams.

Empty yet not unprofitable. But to retire rich, private mad-doctors must work fast and sell hard, because one day it will come to the attention of some ambitious M.P. that not only are there more mad than ever, but also those secret treatments are getting out of hand, and the worst cases of neglect and torture coming to light are far worse than they used to be. That's when those still in the business will sell up and go into something more honest, like pimping."

This to three cheers for Haslam and Bethlem, with a toast of consternation, damnation, and plague upon Tuke and all other private mad-doctors and their houses.

But mostly we tried not to talk business. It was food and fun we had come for. We all got enough of the rest of life on the other six days. And too soon it was eleven, then midnight, and Kitchiner, who'd worked hard all day in the kitchen, would be seen biting down on yawns, and we'd nudge each other and give a sign to the servant who'd been standing by since a quarter to eleven, and he'd go for our coats. And so we'd stand up and congratulate dear good Kitchiner on his having done it once again and shake hands all round and bundle out into the night and hail carriages to take us back to our respective grindstones.

PINEL

On June 28th, Pinel wrote to say he was staying at The George and Blue Boar in Holborn and would arrive two days hence, at ten o'clock. Not knowing his route, I posted a keeper at Moorgate and Jenny at my London Wall door. When she ran in all flushed, I sent Rodbird to signal Bulteel to open the gates. I then took up my position outside the penny entrance, turning the latest version of my mouth-key in my pocket.

I was flanked by Mr. Poynder, to help me with the French language, and by my father. In order to make the first impression, I had told Monro a later hour. The plan was, he—late for everything, and always amazed things had started without him—would arrive, find things had started without him, be amazed, and suspect nothing. With luck he'd arrive so late Pinel would never see him. My father was with us because at dinner on Easter Sunday (which he's joined us for since the struggle to keep a house and home together on what his grandiose schemes provided drove my mother to an early grave), Sarah happened to mention Pinel's visit. He practically begged to be invited along, swearing how much as a physician (as he long ago took to calling himself, though he lacks all credentials) he's always wanted to meet him. Closer to the day he asked me who he was. When it comes to greatness my father has never scrupled. *No man learns from rabble,* he bitterly pronounces, meaning his patients, but I've never seen him bow and scrape without inspecting for flaws.

The carriage that swung through the gate was a coach-and-six. For a man of the people, Pinel travels in style. He disembarked with a secretary, a cool, sleek individual resembling a bewigged ferret; a translator, who might have been the secretary's sallower brother; and a ravishing consort: a specimen of the female sex so resplendent that with her coal-black hair and long narrow face she towered amongst us like a thoroughbred detained by a herd of Shetlands. The name of this tremendous beauty was Sylvie Jouval, a former lunatic, though I noticed the word Pinel used was *guérie,* meaning *healed*.

"Ah, the perquisite of cure!" I cried like an idiot, kissing her hand, which to my surprise was thick and coarse as a scullion's. The translator neglecting to translate, I could have kissed him too.

As for Pinel—has a more charming rascal ever journeyed out of France? As soon as you met him you understood how a man could speed from rustic obscurity to director of the Salpêtrière Hospital. The Revolution had thrown into prominence all sorts of Frenchmen of a sweetness otherwise wasted on the desert air, but surely few with the wit and intelligence of this one. By his coarse complexion, sunk cheeks, and careless dress, he was evidently of low, rural birth, yet who better equipped than a cunning peasant to negotiate the Terror?

Introductions completed, my father's prostrations bemusedly received, Pinel announced the first thing he must do was kiss the hand of Peg Nicholson, the would-be assassin of the King. The second was shake that of our resident friend to the Revolution, James Tilly Matthews.

Shall we talk on the way?

Delighted, *monsieur*.

We stopped only to pick up Alavoine, whom I'd instructed to wait for us in his quarters on the pretense he is always so available. With obsequious ceremony, the old devil went ahead unlocking doors while Pinel, his eyes darting everywhere, flowed with compliments and questions concerning this portrait, that coat of arms, that cornice. Our visitor acted enchanted by everything he saw, yet how could eyes so attentive miss the flaws and decay? How could he not wonder what it meant that our physician should be detained on business and might not appear at all? (As for our surgeon, that for the day was me, Crowther being the epitome of unpresentable.) How could Pinel not ask himself if we always scattered the chloride of lime with so heavy a hand, or was it only on visitor days, so strangers might imagine we no longer subscribe to the necessary conjunction of madness and stinking? How could he not hear the groans and cries and constant jingling of chains? Of course he heard them, but however close you watched him, you'd never know. A better indicator of the effect the place was having on our visitors was the eyes of Mlle. Jouval. The look in those glorious peepers was unmitigated dread.

For fear the anticipation would excite her to extreme behaviour, I'd not forewarned Peg Nicholson a great man sought an introduction. A good thing, for the woman we came upon was a paragon of domestic contentment, sitting on her bed genteelly sipping tea, with a little plate of gingerbread by her. I couldn't have arranged the tableau better myself—though I did have a hand in it. Not wanting her seen eating nothing, I'd given her a packet of gingerbread in light of her aversion, ever since she learned the King prefers brown bread, to the brown bread we serve. Her conviction seemed to be that she should not affirm his preference in bread as long as he persisted in refusing her the Crown.

As soon as he knew who it was, Pinel rushed in and fell to one knee. This being homage befitting the queen she is in her mind, Peg extended her hand. But the timing proved unfortunate, for with the fingers Pinel feverishly pressed devoted lips against, she had just taken up a sizeable pinch of snuff, which he in his impetuosity accidentally inhaling, sent him into violent gales of sneezing. Needing both hands to contain the flying snot, he let go hers. This afforded her an opportunity to finish taking her tobacco and to sit snuffling softly as he, still down on one knee, mopped at himself with a handkerchief slipped him by his secretary. No sooner was he dried off than she once more extended the hand, which he eyed the way a hemophiliac might a rabid weasel. But this time the kiss went off without incident. Peeling away his lips and speaking through his translator, he informed her what a *formidable* heroine of the French people she is and will live forever in their hearts as a fearless fighter against tyranny. Her imprisonment, he added, is a call to action for those dedicated to the overthrow of oppression in all its disguises.

As the translator spoke, Peg smiled upon him with sanguine hauteur, liking what she heard. When he finished, she said simply, addressing him, "I am Queen of England, and you and your raving, grippish friend—" nodding toward Pinel—"are my faithful subjects."

This statement put Pinel at a loss what to say.

Still addressing the translator, Peg spoke into the silence. "You and your friend must now explain who I am to your fellow subjects, so they might understand, as so far they have failed to. And while you have their attention, prithee ask what's holding up my crown."

"Holding up . . . your crown, madam?" Pinel himself asked, in a daze.

"You heard me well enough," she replied composedly. "Be sure to tell 'em that if her Majesty don't have it by sunset Friday, it's off with the heads of every member of the male sex inside ten leagues— What *is* the matter with you? Are you French?"

Pinel confessed that he was.

"Then perhaps you can tell me. When Mrs. Carter, the English songbird, says she's determined if she ever keeps a lap-dog or monkey, it shall be a fish, what d'you think she means?"

Now Pinel turned to me with brimming tears and murmured, *"Prendue foue par son emprisonnement. Ah, quelle dommage, monsieur. Quelle dommage tragique."*

"Indeed, *monsieur,*" I confirmed. "Mad as a March hare."

On our way along the east gallery toward the incurable wing, our next stop being James Tilly Matthews, Pinel's eyes continued drinking everything in, though there wasn't much more to see than occasional sets of eyes looking back at him through the peepholes of cell doors. This was because when I instructed Alavoine to lock up any he considered likely to cause a nuisance, he took this to mean everybody. So we walked along unannoyed by lunatics except for groans, bellows, and curses from behind cell doors—none of which was acknowledged by any of us except Mlle. Jouval, who was a perfect Aeolian harp, vibrating sympathetic to every anguished cry.

Meanwhile, as I struggled against that silliest of expressions that comes over a man's face while he is being praised, Pinel addressed himself to what he approved so much in my work. Principally, my reluctance to theorize. The way I eschewed empty abstractions in favour of direct engagement with the patient. As he correctly reminded me, my book was the very first on the subject of mental alienation to benefit from extensive observation and experience. Where other British practioners—Arnold, Harper, Crichton, and more egregiously negligible dunderheads (my words)—were mere scholastics, metaphysic maze-spinners, stealing from the Germans what they hadn't pillaged from the Ancients (his words), I was active at the front, eyes and ears open, wits about me, discharging my duties with integrity, dignity, and humanity. In the personal treatment of patients, he insisted, I am far superior to the mad-doctors Cox, Perfect, and Pargeter together. Also, in a profession where most, like "King-healer" Willis, jealous of their incomes, kept their methods secret, I freely unburdened my mind on the page, unafraid to tell the world what I knew and didn't, either way contributing to the steady advance of medical science. In a nutshell, Pinel declared me the foremost English mad-doctor, and he intended to say as much in his next book.

Ah, the wonderful power of words, to whisk the soul to a froth of giddy embarrassment, and more wonderful still when you consider that this unutterably moving estimation of your worth is based entirely on your own written account of yourself.

After his eulogy to my talents, Pinel moved with unseemly haste to his own unfortunate pretensions to cure. Surely few experiences are more depressing than to be praised to the skies by one who the next moment reveals he's only seen in you what he imagines to be his own strong suit. But this is putting it too mildly. A severer critic would pronounce the man a fraud and the bulk of his philosophy, what he calls his *traitement morale,* unashamed humbug. Why "moral," or why more so than any other treatment in vogue nowadays, I can't say, unless it's the fact that, like me (as the philosophy of John Locke has taught all thinking doctors to do), he pays attention to the particulars of each case. And while he agrees with me madness is neither a profession for clerics nor a disease of the mind—whatever that means—but incorrect associations of ideas the result of morbid tissue, he takes this so far as to contradict himself, believing anything that shows up in imagination must be curable there, even if it's by doctors' playing elaborate games of sympathy and deception. In sum, the man's a regular Continental Tuke, going too far, preaching the curative effects of soothing words, segregating lunatics by imagined types, inviting them to dine at his own table, and staging dramatic "cures" like an impresario. Now that I'd met him, I would say this last custom was not madness at all but a bold stroke

of self-publicity not unlike striding through a madhouse in the wake of a revolution striking off chains.

Fortunately, we arrived at our destination before he could make his famous
claim to pacify raving lunatics by the power of his eye, because if he did, I was
ready to ask him if he'd like to try it with one of our patients with a history of
vicious homicide. Then we'd see how many body-guards Pinel liked to have
along while he did his ocular pacifying.

Alavoine swung open Matthews' door and in we all crowded, to find our lunatic hard at work at the little table I'd given him, engraving a copper-plate. No
chains, and gripping a potential deadly weapon. Notch two for England.

"James," I said, "it's M. Pinel, all the way from Paris to make your acquaintance."

"Ah, M. Mat'hew!" Pinel cried, pushing past me. "It is such pleasure! May
I beg, sir, the honour to shake your han'?"

When Matthews gave no sign he heard, I said, to smooth the awkwardness,
"Do you see what he's doing there, M. Pinel?"

"Yes, yes, *bien sûr,* I see," Pinel replied impatiently. "*La gravure.* What do
you represent, M. Mat'hew?"

"No, what do *you* represent, M. Pinel?" Matthews shot back, without looking up.

Pinel, once he understood the quibble, laughed so heartily and long you'd
think this the most magnificent piece of wit he ever heard. Sobering, he assumed an attitude of pompous ceremony. "I represent, M. Mat'hew, the French
people. They t'ank you from their heart' for your valiant effort for peace between our nation'."

"Queer thanks," Matthews retorted, "to be made an object of their intrigue."

"You were imprison, I know dat—" Pinel acknowledged with a woebegone
look. "A dark episode in dark time."

"Not so dark," Matthews replied, "as the fact you're a criminal impostor in
league with magnetic agents in positions close by Parliament, the Admiralty,
the Treasury, and this hospital. While you distract us here, your parliamentary
confederates are at work animating Pitt, whose sozzled brain has long been a
deft unwitting tool of their magnetic fluid. But hear me when I say it: Britons
never shall be puppets!"

This speech was followed by a short pause. My father coughed.

"Why are you in here?" Pinel abruptly asked, too amazed perhaps by
Matthews' manner to notice that his raving had already answered the question.

"Same reason you are," Matthews replied coldly. "As a victim of the gang."

"Actually," I broke in, "none of us, *monsieur,* is quite sure why M. Matthews
is with us. The Government has been very close as to—"

Here I stopped. Pinel was looking at me significantly, tapping his finger
against his nose, which Matthews saw, his head having whipped round the instant I broke off, to know why.

"And how do you like it?" Pinel quickly asked, making a deflective show of glancing about appraisingly. "This seems to be a pleasant enough—"

"I'm here to be destroyed," Matthews stated. He'd returned to his work.

"He's mad but harmless," I informed Pinel *sotto voce*. "Normally we let the ones—"

"And who is destroying you?" Pinel asked, in English, ignoring me.

"Him—"

By a jerk of his head, Matthews had indicated me. I emitted a little bark of a laugh, then cleared my throat and said again, "Normally after a year, Monsieur Pinel, the harmless ones we—"

This time Pinel put a hand on my arm and indicated for me to look.

Matthews had just noticed Mlle. Jouval. In a hushed, amazed, grateful voice he said, "You're not a fluid-worker—"

The translator, suspecting I think an indecency, glanced at Pinel—who nodded—before he Frenched it, as *travailleur du fluide*.

Mlle. Jouval could not have known what Matthews meant, but operating along her own private channel of sympathy, she immediately replied something I couldn't catch. Her French was unlike any I ever heard. I looked to the translator, but to my amazement Matthews was already answering in his own rapid French. His too I found impenetrable. Learned in prison, I suppose. He was telling her his mother was Huguenot, *"une tisserande Huguenote avec un fluide magnétique, mais enchaînée par son métier à tisser—"* a Huguenot weaver with magnetic power, but chained to her loom, as Poynder later translated it for me. To this, Mlle. Jouval replied that for all his faults, Louis XVI had been a good friend to the Huguenots who still remained in France.

"Trop tard pour maman!" Matthews sang out in a bright, flat voice.

"Mon papa était Huguenot, et aussi un tisserand," Mlle. Jouval now volunteered, dropping her eyes and colouring all the way to her magnificent cheekbones.

"Formidable! Et aussi un ami du Roi?" Matthews asked, grinning like a cat.

"Pas du tout, monsieur," replied the charming creature, yet more abashed.

"Tant pis!" Matthews trilled, adding in a sudden ferocious growl, *"Ma maman était une tisserande et une ennemie terrible de la Reine!"* Now he pretended to be cast down all pitiable. *"Mais plus terrible de mon papa! Pour ma maman, papa était le fil incorrect, et tout le tissu de sa vie était gâté."* In Matthews' father (as Poynder translated for me the next day) his mother had taken hold of the wrong thread and so ruined the fabric of her life.

Their French continuing opaque to me, I fell to thinking. I should have been prepared for Matthews' ingratitude. Misbehaviour of inmates during visits is common enough and in general not a bad thing: The lunatic appreciates the opportunity to break the rules and the bigwig to witness how tolerant we are. But when Matthews betrayed me before Pinel, I caught a glimpse of his disease and knew that from him all my *kindness* and *consideration*—those precious watchwords of the Tukes and the Pinels—would only ever elicit the bitterest in-gratitude. And it wasn't only myself I was thinking of—at least I didn't think so. It was the bigger question of what Matthews was capable of if he was ever let out. And it seemed to me then that all my hopes of him, all my confidence in his goodness, was only ever my own pride in thinking I knew madness better than I did. How could I predict what Matthews would or would not do? Who was I to go against those in a superior position to know the facts? What but sheer arrogance would have me seeking ways to countermand so unambiguous a direction from above?

These sweaty, guilty, anxious reflections were broke off by a nightmarish-familiar voice booming from the doorway. "What ho, Mr. Haslam! Our incon-tinental visitors could not restrain themselves, what?"

THE MOUTH-KEY

As Pinel's glittering eyes took in Monro's mud-spattered boots, the improbable surtout, the broad-brimmed hat, the object of that gaze, after tossing the party a few general words of greeting, turned his full attention upon Mlle. Jouval, and in a voice loud enough for the entire gallery to hear, set about recounting the almighty importance of himself to Bethlem, nay, of three generations of himself, and still another Monro-ling poised in the wings, though that one as yet but seven years old, ha ha ha! I never saw the man work so strainedly to impress. If, like my father, he didn't know who Pinel was when I'd told him he was coming, he'd since found out. And hearing him now, I could imagine him ha-ha-ha-ing away before the Bethlem subcommittee at his interview for the post, and how they must have said to themselves, Oh, he's the best man for physician of Bethlem, all right. What he actually says don't make any sense, but that will be from two generations of the family in the business. It rubs off, they say, and perhaps just as well. The patients will feel he's practically one of them.

Monro was insisting we all inspect the new shower-baths, and this provided a nice glimpse of the steel in Pinel, who declined to go anywhere until he'd been allowed a private word with Matthews. And so, the door closing against us, we trooped out into the gallery where there was nothing to do but stand and wait and listen to Monro. Poynder and the French looked on impassive as he babbled, but my father seemed ready to bolt. His greatness sensors having confirmed what he already knew, that Monro was littleness through and through, he was not interested to hear how our physician lives and breathes Bethlem, the blood of the patients practically coursing through his veins he's so dedicated to their welfare, and yet another entire part of him is an artist devoted to the sublimities of nature and the beauties of the canvas, and on and on, everybody's eyes gone glassy except, as I say, my father's, which resembled those of a cornered dog.

But more affecting to me was the discomfort of Mlle. Jouval, whom I would say prolonged mental suffering had left more sensitive to pain, injustice, and folly than she could yet well endure. I'm sure her only protection against Monro was a perfect ignorance of what he was saying. I know I should have shielded her from his grating force, but I was too busy straining to hear through the door what tales Matthews was telling of my destruction of him. And which of us would Pinel—a man in the habit of dining with maniacs, a man ready to declare a hero of the French people every deranged anti-royalist he stumbled upon—which of us would Pinel more likely believe? In the eyes of such a fanatic, any ordinary degree of authority must count as oppression. And the more opportunity he gave Matthews to voice his insubordination, the firmer his conviction I was the oppressor if not the active destroyer around here and fell laughably short of the paragon he'd conjured from reading my book.

Through the door I could hear only enough to know they were talking French. Generally, the conversation was low, the rhythms on one side more erratic. This was not improbably the confidential talk of two men conspiring together, one of them happening to be insane. And then, though what he said remained muffled, Matthews' voice grew more strident, the speeches going on longer, and soon after, the door opened and Pinel was stepping out to rejoin us.

"All done your *tête-à-tête* with our favourite republican lunatic, Mr. Pinel?" Monro called to him, by this time too worked up to await a response. Instead, crying, "Very well then! It's heigh-ho and away to the shower-baths!" He made a buffoonish show of presenting his arm to Mlle. Jouval before setting off with her down the gallery. The rest of us followed after, Pinel on my right side, his translator on my left. As I opened my mouth to ask Pinel how his exchange with Matthews had gone, my father, seizing his main chance, began chattering away in Pinel's other ear about the history of public visiting at Bethlem, a subject of which he knew nothing beyond what his imagination had done with what he'd picked up from me. The man is a magpie. As for his speech to Pinel, he must have practised it at home.

"I hope you know, M. Pinel," he began, "you're lucky to be seeing the place. There hasn't been open visiting here since you was a child. As for me, I remember those days very well. But public visiting came to be imagined cruel and inhuman, though I understand from my son John here it brought in four hundred pounds a year, which I'm sure the inmates were as pleased to see benefit from as to know they ranked as popular a sight of the town as Bartholomew Fair or the Tower lions. That's pretty human, I'd say, and hardly cruel. I'm sure they found daily tourists among them a greater source of entertainment than standing on a chair to look out the window at people walking in Moorfields. And when the lunatics put on their antics, it was as much for their own amusement as the gawkers'. Give 'em half a chance, and they'll put them on still. Unfortunately, keepers make a hard audience. To them it's nothing to interrupt a lunatic's tranquillity, but God help the lunatic who tries it with them. One moment they're joking away friendly as you please, the next they're raining down blows. You can see why my son's all for more public access. The plain fact is, there's far worse abuses in here since they've kept out the tourists than there ever—"

Here I broke in to ask Pinel how it had gone with Matthews. My father's envy of anyone not actually in the gutter, even if it's his own son, makes him a menace in company.

Grateful to be delivered from that familiarity, Pinel was quick to shake his head in a dumb show of disappointment. "M. Mat'hew is convince he is the victim of French intrigue."

"Yes, he's a lunatic."

"*Hélas!*"

"And not to be credited," I added redundantly, for something to say before my father broke in again.

At this, Pinel shot me a look of relief. *"Exactement!"*

His emotion emboldened me to ask why he'd chose to speak to Matthews in private.

His chin came up, and though he spoke in French he spoke slowly. "Because I fear, M. Haslam, although M. Matthews' express intention is peace between our nations, his words have potential to do irreparable damage."

"Who's listening?" I asked.

The question surprised him. "You, are you not, M. Haslam, for one? Is not listening the foundation of your treatment of the poor sufferers under your care here? Is it not what has put you at the forefront of English practitioners?"

"I suppose so," I answered with a self-deprecating air. "Unless, I suppose, as Matthews is always assuring me, I listen but don't hear."

He smiled, unamused. "In his case, *hélas,* that may be for the best. Five year ago he was a good friend to the Revolution. Now his mind is in ruin. I confess to you one purpose of my visit here was to solicit his release. Now I know he is where he belong."

As Pinel said these words, we were trudging down the central staircase, he speaking sometimes English, sometimes French, in my right ear, his translator pouring the corresponding English in my left.

"M. Pinel," I said, startled by my own emotion, which to my surprise (because I thought I agreed with him) was outrage, "why is Matthews in here?"

"As a threat to both our nation, I should think," he replied, seeming himself surprised I needed to ask.

"How? Why? Ain't our nations their own greatest threats to each other? Ain't peace between them what he's always fought for?"

"In his mind, yes. But is he sane?"

"Perhaps not sane. But why not harmless? Why give credence to madness?"

"No, M. Haslam. I would say the question, in such time as these, must be rather, Could he be a danger?"

"Not according to my lights."

"But do you know what he's done?"

"No, do you?"

Like a man saddened to think what it might be, he shook his head.

"Then how do you know what he'll do?"

"Is that for you and me to know, M. Haslam?" he asked with a smile of admonishment. "Are we legislators? Are we gods?"

These blithe assurances from one who knew nothing but what was good for the Revolution made me too flushed and furious not to assume the guise of an imbecile. We had reached the shower-bath. Like a spectator at a play, I watched Monro despatch Alavoine to select patients for a demonstration. As Pinel, seeing his chance, stepped away to rescue Mlle. Jouval from Monro, I wordlessly drew the mouth-key from my pocket and held it before him.

He stopped and looked down at it resting in the palm of my hand. He then looked very soberly at me.

I explained what it was and how I had come to create it. I mentioned an early expression of interest from Mr. Wright, the owner of a madhouse in Bethnal Green. As I enumerated several refinements that had come about in interesting ways, Pinel picked it up and turned it over in his fingers. When I was done my explanation he replaced it in my palm, saying in a gentle voice, "Still, M. Haslam. A terrible instrument, is it not?"

"Less so than knocking out teeth," I replied equably, thinking, *Or a guillotine.*

"But more so surely than attempting to find out from them why they don't open their mout's?"

I laughed at this, imagining a joke, for how could they speak if—

He watched me with cold eyes.

"Will *finding out* open them?" I asked, recovering.

"No, but in the course of inquiry, entering wit' dem a little into their suffering may."

Here it crossed my mind I was being played like a British puppet as by one of those French magnet-working agents so vexing to Matthews. Did Pinel imagine we were being great *philosophes* together, as in a *tête-à-tête* at the Académie Française, or was he only toying with me? Surely this was standard French resistance to a straightforward, practical solution? At a loss what to reply, I made a nod to mean I took his meaning perfectly, he need say no more. Yet even to myself the nod felt impatient and dismissive, and I knew he saw it all.

Now Alavoine was back, ushering before him four patients, two men and two women. Cleverly he'd chosen four who not only strip themselves at the slightest provocation to enjoy a cold air bath but are free of the usual licentious habits of such types. Yet on this occasion, as soon as they marked the strange

company, the females grew uncharacteristically abashed. Alavoine having sufficient experience of visiting dignitaries not to threaten violence, those two
ended up taking their shower-bath wrapped in a sheet. But sheeted or not, the
four drooping radishes as they shuffled forward single-file to be hammered by
the freezing spray, made so shivering and dejected a sight that our sensitive visitors averted their eyes. The exception was Mlle. Jouval, who seemed unable to
tear hers away. By the time Pinel put his arms around her to walk her aside, her
body was wracked with sobs.

Fifteen minutes later our visitors, Mlle. Jouval leaning hard on Pinel, were in
such a hurry to climb into their carriage and be gone that they couldn't remember what time their boat left, or indeed what day it left on, though Monro,
seeking to assure them they had hours to spare and must come back tomorrow
and tour our Dead House, asked two or three times.

As soon as the carriage was out of sight, I wanted nothing but to slip along
to my office and mentally review the events of the morning. But Monro expected supper, which he and I took fashionably late and cold, Sarah having re-
tired to her bed not long past noon. This left me to listen to him babble for five
hours while he drank up my red-port. He started out highly pleased, detailing
his satisfaction at how everything had gone, asking me repeatedly wasn't that
something and didn't we show the French bastards. But the more pleased he
declared himself, the more he drank, and the more he drank, the more bug-
eyed aware he grew that Pinel had spoke no more than a dozen words to him
the entire visit. So galling was this realization that a glimpse he'd caught of
Pinel turning away Mlle. Jouval from the ground-breaking spectacle of our
shower-bath expanded in his mind until he was convinced Pinel had stole her
from him. And so tormentingly did this bizarre persuasion operate upon his
sodden brain that by the time Alavoine and I poured him onto his horse, every
forecourt window not boarded up had a lunatic face pressed against it to watch
our physician gallop off cursing the French nation for the most verminous pack
of scoundrels that ever tried the patience of Europe.

HIGHER GROUND

Pinel's visit brought me to several conclusions, all soberer than Monro's. Our strengths showed better on paper. The reality of Bethlem as it registered on a sheltered or biased sensibility was too apt to undo too much good work. There was also my own career to think of. Before I met Pinel I was content to bask in the knowledge he approved my book and my approach. But my satisfaction was based on a convenient assumption of his qualification to judge. Now that I'd met him and noticed he was as implicated as the next politico, I felt the fatuousness of his praise and with it the emptiness of my own self-congratulation, and in seeing that saw, glaringly, the slightness and shortcomings of my little book.

This was how I came to conclude that the thing I must do next, if I was to remain at the forefront of this dirty-faced infant science called mad-doctoring, was publish a second edition more assured and substantial, improved by corrections and additions, something worthy to stand as the authoritative British text for the treatment of madness. Something to confirm my strengths before the world while forestalling the back-handed attack on me Pinel could now be counted on to be drafting for his own next book. In this way our mutual awakening had perfected my resolve to become the foremost English mad-doctor *in fact* that he *in imagination* once concluded me. In this way, my apotheosis to words would serve as means to a most practical and down-to-earth of ends.

As for what to do about Matthews, something was dawning. What it was I didn't as yet quite know. But I did know this was no ordinary lunatic. Not to me.

Pinel's visit falling on a Friday, I had the foresight to obtain written permission of the governors to take the family to Hampstead for a recuperative Sunday ramble upon the plain on top of the hill there, called by the locals the Heath.

After months of working nights on my mouth-key and days overseeing preparations for Pinel to view the place, it was my first time since last autumn outside Bethlem's walls in full daylight, Kitchiner's *converzationes* being evening affairs. All I'd glimpsed of springtime was blossoms on the spindly cherry by my office door.

Had the day not dawned warm and dry, we'd have stayed at home. The last thing Sarah needed was a chill. But the day promising fair, we piled into a hackney and rattled out into the countryside. All London had the same idea, some in coaches, most afoot, walking alone or in straggling family groups, everybody in need of a leg-stretch and fresh air. The closer we came to Hampstead, the more plots of flowers sprang up by the roadside, at the top of each a ragged woman or child with a basket, hawking. Market gardens were also planted along there, neat rows of cauliflower and cabbages, and these too were for sale, or would be soon. Every third house, shed, and barn glimpsable from the road had been converted for the day to an alehouse or tavern, with doors thrown open and tables and benches put out. For an exodus to the peace of the countryside, it was the most festive, mob-filled Sunday morning I ever saw.

But once we disembarked and started to climb, following a broad path where at times oaks and chestnuts made a green canopy, the crowds seemed to fan out and dissolve, and before long we were as good as by ourselves, taking slow steps upward under a sun shining down out of Wedgewood heavens, my dear Sarah on my arm. Indicating the blue, I said, "As soon as I have determined how to translate fame into money and time, we'll spend three months each year in Portugal and that way, my love, spare your precious lungs London winters. Until then, Hampstead Hill on a glorious spring Sunday is the best I can do."

"Still sanguine, John?"

"Aye, my love. Ever that."

Her eyes had been fixed some distance higher up the slope, on Jenny gnawing at a hangnail as she watched over the children, who were picking wildflowers, Henrietta on John's detailed instructions. Now those eyes, shining brighter than mortal eyes shine, fixed on me.

Frightened, I indicated the little party. "Our son, have you noticed, has a genius for natural philosophy—"

"You'll face your disappointments squarely, won't you, John?"

"Oh, he won't disappoint—" A cowardly response, as I knew when I made it.

"You won't grow a monster of bitterness and destruction?"

I laughed. "Why? Am I beginning to show symptoms?"

"The man I love is forthright and has good intentions—" Here she broke off, waiting for me to look at her. When I did she said, "Your honesty has made you and it will break you, and, God willing, John, it will save you."

"What's this? The flesh of his flesh can read the future now?"

"And will the flesh of hers remember what she told?"

"Yes, because every word she utters is rat-tat-attooed on his heart."

And so it was. The life I lived with Sarah in those years was too conscious, with everything composed within the frame of its end. Once a trudge up Hampstead Hill would have set me dreaming. Today I was a watchful, flinching eye.

After a morning of following the breezes, we spread a cloth on the grass and ate a lunch of bread, cheese, fruit. Later we lolled while the children played, then roused ourselves and wandered again, the children racing ahead, and would have wandered longer, were there not now glooming skies in the west. Slowly we circled a massive solitary beech while Jenny pushed the squealing children on its swings, before descending to find a carriage waiting as if only for us, to carry us through a deluge that turned the unpaved part of our route to one long slough—but we arrived home safe, dry, and pleasantly exhausted.

It was a day that even as you live it emanates a luminous remove that most achieve only afterward, as crystal pools of memory.

Monday morning early, after a meeting with Poynder to learn what I'd failed to catch on Pinel's visit, I paid a call on Matthews, who was sitting on his bed eating his breakfast of bread and butter with water-gruel.

"Well, James," I said, crossing idly to the little table where he kept his engraving materials. "How did you enjoy our visitors?"

"The woman was an honest soul."

"She was indeed, and a statuesque beauty—" Saying this, I picked up the copper-plate he'd been working on and slanted it toward the light. "James, you never did tell M. Pinel what this is an image of—"

"Put it down."

"Why, it's a woman—"

"Touch it longer and I'll destroy it."

I set it back down and turned to him. "It's your mother, isn't it, chained to her loom?"

At this, he sprung from the bed to snatch up the copper-plate and graver. He then crossed to the far wall and with his back to me set about scratching the plate all over.

"James, why?"

"Because," he cried, with a glance round at me, tears standing in his eyes, "after being entreated by her so long, you can't even recognize who it is."

"Your wife—? It's not a loom, it's a gate—?"

"Why don't you let her visit?"

"James, I've told you. It's not my decision, it's Monro's, with the governors fully behind him."

"You could talk to him."

"I have, too many times. His back is up."

"You could sneak her in. He'd never know."

"Alavoine would, and tell him. Don't you realize some in here are jealous of the favours I grant you? How many other inmates are secretly given free candles to work at night?"

"How many others burn them while recording abuses of beggars and slaves too frightened and confused even to understand that's what they are, while you labour on your mouth-key so you don't have to hear what the ones who do understand say?"

"James," I replied, trying to be droll, "this look I see is the one a slave puts on behind his master's back, not before his face."

"No, Jack. A fawning look only means he'd be a greater tyrant, if he could, than his master ever was. It must be contamination by the spirit of Liverpool that has you seeing slaves where they're not."

"I know you're no slave, James. And you know I've tried to be a friend to you in here—"

"Your friendship is selfishness and strategy, Jack, your kindness a counterfeit for action. You have no interest in what I have to say, only in whether I still believe it or am yet prepared to abjure it. By what presumption do you dismiss my professions while pretending not only to know but to judge my mind?"

"By my capacity, James, to penetrate as far into the mind as into a millstone, once it is cracked."

"Once it is dead, is all you know. You always was nothing but a shoddy empiric, Jack, and now you're not even that. One sniff of fame has ruined you beyond all reach of humanity. With your pen you've erupted to a greater villain than Monro and his brushes ever was. At least he stays away."

All the time he abused me he was scratching wildly at the copper-plate. I put a hand to my eyes. "I suppose this will be what you told Pinel."

"No, for him I expressed it in more graphical terms, with corroboration by hand-lettered documents. I needed it made absolutely clear you're destroying me, so they think twice before the gang redouble their efforts."

"You shall be destroyed, James," I said quietly, not intending a threat, though I can't pretend it didn't sound like one, "if you persist in this insolence."

"When the mighty abuse their power, Jack, what humbles them?"

"It's hardly a riddle which of us is the madman, if that's what you mean. You know, James, sometimes I think you need to be taught the ordinary forms of things around here, the same as any other patient. In your caudled state, you seem to have forgot that words and actions deserve consequences, even in here. Nay, all the more so in here."

"How convenient your morality should dovetail so nice with your viciousness."

"And this, sir, is the very insolence that shall no longer be tolerated. Dispute our authority, damn you, and we'll soon let you know what our authority is!"

Here I broke off trembling and left him before I made the situation worse, cursing myself that I should have let him provoke me. Before I closed the door I looked back to see a lunatic hunched over a copper-plate destroying the image of his last hope, himself a perfect image of the self-destruction he'd tell the whole world that I and I alone was responsible for.

Well, a clear small voice said, *let him tell it. We'll see who sanity believes.*

My confrontation with Matthews upsetting me too much to proceed on my rounds, I took a walk down Broad Street, to my immediate regret. The city was so foggy and hot, the pavement so thronged with feet and lungs, it seemed a holiday, or Bethlem had exploded. "By your leave," the carman mutters after he's shoved you aside, while a rotting hag recites the beauties of her girls to the jingle-jangle of a tambourine. The City's burgeoning. Every foray out, you plunge into half again as many whores, musicians, beggars, sailors, Negroes, urchins, pedlars, and thieves. The clamour only drove me in on myself, to gloomier reflection than if I'd stayed indoors.

A good mad-doctor does not allow a lunatic to provoke him, if for no other reason than in the heat of the exchange the lunatic goes too far and so brings down on himself an answering discipline, not to punish but to remind him there is a real world out there we all must live in, like it or not.

As I thought this while I walked, for some reason I kept glimpsing Margaret Matthews in the unlikeliest faces. Though our restraint order precluded her approaching Bethlem, it wouldn't stop her approaching me. But she hadn't been camped at my door, and with this fog, these crowds, and the intricate puzzle of London streets and alleys, what were the odds? No sooner had this thought come to me than of course I saw her, truly saw her, in Threadneedle Street, peering into a swag-shop window.

Too shaky from one confrontation already this morning, I slipped into what I thought was Finch Lane, but it was a cul-de-sac and she followed me in. As soon as I saw my mistake, I swung round and nearly knocked her down. Though smaller than I remembered (for so great a nuisance) and looking ten years older, she was still fadingly pretty but exhausted, distracted, and shabbier dressed than on her Bethlem visits.

"The reason he's not answering my letters," were her first words, spoke with grim lack of to-do, "is he's not received them."

I said I didn't know what she meant.

"Your basketmen," she said, with slow enunciation, "are intercepting my letters to my husband, and if not mine to him then his to me. Or both."

I assured her any keeper who did such a thing without cause was at risk of immediate dismissal.

"Does my husband receive my letters?"

"Not that I know."

"Who has charge of the post?"

"Mr. Poynder."

"Could you ask Mr. Poynder if he's received any letters from me to my husband, and could you make sure if he has and has filed them somewhere, he passes them on to their intended recipient? Could you at least do that much?"

I nodded, adding, "You should understand, Mrs. Matthews, it's the keepers' duty to scrutinize anything sent to the patients, including letters."

"The keepers are illiterates. You mean Alavoine."

"Yes, I should think it's mostly Alavoine—"

"Who will have burned or sold them. Nothing is being hatched, Mr. Haslam. These are sentiments of loving concern from a wife to her unjustly incarcerated husband. There is no reason on earth to prevent him from reading what I write him."

"No, there's not. But you should know some have argued letters will encourage an inmate to forget where he is."

This stunned her. "What are you saying?"

"I'm saying, for the same reason it's universally acknowledged lunatics do better removed from their families, some practitioners maintain that correspondence, to the extent it keeps the connexion alive, impedes recovery."

"And are you one of those 'practitioners,' Mr. Haslam?"

"No, I'm not."

"Then what is telling me this but pure cruelty? Why give mad reasons? You have the power to undo the abuse, you don't need to offer a cowardly half-defence of things as they are. Or is this only something you say now, here, to me, out of habit or instinct of survival, and you'll go away and do what surely you understand must be done? This isn't you telling me you won't do anything—is it? Tell me it's not—"

This had in it a note of tearful pleading that was something new from her and I confess disgusted me a little. While I hardly preferred her furious, this was a degree of instability I'd not seen from her before, and it put me in mind of the first law of magic: Like attracts like. For the glints of madness invariably visible in the behaviour of mad-doctors may also be discerned in the words and actions of the spouses of lunatics.

"I shall have a word with Mr. Poynder and Mr. Alavoine," I said in a placatory tone.

At this she squinted at me close a moment, and then said something strange. "Mr. Haslam, you won't ever destroy him, so don't think you can. He's stronger than you are."

"Perhaps he is," I replied lightly. "Perhaps that's the problem. I won't be strong enough to stop him from destroying himself."

"Oh you twister," she muttered, turning away.

"Mrs. Matthews," I said, my words echoing hollow as I spoke them, though they were not in any sense a lie. "Believe me when I say, like you, I only want your husband well."

She looked around. "Is this why you have locked him in the incurable wing?"

"Mrs. Matthews, how dangerous your husband is has not been determined—"

"What do you mean *dangerous*?" she asked in disgust yet with a hint of alarm. "How is he dangerous?"

"His condition changes."

"What are you saying?"

"If anything, he's saner. Only more . . . vicious."

"My God, wouldn't you be? So this *is* revenge—"

"By no means. The viciousness raises the possibility of harm to others, that's all. As well as to himself—" and I thought, *Well, that was easy enough. Why didn't I think of it this way before?*

"I don't believe you," she said wearily and turned away once again.

"Mrs. Matthews, a little faith in us might afford you the peace of mind—if you'll forgive me—you appear in need of just now."

"No," she said, half turning back, shaking her head, too vigorously. "It's too late for faith in you. There must be another way, and I must find it—"

Saying this, she stepped away from me into Threadneedle Street under a shower of curses from a drayman forced to slow up his beast. Though evidently unaware of her surroundings, she somehow achieved the opposite kerb untrampled, and disappeared into the crowd on that side, just another drab on the wander down a London thoroughfare.

I watched until she was out of sight and then made my way through the human ocean home, reflecting how, while I would certainly speak to Poynder and Alavoine about this matter of the letters, nothing would come of it: neither owed anything to me.

But it was only as I placed my hand on my own door that the full solution of what to do about Matthews revealed itself, and when it did I could only think it was emotion and politics that prevented me from seeing it sooner. The key was, I was a man of medicine and this was a medical case, a uniquely challenging one. For if this was a lunatic who suffered not only delusional convictions but hallucinations affecting every sense, the question was, Was this the gradual disintegration of personality usual in so extreme a case or was this the righteous wrath of a patient waxing more lucid under our care? Or put it another way: If you could more easily argue Matthews was dangerous than not a lunatic, then how to explain that most of the time whether hostile or not he communicated with me direct and clear? Never mind how I felt or what the politicians believed, Matthews was a medical question to be solved. Instead of stooping to a Tuke strategy of pretending a harmless lunatic will be perfectly sane if you treat him like a gentleman or a child, or to a Pinel strategy of telling myself his fate must depend on the international situation, as a man of medicine I must honour my *professional* interest in him. So perhaps Liverpool and Pinel were right for a reason they never thought of: It wouldn't be the worst thing for the world were Matthews to stay on with us for the foreseeable future, as a valid case for ongoing study, and so contribute to the next edition of my book—what more dramatic illustration of madness than this?—and so truly do his part, as I would continue to do mine, to legitimate a profession too often a refuge for hypocrites and dreamers.

And it struck me how incumbent it is on one in my position not to let himself be tied in knots by a patient but to use his wit and resolve, and yes, if need be, even harden his heart a little, so he can abstract himself enough to do his work and by the simple strategy of that priority remain high and dry, for the sake of the larger enterprise. Then if sometimes the screams of the drowning draw him back down to the shore to help out if he can, he should by all means go, but he must watch that an arm of the sea or the overwhelming burden of so much misery don't pull him down forever in the depths where they are.

JAMES TILLY MATTHEWS

1809

THE CAMBERWELL FRIEND

Twelve years it's been since The Schoolmaster determined me a specimen for medical study and twelve too since I saw my last outside visitor, my beloved Margaret. Unless, that is, you count Haslam's daughter, Henrietta, who six and seven years ago used to visit me daily to offer chatty reports on her life and more soberly confide her fears for her mother's. I don't think she had anyone else to talk to about those. Henrietta was a fine young girl, in appearance a bonny version of her father, in mind and manner an interesting blend of his dogged immediacy and what I guess is her mother's righteous passion. To my surprise—though I suppose it shouldn't have been, for wasn't I on my first arrival here similarly dazzled?—she was a fanatic of her father, thinking him an exemplarily good and brilliant man and interested in all he claimed to be attempting on behalf of lunatics everywhere. Before I could disabuse her, he set in motion that process himself when, discovering her visits to me, he abruptly put an end to our friendship—or thought he did. After that, her visits, being secret, were rarer. Though she never openly criticized him, you could sense the diminishment of her esteem, until by the day six years ago I last saw her, I would say she hated him, except more likely she only resented his possessive attachment to the little girl she no longer felt herself to be. That same week, owing to the deterioration of the fabric of the family residence along with most of the east wing, the Haslams moved to a house in Islington. In those days there was confident talk of a new hospital up there. The talk has since—

No sooner had my lettering proceeded as far as the above than, befitting the mind-toying agent he is a puppet of, the keeper Davies astonishingly brought in my first outside visitor in twelve years. This was my doughty childhood companion, Robert Dunbar, who has just now assured me that he and assorted others of my former acquaintance are doing everything they can to get me out.

"And Margaret?" I asked. "Is she somewhere in this, I hope?"

Dunbar looked at me dumbfounded. He's no longer the youth on Camberwell Green with tears streaming down his face as he thrashed me for reasons often mysterious to us both. The flesh has settled heavily upon the bones of the face, the emotion showing when it shows at all in compulsive adjustments of his long legs, which are always being crossed and recrossed or braided round themselves. I wonder why. "So it's true," he said in dismay. "You don't receive her letters—"

"Cheer up, Robert. It's not like I ever feared she don't write. What do they say?"

"*I* don't know, Jimmy! How much she misses you, I guess, and something of how she directs all we do."

"Directs because eleven years ago she herself was banned from entering this place?"

"That's right."

We were sitting side-by-side on my bed. Davies was not far away, leaning against the wall eating an apple when he wasn't lumbering off to sow menace in the gallery on the principle that if you want frightened birds you keep the air frightened.

I should explain my cell in the uncurable wing disappeared four years ago when the governors ordered the east wing demolition. I now reside in a sort of recess off a larger room in what remains of the second floor east of the central hall. The room contains six of us. All except Jack Baker and me are chained to the walls. In exchange for a pittance of light and privacy, my alcove offers chilling drafts from a broken casement located so high it can be seen out of only if I place my chair on my table and climb up. The view is of rooftops and southwest to the river and its bridges and shipping traffic. St. Paul's would be visible were it not for a jag of the exterior wall caused by the straw-burning flue.

Something had occurred to Dunbar. "Does no letters from Margaret, Jimmy, mean you don't know you have a son?"

At this last word the floor under me gave a lurch. *"What?"* I cried. "A father—!?"

"Since nearly twelve years—"

"My God, Robert!" I cried, tears flowing. "What kind of news is this? Is he a fine boy? Tell me! What's his name?"

"The finest there ever lived, Jimmy. His name's Jim."

"Jim. Now, there's a name—!"

Dunbar was looking at his watch. When he saw I noticed he cast his eyes significantly at Davies to say we had little time. Though I was bursting to hear everything about Jim, I said, dropping my voice (though it happened at that moment Davies was trundling off), "My informants, Robert, tell me several years ago two letters arrived, one for Monro and one for the governors, both requesting my discharge and both signed by Margaret. Of course, on the advice of the medical officers, the subcommittee said no. Still, it's good of you all to be trying."

"They would never allow a visit by any of us," he said, with a bitter look, "until mine, today."

"But why now?"

By his answer I was brought up to date.

Davies in the meantime was back from the gallery. As he'd passed through the other part of the room, however, little Jack Baker had clambered up on his back and was now perched there naked and howling. Instead of removing the clamorous carrot-pate, Davies was amusing himself by leaning against the wall as casual as before, only now crushing his passenger, who, long convinced he's experienced an unnatural connexion with his father, fell to moaning and gasping, "Oh my God! I'm broken! A taste of the Grinder of Hell awaiting me! The life squeezed out of me just so on the rack of my own nastiness!" etc., which noise happily prevented Davies from hearing Dunbar's account.

With one eye on the Grinder of Hell game, Dunbar explained that for three years Margaret, despite her rejection by Lord Erskine's secretary when I was first put in here, had been writing to him, who was now Lord Chancellor, in his capacity as Secretary of Lunatics (a fitting station, I here insert, for one so imbecilitated by the gang he's practically Monroish). Finally, a year ago, his Lordship was moved to inquire, by a letter sent to Monro, as to my state of mind and the reason I was detained. Erskine's letter inspired the Bethlem subcommittee (owing to arguments, it's been said, by John Haslam, who sometimes attends) at two meetings in autumn of last year to conclude me mad as ever but to observe they'd have no objection to the Parish of Camberwell applying for my release, provided the Lord Chancellor sanctioned their handing me over.

In early December, that sanction being slow to arrive, Margaret sent a third letter, this one requesting on my behalf a six-month leave of absence. And so my case—not me, never me—was yet again examined by the subcommittee, who after they unanimously affirmed I was insane, regretted that since the Lord Chancellor had returned no answer to their official letter, there was nothing they could do, the matter being entirely out of their hands.

I hate to think how many hands the misery of this world is out of.

At last, on Christmas Eve, a letter arrived from the Lord Chancellor's secretary informing the subcommittee that his Lordship could intervene only by a writ of habeas corpus.

A letter from the committee duly informed Margaret of his Lordship's advice.

This was not the first time she had been counselled to launch a plea of habeas corpus. The Bethlem subcommittee itself put the idea to her twelve years earlier. She, however, continued to fear a habeas corpus writ would only antagonize the Bethlem governors and officers and, after it was crushed, prejudice my treatment in here, effectively ending my chances of liberty if not my survival. Instead, this past spring, under Dunbar's name and those of my nephew Richard Staveley and my old friend George Lambeth, she applied once more for my discharge, assuring the committee that if I was released, my friends would confine me until such time as they received favourable medical opinion concerning the actual state of my mind. Further, they would exonerate the Parish of Camberwell of any continuing obligation to maintain me.

"A generous offer," I remarked to Dunbar.

He was watching Davies and Baker and failed to hear. In his distress, Jack Baker had begun to beshit himself. Now Davies, with the mutter, "Had I a monkey like you, I'd hang him," in one swift movement swung him round by the forearms and carried him—writhing, squealing, shitting—back to his bed.

"So now what?" I said as Baker's shrieks rent the air.

"At a meeting of the subcommittee next month, August," Dunbar resumed, Davies and Baker being out of sight, "we present in person our application to receive you, and they examine you, in our presence."

"And that of the medical officers."

"Yes. Haslam and Monro."

"And what do you think they'll conclude?"

"Who can say, Jimmy, but I don't think it's hopeless. They were willing to abide by the Lord Chancellor—"

"Who said he couldn't intervene."

"And this time they're examining you in person."

"The last time I was examined in person was twelve years ago, by Lord Kenyon. I've been in ever since."

"All you need to do is show yourself sane."

"This was never about insanity, Robert."

"Still. If you do, Margaret believes they're now ready to be rid of you."

"Of her, more likely. What they're ready for is a quiet life."

He nodded, thinking of something else. Then he told a story.

In January of this year he happened to run into Jack the Schoolmaster (Haslam to him), celebrating with a bookseller named Callow, at The Sow and Sausage in St. Mary Axe. The Schoolmaster had just published the second edition of his book, its title now *Observations on Madness*, *"Madness"* replacing the earlier *"Insanity,"* the former term more in fashion these days, the condition having grown so stylish as to be widely assumed curable—though he don't believe it. The dedication is a fawning one to Monro's "superior judgment," his "skill and liberality," and the "subsisting friendship" he has with him. That's all a lie too. On the night in question, he was in his cups, and instead of his own book—which he had a copy of in his pocket but wouldn't let anybody look inside, saying they must buy their own—was passing around the table a page of my lettering, showing everybody how it's so neat it can't be distinguished from type. He kept insisting they should see my engravings, which are as good as plates in a proper book.

"There's a poor engraving of his mouth-key in that edition," I told Dunbar. "He wanted me to do it, but I refused."

"Mouth-key?"

"A key to open mouths."

Dunbar looked blank a moment before continuing. Just because you're on a madman's side does not mean you need to hear what he says.

The Schoolmaster, having never met him before, had no idea who Dunbar was, but when Dunbar said he knew me and inquired after my health, The Schoolmaster assured him he saw me twice a week and I'm very well. He said, though he once thought I'd be the cornerstone of his new edition, over the years he'd come to consider me as good as sane. Except for a few delusional convictions (which likely as not are the effect of my incarceration), I no longer touch on political subjects, am as lucid as himself, far saner (making a jest) than his friend Callow, and it was a thousand pities I can't be restored to my family, as I'm a most honest, clever, and ingenious fellow.

It was, Dunbar said, this chance encounter that's inspired them to renewed vigour in the fight for my release. From it they've concluded that if Jack the Schoolmaster would say such things in public to one who admitted he knows me, he's softening if not square on our side.

"He was drunk," I pointed out.

"Still—"

"You don't know The Schoolmaster as I do."

"Haslam? No. But remember, Jimmy, it looks like he was instrumental at the meeting when they said they'd let you go if the Lord Chancellor approved it."

Davies was now back. The wall and floor where he'd stood with Baker being liberally befouled, he'd unchained old Joseph Panter. Joseph believes himself a child of Apollo, engendered by the sun shining near his father's door on a dunghill. For the first two hours of life he was a flea, then a fine boy of nine years. Davies was gripping the back of Joseph's neck to point out Jack Baker's shit to him by pressing his nose in it, telling him, "Go on, kiss your dear old Mum." Joseph was gagging. In his hand, I noticed, he was clutching a rag.

"Here's the thing to understand about our apothecary," I told Dunbar. "His sense of rank is acute. With his soul in consignment to those above, he won't take counsel from the side or below. That's why he resents his betters so much. He suspects but can't acknowledge to himself he's too slavish not to obey their every glance. Also, having on all available occasions declared me mad, as his own wonderful exemplum of that condition, he'll fight to the death anybody who tries to get me out by saying I'm not. He has his principles, you see—"

Dunbar heard this—if he heard it at all—in silence. He was watching Davies and Panter. When his attention returned to me he said, "Jimmy, I can swear out an affidavit Haslam said what he said."

"Yes, you can, and assuming anybody ever sees your affidavit and having

seen it does anything about it, The Schoolmaster can always say he was in a festive mood that night and only pulling your leg, and Callow will back him up."

Dunbar sighed. "We have to try."

"Yes, we do. Will Margaret be at the hearing?"

"No. She's still barred."

"The bastards."

Dunbar nodded, glancing uneasily toward the doorway. "Right royal fuck-
ers, the lot of them."

Davies heard this and looked close at Dunbar, whose eyes returned quick to
me. Evidently Davies had detoured by the beer tap after chaining Baker, but
such grateful draughts only make him meaner. The keepers, of course, are
three-quarters drunk most of the time, the women as inveterately as the men,
but Davies' attitude is singularly disturbing. His watchword—*A drunkard is
mad for the present, but a madman is drunk always*—affords him the conviction
that drunk he can be as wayward and dangerous as he imagines we are. In this
spirit he makes patients his accomplices, as when he compels one to restrain
another so he can force-feed him. Sometimes it's the mouth-key, sometimes the
food jammed in so hard the spoon comes out dripping blood. He also impli-
cates patients by making them watch abuses. I don't know how many he's
taken to the cellar to watch him fuck poor Mr. Carstairs. All the keepers are
wayward and dangerous, but only this one on principle. He especially enjoys
placing his thumbs inside a lunatic's cheeks and vigorously shaking them, particularly if he can arrange it so their head's struck repeatedly against the wall.

"How is she, Robert?" I asked.

"Margaret? Well. She's well—" This with shifting eyes, in a tone almost
querying, or imploring.

"She's got along all right, has she? And the lad—?"

"Well enough, Jimmy. They miss you."

"It's been a long time to miss me. Him his whole life—"

"Aye—"

"Does she have help? Does she still employ Justina Latimer?"

This name seemed to consternate him. Thinking he'd forgot who she was, I
added, "As her maid—"

"No," he said. "Margaret gave Justina her notice years ago, for insolence,
and other crimes—"

"What crimes, Robert? Not theft, I hope—?"

"Not theft—" he said quickly, seeming to curdle into himself.

"There's a piss-pot under the bed, Robert, if you need—"

He shook his head. "You did write Margaret—?"

"I did. From the question I take it my letters have not got past Sir Archy."

Talk of letters reminded Dunbar, and before I could stop him he extracted
from his jacket an envelope and held it out, saying, "Here's one that's getting
through—"

"Is it, now?" This was Davies, as he plucked it from Dunbar's hand.

Dunbar jumped up. "Give that over!" he cried. "That's Jimmy's!"

"Whose?" Davies wondered, horribly intrigued by Dunbar's agitation. Although a thorough unwitting pawn of magnetic agents, and as such the purest case of ignorance-is-force I ever encountered, Davies has never lost the born bully's delicate nose for infirmity. Now he folded his thigh-thick arms and directed at Dunbar a look that communicated consequences too brutal for such a one not to be instantly reduced to a quaking dish-clout. How severely you judge my old Camberwell friend's uncourageous behaviour will depend on how many William Davies you have met in your life in how many dark alleys and what your rate of success in countering those assaults on the integrity of your body and soul.

My hand on Dunbar's arm easily drew him back down. "Never mind it, Robert," I said, but the visit was over. Davies was on top of Dunbar to pull him to his feet and march him out, pausing only to direct a sharp kick at Joseph Panter, who was on his hands and knees, hard at work. Joseph took a moment to recover his balance after the toe of Davies' boot lifted his ribcage high on one side, and then he returned to smearing ordure in loving circles on the floor and wall.

My beloved Husband,

This is not the first letter I have written to you in your imprisonment, but it is too likely the first you will read. Though I know you yourself will have written faithfully, not a single letter from you has reached me. The day I come upon our correspondence hawked in the street, a ha'penny will buy me evidence of what we both already know: Everything that comes to Alavoine leaves only for money. But at least published we can read what we said, and if to increase their value our words have been doctored we'll know the true parts as sure as we know each other's heart.

Dearest Jamie, I write because the governors have granted permission for someone to visit you. Since I remain non grata, our choice has been Robert Dunbar, who will let you know that despite meagre resources and the creaking wheels-inside-wheels of power that run the country while they trap and crush anyone rash enough to attempt to discover how they work, we are doing all we can to win your freedom. But mainly by this letter know that you are father to a son who turns twelve on the 10th of September, your namesake, the most beautiful and intelligent boy that ever walked on this Earth, happy and kind, loving to his mother, thriving at school, praying nightly for your health and long life and the day you come home—

But I break off—Robert's at the door to say he's just heard he visits you this morning or not at all—

Jamie, rest assured Jim and I love you with all our hearts, and with your friends and other honest champions of justice we will prevail.

Your devoted wife
Margaret

Dearest Mags,

Though I caught only a glimpse of my name writ in your precious hand as your letter was plucked from Robert Dunbar's grasp by one of our resident bullies, it was sufficient reminder there have been others before it, each less overtly than this one snatched as it enters the building, just as mine are when they leave it. What heartless predators, to confiscate the loving sentiments of lawful wedded pens!

Your great news must be of young Jim, whose existence Robert had opportunity to tell me of, alas, only the barest fact. Dear Mags, I am speechless—wordless—with joy. My dreams of our boy's future achievements go shooting off in a thousand directions—

There—I have just scored a notch in the wall opposite my bed, marking his height. I don't know what it actually is but shall have Robert (if he comes again) offer a correction. This way I'll track young Jim's growth while I envision every manner of virtue blooming in him as he matures to an upstanding honourable man, as I know he must, being blest by the love of a mother so worthy and true.

Your fond loving husband (all of an instant a doting parent),
James

LUNATICS

This morning I awoke in that anxious state when the most familiar objects assume a hostile cast, and you wonder what on earth could inspire so hateful an array. It was either pace back and forth in an atmosphere of unremitting menace or pass along the gallery and visit our would-be regicide James Hadfield.

I chose Hadfield not for his charms (he has none) but for the magnetic fluid the gang circulate through his cell. The gang's methods of working are as numerous as their victims, but the essential principle is the magnetic impregnation of unsuspecting men and women in order to suck their secrets, influence their actions, or else slowly destroy them. My hope was inoculation against what they plan for my Saturday appearance before the Bethlem subcommittee. The reason I can come and go (on the men's side) was nine years ago The Schoolmaster removed my chains for good. Perhaps he remembered it's discipline he stands for, not punishment. Or wearied of the game of rewarding me by giving me back my engraving tools and punishing me by taking them away again. Perhaps it dawned on him there's something wrong when removal of a deprivation is counted as a privilege. So for nine years I've had the care of a small garden plot among the ruins of the inner wall, and he's let me come and go there as I please.

In my freedom from chains I'm luckier than Hadfield, who though he's got his own room has been shackled the better part of seven years, ever since he knocked Benjamin Swain over a bench and so qualified Swain in the governors' published statement to have died of natural causes. What more natural than a blow from a lunatic? A lie to the public? Four months later, in July, Hadfield enjoyed a brief hiatus from restraint when he escaped in the company of John Dunlop. They got as far as Dover, where a whore they jumped lived long enough to report them to the authorities. After that the governors required Sir Archy and The Schoolmaster to put in writing their thoughts concerning hospital security. This they did to everyone's satisfaction, although Sir Archy's failure at the time of escape to tell anyone two patients were missing the subcommittee found "highly reprehensible." Of course nothing changed. The surveyor was called in to inspect the locks and that was the end of the episode. People are always escaping from here, whether or not they've slipped Sir Archy a quid for the privilege. The more of us on the streets or in private care at private expense or stuck like a pin-auger in the bosoms of our families the better—or so goes the latest thinking.

In this The Schoolmaster's always been ahead of his time, except when it comes to some of us and the private-care-at-private-expense part, hating as he does anyone who'd make a fortune off mental suffering. An international reputation for himself is another matter.

After his Dover holiday, Hadfield was first returned to Newgate, but since then he's been back and forth between here and there half a dozen times. No one wants him, but there's no question they've got him. When he's here, he's as agreeable as the next base malcontent, cleanly in his person, knacky and ingenious in his amusements. By trade a silversmith, he puts his time to good use weaving straw baskets and writing poems, including a very pretty one on the death of his squirrel Jack, which concludes,

So there is an end to my little dancing Jack
That will never more be frightened by a Cat.

Such nimble productions he sells to the few visitors allowed through, his popularity with them that know him by reputation alone running second only to Peg Nicholson's and my own. By this means, combined with his government pension of sixpence per day, he dresses nattily and keeps his birds and cats plump on seed and fish scraps and himself mighty on tobacco.

Unfortunately for Hadfield, visitors of late have been scarce. So too admissions. Despite an influx in recent years of mental casualties of Bonaparte's cannons, our number is now not much over two hundred and dropping fast, most tucked away in chains. Though outraged at the thought of genteel folk shirking the sight of lunatics, The Schoolmaster's an advocate of the soothing power of darkness, particularly for wet or dirty patients, who end up on straw in the basement. The formula for their condition is *insensible to the calls of Nature*. Straw, being closer to Nature, must help them to hear her when she calls. They certainly can't see her. Advice to visitors: Bring a lanthorn, and don't forget a scented handkerchief—in case they let you in. If the place was a ruin when I first came, at least it was a teeming ruin and not a dank, stenchy desolation of whistling drafts and clanging iron. When much of the east wing went, I lost my longest home here and the women patients their tub bath. Now the ones who won't or can't endure the shower-bath you daren't approach for the stink.

So our alma mater moans and begs in the same street she always did, a grizzled, blasted, rotten veteran of a century and a quarter of government neglect.

This, by the way, is largely the result of a Bethlem treasurer named Kinleside absconding twenty years ago—long before either Jack or I arrived—with six thousand pounds. A Select Committee of Inquiry's judgment of Bethlem's record-keeping and accounting as "extremely obscure and defective" has resulted in a government policy as good as designed to deepen and justify the shadow, resulting in ideal conditions for the gang to sprawl together in promiscuous intercourse and establish their filthy community.

Meanwhile, most in here have no conception of the treatment they receive as anything other than malevolent and unnatural chastisement for misdoings they can't begin to conceive. They wake up they-know-not-where, not in their right mind; unable to comprehend anything for certain; unwitting of decisions being made behind their back that yet directly affect their chances of survival; allowed no say, no privacy, no respect for their station—or what was once their station; at the mercy of a cabal of vicious drunks who treat them any way their savage whims dictate. For most it's like drowning in a pitch-black well while their guardians stand around and lob rocks. It's farther in here to justice than to sanity. The fist is always right in our face.

But there was a reason beyond outrage and magnetic inoculation I went to see Hadfield on the eve of my hearing, and that was I sometimes think his case might suggest a legal remedy for my own, if only I could figure out what it is.

Like Palmer Hurst, Kooney Nugent, William Wake, and Urbane Metcalfe, to name four others I've counted as friends in here over the years, Hadfield is with us as a danger to his Majesty. Nine years ago, the King was making his bows upon entering Drury Lane Theatre, when Hadfield fired a pistol at him from the pit, the ball lodging in the ceiling of the royal box. In the traditional course of things, such overt aggression against the ruling monarch would mean instant hanging. But the defence—none other than my sometime supporter Lord Erskine, arguing before four judges, one of whom (Lord Kenyon) had recently put me away for good—drew attention to Hadfield's head. Grossly visible there were the sabre wounds he'd received in '93 as a soldier in the Fifteenth Light Dragoons at the Battle of Lincelles. These Erskine succeeded in establishing as the manifest source of Hadfield's intellectual disturbance. Suffering, as a result, extensive intimations of the dissolution of all human things, Hadfield only wanted to kill the King as a means to his own execution and so avoid the dishonour of suicide. A more frequent motive among the general population of assassins than you might suppose.

Even so, Hadfield would not likely have mustered the necessary resolve had he not, while out for a stroll of a Sabbath in White Conduit Fields, been accosted by the religious fanatic Bannister Truelock. It was Truelock who easily convinced him the Bible's a vulgar and indecent history that fails to contain one solid or sensible argument, the New Testament in particular being a fabric of falsehood and deception of use only for the amusement of its absurdity, whereas for his part Truelock had been pregnant a quarter century with the Messiah, who now stood poised to erupt from his mouth, the only obstacle to this singular advantage to religion being the life of the King.

Such was the argument for the defence. But I should point out Hadfield's action was only in part the work of a sabre-damaged brain under the sway of little Bannister Truelock (no mean rouser of insurrection, as can be testified by the chaos that erupts in here every time he's readmitted). Mainly Hadfield's assault on the King was the doing of French magnetic fluid-working under the direction of Bill the King, who's said to bear an uncanny resemblance to the late Dr. DeValangin. But unlike that beloved Forceps, Bill's a mysterious villain of unrelenting treachery. A celebrated master of the Air Loom for as long as anybody can remember, he's never been observed to smile, except at chess. Bill has his own good reasons for wanting his Majesty dead, but what they are I won't know until I know who he is, by which I mean who he's inhabiting. (A significant characteristic of the gang is, they have nothing to say or do in the world until they introject themselves into a human body. If there's a moral in this I'm not sure what it is, unless it's that one honest man or woman stands taller than all the evil that ever was.)

In the end Hadfield was found innocent by reason of a delusion, however temporary, but since nobody wanted him loose, a new law was rushed through to enable the incarceration of insane persons charged with treason, murder, or a felony, if they're deemable a threat to the State—even when by reason of insanity they've been cleared of all charges. This is how what's called the insanity plea came to be and James Hadfield our nation's first criminal lunatic. Many's the addle-pate's been tossed in here after him.

And before. Which is another way Hadfield's case would seem to touch on my own, for my detention predates that law and is not even, like Peg Nicholson's, a Green Cloth one. My detention occurred in the days when these things were handled more casually, as by a note to Monro from Lord Liverpool saying, Can you keep this one for us till further notice, Tom, like a good fellow?

Mind you, the crimes of Bethlem's assorted enemies of the State vary greatly in enormity. Hurst, Wake, Nugent, Metcalfe, and the rest are merely individuals with a habit of wandering onto royal property without the sense to leave before they're caught. All are sooner or later let go, but most are incorrigible. It's something about the mighty tug that fame, power, wealth, and authority exert on uncompassed minds.

True lunatic would-be royal assassins such as Hadfield are a rarer breed.

So am I. And after twelve years of not being let go, here's something I understand. I'm no more here for threatening Liverpool's life (let alone the King's) than I am for causing a stir in the public benches of the House. It's not anything I did. It's what I know.

Out in the upper gallery it was a quiet morning. Two of our makers and destroyers of universes were hard at work, and I paused on my way to Hadfield to partake of their genius.

The first I came to, standing in the centre of a small crowd, was Alfred Sconser. Alfred has the remarkable talent of eliciting a large amount of green fluid from out of his lungs. Tipping forward from the waist, he drools this ropy, viscous substance in a column a good inch and a half in diameter and perhaps five inches in length. Out of this pendant shaft, in gradual stages, with great care, he blows a grey-green bubble that on a good day reaches three feet in diameter, to general applause. The surface of Sconser's Sphere, as it's known, is smooth, with continents of thicker, duskier phlegm in relief upon it. Watching Alfred at work you find yourself witness to the generation of a globe not so very different from the one on which you are standing. When he has got his creation as big as it will go, he maintains it a few minutes (I have never known anyone, however excited they become at the sight of it, to offer to burst it), then with equal painstakingness collapses it, at last drawing the entirety of the heavy fluid back into his mouth and swallowing it all down, with a gratified smile.

This is an accomplished performance, and Alfred has his hat on the floor beside him the while. But unless there are outside visitors present (ones, that is, who don't recoil in disgust), he rarely receives more than the heartfelt admiration of his colleagues. Lately, it happens, I've earned a little from the sale of my engravings to our infrequent tourists, and so today when Alfred finished and the world had been swallowed back down, I placed a ha'penny in the hat before passing on.

Next I spent a few minutes in the company of that other serial destroyer and remaker of universes, Richard Pocock, whose conviction it is that as soon as he thinks of something, it's destroyed or, as he says, *thrown up*. Pocock knows he can't help all the destruction he's guilty of, because what man alive can stop himself thinking something once he's set his mind not to? But today he was working away, as he sometimes does, to undo the damage. To accomplish this, he stands with his eyes closed and his body bent double and his hands and arms extended in front of him, like one groping in the dark. He then decries all his previous thoughts, saying, for example, "I never thought of America, nor Jersey, nor Spain, nor Portugal, nor Plymouth Dock. I never thought of a pigsty, nor of Guildford. Oh, poor Guildford! and poor, good Mr. Hastings—" his former master—"and his family, my good and worthy friends who, thanks to me, alas, are no more! I never thought of a ploughshare, nor yet of a knapsack, nor yet of a summer house, nor of a sprocket and faucet, nor a monkey's beard, nor a hen's foot, nor a finger-organ, nor a boar's bristle. I have never thought of a parson, nor yet of a hedgehog, no, nor of a flying squirrel in America, nor of a monkey shaving himself, nor of the hinges of Mr. Hastings' cellar door, nor of the Polinac River in France, where I sailed from—" etc.

And so I left Richard Pocock to restore one universe even as Alfred Sconser was preparing to disgorge another.

Two doors this side of Hadfield's cell I next stopped a moment to offer an encouraging word to James Norris, a homicidal American sailor who's been locked up near a decade now in an iron apparatus special-designed for him by our medical officers after he plunged a knife into the keeper Hawkins, attacked with fatal intent a patient named Thompson rash enough to come to Hawkins' rescue, and had just bit off Thompson's finger when he was stopped from doing worse by having his arm smashed by our friend Davies with a shovel. Owing to an oddness of physiology, Norris's wrists are thicker than his hands, so to him a pair of handcuffs is the gift of a deadly weapon.

The merciful and humane apparatus in which our medical officers have Norris confined is a series of riveted iron rings that encircle his neck, trunk, and upper arms. The neck ring is attached by a short chain to an iron hoop that slides up and down a six-foot iron bar. The trunk and arm rings, which are fused, pinion his arms tight to his sides. All three varieties of ring are connected by two-inch iron bars that pass over his shoulders. A chain around his ankles prevents kicking. For nine years, our American has been able only to lie on his back or else, on account of the shortness of his neck chain (twelve inches), to stand on his bed against the wall. Now that he's grown emaciated from lack of movement, he can draw his arms from the circular projections from his trunk ring and hold reading material. If he doesn't, he has no choice but to rest them on the edges of those projections, a position he finds more painful than keeping them inside. These same projections are what prevent him from sleeping on his side.

Norris has the care of a badger-dog-and-terrier cross named Philadelphia, of whom he's exceeding fond. He's also a voracious devourer of newspapers and books, which the keepers out of pity (as a cat pities a mouse) supply him with daily. He speaks rationally enough, at times expressing gratitude for his restraint, since he says he don't feel entirely able to answer for his conduct and otherwise might commit more mayhem in the world than he already has.

Still, it seems a drastic confinement for one so sensible of his condition.

"Heigh-ho, James," I said as Philadelphia trotted over to sniff at my ankle.

"Heigh-ho, Jimmy," he replied, setting down his paper. "I see my countrymen are overjoyed this nation's promised to renew trade with them next spring. The question is, Do they imagine President Madison has conceded, or are they aware you British finally acknowledged Holland's a free country that can trade with whoever it wants?"

"Whatever your countrymen know, Jim, it'll be only what they've been told."

"And in that no different from yours, I'll warrant."

"No, no difference here."

"So where are you off to, then, Jim?"

"To see Jim Hadfield."

"The three Jimmies, we are."

"That's us."

Hadfield I found shackled as usual in his cell, weaving a placemat of straw. Though too insolent, daring, and violent to be unchained, Hadfield since his murder of Benjamin Swain has run the largest manufactory on the premises. Swain at the height of his activities oversaw a sizable industry in baskets and tablemats but was never a fair employer, choosing as assistants only those well chained. So when he refused to pay them, saying their work was no good, or told them he'd paid them when he hadn't, or paid them in bad coin, they were not well positioned to come after him. Hadfield, while more dangerous, is fairer, working mainly with his nemesis Bannister Truelock, himself a cobbler by trade, the two of them together by better taste and greater skill far surpassing the former productions of Swain and his iron-indentured crew. (By the way, Hadfield maintains he's unfairly accused, that he never struck Swain a blow that sent him over a bench head-first into the floor, but rather Swain, jealous of competition, was gathering his force to deliver a fatal blow to Hadfield as he sat innocently at work on a rag doily, when suddenly he dropped to the floor and expired, his head having exploded from the intensity of his rage.)

"Hello, James," I said. "How goes the trade in placemats?"

"Poor."

"No gawkers through?"

At first he made no response. He's one the gang prefer to keep in a twilight state. Six feet from his cell as I'd approached I could feel the insinuation of their magnetic assailment. Like many, Hadfield is so little aware of the primary source of his intellectual darkness that he'd sooner strike you down than acknowledge he suffers any at all. But on occasion he's been heard to complain that someone's trying to annihilate his "thinking substance," and that's a pretty accurate statement of his case. But he can work, and who will believe himself terminally afflicted who can still work?

"Just as well no bloody gawkers," he said.

"Why is that?"

"*Look* at me, damn thee," he growled.

With his gouged cranium, the bone smashed entirely away on one side, the membrane of skin there palpitant with each throb of his thinking substance, and with his head on a curious permanent angle owing to the position it lay in when surgery became imperative after the muscles of the neck were severed by the same or a different swordblade that penetrated his skull, he is undeniably a grotesque sight.

"You look as you did ever since I first knew you," I said, to reassure him.

Now he lifted murderous red eyes at me and passed a hand across his shattered skull. "You don't perceive, I suppose, I am *losing my hair*?"

"Perhaps a little," I conceded. We have this conversation often. His hair has grown thin on the diet here, he believes, and no longer has body enough to soften the horror with which the sight of him is apt to strike the unaccustomed eye. I know he has a request in for a wig—because I lettered it, at his dictation. His contention is, he no longer enjoys the same degree of *mental binding* as the rest of us. Besides this, a good wig would improve his appearance. And yet, while no one ranks higher on the list of Hadfield's admirers than himself, I suspect his lack of comeliness is of no tangible loss to him except as it might dissuade any but whores from having congress with him. But I can't imagine what other sort of woman would come near him. It's not as if he needs to pay whores more because he's grotesque. They're used to that. In any case, as long as he has his pension and can work and sell his manufactures, he'll keep himself sufficiently in pocket to purchase from Sir Archy private time in the visitors' room and doxies aplenty to visit him there for the satisfaction of every convolution of his lewdness. Of all in here for an incurable term, Hadfield is perhaps the one with least to complain about. But a feature of his condition is that he does complain, constantly. In this he's like a hypochondriac, who will complain, and live, forever.

"I am losing time," he told me. "Wasting my best days. I believe, here—" again passing a hand over his skull—"is sufficient proof of the consequence of my confinement."

Sometimes he groans that for the same reason the teeth are crumbling in his mouth.

"James," I said. "Let me remind you we're both victims, to a degree, of a force far greater and of more intrusive malevolence than was ever a product of British justice."

This only annoyed him. "Bugger off with your French agents, Matthews. I have no patience for your raving at a time when the hair lies so thick on my gown and the floor round about me, I feel I'm at the barber's."

Even as Hadfield rejected my reminder, I could sense by a shift in the quality of the force in the room that one of the women (of whom there are three in the gang, to four men) had just taken charge of the Air Loom. My guess was The Glove Woman, who never speaks but is remarkable for her skill in managing that terrible device. Certainly it's well within her powers to use it to cause loss of hair and have us blame it on the diet. Her own locks have lately been fleeing her upper head for the damper climes of her nostril-aerated lip and night-drool chin, and for this reason she now wears at all times a chip hat draped with black silk. Embalding others is just the kind of game she'd warm to. I can see her now, expertly working the machine while the rest of them banter and pluck at her like rooks at a strange jackdaw.

"There's talk Lord Sidmouth wants the governors to open two criminal wings that would hold sixty," I told Hadfield, changing the subject.

"Wings? Good. I'll fly away, ha ha!"

"These would be part of an entire new building."

"Where?"

"Nobody knows."

He grunted.

"I'm before the governors' subcommittee Saturday," I next informed him.

This having nothing to do with him, he made no reply. In here you grow accustomed to a relaxed approach to conversation. A person will walk away in mid-sentence and neither of you thinks anything of it. The only reason Hadfield hadn't already walked away was he was chained to the floor. In fact I would say the explanation for why, aside from the similarities of our cases, I've fallen into the custom of visiting him despite no discernible pleasure in his company is the same as why you will fall into the habit of visiting someone you can count on to be always at home and dependable in their reception, however dull.

"At least you're in by law," I said.

"I don't like the way this is going," he muttered.

"How is that?" I asked, thinking this might be a conversation.

"For God's sake, can't you see I am losing my hair?"

Inoculated yet or not, I soon took my leave of James Hadfield. A little of him does me for days. Though less confined than James Norris, he lacks the American's generosity of mind.

As I passed back along the gallery, I came upon Alfred Sconser completing the deflation of a Sphere. He seemed exhausted. All but one or two of his earlier audience had wandered off. Even lunatics grow tired of the same thing over and over. Suffering at that moment an overwhelming sense of the futility of all human endeavour, I tossed another ha'penny in the hat, which was empty, as before.

As the last of the column of green phlegm retracted slowly into Alfred's mouth, his eyes fixed hard on me. After swallowing down the entire gob, he bent to retrieve the coin, which he firmly replaced in my palm, saying in a voice of dignity, "I do clean out the hat."

Dearest Jamie,

Though I know unless the Bethlem door that opened a crack to let in Robert Dunbar is now also admitting my letters, this no more than the last will be the first from me you read. Yet I must write, for tomorrow you're alone before the committee. Our every attempt to persuade them to suspend, even temporarily, the sanctions against me has failed. They want me to regret I was a nuisance in the early days of your imprisonment and seem to take pleasure in reminding me how much it's diminished my capacity to help you. In this way they'd make me to blame for their failure of compassion. All I can do now is launch my counsel into the abyss like a desperate atheist a prayer, an atheist with every reason to fear hostile surveillance.

Jamie, first, you must face your inquisitors in a calm, reasonable manner. Though we both know you're not in for being mad, you must take particular care not to appear so. Committees, like water, seek their own level, i.e., the precedence of former rulings. Or think of it this way: Those made accountable for others' behaviour tend to judge according to what they construe others' good and not according to their own felt intelligence. Their duty, in other words, makes them rarely wise and frequently arbitrary.

Second, you should not anticipate effective support from John Haslam, whose prime concern will be to defend his medical judgment of your case. Not understanding the reason you are in, and feeling in consequence (if he feels anything at all) susceptible to a charge of ignorance in the matter, he will cloak himself in the power of what he knows—medicine—even as he also knows it's not the issue.

Third, for your own good you must speak as little as possible of what you *did in France. Though your sole intention in peacemaking was the good of your country, any such dealings are lately as much as ever considered traitorous, and you can no more afford to be seen to be concealing your supposed revolutionist connexions than can Bethlem those of an inmate. Jamie, this last advice is extremely important, for a single misstep could mean you not only don't get your freedom but are hanged for treason. How painful it is to write these words, but the matter is so extremely serious that were the chances you read this a thousand times less than they really are, it would need to be done.*

Finally, Jamie, I hope what isn't necessary to be said is the hearts and thoughts of all who love you will be with you tomorrow.

Your ever faithful
Margaret

BEFORE THE COMMITTEE

My first appearance before the Bethlem subcommittee after twelve years and six months at their pleasure took place on the morning of Saturday, August 12th, 1809. Sir Archy walked with me—or I should say I supported him—all the way down to the first-floor hall, which I never saw before. There we settled ourselves in silence on a bench rubbed smooth by the bums of a century of lunatics and their families. Otherwise there was little to admire. From where I sat, the light was too poor to make out what plaques and pictures hung on the walls and up the stairwell. Such glazing as there was streaked with grime.

Our silence was both vocal and mental. For the most part, Sir Archy communicates with me direct, by brain-saying. Yes, he's just as quaint and indelicate in thought as in word and deed and no less obscene a blackguard on the inside than he looks and sounds. Following a particularly vicious assault on me, he likes to lurk at the Air Loom controls, stroking them with his bony fingers. After several minutes of this, he'll turn with a hooded smile to The Middleman and in a filthy tone remark that I am the talisman.

"You have plucked the very word from my mouth," is The Middleman's invariable facetious response.

We're all talismans of those two. Sometimes as they impose their will on me, Jack the Schoolmaster stands in the shadows. If asked what he's doing, he shrugs and replies, "I'm here to see fair play," which always brings down the house.

That said, of late Alavoine (and I do mean Alavoine and not his inhabitor Sir Archy) has grown, when he can manage it, something like a friend. But not today. Today he was but a failing old man.

"The wheel's fallen off your cart, Sir Archy," I'd said as I helped the old body down the stairs. "Is it not time you transferred to another vehicle not so decrepit?"

He smiled at this and brain-said me only, *Power and access, laddie, power and access.* This came out, *P-hohr hehn hahk-sehss, lehdhie. P-hohr hehn hahk-sehss.* Even brain-saying, Sir Archy affects a provincial jargon. Affects because it's not his true language. At one time I'd have understood him to mean the gang's power of access is limited. But now I know it's the rare one they can't take over, once they apply their instruments to the task. Sir Archy inhabits old Alavoine for one reason: the steward's power on the men's side of the building and his universal access otherwise. Where better than in the steward of the place, however geriatric, to locate an agent? Add to him Jack the Schoolmaster, who took control of Haslam a long time ago, and The Glove Woman, who's constantly in Matron White and whose villainy could fill the British Library, and you begin to understand how thoroughly they have us covered.

For the hour Sir Archy and I waited on the bench, him slumped roupily against me, I fell to mentally reviewing certain crimes by keepers I'd lately been lettering, as when last summer The Glove Woman spent a fortnight at Worthing with one of her patients, a Miss Beddoes. This is worse than it sounds, for while The Glove Woman came back with two dozen brand-new pairs of fine-quality kidskin gloves, Miss Beddoes came back pregnant. This and other outrages I was turning over in my mind, when, to my horror, worse than the terrible breathing at my ear, the terrible breathing ceased.

Frantic, I fumbled fingers to his neck: no pulse! For more than a decade all but extinguished, and now the decrepit vehicle too! Alas, poor Alavoine! Over the years I had been beneficiary of enough signs of kindness from my old friend to now feel a burn of tears—when suddenly the ancient carcass give a great gasp, and after a carriage-wreck of wrenching heaves and phlegmy hacks, resumed its ragged rhythm. I blew my nose. Soon after, we were called into the committee room. I was almost on my feet when I had another surprise, as recipient of one of those startling small gestures that indicate old Alavoine is still among us. Waking with a jolt from his slumber, in a space of seconds before Sir Archy surged back in, he leant over and kissed my forehead whispering, *Ghahd bhuh-lhass yho, lehdhie.* Before I could whisper, *Thank you, Peter,* I was through the door.

You can imagine how badly shook I was on entering the committee room, an unfortunate circumstance with so much riding on my appearing sane. Besides, after the drafty hall, and with blazing fires in both fireplaces, the room was too hot. Immediately inside the door I was sat down at the foot of a long, broad table, facing seven men ranged at the other end. Of these, four were governors, and of them it was immediately apparent two were inhabited. Put them and Sir Archy together with Jack the Schoolmaster; the clerk Poynder, an amiable fellow but indecently impressionable; and Monro, whose brain is so weak he can't locate his cock without magnetic assistance; and you had as good as six agents in the room.

Glancing hard right behind me, I saw, seated along the back wall, on the other side of the door from Sir Archy, Robert Dunbar, seeming queasy. By the look of him he'd just been before the committee. Next to him was my nephew Richard Staveley, now a Cheapside druggist, as Dunbar had told me. Staveley mouthed *Halloo Jim* and I mouthed back *Halloo Dick.* On Staveley's left sat, of all people, Justina Latimer, no longer young but not old either, and no longer looking like anybody's maid outside a Parisian bordello. Now, why would she be here? Under a scarlet bonnet spilling papier-mâché green-grapes, she was every inch your powdered, tousled whore but beamed at me for a reason I could only wonder at. A fluttery enticement of feminine frippery, but get on the wrong side of that one and you'll soon know the meaning of rag and tag. Next to her was a man I never saw before but with a baboon face. Was she here with him? He looked at me mildly and nodded. The one I didn't see was my other old friend mentioned by Dunbar: George Lambeth. I guess George had other plans. He was one of those people you continue fond of after quickly learning never to count on.

That made it six against five, with three to be determined. Fair enough odds, at least on the face of it. Had Lambeth bothered to show, they would have been even.

I wondered if the gang had moved the Air Loom in closer, even so far as into the building, or if they'd bother, being already well represented in person, as it were. Closer is better, inside is best, but no man or woman within a hundred feet of the machine is safe from its worst effects.

"Shall we begin?" The chairman's name was Wood. Having every appearance of a London broker doing his duty on a public committee that he never wanted to be on, he was one of the two governors manifestly inhabited. Anybody unwilling to do what he's doing is easily taken over. In this he resembled Haslam, with the significant difference that by the time Wood is more than a hundred feet from these premises, he'll be himself again. Haslam it'll take more than a walk out to free of The Schoolmaster.

I nodded, peering at him close, trying to make out which agent it was.

He cleared his throat but never swallowed. This was a ploy, for inhabited ones swallowing make a tell-tale sound like the creaking of a wicker basket when you compress it with both hands.

"Very well—" He was scanning down a list of questions undoubtedly prepared for him by The Schoolmaster, the only one in the room with anything like full knowledge of my case. (The gang sometimes refer to him as The Recorder, for his skill in shorthand, and indeed he pretends to register everything that passes. These exertions he calls *dictating,* by which he endeavours to intrude his style of being upon my own.) "May we ask first, Mr. Matthews, your views on the current political situation in France?"

"I have no views on that situation, sir," I soberly replied. "My own affords me no prospects of it."

The subtlety of this answer passing Wood by, he seemed satisfied. As he looked to the next question on his list, I turned to my friends to see how I was doing. Staveley, who used to be so dropsical I never expected him to live to be thirty but looks fine now, give me a thumbs-up.

"But you have in the past concerned yourself with that situation, have you not, Mr. Matthews? Did you not on more than one occasion travel to that country, and were you not imprisoned there for your activities, indeed for some time?"

"Yes, I was. And now bitterly regret that involvement."

"And why is that?"

"Because it's parted me from my family and friends."

The elision confused him. "But you're not still in France—?"

"No, sir, only still imprisoned."

"And this has been a source of suffering for you, has it, Mr. Matthews, this im— this separation from your family and friends?"

"Yes, sir, it has. And remains so. Most grievously."

Now Jack the Schoolmaster, who was sitting next to Wood, with his arms crossed against his chest and his chair tipped back on two legs, thudded forward and leaned over to say something in his ear. It was as Wood tipped his head to hear what The Schoolmaster had to tell him that I caught a glimpse of the agent in charge there, and to my amazement it was the one they call Augusta. I would know that sharp, powderless countenance anywhere.

Having apparently been directed by The Schoolmaster what line of questioning to pursue next, Wood (or I should say, Augusta) said, "Mr. Matthews, do you know why you're a patient in this hospital?"

"I do." Again I looked around and was heartened to receive encouraging looks from my friends.

"And what is that reason?"

Though I next had every intention (having every need) to say clearly what my reason was, the question even as I made to answer it was toppled from view by a succession of mental cascades not unlike diarrheal purges.

"The reason—ah—" It was no use. I had forgot the question. Worse, by a mounting paralysis in my tongue I knew I was being not only brain-said but *fluid-locked* (as they call it), which means they were simultaneously working the Air Loom to constrict the fibres of my mouth-parts. I couldn't have spoke even if I had any idea what I wanted to say. This must have been the doing of The Schoolmaster, Augusta having nothing like the necessary skill.

"Yes, sir. The reason. Why you're here."

Monro's hat was pulled down over his face so I couldn't see who was in there. To further throw me off, he was pretending to sketch away. On his right hand The Schoolmaster sat hunched, swarthy-jowled, his eyes drilling into me, insinuating his influence. Here it might well be asked how he could be right in front of me, effectually brain-saying me direct and yet at the same time fluid-locking me by means of the machine, and I admit it was unaccountable, like a contradiction in a nightmare—but does it wake you? I can only think another gang member was working the machine, one, like Augusta, under such strict supervision by The Schoolmaster that her fluid-locking was emitting waft after waft of *his* mental effluvia. I confess it surprised me to realize that as merely the gang's recorder, not to mention one not very skilled at the machine—which for that reason they seldom let him near—he was capable of so much influence. Then again, I should not forget the victim was myself, who as a recorder in my own right have long been his particular prey.

Once more I glanced round at my friends, whose faces now showed not so much encouragement as consternation and alarm. If Dunbar looked queasy before, he was nauseated now. Staveley looked in dire need of a drink. The baboon man gazed back at me impassive about the face, but in his eyes was something like concern. As for Justina Latimer, she glanced at me smiling when I turned, but I would say this was less to do with me than a studied pose for the admiration of those members of the committee who kept sneaking peeks.

Shaken, I turned back to Wood. As I did, a drop of that same sweat departed the end of my nose, and my tongue caught it. A good thing, for the salty elixir seeming the courage of my own mother's unending labour distilled, it had the magical virtue of instantly unlocking my mouth-parts. "I'm here," I declared, "for you to do your worst, you hard-favoured, magnet-working cunt."

Mr. Wood blinked at this and seemed to take note of the appellation.

Strictly, what I had said was untrue. Augusta's principal duties are keeping in touch with gangs in the West End and influencing the female sex with her brain-sayings, which by the way are invariably in French, a language cunningly devised to insinuate depravity in the female mind. She seldom takes a hand at the machine, let alone deploys the magnet, and clearly she was not doing so at this moment. But I felt it was best, everything considered, and with Jack the Schoolmaster so fierce on the job, to strike back hard as I could. Though Augusta is every inch the country tradesman's wife and always starts out friendly and cajoling, the instant she knows she won't get her own way, she spews at you the most scabrous malignance. I knew full well I'd pay dear for my blunt taunt, but I was heartily sick and tired of being pushed and pulled every which way by these dreadful bullies.

I didn't have long to wait. Already probing for attention was a mounting tickle in my anus, by which I deduced they were *pushing up the quicksilver,* as they call it, a means they have (among many) of disarming any expression of indignation at their perfidy. Still I resolved to fight on.

"You know as well as I do," I said, "I'm here to be destroyed by a notorious gang of Air-Loom–working magnetic spies, of which you yourself are not an unsignificant member."

"I beg your pardon?" Wood said. "Heirloom-working spies?"

"Air-Loom–working spies, yes."

"I see."

"Do you."

"And how, Mr. Matthews, do these spies 'work' these heirlooms?"

"I am unable to respond to that question," I told him.

"And why is that, sir?"

"It would not serve the matter at hand."

This answer elicited from The Schoolmaster a lively outpouring of whisperings into the ear of Wood, who scarcely had patience to hear him out before he declared, in a state of heightened irritation, "The matter at hand, sir, is your mental competence. Whether these spies exist or not must surely have bearing on that fundamental question."

"No, sir," I replied. "It's universally acknowledged there always have been and always will be spies among us. That, alas, is not enough to prevent anybody from being a lunatic."

"But if a fellow believes there are spies of a kind and in a place there ain't," another governor put in, "mayhap he just might be a lunatic?" This was uttered at a high pitch of nervous exasperation, but so struck was the speaker at the sound of his own whinging voice in the room he immediately lost heart and ended weaker than he started. But at least you knew he spoke direct for himself and was not one who'd been taken over.

"But if," I said, addressing him in the tone of gentle reasonableness one assumes with a feeble-minded friend, "he believes there ain't spies when there are, surely he's the madder, when everybody knows there have been, are, and ever will be."

Now another spoke up. "But what of these gangs? How do you mean they *work* heirlooms? What are they? Antiquaries? Smugglers? That's a straightforward question, by God!"

"And here's a straightforward answer, sir. Our politicians are lackeys and traitors and the royal family a set of treasonous usurpers, and the reason—"

Here again what I next meant to say crumbled and fell away out of view. As on occasion one will fade from a pressing scene of affairs into a succession of lethargies, I found myself in a slow tumble from one swoon to the next. Evidently, Augusta had chose to wreak her vengeance on me sooner rather than later. To this end she'd brazenly taken over The Schoolmaster's saying of my brain by sucking it. (*Brain-sucking* is a process by which, after first using the Air Loom to apply a magnetic attachment from their brain to yours, they make a vacuum out of their own and so withdraw from yours the entirety of its thought-contents.)

"Sir? You were saying? The reason—?"

That Augusta should have hit on this moment to do what she was doing was shocking in the extreme but hardly surprising—unlike what happened next, though even it had many precedents in the shameful history of this gang.

"Mr. Matthews, will you please answer the question?"

"I cannot, sir. I have lost my—"

"Power of intellection, sir? Is that what you mean to say? And is that not the reason you're here? Yes? No? Won't answer? Then let me ask you this—"

Though at first sight, The Schoolmaster's and Augusta's impositions might seem as nonsensical as they were shameless, they did have a consequence in keeping with their ultimate goal, for the question Wood next asked was so preposterous there was nothing I could say or do but pour my every ounce of strength into a straight face.

What question was it, you ask? Reader, hold on to your hat.

"Do you count yourself grateful, Mr. Matthews, for the treatment you have received while at this hospital?"

The extreme effect of this question on me owed less to its preposterousness than to the immediate solution it provided to the mystery of twelve years of random kindnesses from The Schoolmaster: all to engineer at this moment a touch of the forelock (were it not shaved off) and a "That I do, sir." It's marvellous how an entire history will come pouring into a single instant.

A proper understanding of what happened next was granted me only days later, on a nauseous sick flood of horror. For that tickle at my anus had not been them pushing up the quicksilver, as I'd foolishly imagined, but rather someone at the machine—likely The Glove Woman—insinuating into my fundament an exotic form of the magnetic fluid, obtainable only by an unspeakable process called *gaz-plucking,* by which such fluid, having been rarified and sublimed by its continuance in the bowels of a lunatic, they make use of the Air Loom to extract in a gradual way, bubble by bubble. This, reaching my vitals at the precise moment Chairman Wood put to me his outrageous question, caused the muscles of my face to screw into a fixed grin. It's a process the gang call *laugh-making,* and in my weakened mental condition, I was its helpless victim, falling off my chair with my face locked in such a horrible grimace of hilarity as to throw the entire proceedings into unadjournable uproar. By the time I was carted from the room, my face, tongue, and brain were froze fast, with nothing remaining in my mental realm save the dumbstruck faces of my supporters, like kites snapping stiff against vanquished skies.

Dearest Mags,

I know by my Air-Loom-induced susceptibility to that Influencing En-gine how sorely I have disappointed you all. No words can express my regret in having done so, and undoubtedly no words will, for the chances you ever read this are as good as nil. But even inside here, hope like a precious plate keeps springing from the shelf to smash again, and so I take up my pen to beg that you assure Jim I did everything in my power to withstand their brain-saying, thought-working, etc. If it had been only (only!?) The Mid-dleman at the controls and the rest of them simply queering the game by owling me from the safety of the living empty shells of selected governors, I might have prevailed, but with the double-barrelled assault on my thinking substance by The Schoolmaster and Augusta, plus The Glove Woman laugh-making me by insinuating fingerlings of hilarity into my lower ori-fice, it was more than any human being could hope to withstand.

But rest assured, my Dearest Ones, I am recovering, though slowly, and yes, even learning to grow a little reconciled to the now certain knowledge I shall never leave this dreadful place again. Please tell Jim how sorry I am to have let him down.

Your husband lately doomed by
a shocking alliance of superhuman forces,
James

P.S. Why was Justina Latimer there?

TWO VISITORS

As another has said, I am not mad but my thoughts sometimes are.

This unfortunately was not the opinion of the Bethlem subcommittee in the wake of my gang-infested hearing. They now declined to believe my friends would hold me, if they'd so adamantly argue I'm sane when I'm so manifestly not. My friends' lack of judgment was considered by the committee a sign as bad as the one that in twelve years of punishment (in their word, treatment) for insanity, I have steadfastly refused to admit I suffer from that condition.

In the weeks after my hearing, Robert Dunbar was allowed two visits to my sickbed. On both occasions the letters for me from Margaret he carried were taken away before he reached my cell, with assurances I'd see them once they were scrutinized. I'm still waiting. During Dunbar's second visit, he reported that Camberwell Parish, which had high hopes my hearing would win my freedom, in their disappointment now refuse to pay the continuing cost of me, and are full on our side in support of my release at their discretion. This is why Robert Dunbar, in the company of William Law (a Camberwell churchwarden) and the baboon-faced man at my hearing (who it turns out is the new Camberwell overseer of the poor, one Joseph Sadler), waited on the committee to demand my release, suggesting I be removed from Bethlem and placed, until my harmlessness be established, in the Camberwell workhouse strong-room. (Justina, by the way, was not there with Sadler. Her presence remains as consternating a puzzle to Dunbar as to me.) When the committee's response to Camberwell's generous-minded offer was assorted demurrals and evasions (its composition being in the course of the usual rotation different from that of the one that first suggested I be handed over to Camberwell Parish for safe-keeping), the Camberwell officers declared, "In that case, Gentlemen, we have nothing more to do with him. Let us know the amount that is due, and we'll tender it in bank notes. If you hold him, you hold him at your own expense."

As Sadler afterward reported to Dunbar, the committee's response was hastily to refer the entire business to the next meeting of the Grand Committee, which was at Bridewell on October 4th, when Sadler and Law were a good deal surprised to hear several of the Bethlem subcommittee who attended declare I'm not only as insane as ever but too intransigent a lunatic ever to be allowed at large. The last of these to speak was Wood—or should I say Augusta—who stated outright he considers me highly dangerous to the safety of his Majesty. Haslam and Monro were there to grimly concur. Topping off the proceedings, the chairman of the Grand Committee stood up and read out a letter, dated September 7th, from Lord Liverpool (not the 1st Earl, who died last year, but his son, the 2nd Earl, as home secretary—the grave is nothing to these people), who recommended I be detained as a fit and proper patient of this hospital. Further, he committed the Government to relieving Camberwell Parish of all my expenses, including those of my funeral, should I die here.

Where else do they now expect me to do it?

Liverpool's letter was the clincher and the matter settled. All my champions off the hook and not the shadow of a continued charge on anyone except the Chancellor of the Exchequer, who can afford it.

So here I remain in my dank corner with an ulcer in my back that promises to kill me yet. Luckily my brain was so abused during my subcommittee interview that death itself has come to seem a little agreeable. So many lice—why go on scratching? Like all weavers, my mother was Melancholy's shuttlecock, and so these days am I. The Schoolmaster says Melancholy's a mosquito: Brush it away in haste and it leaves a festering sting. Allow it to drink its fill and it lumbers off harmless. I'm allowing it to drink its fill. Five weeks it's taken me to letter the above account of what Dunbar reported on his two visits, every penstroke an application of will. As for engraving, it's out of the question, I'm at too low an ebb. I confess at my darkest moments I wish I never had a son or was told I do, when it means my life in here is so grimly shadowed by the absence not just of Margaret but of one I never knew. Night and day I lie curled in a condition of mental torpor. The simplest thoughts and routinest sounds from the gallery arrive hedged with mystery, while every item in every newspaper touches on me. I never knew so many special editions.

My next visitor was Jack the Schoolmaster, who hadn't spoke to me since his annual drop-by last May to inaugurate the summer's regimen of bleedings, blisters, vomits, and purges, which as usual he inflicted on every patient they wouldn't kill while cheerfully declaring them useless. He gave me a medicine I swear was copper shavings in a chloric paste. I was incontinent for two weeks. It's a kind of depletory care they practise in here: drenching to diminish the evil their system excites. Since his move to Islington, The Schoolmaster is here four hours a day at most. The rules say he must be here every day, but they don't say for how long. Rumour has it his wife is dying and requires constant attention.

Otherwise, his time has gone into the second edition of his book and various other publications in a vain struggle, *a,* to grow rich enough to remove his wife southward and so rescue her lungs, *b,* to put more distance between his reputation and the appalling truth. Struggle *a*'s vain because there's no more cure for consumption than for madness, and *b* because the better he sounds on paper, the wider the gap between reputation and reality. In any event, I rarely see him now. He's not as absent as Monro, or when here as elusive as Crowther, but he's three times more absent than he used to be. On his visit he let drop he gets more work done in his library at home; there are too many distractions here.

"Distracteds, did you say?"

"Oh, cut it, would you—" In our normal exchanges he addresses me aloud. There is none of the brain-saying of his ostensible satellite Sir Archy.

"How does Henrietta?" I asked next.

But this reminder of the damage he did his daughter's love for him when he cut off her friendship with me only annoying him, he scowled and said, "As a good daughter to her ailing mother."

"I'm sorry your wife isn't well, Jack."

He acknowledged this by a nod but with his face averted as if embarrassed lest I see how much her suffering affected him, or perhaps fearful lest affirming the disease hasten its course.

The pretense for his visit was to apologize for my unending incarceration. More accurately, to reaffirm it without explanation. This a week after he damned me before the Grand Committee. The real reason he was pacing my little corner in such agitation is he's compromised down to his bootsoles, which as any honest soul will tell you is nine-tenths of the way to Hell.

When I pointed this out, his back was to me, his head tipped back like an actor's whose lines are tacked to the ceiling, but he made no answer. When he faced me again, I suggested he examine the ulcer in my back, but he was thinking about something else.

"You are a medical man—?" I said.

"The matter's now beyond the subcommittee's purview," he stated, meaning my release. "The letter from Liverpool has made that clear."

The Schoolmaster's heavier now, and looks older than his forty-five years. Success has proved a harrowing mistress. The poundage testifies less to constant intake, damped flame, than to insulation against conscience. More weight suggests Haslam continues to stir. Buried but alive, which means enough scraps of truth lobbed past The Schoolmaster could mean Haslam snatches enough to grow strong and so fights his way back to the helm of his own being. But I must say there was nothing in those eyes to indicate he was anywhere present. If you ask me, The Schoolmaster had come to see me out of neither guilt nor interest in my freedom but merely curiosity to see what use the gang could put me to in their scheme to murder England, Wales, and Scotland, and let Ireland go hang.

"The problem is, James," he said, "the Government still wants you in."

"Yet you happen to believe I'm sane as the next man."

If this was a hit he only shot back the quicker, "The next man in here, yes." Then, for all the world as if more kindly, "When, James, did I ever tell you you're sane? And what do you expect me to stand up and declare after your performance before the subcommittee?"

"You could explain I'm a victim of systematic mental abuse."

"Which would only make you sound not in control of your actions. No, James. This is what happens when you call people cunts to their faces and denominate politicians traitors and lackeys and the royal family treasonous usurpers." This too seemed sympathetically enough said, but I also caught in it the tenor of gang sentiment and was reminded how much they'd love to see Napoleon Bonaparte crowned Emperor of England. They've told me too often they intend to work that monster up to as high a pitch of grandeur as they will degrade me below any common level of human nature.

When I made no answer, only shook my head, he said, "James, I don't need to remind you, if you would only tell me why you're in here, there might be something, even now, I could do."

When I made no answer, it was as good as the end of Jack's visit, and he soon took his leave.

MOTHER AND SON

My next two visitors arrived together the following Wednesday.

Being in a doze when they entered, I at first mistook them for figments. But unless the gang is *dream-working* you with grotesque phantoms of their own making, a dream, however fantastical at first, when examined close is only ever yourself, and no less familiar. This was two other people. "You've come," I whispered, or thought I did, before I opened my eyes.

There was no reply, only a rustling of skirts and a scrape as of something set on the floor.

Our embrace was a dissolve of tears. When she sat up, she looked to the one with us. I looked too.

"Hello, Papa."

These words issued from the fairest mouth beneath the shapeliest nose and clearest eyes I ever saw. When the lips floated in for a kiss, I saw his mother's, but those eyes spoke of my own mother's too. "Hello, *my son,*" I whispered, groping for his hands, tears brimming, babbling and squeezing, hardly knowing what I said.

Margaret's fingers were in my hair-bristles, then softly smoothing the creases at my brow.

"Your health, Father?" he asked. "Do they treat you well?"

"They treat me just as they know how to, my darling Jim—"

He smiled at this uncomprehending, but Margaret looked at me dubiously, with her old face. She's an old woman now, and she regarded me as sceptically as I did her poor greenish-black gown and threadbare jacket as she stood behind him, with a hand on his slender shoulder. He was a flax-haired angel. Small, like me—I must adjust my wall-notch—but I would say eleven or twelve years of age, which is what he would need to be. "Do you go to school, Jim?"

"I do, Papa," and he prattled awhile about his school and the teachers and friends he had there, until the tears flooded my cheeks, alarming him. "Is every-thing all right, Papa?"

"It is, Jim," Margaret gently assured him (causing him, with a manly impa-tience, to shrug off her hand). "Only very happy to see you. Now you must let your father and me talk."

"Before a keeper appears—" I confirmed, squeezing his fingers.

Sighing, Margaret sat on the edge of my bed to recount how for a decade she retailed tea, but the East India Company showing scant mercy for the indepen-dent shop, two years ago, to pay her debts, she sold all stock and furnishings to our long-time suppliers Crump & Co., who have hired her as book-keeper at their Holborn offices. Now our shop is the premises of a bespoke tailor named Hodge. Hodge of Leadenhall.

Bespoke put me in mind of Justina Latimer's hat. My question of Margaret why our former maid was at my subcommittee hearing seemed to nonplus her. "I can't imagine but don't like it," she replied, looking perturbed. "All I know is when we pass in the street she pretends not to see me. Someone said she was modelling hats in the Burlington Arcade."

"The scarlet bonnet with the green-grapes—"

"You should see the sunflower one."

"She was friendly enough."

"The more our concern. Something's up, but I don't know what. Did you know her former husband, the one murdered in his bed, was a republican sympathizer—?"

"And who are her associates now?"

"Gentlemen."

"That could be our answer."

Margaret looked at me close a moment and then provided a synopsis of her efforts to win my release, saying I could read it in full in the copies of her letters she'd brought. Her efforts stretch back twelve years and are more extensive than Dunbar ever dreamed of. She even once solicited the help of David Williams, who has done nothing. Now I understand how despite two sources of income she has no money.

"I'm sorry I was overcome before the subcommittee," I said. "After all your work to get me so far, it would seem they've won the game."

"Not yet."

"Mags, no. You can't spend the rest of your life on me. We must concentrate on family visits." I squeezed Jim's hand. "From them I'll draw the strength I need to work on The Schoolmaster direct. I think part of him—I mean the Haslam part, such as remains—regrets I'm still in here."

"Haslam can afford a spate of remorse. But once he's immured in his next book, the mood will pass, and soon as that one's finished, it'll be on to the next. All he must do is stay buried in words until Death collects all Conscience' pricks. There's no peace of mind like the grave."

"So what's to be done? A quid to Alavoine and over the wall?"

"No, you're too famous not to be pursued till capture. There's only one way left: a legal challenge of habeas corpus, before the Court of the King's Bench. Why do they have you? But it's dangerous. If we think Monro and the governors are unsympathetic now, wait until we come at them with this. And if we lose, you won't be going anywhere you can escape their revenge. Robert tells me Haslam's kept you supplied with candles, paper, and such-like. All that will end."

"No it won't, Jack's not petty. But we do need to have him full on our side, as the one who knows most about me. Then it'll be up to the governors to say why I'm in, and they can't do it because they have no idea, and those who have and are still alive can't reveal it."

"Why? What is it?"

"Oh. Mags, don't make me tell you what I know. You're the poorest liar I ever knew." She nodded, aware she was.

Her candour inspired me to explain. "The trouble with knowing things so far beyond top secret they sound like fantasy is that the constant exposure to the deluded inadequacy of others' understandings makes you feel mad and alone. At first you ask yourself, What instead of this poppycock would he be telling me if he knew what I do? But the fact is he don't and never will, and the repeated mental exercise is so hard on your brain you give it over, and that's when it dawns on you he's a puppet controlled by forces he'll never understand and you will be too if you don't watch out."

Perhaps Margaret knew what I meant, perhaps she didn't. Her attention was on another effect of knowing too much. "But, Jamie, if you know why you're in, you must have some idea who wants you in, which means you can guess their reaction to a habeas corpus proceeding."

"They'll try to stop it."

"But how? It's a purely legal undertaking—"

"Mags, I'm not in by law. This is bigger than the courts."

"So politicians influence judges?"

"Is the King shy of snipers?"

"Will they stop at habeas-corpus-fixing?"

"Won't that be enough?"

"I'm asking, will we be putting you in danger from without, Bethlem reactions aside?"

"Not, I should think, as long as I'm in here. Out will be another matter."

"Out I'll guard you with my life. Out we can leave the country. First things first. We'll try not to lose, Jamie, but we could, even if they don't interfere. Even with Haslam on our side, for he knows too little. All we can do is bring in witnesses to your character and outside medical experts to examine you and trust that together they provide affidavits strong enough to convince a judge."

"The question," I said, "is whether The Schoolmaster cares more about his position than the truth."

"Don't forget there's also the truth of his public portrait of Bethlem, which his honour will require him to defend."

"Put that way, our case does seem hopeless—"

"Hopeless, are we? Not in here, surely?" This was wit from The Middleman, now looming over us like a vulture.

With a quick glance to see he wasn't interfering with Jim, Margaret threw her arms around me, but the ulcer in my back causing me to flinch, she pulled back. "Jamie, what is it? What's wrong?"

As she said this, The Middleman placed one bony claw on her shoulder and the other on Jim's. I squeezed Jim's hand tighter, but mine was sweating and our grip slippery. "Hour's up, Silly-Tilly," muttered The Middleman, never one to allow a space of compassion.

"It's not been an hour!" Margaret cried, looking frantic at me. "Jamie, *what—?*"

"I'm all right, Mags. It's nothing—"

With a tug at her elbow, The Middleman pulled her away. At the same time, he used his knee to break my grip on Jim's hand. Then, holding Margaret at bay, he reached down for something alongside my bed: a wicker hamper.

"That's for my husband!" Margaret cried, knowing what was coming. "Leave it!"

With difficulty I struggled to stand, but in a feat of balance, as he gripped Margaret's arm in one hand, the hamper in the other, The Middleman placed his boot sole flat against my chest. I flew across the bed and slammed the brick wall. When my senses returned, I saw Jim belabouring The Middleman with childish blows as Margaret fought the brute for the hamper until, growling, "Damned bitch," he yanked it from her with such force its contents ascended in air: linen, fruit, cutlery, books, paper, ink, letters—a good dozen packets of letters, tied with string.

Some items hit the wall and fell, the ink smashing. Others scattered along the floor.

Margaret swung on me beseeching, *"Jamie, tell me!"*

Roughly pushing Jim ahead of him, The Middleman was using his foot to sweep the hamper's contents out into the larger room. Over his shoulder he said, "Come for these, Silly-Tilly, and you know what's up for your arse."

"I have an ulcer in my back," I told Margaret quietly.

"Are they treating it?"

Looking to Jim, I shook my head No.

Margaret looked too, in time to see The Middleman disappear round the corner with him. She kissed me and flew after.

Which left me to rock on my bed, listening to my wife's imprecations and son's sobs fade together down the gallery.

Dearest Jamie,

If only there were a better way than a letter you'll never read to let you know Haslam had an ear cocked lest I was offered trouble and when I was, himself escorted Jim and me to the gate, with a vow to discipline Rodbird for his abuse of us and to see that Alavoine passes on my letters, once they're approved—

Jamie, we have every reason to expect our habeas corpus will go ahead. We're now in search of the most sympathetic and persuasive medical men to examine you and pronounce on your case. Our thinking is if the judge can be persuaded you're not in on medical grounds, he'll want to know what grounds you are in on.

Beloved Husband, today as Jim was helping me prepare our dinner he asked if heroes often go unrecognized. His classmates knowing you better as a lunatic than as saviour of our country, he's now old enough to suspect more in this than schoolyard malice. My answer was yes, heroes nearly always go unrecognized, when they're not despised or resented as naifs, fools, prigs, or troublemakers. The greatest—and luckiest—achievement of a hero is to be hailed as one. For that he must be commonly agreed to have risked or (better) sacrificed his life to save or signally benefit the lives of others. Failing this, courage and honesty seldom please, seeming self-righteous rebukes to everybody else's sly small way of sidling along.

In answer to this he smiled and said, "I think sometimes the more I know of the world the less I want to be in it—"

"But you are in it," I cried, "because of one thing: love. Love's the complication and you must let it always be—!"

Jamie, how I wish you had been here from the beginning for the succession of miracles that has been our Jim's youth, as he's ascended from one level of mind to the next, now and then gazing around him exhilarated, like a mountaineer taking in a prospect. And when he's been too long on one plateau before his next ascent, you know he's in its shadow because how restless and moody he grows—Then all at once, before you realize it, he's reached another summit, and O then to see the sunshine in his face! This has been the hardest part of all, my husband, harder I think sometimes than our own separation: to know how much you and he have missed in missing your lives together.

I pray you forgive this bitter reflection—
Your loving
Margaret

FRIEND TUKE

It's been a month now, and I've not seen Margaret again, only two thin packets of her letters, the first retrieved from the gallery doorway by Reverend Jupp (a Methodist in for melancholy) before The Middleman returned for his spoils, the second by way of Alavoine thanks to The Schoolmaster—or should I say Haslam. With something more in his eyes than the usual desolation, Jupp slipped me the first packet two days after Margaret's visit, as we passed in the gallery. The second was tossed onto my bed last week by the keeper Davies, our whistling postman from Hell.

Now that I've read Margaret's letters, I know my own are a beggar-boy's, whinging and cringing, and I wonder if this log of abuses is not my more manly love letter to a woman so dogged and strong. Judging from the few of hers Jupp's kindness and Haslam's justice have enabled me to see—thirty-four in all, the Jupp-saved written between March 4th and August 17th, 1804, the Haslam-provided between December 4th, 1808, and February 15th of this year, I mean 1809 (the narrow time span of the latter packet owing I should think to Haslam's having no way to know how many Sir Archy's held back)— Margaret's letters in their own way are as lovingly rendered as this chronicle, and no more fit for public eyes. Documents of loss, humiliation, resolve, longing, lust, fury, despair—all at a pitch certain to outrage those for whom sanguine views promise every advantage of hope, prevalence, and comfort. You build your world on sunny principles, and lo and behold ain't life sunny, except for how much you hate the guts of anybody who'd prick your bubble.

I was lying on my bed thinking these ungenteel thoughts while wondering if habeas corpus will deliver me back into the world wiser than to be a blind drummer for human nature, when Mr. Ailey, a promising mathematician until he strangled his mother, stopped by to report that the Quaker William Tuke was in the building, with another gentleman.

I sprang from my deathbed.

Tuke is founder of The Retreat, the private asylum that's been making such a racket at York. Even the London papers have been full of it for years. By Ailey's account, the purpose of Tuke's visit to The Schoolmaster was to learn how we do things here. Tuke's been reported as saying he was even more impressed by the second edition of Jack's book than by the first. But you don't need to find the Tuke approach a good one to consider his errand, if not a fool's, more mysterious than it appears. Who can predict what strangeness will issue from a Quaker silence? Yet Tuke's visit whether strange or not promised to reveal something of the prospects of our habeas corpus.

Reaching the lower gallery, I ducked down quick behind the lunatic Phippard, an old sailor in the habit of gleefully swagging on the spot while he scans the heaving main. Adjusting his position, I got him between me and The Schoolmaster's back, close enough so I could hear what Tuke was saying. Though tall, Phippard makes poor cover, for every twenty minutes or so he stamps his foot and booms out something like, "God bless the King and all the, admirals! I would fight up to my neck in blood for them!" before he returns to scanning. Such behaviour is apt to draw the attention of the unaccustomed. Fortunately, being moved by me a dozen feet failed to rouse Phippard from his anticipation of war at sea, and Tuke and The Schoolmaster remained locked in conversation.

By the pitch of The Schoolmaster's shoulders, it was not one he was happy to be in. Beyond his right shoulder I could see Tuke's ordinary, impatient face and the clipped movement of his pursed mouth with its chunks of yellow teeth. From the neck down, Tuke is a plain, drab-outfitted squab of the sort so intent on making his appearance unenviable that you can't forget it. He's exactly what you think of when you think of a Quaker merchant. Why does the nonconformist always have the best uniform? Yet I felt an immediate connexion to him and thought at first this must be because he's made his fortune in tea, an ambition once my own, queer as it was just now to watch my hand letter the fact.

But there was something more in Tuke's face than tea, and something of disguise in that Quaker outfit.

As to who the third gentleman was, owing to the position of The Schoolmaster, I couldn't see. If it was Bryan Crowther (who's an unabashed admirer of Tuke and his methods), Mr. Ailey would have known it, and if he didn't, there's the fact The Schoolmaster so loathes our surgeon it's the rare occasion he'll remain in the same room with him. For all Crowther's eagerness to be a contributing part of things around here, he ain't and never was and in his disappointment has too often retreated into drink, which has done nothing to enhance his prospects.

But harkee, Tuke was talking.

"There is much analogy, don't you think, Mr. Haslam, between the judicious treatment of children and that of insane persons? As the most disruptive lunatic, one might say, has much in common with a two year old?"

"An insane two year old—?" was The Schoolmaster's murmured response.

Having the dogged, no-nonsense air of a man with a sizable store of pronouncements to get through, Tuke didn't seem to hear what The Schoolmaster
said. Or perhaps Jack smiled as he spoke, and Tuke, thus cued, made the mental note *jest,* only himself omitting to smile, as one does who, having no sense
of humour, assumes any sign of one betrays a tendency to instability best not
encouraged.

As for the third gentleman, he shifted his weight like a man uncomfortable
with a joke. But he didn't speak, and he didn't shift far enough to afford a view
of who he was. Perhaps, I thought, it was only Tuke's son—or even grandson.
Old Tuke's no spring foal.

"Which is not to say," Tuke continued unflapped, "we should address them
in a childish or domineering manner."

"By no means ought we to *domineer,*" The Schoolmaster drawled, as if half
asleep. "When it's always been quite enough to *dominate.*"

Now Tuke shot Jack the scrutinizing look of one to whom it's just occurred
the other could be vibrating at a frequency different from the one he thought.
Just to be sure, and revealing the obtuse confidence of fifty years' freedom from
doubt, he waded in deeper. "Dominate, Mr. Haslam? I wonder if we ought to
use even a word like dominate."

"Well," The Schoolmaster answered, practically in a yawn, "only for Truth's
sake—" Picking up speed, he continued, "Two things, Mr. Tuke. One, these
people are indeed in a condition of domination. Their confinement, however
mild its acceptation, as at your celebrated house—" bowing—"amounts to an
incarceration equal to that of the inhabitants of the King's Bench, or Newgate
Gaol. You do after all require they keep their madness to themselves. Ha-has,
so to speak, are fences too. So why should not the manner and discourse of
their dominators fit the circumstance?"

Before Tuke could make answer to this, Jack went on. "Two, thinking now
of our own personal comportment as it must encourage in our patients that rational calm we agree is our common goal: Unless we'd be self-defeating hypocrites, surely we ought to display the authority invested in us and not, by
pretending to be like them (as all too often happens), out of our own sheer lack
of self-control in an insidious environment, sink to a level grotesque and dreadful as theirs and so lose their awe and respect altogether." Here he meant
Crowther, but Tuke had no way to know it. "Mind you," again cutting him off,
"if our concern here is only words—because your house employs strait-
waistcoats as much as the next, but how in this day and age can anybody expect
to attract paying customers with talk of shackles and severity—then I do sym-
pathize, for such meal-mouthedness is only an understandable consequence of
lunatic advisors turning hoteliers and so transforming human suffering to a
business."

This attack was vintage Schoolmaster, and I was curious how Tuke would
take it—which was slow and deliberate, as he marshalled enough control of

himself to make a generous-seeming, let's-get-back-to-why-I'm-here response. "What I most value about your book, Mr. Haslam, is the impression you convey in it of your energy in doing what's necessary to initiate a fraternal rapport with each patient. Like the great Pinel—" by a stiffening of his neck you could see how little The Schoolmaster relished the comparison—"you inquire into the particulars of his case, how he acts, how he's come to be in hospital, and so forth. It's my belief, as I know it must be yours, that if we would seek to cure—"

"*Cure?*" The speed with which this syllable shot back at Tuke streaming sarcastic incredulity was remarkable.

"Yes, sir," Tuke returned, practically as fast. "Cure. Cure of their insanity."

"Ah, *cure,*" The Schoolmaster replied, this time like one too innocent not to be a little slow to grasp a point of such diabolical cunning. "Tell me, Mr. Tuke, would this be more politics? They do better if they imagine their time with you well spent? A profitable investment on their part, is that it?"

"Why, what more profitable to a man, Mr. Haslam, than his sanity back?"

"Funny, I thought you'd say soul." And before Tuke could pick himself off the floor after that one, The Schoolmaster concluded, in a long-suffering voice, something like a fond nephew's as it finally dawns on him his favourite uncle is a jabbering idiot, "So you do believe you can cure the insane."

"I do. Here's why. At The Retreat we see monthly occurrences of it. Weekly occurrences."

"As do I, even in this poor place."

"Well then—?"

"Perhaps the difference between us, Mr. Tuke, is you've discovered how it's done. Your innocence of medical rigmarole has afforded you insight unavailable to those of us still fettered by Hippocratic scruples."

Now, this was going pretty far, even for The Schoolmaster, whose world fame (ever since Pinel, in the book he wrote after he was here, as good as called him the greatest English mad-doctor that ever lived) has for some unaccountable reason done little to curb the effects of his insecurities. It's as if he's more impatient than ever with people slow to appreciate how right he is. Yet I wondered if that unease wasn't blinding him to what he's up against in the mighty Tuke. Sometimes you'll half pity a man his crackpot beliefs, and yet what indomitable courage they may be all the while affording him. Enough easily to destroy you and everything you ever stood for.

"I'll tell you how it's done, Mr. Haslam."

As he said these words, Tuke shot a glance at the third gentleman. It was a quick one, the kind by which a man will deflect attention from himself while he frames what he's going to say next. But for me it told everything. Because *even as Tuke glanced at his companion, he (Tuke!) continued to gaze hard at The Schoolmaster.*

At first I thought this must be my imagination, yet I knew what I'd seen and so knew it could mean only one thing: Tuke's been taken over. That connexion I felt to him, what I was seeing in his face, was tea all right, but more essentially it was this: He's in the power of the gang.

But which agent? If you think I watched him close before—

"The way it's done, Mr. Haslam, is simple. We must love them."

A silence ensued from these words, the gentleman next to Tuke once more shifting his weight from one foot to the other, this time (I imagined) in nervous approval, as Tuke's eyes continued to bore away into The Schoolmaster's face while The Schoolmaster's head remained bent. What expression was on The Schoolmaster's face I had no way to see and couldn't guess if he'd be bold enough to be meeting Tuke's gaze.

"Love them—" The Schoolmaster murmured at last, in a doubting tone.

"Yes, sir. Love them. Only by love can this most devastating of human pestilences be cleansed from the face of the earth."

"Love," The Schoolmaster repeated again, this time in such a way as to produce an animal sound you would not believe any human language had been vulgar enough to distinguish with meaning. If *cure* was a term The Schoolmaster found incredible, then *love* from his mouth was a loathing, unsignificant grunt.

"Love them, sir," Tuke insisted once more, and added, *"for the troubled sinners they are."*

And there it was, as The Schoolmaster had all along known it would be. Even from a Quaker, the sick-sweet incense of priestcraft.

Now I looked at Tuke, who kept his eyes fixed hard on The Schoolmaster as if he would stare him down. At that moment I was struck by how much he resembled the late Sir William Pultney. A certain Roman aspect to the nose, and the sunk cheeks, though admittedly from a coarser mould. And then, by an association I at first assumed superficial, I found myself thinking of Dr. DeValangin, Old Benevolence, as we used to call him, who treated no man as a sinner, troubled or not. The resemblance was not with Tuke himself, but—*Uh-oh.*

Stop right there. Now I knew. And a good thing it was I had Phippard to hold tight to, because the knowledge, when it hit me, buckled my knees.

The truth of the matter is this: The agent currently in charge of the Quaker William Tuke is none other than the leader of the Air Loom gang himself, that archvillain of murderous deceit, the one who's never been observed to smile except at chess: Bill the King.

May God have mercy on us all.

BILL & CO.

But that wasn't the half of it. Once I'd regained sufficient control of myself to extend my attention beyond the poor bare stinking weave of Phippard's blanket-gown, the first thing I noticed was Urbane Metcalfe. Metcalfe is an obstreperous little complaining lunatic, a roaming pedlar who says he's heir to the throne of Denmark, a delusion that could explain his chronic weakness for royal trespass, mentioned above. He was crossing toward the window, which stood wide open. Outside, a freezing rain cascaded down, and from Metcalfe's ensuing pantomime I understood he could see a female patient standing drenched in the yard and was attempting to alert The Schoolmaster, so she might be brought in before she contracted pneumonia.

But The Schoolmaster being horn-locked in debate with Bill the King, Metcalfe's exhortations were going unheeded. Nothing short of plucking The Schoolmaster by the sleeve (something even Urbane Metcalfe would hesitate to do) was likely to draw his attention, and I begun to fear Metcalfe, who has a stiff importunate beard and the penetrating black eyes of a water-rat, would come after me to do something, for those eyes had taken note of where I was. But just when Metcalfe seemed ready to make enough commotion to get himself thrown in chains for a month, the mysterious third man broke from Bill and The Schoolmaster and walked over to the window to see what Metcalfe wanted. And that was how, to my utter amazement, I saw who it was, and this was none other than the individual who first overturned everything I ever believed in, my former tutor, mentor, lodestone, and friend, that sometime-noteworthy man of light and leading, the celebrated republican and revolutionary, David Williams.

First Bill the King in Tuke, now David Williams in the company of Bill the King. Has anybody during one brief crouch behind a lunatic experienced in such rapid succession two conjunctions so astounding?

Not only that. As soon as David Williams saw what Metcalfe wanted, he

called out to Bill and The Schoolmaster to come and see. This was a reflex of
his goodness. Him of course they immediately heard and went over. After that
there was nothing to be done but The Schoolmaster must send Metcalfe to find
the keeper Davies to bring her in. Except, the bustle of these arrangements im-
pinging on Phippard's nautical reflections to a degree my use of him as a human screen had not, he give a sudden start and shouted out, "Glory be to his
Majesty's Navy! May the blood of a thousand Frogs turn the Channel to
ketchup!"

For Phippard this was a normal sort of thing to say, and The Schoolmaster
and Bill the King never even bothered to look around, but David Williams did,
and that's how he come to see me. Only, then he looked away, and I was struck
to the heart to think he'd pretend not to know me, until I considered I must be
too altered by time and illness for immediate recognition, even by a former intimate. I appreciate my actions in both London and Paris had caused him no
little embarrassment, but for all his faults he was a bigger man than to cut me.
And I was right. If his first impulse was to look away, he soon enough looked
back, and when The Schoolmaster and Bill the King, still arguing, begun to
move down the gallery, he broke from them and crossed the floor to me.

So it was in a wash of bliss I witnessed the approach of the dear, slight figure
of my once beloved friend. But as he drew on, his wan features and grey, thin-
ning hair and seedy coat caused me to ask if this could be the same firebrand I
knew seventeen years ago, when we was shining-eyed young Turks together,
knee-to-knee over tea in my parlour as he tutored me in the philosophy we so
fervently believed would change the world. Was this the man who travelled to
Paris in '92 to help the Girondin faction frame a constitution worthy of the true
republicans they were puffed up like turkey-cocks with calling themselves?
Was this the man I followed there to learn first hand what he'd been teaching
me, for those were desperate days: If France went down in chaos again, who
could say English liberty would not go with her? Was this the man I followed
because he was the first I ever knew to embrace the good of all humanity, who
first taught me love and freedom in universal fraternity?

David Williams never trumpeted his egalitarian principles. Instead he was
satisfied to argue with quiet lucidity that if humankind is ever to deliver itself
from bloodshed, then every person must understand they have the same worth
as the next and each a free and full say in the common good. Estimate another's
worth as greater than your own, and it follows that another's is less. From ine-
quality it's a slippery slope to intolerance and from intolerance to resentment
and resentment to oppression if you can and slaughter if you can't, so why
make that first mistake? Until this primary human principle has been understood, how can the future not be perfect mayhem?

This was the innocent philosophy of youth that flooded back as I stepped
from behind my sailor to reach out trembling hands and feel once more the
press of my sometime boon companion's. Like Margaret's and Jim's, their

touch put me in mind just how much sanity and goodness there yet exists beyond these walls. Like theirs, it turned me a sponge, and when his fingers squeezed mine, the water gushed from my eyes.

"Alas, *mon compère,*" he murmured, "that it should be in such a place we meet again." As he spoke he meant to illustrate his regret with an eye-roll round the gallery, but it snagged on Phippard's ecstatic swagging. From the grimace on Phippard's face you knew it was a glorious day at sea, all blazing sun and salt spray.

"None, Mr. Williams," I assured him, "join you in that emotion so ardent as myself. But even as I was busy serving my country, I was flung in here."

"You made too-great demands on yourself, my friend. Super-human demands."

Did I? a voice inside me retorted. *Was that the only error made, then, David?*

Now more than our old philosophy came flooding back. All of a sudden it was February 11th, 1793. This was the day after we declared war on France in response to their starting the month by declaring war on us. In my own carriage I had driven David Williams, fresh back from Paris, to meet the British foreign secretary, Lord Grenville, at an interview I'd personally arranged. The plan was Williams would deliver a letter and oral message from Grenville's French counterpart, Lebrun. The letter was Lebrun's sincere apology for the French declaration of war and a moving plea for peace. Considering war had only just been declared, this was an extraordinary thing for a foreign minister to do. When Williams explained to Grenville's under-secretary, Mr. Aust, that the purpose of our visit was nothing less than a French overture for peace, Aust looked at him in wordless astonishment.

"The French government," Williams repeated into the silence, "is prepared to make great sacrifices to preserve peace."

But having said this, he pretended to accept at face value Aust's coldly formal expression (once he recovered himself) of regret that Grenville was at the last minute unavailable to meet with us. Instead of objecting to such treatment, Williams merely left his name and address and walked out. They could contact him for the letter when they were ready to read it.

As soon as we were back outside on the pavement, I importuned him, saying, "David, for God's sake why didn't you give Aust the letter, as you've travelled all the way from Paris to do?"

"Because," came the agitated reply, "it's too evident our government's as intent on war as France is. If I deliver this letter, Lebrun will go to the guillotine. This is collaboration with the enemy."

"But he won't if the letter brings peace!" I wailed. "And it's now the only hope for that! David, you can't go by the behaviour of a man's under-secretary! Aust knows nothing! Give the letter to him now! Believe me, it's not too late! He'll pass it direct to Grenville, who, don't you remember, is the Prime Minister's cousin! You know as well as I do his Lordship's up there and will take it direct to Pitt, who will want to see you, which will give you a chance to deliver Lebrun's oral message!"

But Williams refused, declaring that nothing could persuade him to place a human life in danger for a hopeless cause.

"David, listen to me! How many more lives will be lost if you don't act now? I assure you, Grenville won't disappoint us, but it's imperative that he see the letter! Please, I implore you! If you would only exert yourself, you could prevent the war!"

But Williams laughed at this, and however much I pleaded, he remained adamant. This behaviour was owable in part to genuine concern for Lebrun, who after he was apprehended in a hayloft, disguised as a farm worker, did in fact go to the guillotine, in December of that year, singing "La Marseillaise." But mostly Williams was a timid man. Not every republican is cut out for revolution. In his view, politics should proceed like Nature, by degrees. He'd attended the French king's trial in December and was as horrified at it as at the Paris chaos. Back in London he was doing his best to appear calm and reasonable, even as he was trembling so wildly he could hardly speak. What terrified him was the prospect of Government prosecution as a traitor, for communicating with his Majesty's enemies. We both knew what they'd tried to do to Tom Paine. David didn't want his next book suppressed; he didn't want to be gaoled for sedition. He didn't want to be half-hanged and his entrails removed and burnt while he was still alive, as required by the *Traitorous Correspondence Bill* that Pitt had rammed through. Who in those days wasn't afraid? Yet in his case, any fear was groundless, for I had already placed French money in British hands to ensure, among other things, his safety from prosecution in this country. I could have told him that, but he wouldn't like it.

When he continued refusing to give Aust the letter, I was left no option but to feign a sudden resolve to settle in France, dropping to my knees to beg letters of recommendation to the French ministers. These he absolutely refused to provide. Refusing then even to climb back into my carriage, he turned on his heel and walked away.

And that was the last I saw of him, until now, when I thought, *And how staunch a defender are* you, *David, of what* you *believe in?* Aloud I said, "I apologize, sir, if my behaviour when we knew each other ever caused you inconvenience."

If he suspected irony in this (as well he should), he didn't show it, only shook his head. "There's nothing to forgive, my friend. You were not in your right mind."

Oh, was I not? *And how right in your mind are you, a republican fart-catcher to an enterprising Quaker?* "May I ask, sir," I said, bowing, "how it is you come to be here with Bill—ah, Mr. Tuke?"

"Oh, I'm on The Retreat's board—" came the reply, so offhand you'd think being caught bare-faced in the company of Bill the King counted for nothing.

But then, did he even know it was him? "It's long been Mr. Tuke's hope," he continued, "to discuss treatment with Mr. Haslam, whom he views as one of the nation's most enlightened providers."

"And how have you found him yourself?"

"A more compassionate warder than he wants us to know. His gruff wit's most exhilarating, don't you agree? I always did appreciate a man unafraid to stand up for his convictions. With a clientele so many and brutal—worthy exceptions notwithstanding—" and this time I bowed so low and long the blood filled my head like a butcher's calabash—"I should think you'd learn pretty quick to be brusque."

These statements I could make nothing of. *Clientele?* So we were customers now? Yet if this was a business, what quality of service did he think naked beggars queue to receive? And what was this about appreciation of a man ready to fight for his convictions? A gracious compliment or a self-damning gap of memory?

"You look excellent well, James," he next threw out. This one so nonplussed me I was tempted to spin round and flap my shirt-tails to give him an *excellent* whiff of my abscess. It was now apparent he had no intention of acknowledging Margaret's visit to him. Having done nothing for me, he considered the matter dead and buried. Why else did he not fear I'd wonder at his shocking silence? "After everything you've been through, James," he went on, "hospital life evidently agrees with you. I never saw you half so collected in Paris, nor the last time we spoke in London. Mr. Haslam, I daresay, is doing something right."

Before I could blast away at this wretched drivel, a call echoed down the gallery. "Mr. Williams, will you catch us up, or do we wait?"

Even at this distance you could smell Bill's fury: fumes of night-shade and hellebore. I'm the last person he's going to want David Williams talking to.

"Coming, Will!" David called out—*Bill* I heard at first and give a shudder— and with a brief glance at Phippard, as if politeness might enjoin a farewell there too, he pressed my hands once more. As he did, he dropped his voice to utter words that though they resembled specious babbling and as such failed utterly to qualify as the apology he owed me, did offer grounds for hope: "I pray the next time we meet, my dear Matthews, it's someplace more congenial." And adding, louder (the public part, the former for my ears only), "Keep well, old friend—"

And so, as I watched my hero canter down the gallery like a grateful dog to a new master, I said to Phippard, "Well, Midshipman, what was that about? Could it be my old friend is now a craven pawn of Air Loom instigation?"

The exclusively naval nature of Phippard's concerns precluded any actual reply.

"Or is he a great man yet?" I murmured, after watching the three of them pass single-file through the gate in the wall of iron bars and disappear from view.

Again Phippard gave no sign he understood, but I think he did. His world is full of great men.

My Beloved Wife,

Can you guess who's just been to visit? Bill the King—in William Tuke! And if that wasn't enough, who did he bring with him? Brace yourself: David Williams.

Intending no more than to sound from the tenor of Tuke's visit the prospects for our habeas corpus, I stumble upon my oldest and once dearest friend teamed with the leader of the gang in control of this very hospital. No wonder, though you begged him, Williams has done nothing to get me out. Face to face with him in the lower gallery was like running into an old friend when you're abroad without your illusions. The former wholesome façade detaches and falls away to reveal a ramshackle edifice. Though his conversation had every appearance of a succession of low, convoluted brain-sayings—addressing me, for example, as mon compère *(as if slyly to acknowledge our French time together)—the fact there was no hint of a presence in him, along with the fact he uttered every syllable aloud, suggested he hasn't been taken over. Not yet. More likely his guilt for abandoning me years ago, and again more lately by doing nothing to get me out of here though you begged him, had him blurting with each word he spoke the last he intended. He's only human, after all, which is one way to say why it's only ever been humanity in the abstract he's fought for.*

As for Bill the King, word from the gang has always been he stoops to human form only when confident of widespread human desolation. Probably he's achieved access to the old Quaker because like him he's out to destroy this place and substitute something more covertly oppressive while it shows the world a happier face. Bill's habitation of Tuke must also owe something to the affinity between, on the one hand, his own desire to engineer the death of our true monarch George and, on the other, Tuke's Quaker abhorrence of rank. (Though if Tuke truly abhorred rank as much as he thinks or pretends he does, then Bill could never touch him.)

Of course, none of this begins to address the question how The School-master could dare to go against Bill the King. Brain-saying Augusta at my committee hearing is one thing. Openly defying Bill, whatever body he's in, whatever sentiments he's espousing, is another. Because this was no mistake of identity. If I could glimpse Bill the King in Tuke, The Schoolmaster would know he was in him as soon as Tuke's shadow brushed London Wall.

Still, the question—like a Liberty Bell proclaiming a riddle (Life, Liberty and the Pursuit of what!?)—goes on pealing: What is going on? I have no idea, though I do confess to a hope our habeas corpus will succeed. All I must do is satisfy my medical examiners of my mental health. And once we win and I'm back, O my Life's Love, with you and young Jim in the tran-quil privacy of our parlour, the true history of who I am and what I have done will unfold like a revelation, and I shall be its letterer. And unlike my log of madhouse abuses, it's a story people will be pleased to read, as in it they discover a glimmering testament of honour and courage racing to and fro in a midnight of intrigue, lettered in plain ink upon plain paper by one of their own, and know there lives and breathes among them a man who with Cicero asks only, Let me die in the country I have often saved.

Until that wished-for time of home lettering,

your loving

James

Dearest Husband,

    I have only this minute got in the door from my first meeting with Drs. Birkbeck and Clutterbuck of the College of Physicians. Having seen you but once, their reluctance to make a definite comment on your case is understandable, but one thing is clear: They like you, Jamie. Which gives me every hope they'll judge in our favour. When I just now told Jim this, he spun me in a dance round the kitchen. Your son having lived his life under the weight of his mother's sighs, any prospect of her happiness makes him positively giddy.

    That's all I wanted to say: Your examiners seem such generous, fairminded men that I have sunny expectations of our habeas corpus—if, that is, the judge can be counted on to hear them, and if there's any justice in England he can.

Your loving
Margaret

    P.S. Jim has something to add.

Dear Father,

    Mum and I—did she tell you?—have twenty fingers crossed for you! And twenty toes too!! (And it's not easy to cross all your toes!!! Did you ever try it????)

Love,
Jim

EXAMINATION BY EXPERTS

Here it is not yet December and already Drs. Clutterbuck and Birkbeck have paid me four visits together, sometimes the one asking questions, sometimes the other. In addition, Dr. Birkbeck has paid me two visits solo. These men are the two ascendant meteors of the Royal College of Physicians that Dick Staveley has persuaded Monro to allow to examine me, so they can provide testimony in favour of my habeas corpus challenge. Between them they've plied me with every modern stratagem of mental scrutiny. The more I said, the more there was to say. Yet just when the pieces were starting to fall into place by the discipline of the telling, they assured me they'd heard enough. Each has now separately mulled over his findings and concluded I'm perfectly sane and intends to say as much in his affidavit before the court.

Their confidence in me has been gratifying and offers further hope of a positive outcome to our case.

For fear they'd think me credulous or deluded, I neglected at first to mention anything involving magnetic workings by French spies. But Dr. Birkbeck (who was first to question me) proved so sympathetic a listener and so manifestly holds the welfare of the ordinary man tight at his heart, I soon told him everything, namely, "A London gang of event-working assassins, finding my senses proof against their fluid-working (as they term it), have appointed French magnetic spy-workers to actuate the proper persons to pretend I am insane, for the purpose of plunging me in a madhouse, to invalidate all I say by confining me within the measure of the Bedlam-attaining-airloom-warp, making sure by the poisonous effluvia they use that I'm kept fully impregnated, so as to overpower my reason and speech and destroy me in their own way while all should suppose it was insanity which produced my death according to the principle *Whom the gods would destroy they first make mad,* a running joke with them they dolefully intone then burst out laughing."

Yet even as I thumb-nailed my case, I wondered, *Why on earth risk damning myself out of my own mouth?* Then I thought, *If you can't tell an honest man the truth, who can you tell it to?* And so I explained all, setting forth the complicated matter of the various procedures of the various gangs and some things that happened to me before I was thrown in here, and how I'm on their calendar for destruction, and the only thing that will save me is if I more than forgive, if I *thank* them for their treatment of me. Otherwise, as they constantly inform me, I should not expect to escape their clutches alive. Yet what they want of me I can never give them, for to thank them would be to betray every principle I ever stood for and so would spell my destruction another way.

On a different occasion, after listening to my account of my Paris years, Dr. Clutterbuck—a forceful, manly, handsome fellow with a thick, strong nose and impressive underbite—broke a long silence by reminding me who it was that Dr. Mesmer, when his science was rejected as charlatanism by the French Academy, appealed to but the people? And wasn't it true that Mesmerism salons were frequently fronts for radical societies? And he assured me with a knowing look he has it for a fact that M. Brissot, the French Girondist-revolutionist leader, was a Mesmerism devotee, at least he was until he came to power. Then there was Lafayette, who fought in America alongside the colonists at Valley Forge and has been quoted as saying the main force behind that revolution was Mesmerism; Bergasse (converter of Brissot to Mesmerism in the first place); the husband and wife revolutionists the Rolands; and a dozen others, including, of all people, Marie Antoinette herself, though he guessed a queen can afford to dabble, or might imagine she can. After confessing he'd always wondered if she was behind the Mesmerism plan to free the King from prison by a magnet beaming an escape plan, he asked me if when in Paris I was ever in contact with Dr. Mesmer himself, or M. Puységur, or with Restif de la Bretonne, or Bonneville, or any of the former Cercle Social? Abbé Barruel, perhaps?

Though surprised at Clutterbuck's original train of association, I paid his sympathy the courtesy of a straight-faced answer, assuring him that while I was never in contact with any French disciples of Dr. Mesmer that I was aware of at the time, from what little I've been able to understand of his theories, I would guess he might be on to something. Certainly his strategy of cloaking his doctrine in mystery accords with the methods of the gang, as it does with the policy of a republican like Brissot, who always argued that to produce revolution out in the open is to doom it to failure.

I added I've sometimes wondered if Mesmer's technique of having people grip iron bars plunged in tubs of magnetic filings and so pass into swoons and orgasmic ejaculations could have served as inspiration for the two metal rods I've lately noticed affixed a-top the Air Loom. (These enable the one at the controls of that machine to reach up and grasp them and so weaken the force of the magnetic assailment on anyone who's just glimpsed a gang member inhabiting a victim. In this way the member appears to the glimpser to *step back* inside the victim, which is what Augusta did when I saw her inhabiting Wood. But nobody swoons.)

Dr. Clutterbuck greeted my attempt to humour him by smiling in a vague way before charging off on a tangent. "You know, Matthews, one thing I've noticed about Mesmerism, it makes people honest. Any English follower of Mesmer I ever met, while he might be too suspicious of the five senses for the comfort of a dull, plodding Forceps like myself, you can be sure he won't be out to deceive or flatter anybody. The simple fact is, Mesmerism may reduce the human body to a puppet or machine, but I never met a Mesmer advocate who had time for the empty forms and silly conventions of common life."

I confessed I never knew any English Mesmerism practitioners or even that they existed.

"Whether it all be imagination or no," Dr. Clutterbuck concluded enigmatically, "there were many in those mad times who thought it wasn't. And I don't think you should be punished just because it happens you're still one of 'em. Don't the doctors in this place understand there's no better way to fix a man in a conviction, however absurd, than to persecute him for it?"

That was Dr. Clutterbuck.

Dr. Birkbeck, the second last time I saw him, cut short my tortuous account of the weeks preceding my imprisonment at Lille, observing only, "What happened in France was a mad business start to finish, eh Matthews? You know what Mr. Coleridge called it, don't you? 'The Giant Frenzy.' As one tumbled head-over-heels by that tumult, you concur, I trust, with our poet's designation?"

I said I did.

Later, as they were leaving, Dr. Birkbeck, who is a short, sturdy, jaundiced-looking fellow with a long chin, pumped my hand with terrific vigour, saying, "Matthews, if you're mad, believe me, so was our mighty opponent of revolution, Edmund Burke."

Who foamed like Niagara, it's been said, but I held my tongue.

"To put the matter in a nutshell," he concluded, releasing his grip, "you shouldn't be in here."

Telling me this seemed to cheer him enormously, but he has a restless conceit about him, which over the next several days the injustice of my situation must have enflamed, for on their last visit to me, he and Clutterbuck brought along Monro himself, and as soon as the three arrived in my corner, Birkbeck rounded on Monro saying, "Tell us, Doctor, is there any particular subject apt to cause this man maniacal hallucinations?"

Caught off guard by the question, Monro replied that to his knowledge there was not, though he did believe me unhinged.

"I take it then, sir, you judge this Air Loom business to be more than a philosophical point?"

Monro asked what heirloom business he referred to.

Looking vexed, Birkbeck said, "Could you please, Dr. Monro, tell us in plain words why you think Mr. Matthews is insane."

Evidently Monro had no warning of anything like this on its way, or if he did, had been too busy floundering around in the usual birdlime of his understanding to heed it, for he only blustered out that while it might not convince any of us to hear him say it, he had a feeling he could positively rely on that I'm totally insane.

Now Birkbeck drew himself up. "From what I can see, sir, the main proof you have of this man's insanity is his inflexible resistance either to admit he's mad or to render thanks to the medical officers of this hospital for the injustice they've done him in keeping him here. From my discussions with him, it's evident he harbours a profound antipathy toward both yourself and Mr. Haslam, whom he holds primarily responsible for his twelve-year confinement. In the circumstances, sir, I find such antipathy so far from evidence of his madness as to constitute certain proof of his inviolable sanity."

Monro's response to this outburst was briefly to look a little sheepish, particularly like one who has just received a short, sharp rap to the skull. He then emitted a series of protesting bleats.

The two medical gentlemen have now submitted their affidavits, in which they make the strongest possible case for my sanity.

So too have Mr. Sadler and Mr. Law as representatives of Camberwell Parish. Theirs gives an account of their interviews before the Bethlem and Grand Committees and also of what happened last week, when, still not giving up, they came again to demand my release and were told by Mr. Poynder—or so I was brain-said by Charlotte, luckily at the time freed from her chains long enough to be on her hands and knees scrubbing the clerk's office floor, having just provided The Middleman a similar service performable in the same position—that I'm now considered a state prisoner (which I always was) and therefore officially out of Camberwell's hands. While this is neither good news nor any kind at all really, at least such a statement included in the affidavit may rouse the judge to ask himself why on earth I'm a prisoner of the state.

I understand there's also an affidavit from Robert Dunbar declaring the Bethlem damp is destroying my health. This will be Margaret's doing, inspired by my telling her I have an ulcer in my back. Another Dunbar affidavit—how he ran into The Schoolmaster at The Sow and Sausage and Jack mentioned I'm as sane as he is—is also in the file. Apparently Dunbar told the story to the subcommittee before they saw me. Let's hope it counts for more in writing. As for The Schoolmaster, he won't block my release, but he won't enable it either.

The affidavits go next to the judge, a Justice LeBlanc, of whom nothing is known. He decides if he sees me or no. If no, our habeas corpus has failed.

I expect The Schoolmaster will file a detailed, explicit affidavit saying the court must ensure this *automaton* on whom he is the world expert should not be allowed to join too many others like him roaming the nation at the expense of royal safety, with an addendum to defend his honour, swearing he was never in The Sow and Sausage on the night claimed by Mr. Dunbar, who's evidently been imposed on by a stranger cunning enough to tell him what he wanted to hear.

There will also be an affidavit from Monro, a terrible flood of self-inflating gabble that will spell out the ways I'm a living menace to the royal family, the Government, and the public, and conclude by declaring me the most deranged lunatic he ever met with in a career dating back to the birth of his grandfather.

One affidavit I do know of (by means of Charlotte) is from the wretched puppet of a French magnetic agent who accosted me on the Channel boat my last trip home from France. In it he declares me a danger to his Majesty and his subjects. This Mortimer it turns out is not only a Bethlem governor and member of the Grand Committee that recently refused to discharge me, but the very same wretched puppet of a French magnetic agent named Chavanay who accosted me on the Channel boat, stretching himself beside me on the deck and whispering, "Mr. Matthews, are you acquainted with the art of talking with your brains?"

When I replied in the negative, he said, "It is effected by means of the magnet."

That, I now learn, was my induction to the horror, but try telling that to the Bethlem governors.

Of course, Liverpool's letter instructing them to keep me will be part of the package.

From the pens of what other enemies, that I never even knew I had, affidavits will flow, I don't know.

No one in here has any information. Even Charlotte's brain-sayings have grown intermittent and unhelpful. I don't know why. She was always good at keeping in touch.

It's a waiting game.

With the ulcer in my back now a weeping suppuration, I no longer recline like the carved perpetual maniacs above our gates but lie curled on my bed, staring at the wall. Each brick and the pattern it makes with the rest is familiar to me as the image of my own hand, or soul. If there's a distinction between brick, hand, soul, I no longer know what it is. Thus my imprisonment *informs* me. Instructs me to mouth *Goodbye Mags, goodbye Jim.* And wonder how even for a little while I could have imagined these bricks won't be all I'll ever know again.

Sometimes too I wonder if I should have gone to France in the first place and done there what I did, seeing as how it's enabled them to pretend the purpose of my imprisonment has been to let me know I should not have, when its true purpose has been to save their necks by shutting me off from the world, thereby seeking to perplex my understanding of who I am. They think if only I lose sight of my identity, I'll lose sight of theirs and, if I do happen to remember it, will have no sane audience to inform, and on the rare occasion that I do, as an inmate of this place will command no authority to be heard. By this tortuous punishment they pretend to tell me, *Now, don't you ever do that again.* A curious injunction, even were it not a fiendish ploy. Well, would I do it again? Now that by that same "punishment" I am in a position to observe first hand how such daily coercion operates, of course I would. Who could call himself a man who wouldn't?

Unfortunately, getting out is another story. We have a lunatic in here named Barrington who's convinced he can see and breathe and travel underground. Every other day he needs to be stopped from digging a hole in the yard to bury himself. I think sometimes I must be his unhappy brother.

Dearest Jamie,

And so we arrive at the eve of the Court's decision, which should be to-morrow or next week but in any case soon. Jamie, we've done all we can, and nothing remains but to hope. With Truth on our side, Justice should be too, but if there's one thing I've learned these twelve years, it's the Law doesn't work that way.

Here, in short, is my worry: The assumption of all knowing parties when informed of your case is that those who want you in will justify your imprisonment under the Traitorous Correspondence Bill *of 1793—viz., your supposed correspondence with French revolutionists—for this is their best (if not only) legal means to counter our medical argument. Yet, so far as we can determine, they haven't done it. Which means either they're incompetent or like the Bethlem governors and medical officers they don't know why you're in, or have forgot, in which case we've won. . . . Or else you remain so great a threat to them they don't dare invoke that bill lest it open the door to revelations too damning to themselves. If this latter is the case, their position may be securer than we know and their influence, as you have feared, extend deeper than the courts, in which case we were defeated before we began.*

Jamie, I indicate the matter so nakedly only to see it sharp and clear for myself. I think you know it already. In any case we shall both know the outcome of all our efforts before you read this. Let's hope when you do read this you're home again, and we can laugh together over what I can only pray are unfounded fears.

Your loving
Margaret

CHARLOTTE

The most fascinating part of telling the French segment of my story to Dr. Clutterbuck, aside from the little impression it made on him, has been how the discipline of the telling has marshalled my memories to a coherence they never knew. Lately individuals from those years have populated my mind like denizens of a *camera obscura*. I shall here letter them, and so put to better use than roaming my cell the hours to our habeas corpus outcome.

When, in February 1793, David Williams abandoned our shared cause of peace, leaving me stranded with my hired carriage, he broke my heart. One day your beloved brother, the only hero you ever had, departs forever the parental strife, leaving you guilty and abandoned. What can you do but throw yourself weeping at the legs of first one parent then the other, your world split wide open, and who will be left to love you tomorrow? What can a child do but peacemake? Knowing what Williams' undelivered oral message must be, I went direct to Lord Liverpool—in those days still Baron Hawkesbury—and laid it all before him; information even more remarkable than Lebrun's begging letter for peace. What was it? That Lebrun's government sought the assistance of the British government to crush their then-opposition, the blood-thirsty Jacobins, and so end the war and the mounting Terror.

With Hawkesbury I had a connexion, having already delivered on his behalf letters and valuables to the French government, and vice versa—services for which, as I reminded him, I'd not been paid. He received this information in a noncommittal, I would almost say doubting fashion, as if he hardly knew who I was. Superciliously he informed me the Government, if it saw any point, would form an answer in due course. Once it did, and I was the one chose to convey it to France, they'd contact me. I told him I'd wait. But when a month passed and nothing happened, the news from Paris growing daily more dire and rioting spreading through the French provinces like grass fires, one morning toward the end of the second week in March I proceeded to Hawkesbury's office frantic for an answer and was denied access even to the building. This telling me where things stood, I shot straight back to Paris. Answer or no answer, papers or no papers.

My arrival occurring on March 19th—the very day after the French commander Dumouriez' defeat by the Austrians at the Battle of Neerwinden—Lebrun, still French foreign minister, was tail-wagging eager to receive any friend of David Williams, and a regular beagle of despair when he learned I carried no message from Grenville.

Perchance M. Matthews can himself provide some inkling as to British demands for peace?

Mais oui, I sighed (lifting a trembling hand to my brow). But might I first impose on Monsieur for a bed for the night?

Bien sûr, M. Matthews. J'ai agi sans aucune consideration, vous êtes épuisé. Demain, c'est assez bientôt.

Next morning, over a late breakfast in my stateroom, I provided Lebrun with a hand-lettered outline of the Allied campaign (including diagrams for an attack on Toulon), along with a step-by-step guide for France to negotiate peace with England.

He went away rubbing his hands like a cuckold in a farce.

After lunch he was back, for clarification of the step-by-step guide. Over breakfast the following morning, I presented him with a thirteen-page memorandum in question-and-answer form, the questions British demands, the answers positions France would do well to adopt. I wish I could say this memorandum and the outline of the Allied campaign arrived fluidically. In fact, they cost me two entire nights of thinking and lettering. I was feeling my way in the dark.

But we did attack Toulon. In the course of my London interviews I had picked up certain hints. An informed guess.

The documents passed. Though the French executive council refused (as my "guide" required them) to admit responsibility for the war; transfer what remained of the French royal family from prison in France to England and provide £500,000 for their maintenance there; move the Assembly out of Paris; restore Avignon to the Pope; give England a few islands, one of them Tobag; and entirely disarm, in which event England would immediately follow suit; the French council did declare themselves prepared to grant various concessions involving the frontier, as well as the indemnification of Savoy and of the German princes. On April 2nd, they voted to respond in good faith to the "British demands" and so obtain peace with England.

With this in writing and sealed with the French seal, I returned to London, but the British government in its wisdom rejecting the overture, I met again with Hawkesbury (who lo and behold would see me again). But from his reluctance to acknowledge I ever did any service to the country, as well as from certain things he arrogantly let drop at that interview, I glimpsed the abomination of our Government's larger intention. I staggered out of there horrified at the iniquitous gulf this country was hunkered at the brink of. All night I wandered the Thames bank, trying to think why I shouldn't fill my pockets with rocks and wade in. The plain fact was I'd been used. And Williams too. The bastards' nefarious workings infected everything they touched, and they touched everything. But as the sun come up over Redriff, I knew what I had to do: gallop back to Paris, like a horse to battle demons in a flaming stables.

The above was as far as I got last week in my lettering when Margaret come in to tell me how our habeas corpus went. At first as she approached, seeing she carried no hamper of goods to ease a continued stay, I imagined good news. Then I saw her face: blank shock—and something else, or was it?

The writ has failed. The judge has ruled I'm wholly unfit to be at large. Margaret's twelve years' struggle has come to this.

Solemnly, after she next told me the good part—that the judge ruled I be given my own dry upper room, to be fitted out at moderate expense by the steward (meaning Sir Archy), with my own fire, and my health seen to—she recounted the interview with The Schoolmaster she had just come from.

As soon as he sat her down in his office (now the small room off the main-floor hall, where he used to only see patients), he set about to impress upon her how he's wanted me out since the day I arrived and what a shame it is for all concerned that Liverpool's letter has now rendered my release impossible.

This was flim-flam, pure and simple. "You sought that letter," she said.

Well, yes, they did, he acknowledged with guilty haste, Monro insisted upon it, but only after the committee doubted my friends would secure me. And he explained how at the time I was admitted, there was no official procedure, but as a matter of fact it was the magistrates of Bow Street that first charged I be held, with Camberwell Parish only paying my keep. For this reason, the Bethlem governors always considered me in by government direction. That's why a letter from Liverpool had been sought, to regularize (*read* legalize) the arrangement and put the finances of my keep on a solid footing. Still, they were ready to let me go, if only Justice LeBlanc ordered it. But he didn't. The matter thus clarified, The Schoolmaster fixed upon Margaret a look (it seemed to her) a sublimely uneasy balance of sympathy with us and complacence with the *status in quo*.

"But there was something else," she told me. "A relief he couldn't conceal. If I didn't know better, I'd say that over the years he's grown too attached to let you go."

"That'll be Haslam," I said, meaning, not The Schoolmaster. Though I knew that if I said no more, what I did say had the appearance of an empty rejoinder, I kept mum. The matter was too complicated: Haslam would also want my freedom.

Rammer-straight on her wood seat, directing a cold stare at The Schoolmaster, Margaret had said, "What happens now?"

"Nothing, I'm afraid. Mrs. Matthews, you must believe me when I tell you that habeas corpus was absolutely the only way to fetch your husband home. LeBlanc's decision has been in every respect unfortunate. But I must say your husband's cause wasn't helped by the fool's-cap investigation of Butterclerk and Cluckbeck. If those two comedy-clowns hadn't aggravated Monro with their deafness and blindness to lunacy, your husband would be with you today."

"Their conclusion he's sane seems to have annoyed you."

"Annoyed, Mrs. Matthews, and amazed. When you consider a person cannot correctly be said to be *in* his senses and *out* of them at the same time, or when you consider madness is opposite to reason and good sense the way light is to darkness and straight to crooked, don't you think it's truly wonderful when medical professionals fail to discriminate transactions of daylight from materials of a dream? When, after a few visits with a lunatic, they, in full public view, entertain opinions diametrically opposed to those of men who after twelve years of his company and careers spent observing madness can be expected to know him better than they do and can diagnose his condition better than they can? And don't you also marvel that the convenience of being disburthened of the expense of a pauper lunatic should never once have entered the thoughts of officers of so poor a parish as Camberwell?"

"Mr. Haslam, it appears this result has touched you in some personal way I don't fully understand."

"Then understand this, Mrs. Matthews. Your husband is too intelligent to give himself away to an interviewer whom he has every reason to convince of his sanity. How harmless your husband is may be debatable, but whether or not he's a lunatic is not. What offends me is that your comedy-clowns should hold this hospital and its officers in such contempt as to fail to recognize a fact so obvious as your husband's insanity. The world didn't need to be assured yet again that a lunatic can be rid of his condition as easy as being declared he's not one."

"Even if that declaration procures him the care he needs? The care is real, Mr. Haslam, the rest is words, vanity, and politics. Why cling to impotent distinctions when a human life hangs in the balance?"

"Mrs. Matthews, as a man of medicine I can't declare a man sane when he's not."

"You don't need to. The puzzle is why others' doing it should so incense you."

"Puzzle? What puzzle? My life in medicine has been devoted to fighting against public deception concerning lunatics. Declaring your husband sane is for the Butterclerks and the Cluckbecks, who have the hunger of their ambitions to feed. I'm as sorry as you are they couldn't help him—"

"No, Mr. Haslam. At the end of the day the hunger of ambition is your own.

What has finally kept my husband in is the letter from Liverpool. In the wake of it, the medical arguments have counted for nothing. You can blame Birkbeck and Clutterbuck as much as you like. The rub for you is nobody—not the doctors, not the politicians, not the judges, not the governors—cares a fig what you think about madness. And I must say I don't either, because it's long been too evident that you care less about my husband than about your own self-advancement." Margaret stood up. "Now let me speak to him."

Before he rose as if exhaustedly to escort her upstairs, The Schoolmaster only directed at her, she said, eyes like two empty jam jars.

Now, that interview over, she was sitting on my bed, her emotion communicating in the fierce, rhythmic way she was pressing my hands.

Presently she inquired after my back.

Curled on my side, my head on my pillow, gazing at her skirt tenting dark over her knees, I admitted it felt now and then a little uneasy.

She sighed. Then she told me two awful pieces of news.

First, last night Justina Latimer, whom she hadn't spoke to in a decade, had burst in on her in a state of clamorous alarm, saying certain parties in Government, alerted by our habeas corpus endeavour to my continuing existence, were prepared to do harm to her (Margaret) and Jim if I didn't from this day keep my mouth shut.

"What?" I cried. "They sent Justina to threaten us?"

Not according to our former maid. By her account she'd chanced on the information through a gentleman friend, an intimate of the Duke of York.

"Dear God. Not York—"

"Why, Jamie? Do you know him?"

"The King's son. A dolt—"

"So not involved—?" she asked hopefully.

Oh yes, involved. Involved as can be. But I didn't say it, only shook my head.

Margaret looked at me doubtful a moment and then seemed to resolve to be satisfied, continuing with the rest of what she needed to tell me, namely, that from a quality of menace intermixed in Justina's manner, she (Margaret) had a darker suspicion that our former maid, as a victim of blackmail concerning how her husband really died, was herself expected to play a part in the harm. This forewarning from Justina was the better, or perhaps only the more frightened part of a bid to preclude the occasion. When she begged Margaret to flee with Jim, she also begged her to take her with them, begged like a woman in fear for her life.

"If Justina's part of the plot, she must move in high circles," I commented, "where it seems madness is now so much in vogue a lunatic's word can strike fear in *beau monde* hearts. Flee where?"

Margaret shut her eyes before she spoke—at least, I think she did. *Eyes closed, eyes stayed open.* My blood ran cold.

That's when she dropped the second bomb-shell. On her way here she'd stopped at a shipping agent's to put down payment of passage for her and Jim on a schooner leaving at week's end for Jamaica. Our house was already in the hands of a rent agent, who would oversee Hodge the tailor's tenancy of our shop.

This second piece of news took away what was left of my breath. "No—" was all I could whisper, looking down to see my hand clutching a piece of paper with a Jamaica address on it.

"Forgive me, Jamie. I wouldn't tell you any of this, but you must understand we need to leave. Either Justina's telling the truth and Jim's in danger from Government agents or she's lying and he's in danger from her. I can't—I won't—risk his life—"

"Give me something to sign," I said hoarsely. "Sell the house and shop. David Williams has been here—" My voice sounded faraway, hollow and pleading. "He's going to get me out." If this was true, it changed everything. "We'll emigrate as a family. The gang never mentions Jamaica—" Not by name, no, but their affiliates operate throughout the West Indies, magnet-working in the sugar trade (which they dominate much as they do the corn and cotton in America), boasting obscenely of *sucking the sugar stick, black jokes to be cracked*, etc.

Again she sighed, or someone did. "No, Jamie. Not even your mighty David can help you now. And I can't sell the house—it's yours and you're in here, there's no time— We must leave quickly—"

To ease the brute finality of this, she leaned in to kiss my lips, her own warm and dry and myself docilely compliant, when, to my horror, from between those chaste lips (or so it seemed) came the outrageous probe at my teeth of a brash French muscle.

Dear God, it was Charlotte. I'd know that tongue anywhere.

"Margaret," I said, and just to dredge up the name was me fighting for my life, "you don't want to go—"

"Jamie, you must understand I have no choice, only please don't strain yourself to believe I'm not failing you— It will only aggravate your condition—"

"Salope—!"

"No, Jamie—" She was wiping at tears. "You must remain strong of mind. Please. For Jim and me and yourself and everything you ever believed in—"

What was this but a nail's wail for the hammer? And yet I could only close my eyes, remembering how twelve years ago Charlotte showed herself outside the gate when The Middleman and a French agent disguised as Bulteel came bearing down on us, except this time I could only sigh, "Begone, harlot—" to which, beyond a sob and a shoe-scuff and the insolent solace of a lingering phantom squeeze at my testicles, there was no response. When I could see again, I was alone, and could only wish the encounter start to finish had been some newfangled prank by the gang, but it wasn't, and I had just broke my own heart in two.

JOHN HASLAM

1816

PLUNGING

Twenty years it's been since I first took up my Bethlem post. Twenty years that on a retrospective springtime Sunday morning in neat suburban Islington, my library windows open on a June blue sky, seem as many weeks. A daily headlong press of business, with all the hurry and confusion of a madman's thoughts, a rolling tide of sights and uproar and smells and fleeting ragged reflection under swift grey clouds. A man in full career, oh yes. Only a few minutes now and then does he have to stare through a telescope at the night heavens, or at the end of it all, as now, in the lucid calm before the breezes of a new day start up, gaze behind him at the dying turmoil and discover his own storm-tossed progress and ask himself, *My God, what was I thinking?*

About the proper treatment of lunatics, constantly, for to stop would have unleashed a flood of grief and fear I was too caught up with exhausting myself to endure and exhausted could endure less. My wife was dying, and what for me then? How much of a present shadowed by that could I bear? Better to slip away into work, away from her cough in the hallway, from presiding with paternal cheer over the family meal hardly able to meet the frightened eyes of my children, from sitting with her evenings pretending to delight in her unnatural animation, from allowing her heart-rendingly to believe (because it gave her such hope) that I was a hair's breadth from taking Christ as my Saviour, from discussing together the shining futures of our beautiful Henrietta and brilliant John (soon off to Glasgow to study medicine) and thereafter the Glad Day we'd be reunited as a family, gazing out from our celestial home at azure sky and passing cherubim.

One night six weeks before the end (John had been in Glasgow eight months), I invited Henrietta into the library to let her know how little time remained to her mother. She only looked at me. Returning the look, I wondered how I could have thought she didn't already know this. How old was she? Seventeen? Eighteen? Her look seemed to ask, What more do you want from me? Tears at least, I wanted to say. Anything but that insolent little smile, that so-be-it shrug.

Lamely I said, "That's all. Just so I know you know—"

"I do," she replied. "Who spends every day and night with her while you hide away in here? Who sponges her four times a day and when she coughs performs sleight of hand with the handkerchief to conceal the red? Who reads to her from the Bible because she no longer has strength to hold it herself? Who has promised hand-on-heart to devote her life to a God who'd do this to so good a woman?"

"I can't hear you. You're unhappy. We all are. There will be too few more of these days and nights—"

"If that's all, Father. I hear her bell—"

As I watched Hetty leave me, I wondered how it happens a child's grief for one parent will reverberate as rage at the other. Any small curb, it seems, is enough to rouse fury in a heart conscious of servitude. Ever since I'd prevented her visits to Matthews when we lived at Bethlem, she'd been kicking against me in small ways. More lately I'd incurred her unmistakable wrath by refusing her permission to walk out with her "friend" Mr. Felpice. Yet surely these were trivial losses compared to her mother's dying, and only extremity of grief could turn a loving daughter's values so topsy-turvy. Still, I was at a loss to know how my darling girl could become this bitter young woman, who'd accuse me of hiding away, in her presumption to know this was not me desperately doing what I must to keep a hopeless enterprise going.

On the night of May 7th, 1810, Sarah passed mercifully to her rest. I almost wrote *died in agony in a bed filled with blood*. The bland formula is a drape over that, but the deceit shocks in its own way. Sarah did not pass *mercifully to her rest*. Long before she finished dying, there was no Sarah to pass anywhere. And *rest* is not the word for what a corpse is *at*. A corpse is at full speed back to the dust it came from.

Sarah died and the world went black.

But not black enough for the gods. A month after the funeral (Methodist; it was for my wife, not me), Jenny sobbingly handed me a note in my daughter's hand:

Father—

I am now married to the man I love and have left London forever. While my sincerest wish is when you read this you will rejoice on our behalf, you must appreciate that only the certainty of your objection could have inspired us to so drastic a recourse.

Your dutiful daughter before this, and loving
daughter always, whether this union
has your blessing or no,
Henrietta Felpice

Frantic, I made every inquiry: nothing. Who was this monster? What kind of name is Felpice? When calmer, I wrote John, just returned to Glasgow. By the scant surprise his answer evinced, I guessed she'd confided what she intended. Leaving me to derive what solace I could from his manly reticence.

I was not much consoled. Neither was I by thoughts of remarrying. While it's true the circles I moved in were mostly male (if you didn't count the women's wing, which you shouldn't), the fact was I never met a woman to compare with my late wife. A too-convenient conviction, you might think, and even if true don't expectations have a way of accommodating to circumstances, when the desire is there? But it wasn't, and Sarah's incomparableness was the sort you don't—because you can't—replace. The result was that first year I spent not in fantasies of new-spouse pleasures but shuffling so drearily through the house I drove out even poor Jenny—more tears—to work for a luckier family. After Jenny there was old Mrs. Clark, who came in days to wield a duster and deliver tea and cakes to my desk, silently taking the stale, cold, untouched things away. All I needed of the female now were Sarah's expressions, habits, and opinions, which filled my head and informed my actions. Not keepsakes but salvage from the deep, freely claimable, the vessel sunk. If they'd fit me, I'd have worn her clothes. After walking around with my head ready to burst, it took burying my face one desperate night in her dressing-gown to undam my tears.

It was not long after Sarah died I published several things that bother me still. The first was a small volume devoted to Matthews' delusional system. After Butterclerk and Cluckbeck, by testifying he was sane, had everybody thinking we were the ones medically incompetent and doing less than we could, I wrote another book, *Illustrations of Madness,* to establish once and for all the nature and extent of his insanity. But though that book has the merit of accuracy and originality and includes an engraving of the Air Loom by Matthews himself, with explanatory notes and frequent passages in his own words, it's marred by the bitterness of the occasion, for I indulge in a sneering tone and conclude with an unadvised, categorical defence of the habeas corpus decision, a defence that would later do me no good at a juncture I would need every good done that could be done. More than this, even at the time I reflected, *Is this what my decades' study of Matthews has been for?*

The other pieces, though more minor, in having nothing to justify them bother me as much. At the time they seemed harmless pranks, holidays from care. Now I can only wonder what flailing state I was in. My friend Kitchiner having published his expansively titled *Art of Invigorating and Prolonging Life by Food, Clothes, Air, Exercise, Wine, Sleep, Etc.*, I at first wrote two satiric articles on it, both anonymous, both published in the *London Gazette* by our mutual friend Jerdan, who didn't know who their author was but like me considered the pieces good-humoured enough for print. In the articles I made sport of such Kitchiner enthusiasms as his "Peristaltic Persuaders"—laxative pills of rhubarb, oil of caraway, and syrup—and fired off squibs like, "If all the puny children in this country were brought up to the study of physic, it might conduce to beneficial results, both to themselves and the community, or it might not," and, "Contents of the several chapters do not correspond to titles, but this trifling informality introduces greater variety."

Good fun, what? Reading the pieces now, I find something nasty in them, a quality even of misdirected rage, that so sweet a man as Kitchiner was no deserving victim of. Yet at the next meeting of the Committee of Taste, seeing how exercised he was by what I had wrote and being the one he hit on to demand what he should do about these vicious attacks, I, still thinking they weren't vicious at all and amused to see him fired up, cruelly stoked the flames, exhorting him to face Jerdan (whom he'd banned forever from our dinners for publishing the attacks) in a duel. I can only thank Christ the two best friends I ever had were not the sort of men to take up weapons. It was bad enough I'd estranged them. Yet still I wasn't satisfied, for at the beginning of June I published—also in Jerdan's *Gazette*—a supposed autobiographical essay by Kitchiner, debating whether it was my lack of interest in women or my pearlike corpulence that had been the greater persuasion to a hermit bachelorhood whose solemn mission in the world was to "invent new dishes, and devour them."

Is this how you repay a man who's generously fed and wined you in the best company every Sunday for a decade? No, it's how you come to wonder if you know yourself at all. Why did I do it? The fury of grief? Rage at the universal assumption, in Matthews' habeas corpus case, of the irrelevance of medical opinion, whether pro or con? Or did the idea for the prank—as well as the anger that fuelled it—come from Bryan Crowther's conviction that I was the author of a dismissive *Medical and Physical Journal* review of his book *Practical Remarks on Insanity,* in which he denies any necessary connexion between lunacy and physical symptoms in the brain, declaring that what he calls my "experiments" have utterly failed to establish it? As soon as I caught wind of Crowther's suspicions, I had made every effort, through letters brimming with the friendliest assurances, to convince him I was never guilty of the betrayal he was accusing me of. To no avail. As for my own behaviour, one thing about the Bethlem keepers, it's the lovable patients, not just the unruly ones, who bring out the worst in them. The feeling at such moments is that nothing could be more natural than to teach innocence a lesson. But what is this but the serpent saying to the loving woman or man, "Here is something you should know about a world that contains a creature in a state of pain like mine."

Throughout this period, Bethlem continued her dizzying descent, as was too evident even to one so intent on his own. Though on the premises daily, I rarely stayed long. By then we were down to scarce more than a hundred patients yet not so few I could be there so little. I should have done more, particularly for some, like Matthews (though none were like him). Then again, sometimes I wonder how I found time to do so much as I did. For God's sake, my wife was dying. Besides, *I had enough materials.* Nothing could save Sarah now, but as long as she was alive so was the hope of Portugal to prolong her days. The plan remained to publish more books, grow more famous, and graduate to rich and influential enough to secure the Haslams two annual winter months in the warm south. Except for this third step—how or why it should follow from steps one and two—the plan was a good one, not least in offering the writer's singular advantage of being so busy putting the finishing touches on yesterday's suffering while telling himself he's mitigating tomorrow's that his exposure to today's is mercifully reduced.

But this is mere second guessing of former motives and no less fantastical than dreams of Portugal. What does hindsight know? What difference did it make really that I once tangled with William Tuke? Didn't his grandson Samuel in his *Description of The Retreat* deal with me fairly—as fairly almost as Pinel (to my amazement) in the book he wrote after his visit with us—asserting I treat the insane with judgment and humanity? Young Samuel understood that in speaking candidly to his grandfather I was only demonstrating a professional regard. Like Pinel, old Tuke was discerning enough to have seen through me had I maundered on about what we once were or could be again if only the Government would give us more money. Why argue there's no difference between The Retreat, where the pretense is good manners and no chains because reputation is all, and Bethlem, where such play-acting when it happens only the lunatics do it, and the physical restraint is not administered behind locked doors because nobody at Bethlem was ever foolish or cunning enough to pretend insanity is anything other than the most awful and terrifying disease that ever afflicted humankind?

No, my professional problems do not originate with the Tukes but with how their London disciples have used The Retreat to pander to the modern fashion of pronouncing all well when we are wretched. For we are now entered into the high gold age of the mighty reformer-projectors—the Wilberforces, the Whitbreads, and the Romillies—strutting and declaiming on the public stage as they vow to eradicate insanity from the earth in a generation. And most visible of them all, a crusader for compassion as that principle can be understood by a disciple of smiling madness, is the tall beautiful Quaker Edward Wakefield, a true Tukeite in the modern mould, for whom happiness in conformity is guarantee of cure of insanity. And who better to appreciate the tear-extracting loveliness of The Retreat than one by occupation a Pall Mall estate agent? Meanwhile, like all Quakers, he keeps one soulful eye out for opportunities in kindness, the other for his next coup in business. So it was no surprise when he publicly announced his plans to set up a new London asylum on the model of The Retreat. Or when he struck a high-power committee to raise funds. Or when the same committee, to drum up publicity to that end, appointed itself to investigate the wretched conditions lunatics must endure at Guy's, at St. Luke's, and at Bethlem.

While awaiting their scrutiny of our inadequacies, at a time when our inadequacies were unglaring only on paper, I spent most of my time here at home in my dressing-gown—my wife dead, my son in Scotland, my daughter thrown away in marriage and living who-knew-where and in what circumstances, Matthews no longer speaking to me, Margaret Matthews by all reports in Jamaica (if not already [as no letters from her to her husband ever arriving had me fearing], God forbid, in her grave from yellow fever), my ever-cheerful maid Jenny quit, Crowther loathing me—sitting here at my desk, rubbing my temples, hating myself. I felt like the man falling from a steeple-top. Experiencing a certain excitement in his sickening plunge, he thinks, *Really, this is bearable enough, if it would but last—*

Dearest Jamie,

Ever since Jim and I left England, my letters to you have been scribbled in what at this hour looks to have been an unrelieved condition of one or more of sea-sickness, disorientation, heat, exhaustion, and despair. This hour being the first in almost a year I find myself cool and becalmed, I intend to celebrate by starting over. So make believe this is the first letter you receive from me. It's the first I'll address to you c/o Mr. Poynder—who has always seemed a friend, don't you think?—and who knows? it may just be the first you do receive, if you receive any at all.

After nearly three months' travel, two and a half to reach Black River Bay, a fortnight awaiting the wind to let up sufficiently for the thirty-mile trip west along the coast to Savannah la Mar, whence by wagon the five miles here, Jim and I arrived safe and sound on February 25th of this year. "Here" is Cornwall, the westerly of two sugar plantations owned by Mr. Lewis of the London War Office. Though born in Jamaica, he no longer resides here; his connexion to the island at this late stage of his life is entirely commercial. (Our war with France has meant there's good money to be made in Jamaica sugar.) The estate—a fine one of near 1,700 acres worked by 250 slaves—is managed by an overseer, an agent, a book-keeper, and me, whose domain is the kitchen-garden and main house, a pleasant, mahogany-floored, teak-shuttered, deep-verandahed (here called piazzaed), tamarind-shaded villa situated in a clearing of the forest with a distant view of lilac-coloured hills.

As I write, Jim translates Pliny aloud in the next room, with prompting from his tutor, Mr. Pullen. I sit at a small orangewood desk before a window of the parlour, a cool dark room scented by occasional breezes through the log-wood (like the hawthorn but more fragrant) that overhangs the west side of the house. I am squinting out through the shutters into blinding sunshine where a hedge called "penguin," resembling a row of giant pineapples, marks the perimeter of the yard. Sleeping against it, like tossed dunnage, is a six-foot serpent with the girth to swallow a kitten. If I lean forward, tilt the shutters, and look upward, I can see, huddled in a corner of the piazza ceiling, a land crab—a rat in armour—poised to drop down and scuttle indoors the first chance it gets. It's a strange Eden Jim and I have come to, Jamie, yet all in all benign enough, for those who don't falter. The serpents are big but somnolent, incapable of serious mischief. Worse are the mosquitoes, the humid heat in summer, the human settlement, and our distance from you.

Of the mosquitoes I'll say only I've seen two Negroes walking in the dusk through a swarm of them. The man behind placing his hand against the white shirt of the other, when he drew it away he left a palm-print of blood.

The heat is like being cocooned in a wool blanket and steamed. Every object the desperate eye fixes on inspires a queasy loathing. Because of the heat—though the weather has been cooler lately—I now wear my hair close-cropt, under something like a habit. You wouldn't recognize me.

By human settlement I don't mean our countrymen, who by and large are rough, amiable sorts caught up in the race between a quick fortune and a quick death, or our Negroes, who live peaceable, boisterous lives in their neat rows of thatched huts like English cottages (only better, with mahogany furniture and each having its own garden and fruit trees), I mean the low, mean, stinking, fly-blown, dusty, gloomy, plaguy, huckster-ridden, ramshackle towns. But out here four miles from Savannah la Mar, one can forget—until market day—that such desecrations of nature exist.

The only other human torment here is the Methodists, both white and brown, who by their preaching cause the poor Negroes to tremble at the name of who but Jesus Christ. Mercifully, at Cornwall we have a tradition of no forced church attendance of any denomination. Life for the Cornwall Negroes is hardly perfect, but at least for them Sunday is truly a day of rest and recreation.

All seven days here are filled with Negro song and Negro laughter. It's like Bedlam, except with everybody mostly sane and mostly happy. As for the nights, when darkness falls it's a black stage curtain. If it's cloudy, all goes in three strides to pitch, but as often the moon or a panoply of stars or pale blue sheets of lightning fill the sky and illuminate everything outside and in as bright as day. But dark or light, the night here is more raucous than any Negro fun: screeches and screams of wild parrots and clucking hens and who knows what else. When I ask the English what it is makes such-and-such hair-raising sound, they have no idea, tell me merely I'll get used to it, while the Negroes know only their own names for the creatures and their descriptions are tailored to keep children inside at night, not to calm adult fears. So now I'm part nocturnal myself, but while the beasts are only going about their blood-curdling lives, I'm lying stiff and mute, clutching at my sheets, imagination working away.

But the big fellow against the penguin-hedge begins to stir, our crab grows impatient in its nook and needs to be unseated with a broom before it essays a window, and by Jim's more frequent and audible yawns I would say the lesson next door is winding down. And so must I—

Your close-cropt loving
Margaret

QUAKER WAKEFIELD

The first time the Tuke-inspired Edward Wakefield and his Tuke-inspired committee gained access to Bethlem, no one bothered to tell me. Somehow their visit was arranged direct through one of the governors, an alderman named Cox, who accompanied them, as the rules said he must. This was two years ago this month, which would make it April 1814. Unfortunately for everybody, Alderman Cox, though a governor with two years' experience, had never once walked through the place. Unprepared as he was, the first few sights Alavoine showed them on the men's side so distressed him he collapsed in tears and had to be helped back to the steward's office.

There, with Cox sobbing into his hands, Alavoine (interpreting the rules a little severely) informed Wakefield that their guide being out of commission, he and his colleagues must depart the premises immediately. When Wakefield asked if there was another governor in the building who could accompany them, Alavoine, expressing amazement at the question, assured him there was not, and added (patting his pocket) that though he happened to have on his person a printed list of every single governor and his private address, it would take exceptional circumstances for him to reveal a single name on it. When Wakefield only looked at him uncomprehending, Alavoine tried again, using different words. It was no use. According to every means of reckoning known to our steward, the Quaker was a senseless blockhead.

Alavoine next intimated that if a list of governors was wanted, it must be got from our clerk Mr. Poynder. Accordingly, Wakefield (who was too busy himself comforting the hysterical Cox) sent his assistant with Alavoine to Poynder's office to fetch the list. But when they got there, Poynder's own assistant regretted he could provide nothing without permission from his superior, who was just then, he said, detained in another part of the building. *Sotto voce* (not thinking Alavoine stood right there) he indicated the fee was a guinea, payable in advance to himself, so he could enter it on the books.

Wakefield's assistant was still marvelling at this extortion when Poynder walked in and, being apprised of the request for the list, outright denied it, refusing to supply any explanation or defence for doing so. This left Wakefield's assistant no choice but to return empty-handed to Alavoine's office, where the steward repeated his demand they all leave the building at once. As you can imagine, it was an unhappy posse of reformers our steward accompanied to the front gate, with Wakefield and his assistant each supporting an arm of the incontinently blubbering Cox.

Now, Alavoine had not got very far with this grisly tale before a schoolboy could have told us we weren't off to a dazzling start with our latest band of Christian scrutineers. As soon as I heard out Alavoine, I quick-stepped to Poynder's office to tell him I understood perfectly why he'd acted as he did and assured him at a time like this, when we were dependent on private and government funds for the building of our new hospital, I welcomed adverse publicity no more than he did, and that's why he must immediately deliver, by his own hand, to Wakefield at his private residence, a complete and up-to-date list of our governors, *gratis,* and make sure it was *gratis,* because if I ever heard money was paid for it I'd have double the amount out of his wages.

Then we all braced for the next assault, which was not long coming. On May 2nd, Wakefield was back with a seven-member party including the revolutionist David Williams, who had once visited here with Tuke; Charles Western, M.P. for Essex; and Mr. Arnald, the artist. Their guide this time was a governor with a tougher hide than Cox's, Robert Calvert, who I've never spoke to in my life and now never will. Though I myself had every intention of being there, for insertion of the occasional prophylactic word, a previous engagement at Bridewell ran long, and by the time I rushed back to Bethlem, our inspectors had been and gone. These Quakers rise early, dash about like farts in a glove, and vanish in a shimmer of silence.

On this their second visit, by a mistaken policy perhaps of easy-in, they instructed Alavoine to take them first to the female gallery, where, in one of the side rooms, they found ten mainly naked women, each chained to the wall by one arm. All were barefoot and some missing toes owing to frostbite. As the visitors stood gaping, one of the women, Arabella Fenwick, lifted her head and to their amazement addressed them in a polite and coherent manner. She told them her maiden and married names and said she'd been a teacher of languages, a circumstance Alavoine corroborated with a nod after they turned to him as one man when she said it. To all appearances, Mrs. Fenwick was perfectly sensible of her brutalized condition. In answer to a question as to what she and those chained alongside her did all day, she replied with a smile, "Why, sir, we do nothing. Like the immortals."

The stench in that space being pretty bad, the interview drew to a rapid close, but first, taking a cue from Mr. Arnald, who'd been sketching away, Mrs.

Fenwick begged her guests to leave her with pencil and paper, so that with her free hand she might draw a little, and so pass the time.

But no one except Mr. Arnald carrying such instruments, and he needing his, Mr. Western, the M.P., made a little ceremony of slipping some money to Alavoine, to see the lady got what she asked for.

I've since released Mrs. Fenwick from her chains and given her pencil and paper, for I can see too clearly the leer on the old steward's face as he pockets the cash. *Hhay hahshuhr yho, s-hayhr, shee-huhl gheht whahts c-hoomhing t-hoh hayhr.*

In the cells on that same side though they found (as they reported) women "in as clean and wholesome state as it is possible to preserve them," they discovered others (all wet or dirty patients) naked and chained on trough beds of straw. More than one of these latter patients complained very bitterly, though not about her nakedness, her dirtiness, the stink, the vermin, the cold, or being chained to the wall, but about the plot among the female servants to embezzle her tea and sugar.

By the time the tour was done on the women's side, more than one member of the party was honking in a handkerchief or dabbing at tears. But nobody was doing a Cox.

In the men's gallery they chanced upon five patients handcuffed on a bench along the wall of a side room and one very noisy patient chained tight by both his right arm and right leg. All being barefoot, one of them, described by Wakefield as a mere lad—Arthur Jackman I think it must have been— complained bitterly of his cold feet. (When David Williams reached out and felt them, yes, they were very cold, black and cold.) All except Arthur and the noisy patient were, in Wakefield's opinion (as he murmured), "dreadful idiots." Their mode of confinement combining with their nakedness (except for the blanket-gown or in some cases a small rug laid across the shoulders) gave this room, as the reformer would memorably express it at the Inquiry, the appearance of a dog kennel.

You can see what's happening. The disciple by uncovering dreadful evil enacts his master's example, only outdoing him by "discovering" abuses at respected, world-famous Bethlem Hospital and not mere York Asylum that nobody cares about.

In an interesting irony, our republican visitors—being of the school that madness is a neat and classifiable affliction and it's inconceivable your soft-spoken madman today will be throwing furniture tomorrow—took particular offence at our democratic distribution of the furious and violent patients amongst the mild and convalescent. What especially disturbed them was witnessing a quiet, civil man, a soldier and native of Poland, brutally attacked by another patient, also a soldier, who (as Alavoine explained to the company) always singled out the Pole for particular resentment, calling him a "lousy Spaniard."

You can be sure at Wakefield's London Asylum those two will be strictly segregated. The Pole in his uniform in the window with a teapot, the other who-knows-where. This is if cannon fodder can be assumed to have private sponsors with deep pockets.

Later, as the party stood gazing at a group of bed-lying patients, one man rose naked and walked quietly a few paces down the inside wall of the gallery before he was set upon by two keepers. Without inquiry or observation, not a syllable spoken, they threw him forcibly back down on his bed, leg-locked him, and walked away.

Among those patients granted licence to move at will through the galleries, the chief source of amusement that morning was a louse race enlivened by ha'penny wagers.

Well, you have only to compare conditions at Bethlem to those at The Retreat—where not only do the patients dwell in vales of loving kindness but no one has lost a toe in twenty years, all are issued decent clothes so they can feel themselves on a level with their keepers, and everybody is provided with recreative occupations that assure a pitch of worthy endeavour appropriate to the halcyon spirit of this restorative interlude in an industrious life—to notice we weren't doing very well.

And that was before Wakefield's party came upon our American sailor James Norris, decked out a dozen years now in his contraption of iron harnesses and bars and riveted collars.

The reason Norris was kept this way was the murderousness of his rages combined with his wrists being thicker than his hands, rendering handcuffs useless. Still, none of this hardware would have been necessary had not my own more humane suggestion, that he be kept in two cages and simply driven into the other when one needed cleaning, been overruled by a majority of the sub-committee. (To be fair, their decision was principally owing to a lack of space, the Government requiring us in those years to take in dozens of our soldiers and sailors whom the war with Bonaparte was spitting back out as lunatics when not in a spray of gore.) The result was, by the time Wakefield et al. laid eyes on Norris, for nine years he'd been unable to do more than half-recline on his bed, and then only on his back, though sometimes with difficulty he could achieve a standing position against the iron pole his neck-ring was chained to. But whichever of these two attitudes he assumed, a keeper on the other side of the wall could use the neck-ring to pull him close against it any time he wanted.

Even when Norris was still powerful and raging (and let me emphasize this was the most determined, ferocious, and malignant maniac I ever encountered in my life), the restraints decided upon seemed too elaborately severe, and now that he was fifty-six or -seven years of age and consumptive, with muscles atrophied from lack of use, and no longer verging at every moment on the utmost pitch of violence, those restraints appeared ten times more elaborately severe than they needed to be. And a thousand times more if you happened to believe that no restraint at all is ever necessary, on anybody.

On the May 2nd visit—while Arnald, thankful I should think to have a sitter so accustomed to keeping still, set to work at his sketch—Norris, when he wasn't coughing, discussed with his visitors a variety of topics, especially those touching on the war, in which he displayed a lively interest. By all evidence he was fully aware of his situation, as he was of his lifelong proclivity to violence, freely admitting he wasn't fit to be trusted without some sort of restraint, since no one was less able to answer for his actions than himself.

It's interesting how the more lucidly a patient expresses his understanding of his condition, the more likely others are to doubt its reality. In being never actually believed, or believed only so far as the preconceptions of his self-appointed saviours allow, an honest articulate lunatic such as a Norris or a Matthews must ever be a poor advertisement for those charged with his care. Meanwhile, his would-be saviours, who have no such responsibility, will always find it easy, before they move on to their next self-gratifying act of public virtue, to make a great deal of noise about how much more concern they feel for him than his caretakers ever did.

Still conversing with Wakefield's party, Norris proceeded to enumerate his social enjoyments, boasting what a voracious reader he'd become in his confinement and how generous his fellow inmates, the keepers, and I (though he didn't mention me) had been in supplying him with newspapers and books. Histories and lives, he said, were his favourite, and he would read them cover to cover, always more than once. His visitors were still making noises of admiration at this when he inquired their opinion of the historian Gibbon's assertion that a man need only read something over twice to avoid the inconvenience of notes. After everybody looked at each other wondering what to answer, a Mr. Bevans cleared his throat and suggested that Mr. Gibbon as a man of genius might perhaps be a special case, though for himself he'd never tried it.

Norris's eyes narrowed at this. They then went to his dog, Philadelphia, which had been busy sniffing at ankles. Besides his books, Norris declared, he had a sincerer friend in Philadelphia than most people can boast in a lifetime.

No one said anything; most just looked at the dog and smiled. The only sound was Arnald's pencil. David Williams bent down to give a scratch to the head of Philadelphia, who received it luxuriously.

"And who, then, Mr. Norris," Charles Western, M.P., called into the silence, from the other side of the room—for he had crossed to the window and was looking down on London Wall—"would it be you know in Philadelphia?"

"A sincere friend," Norris answered, calmly enough, though as the politician turned back round to the room, his eyes were on him pretty sharp. "The best on this earth."

"Yes, but would you be willing to tell us his name?"

"Certainly," replied Norris, still calm. "I just did. His name is Philadelphia."

"Ah yes, of course—" Western darting waggish glances at the party. "Mr. Philadelphia . . . of . . . Philadelphia!"

"If you like, sir." This was spoke in a whisper, owing to chronic shortness of breath. Yet feeble as he was, had not Norris at that moment been shackled head to foot, he'd be hurtling through the air like a flying monkey to grip Western's fat head and smash it against the wall until its contents spilt like a rotten gourd's. Instead, the breathing slowed, the eyes dulled. That's the look you see in Arnald's broadside image of Norris, a blank gaze off into empty space. After that, the eyes returned to the newspaper in his lap, which, for some reason, perhaps because it was too difficult to render or might over-complicate his meaning, Arnald neglected to include.

Even Western could understand the interview was over. Perhaps he wondered if it was something he'd said.

The party trouped out, leaving James Norris to read things over twice and so avoid the inconvenience of notes.

I don't know all the sights taken in by Wakefield and his companions on that tour. I don't think Alavoine has told me everything, and some of it about Norris I heard in person from Wakefield's testimony at the Inquiry. But another visit Alavoine was concerned to describe to me in some detail was the one they paid to James Tilly Matthews, in his private room.

MATTHEWS

For several years by this time, Matthews was raving as wildly as he did when first admitted. After the departure of his wife and son for Jamaica, he'd fallen back on his old conviction he was Omni Imperias Grand Arch Emperor of the Universe and all terrestrial heads of state mere strutting impostors. The latter was a corollary as agreeable to an Emperor of the Universe as to a republican and in either case convenient for overruling the tyranny your madness has you daily convinced you're a victim of.

More productively, during those same years, Matthews was putting his engraving talents to use designing the Omni Imperias Palace he planned one day to make his residence, while working on a set of architectural drawings to enter in a competition for the best design of the New Bethlem. Though his qualifications as a lunatic might be thought a handicap, in fact they conferred a unique advantage: four years without his own Bethlem room had afforded him a wealth of hints how best to accommodate lunatics if you cared about their well-being. In the end he did not win but for his efforts was awarded thirty pounds by the Building Committee for his "benefit and comfort." His entry was four watercolour architectural plans (offering alternative details) in a fine folio set, plus fifty pages of notes in his meticulous hand. These are fascinating documents for those curious to know what sort of place a madman thinks a lunatic hospital should be. Not once do the governors consult Monro and myself about the new hospital but are so scrupulous to solicit the opinions of a lunatic in our charge that they escort him to the site of construction to benefit from his architectural criticisms. (As a result of his architectural enthusiasm, the next year Matthews published the first issue of his own magazine, *Useful Architecture,* containing plans of private houses and municipal buildings for a general readership. A second volume ensued, but sales, never vast, precluded a third.)

Beyond this, though it might be thought a curious circumstance that a madman with delusions of grandeur should design a madhouse, one needs only consider the resemblance between Bethlem at Moorfields and the Tuileries Palace to be reminded that grandness and lunacy have always drifted through history in some essential consanguinity. I don't know if this means only that power more than corrupts, it makes men mad; or that madness gravitates to grandeur because the common fate of insanity is squalor; or that the history of madness is one and the same with the history of politics (the two effortlessly swapping back and forth from each other's ranks); or if there's some other, deeper communion between those two that the follies of any age will tend to obscure but the human heart has always known and must assent to.

Maybe it's simple. Maybe we're all great, and mad too. And all know it, but appalled at the thought of so much absence of limitation in either direction, we choose the greater comfort of habit and received opinion, and so reduce ourselves to being ordinary and dull. In this we're like madmen subdued by depletory treatment, but also, at the other extreme that's really no extreme at all, like the great, debilitated by the luxury that consoles them for the narrow burden of constantly needing to defend not only what they have but having so much of it.

As Wakefield's party entered Matthews' room, no one among them could fail to be aware he was coming into the presence of Bethlem's most famous living lunatic, if you didn't count James Hadfield and Peg Nicholson, who enjoyed the unfair advantage of having tried to kill the King. While no more than two in the party—I mean David Williams and Wakefield himself—were familiar with the particulars of Matthews' story, its unmistakable republican gist would have predisposed to sympathy all members of that hand-picked company. And even had Wakefield and Williams been aware that the work their favourite mad republican sat hunched over was designs for his own personal palace once he assumed his rightful place as Emperor of the Universe, they would not have been fazed. First of all, any industry in Bethlem (though there's plenty of it: enterprising manufacture of gewgaws to extract coins from our trickle of permitted tourists) would have struck them as the human spirit triumphing over shocking adversity. Second, wasn't it tyranny that drove Matthews mad in the first place? Third, so what if he happened to be convinced he's greater than all the world's leaders rolled into one? Ain't everybody?

Yet there was more to it than this. Even in the darkest night of his most pathetic megalomania, Matthews never stopped being a favourite with everyone in the place. By that time old Alavoine had been his faithful defender for nigh twenty years, and Alavoine would sell you his mother's corpse for fertilizer, and at a good price too, for what could be the demand?

As Wakefield's party shuffled in, Matthews remained hunched over his work table. But the instant Wakefield said quietly, "Mr. Matthews—?" his head shot up like a deer's in the forest. Then slowly turned.

"An honour, sir—" Wakefield began, and stopped, for in Matthews' face was manifest the look of one discovering something dreadful in another's.

Though he was salesman and politician enough to know the best antidote to public distress, alarm, or inconsequential talk is blithe good humour, Wakefield was at this date as yet too green to manage it. His mouth moved but nothing came out.

Meanwhile Matthews' eyes had moved on and stopped at a face he knew. "My God!" he cried. "David Williams! The c-company you keep!"

It must have been the tension in the room, but this caused a laugh to boom out and take a long time to die down. Before it did, Alavoine, who understood the cause of Matthews' reaction to Wakefield had been the glimpse of an Air Loom agent in him, asked him in an aside, *Whoh hiss hay, Chimhayh?*

A question intended as sympathetic but with a drastic consequence. In reply, Matthews clapped both hands over his left thigh (the side of him Alavoine approached him on) and muttered ferociously, *"Don't start, Sir Archy! Don't bloody* thigh-talk *me now!"* (In my *Illustrations of Madness* I explain that one way the gang used to torment Matthews was by directing their *voice-sayings* [as he called them] at his thigh, in which, to force their reception, they would temporarily embed his organ of hearing.)

Nhoh, Chimhayh, Alavoine assured him. *Hhits hohnlhayh Mhisthayhr Hedhoowharhd Whayhk-fheehld, c-huhm t-hoh s-hayh howh yho hahr heerh.*

It was too late. A terrific grimace was stretching Matthews' features. Repulsed by the bizarre energy of that distortion, the company fell back as, clutching at his head and uttering a series of rending shrieks, the madman came up off his stool and went staggering this way and that before collapsing senseless to the floor.

Over the years, Alavoine had come into a kind of implicit faith in Matthews' delusions. What he alone now realized was the thigh-talking had been succeeded by a classic Air Loom assault of *apoplexy-working with the nutmeggrater,* a process by which the gang use that machine to force magnetic fluids into the victim's head with such violence that in the rare event he's not instantly destroyed, constellations of tiny pimples erupt from his temples. These resemble the black pinholes left by a bolt of lightning as it exits a human body, except they're closer to a rich dark-gold in colour than to sooty, and also raised and rough, and may accurately be compared to the appearance of a nutmeggrater after use.

Alavoine further realized that Matthews had been too immediately overwhelmed to recognize the hand at the controls of the machine. But judging from the speed, accuracy, and strength of the assault, he understood it had to be a consummate expert such as The Middleman, or even—and here he did not forget the notorious villain whom Matthews had once glimpsed in William Tuke, whose reforming career was, after all, Wakefield's principal inspiration— Bill the King himself.

But if it was Bill, who was he here in league with? What agent had Matthews just now spotted in Wakefield? The answer to this question, as Alavoine told me the next day, he discovered only later, after he had separated Bryan Crowther from a bottle long enough so he could tend to Matthews, escorted Wakefield's party to the front gate, and returned to find Matthews slumped on the edge of his bed with his head in his hands and Crowther slouched on Matthews' work stool, arms folded, gazing at him.

Whoh whass hay, Chimhayh? Alavoine asked again, sinking onto the bed next to Matthews and draping a filthy-red-jacketed arm around his neck.

The madman made no objection to the intimacy. Neither did he answer.

It was Crowther who said who it was: "Blue-Mantle."

Hoh Chays-huss *Khuhrayhst, Chimhayh!* was all Alavoine could exclaim at this information. Both he and Crowther were familiar enough with Matthews' fantasies to know Blue-Mantle as a free agent not a member of any single gang, who many in the Bethlem one had always insisted was the agent who'd persuaded Hadfield he must kill his Majesty, that it was never Bill the King at all.

Still shaking his head at the implications of so odious a being at Wakefield's helm, Alavoine cried again, *Hoh, Chimhayh!* as he tugged Matthews closer to him and tipped his old skull to touch the madman's.

The two of them remaining in that attitude, Crowther took it on himself to sum up, for Alavoine's information, the point he'd just been trying to impress on Matthews. "A closeted republican Wakefield may be, or inclined in that direction," he declared, "but a king-slayer, Jimmy, I don't think so."

"It's not Wakefield, it's Blue-Mantle," Matthews replied simply, not lifting his head. "Wakefield's the vehicle only." Listlessly he added, "First David Williams shows his nose here in the company of Bill the King—"

"What?" Crowther interrupted him. "The republican David Williams, who's on the Board of Tuke's Retreat? He's been here before?"

"Five years ago," Matthews said. "And today he pops upon us hand-in-hand with Blue-Mantle. You can't tell me these are innocent pairings."

As Matthews spoke, Crowther fixed a querying look at Alavoine, who saw it when he opened his eyes. *Chimhayh s-hawh Bhill theh Khingh hinh Whihlyhahm T-huhkh,* he explained with a sigh.

"Tuke himself, now, has been here too?" Crowther cried. "Jesus Christ! Why didn't anybody tell me?"

"The Schoolmaster talked to him," Matthews said quietly, still addressing the floor. "Why would he tell you, Bryan, when he doesn't tell you anything?"

"Haslam can go to bloody Hell!" Crowther shouted. "Do you know what that bastard did to me?"

Yahz wheeh dhooh, Bhrayhahn. Hiht hahp-hend fohr yheehrs hahgoh.

But having been drinking, Crowther launched into an extended revilement of me for attacking his *Pitiful*—excuse me—*Practical Remarks on Insanity* but soon losing his way, that ground being too criss-crossed by previous excursions, fell into a corollary track, also a long-time favourite with him: that the

Bethlem damp was shortening Matthews' life, and if our madman was to live another six months he must be found a new place to live.

When Alavoine (who I think preferred not to lose Matthews before Matthews would lose him) shot back irritably that this was no more than a truth universally acknowledged and everybody knew that, with the habeas corpus rejected, nothing further could be done about it, Crowther fixed a bleary red eye on him and intoned in a voice of doom, "It's now more than an abscess he's got, Peter, it's a bleeding tumour."

Hoh Chays-huss, *Bhrayhahn, hahr yho sh-hoohr?*

To confirm he was, Crowther gave a nod that, proving too strenuous for his unstable condition, required a foot shot out to the side. Balance recovered, he went viciously at his face with both hands, rubbing it hard all over, as he liked to do, the way you might manipulate and bat away at a rubber mask, flopping it this way and that until at last you desist, and it springs back to its original shape, only bright red, while for good measure you go on flicking at your ear, like a dog snapping the flap of it with its paw until it cracks like a whip. Then he spoke.

"I was fag at Eton of George Rose, who's lately been saying publicly he don't like the state of our madhouses. I say we conscript him and Friend Wakefield to our cause. Such allies will gain the attention of the press, which these days has grown capable of inciting sentiment for change."

Now Matthews' head came up and Alavoine's with it as if they were hinged at the temple. "Wakefield's no friend to the lunatic," he muttered darkly.

"Then he must be a friend of yours, Jimmy," Crowther replied. "Ain't you always telling us a lunatic's the last thing you are?"

Ignoring this, Matthews observed, "It's no accident hack-rabble Grub Street's direct around the corner."

"No accident, you say—?" Crowther muttered.

"Grub Street printing presses are Air Looms refitted for typesetting. A newspaper's an Influencing Engine from masthead to auction sales."

"Oh, now, Jimmy," Crowther chided him. "You only say that because you consider your own lettering the work of the greatest Omni Imperias Engine that ever grasped a pen and made stroking motions."

"Believe me, Bryan," Matthews answered calmly, "I never flattered myself they don't have more fish in their fryer than this one."

"There's room, is there?" Crowther said, yawning.

"What?"

"Flim-flam-flum," Crowther said and pushed himself to his feet. "Let's see, shall we, if we can't get you out of this stinking sink-hole."

Now Matthews looked at him hard. Even Alavoine's eyes opened, and he looked at him too.

"I'm going to find you a healthier place to live, Jimmy," Crowther announced. "Somewhere your wife can visit you, if she ever—" Though he could hardly stand, he did here break mercifully off (for who could know if she was alive or not?), adding only, "It's my duty as your surgeon—" When still neither would release his pop-eyed stare, he added, with the haste of one tending to panic at the first sign of a moment turning poignant, "But first things first, I must attend to this devilish thirst—"

Which is what, as Alavoine replaced his old head on Matthews' shoulder, Crowther staggered off to do.

And so ended another ingenious confabulation of our Three Wisemen of Bethlem.

Dearest Jamie,

 It's two-thirty in the afternoon, forty-two degrees in the shade, I'm alone in the sweltering cook-room, where we just finished clearing up after what's called here "second breakfast." I have an hour before dinner's to be set out, and I feel inspired to use it to tell you about the food we eat here, which as overseer of the kitchen-garden and cook-room I have a particular interest in.

 Owing to a Jamaica tradition of frequent fires, the cook-room is in a building separate from the main house. Here I and my staff of three slaves—Christabelle, Joan, and May-Beth: fine women all, we keep each other in stitches—prepare four meals a day for the overseer, agent, book-keeper, and their families, who have their own residences but usually take their meals together in this, the main house: First comes breakfast, for nine; second, the repast we just finished, second breakfast, for noon, the main meal; third, dinner for four o'clock, a small meal; and fourth, tea for eight o'clock.

 As to produce, the only northern vegetables that flourish here are cabbages, lettuce, and echallots, though given the heat, disease, insects, and animals, they need hourly watching. Of the local produce we rely on yams and plantains for poor potatoes, ochra for poor asparagus, abba (from the palm-tree) for poor artichokes, and calaloo (a prickly green) for poor spinach. In fruit we do better: oranges, shaddocks (a large citrus also called pompelmoose or forbidden fruit), grape-fruit (called cluster-fruit), passion-fruit (called granadilloes), achie (large and scarlet, that's all I know, I never tasted one), pomegranates, mangoes, coco-nuts, jack-fruit (which can grow big as pumpkins, direct on the trunk of the tree), bread-fruit, and avocado pear (which here they spread on toast instead of butter). In fish too we do very well, despite universally unappetizing names, viz., boney-fish, groupas, grunts, hog-fish, jew-fish, mud-fish, old-fish, parrot-fish, snappers, and snook!

Jim loves it here. Even the summer heat doesn't faze him. He has friends both English and Negro and is a mighty favourite around the place. This morning he announced his ambition is to be an overseer, which reminded me our actions are not without effects, are they? You bring a child to Jamaica and before you know it he's thinking in childish, hopeful Jamaica terms. I reminded him that to be an overseer he'd first need to apprentice as a book-keeper, which would mean direct supervision of Negroes.

Well? his look seemed to say. I can do that.

"Jim, these people are slaves. Five days a week they spend every daylight hour in the fields. What do you think when you see the heads of suicides displayed on the bridges to town? How would you feel if a Negro grovelled before you and cried, 'Massa Jim, me your slave!'?"

"But I would be the best kind of master!" he objected. "I'd never use the cart-whip! Ever!"

"Would you free them?"

"If I was rich enough to own them—why yes I would, first thing!"

"You'd give all your property away, just like that?"

"I'd still have my land—"

"Could you afford to keep it with no slaves to work it?"

"Mummy, if I had money enough for land and slaves I'd have money enough to pay somebody to work it, wouldn't I?"

I would say his exasperation was less with me than with himself for too-little thinking of the too-hard lives of his friends and their parents.

There is a joke here, Jamie, that sums up the place. A courtier in Hell is asked by the Devil how he likes it. "Not at all disagreeable, Mr. Satan, sir," he replies. "Upon my honour, rather warm to be sure!"

> *Your wife who misses you*
> *more than she can say,*
> *Margaret*

James Norris seen through Wakefield's eyes reminding Monro how cruel he made us look, he ordered him freed from the bulk of his restraints and the chain on his neck-ring extended from twelve inches to twenty-four. But this solicitude only made us look guiltier when, on June 7th, 1814, Wakefield and his party returned for a third visit and saw how quick we'd been to act after ten years of doing nothing.

It was too late another way. On the basis of his drawing, Arnald soon had an engraving underway of Norris in full iron regalia. As a broadside published that autumn, this made a shocking picture of a lunatic all sickly and woebegone, drooping like a parched tomato plant in a cone of guide hoops, a perfect image to illustrate Wakefield's allegations of our unspeakable cruelty. Over the next several months, picture and allegations together sold a great many editions, tongues were set in motion, and by the usual course of these things, questions came to be asked in the House.

You can see where this is going.

The next Saturday the Bethlem governors met to horrify each other by reading out attacks on us in *The Times* and *The Morning Chronicle*. Inside an hour they had whipped themselves to such a lather as to appoint an emergency subcommittee to look into Wakefield's allegations, for example, our patients were chained naked in their beds not for purposes of medical cure but revenge. The subcommittee consisted mainly of our own governors but for substance included three M.P.s and three peers, most notably the 6th Earl of Shaftesbury. The following Saturday, myself, Monro, Alavoine, assorted attendants, and several governors who'd served on the weekly subcommittee were called on the carpet.

From their questions, the committee wanted us assured how much we were appreciated. The response of the others was fawning gratitude, but both behaviours seeming to forget the enemy at the gates, when my turn came I reminded everybody it was the governors mainly to blame, for not putting pressure on the government to support us in a manner sufficient to make Bethlem work. A hard truth, for which I expected no thanks, but neither did I expect a cousin of Matthews named Staveley, who called himself a chemist, to stand up at the back and query me from a trembling piece of paper. "Mr. Haslam, on what grounds can you recommend still to persevere in the keeping of Mr. Matthews, after your assertion in The Sow and Sausage on the night of January 18th, 1809, that he was as well as you, and there was no more reason to confine him within these walls?"

Here I could have lied. I had already been publicly embarrassed on this point six years before, and it later showed up in an affidavit in support of Matthews' habeas corpus challenge. On the public occasion, not knowing what else to do and hating myself as I did it, I swore up and down I was never in The Sow and Sausage that night, it must have been somebody else. My accuser that time, and the one in the tavern, had been a friend of Matthews named Dunbar, since then sadly—so Staveley informed us—deceased. Who was left to gainsay me? But it seemed I was now too inflexibly either in the mode of truth or too proud another way to contradict myself, with the consequence I said nothing, only sat perfectly still and waited for the moment to pass.

It never did, only infinitely expanded, like a vapour.

When a break was called, Shaftesbury, who'd sat frowning through my performance, leaned across the table and like a headmaster counselling a new boy in a slavish principle growled, "Don't you know, Haslam, in any dispute those who understand nothing are naturally going to assume the innocence of one of the parties—"

"Yes, my Lord. Simpler that way—"

"So let's not forget, shall we, which party this is."

"Would that be the innocent one, my Lord—?"

"That would be the one," he replied in a venomous tone, thinking—rightly—I mocked him.

"But haven't you noticed," I blurted, a swath of fear through my bowels, for nothing about the old grandee invited debate, "when everybody puts only their best furniture forward, the know-nothings come to assume the function of appearance is concealment? So the charge-layers, having that prejudice to their advantage, as well as a press daily more eloquent on the theme of fine exteriors and hidden vice, are too apt to carry the day."

"Nonsense," was his Lordship's reply. He'd been making to stand. Now he sank back down. "The only reason the charge-layers have been carrying the day is the know-nothings are now corrupted by these republican elements. You'd think old Liverpool was still alive—"

Confused, unless he meant only that republicanism was as rampant now as then—"The 1st Earl, my Lord? No republican he, surely—"

"No, but he played with 'em."

"Played with republicans, my Lord? Not Liverpool, surely—"

"*Surely,* Haslam? You know about *surely,* do you? *Surely* Liverpool was ready to keep a lid on Europe by propping up the Revolution in France."

"I never heard that before," I could only say, for it genuinely flabbergasted me. *Liverpool? Playing with republicans?*

"No? And neither did you hear it just now. It's history, Mr. Haslam. Unofficial, unwritten history, that's all. Nobody that does know it cares. But if you ask me, it opened the door."

"To what, my Lord?"

"Have you been listening, Haslam? Do you have any idea what this conversation has been about?"

"I believe I do, my Lord, in broad outline—"

Briefly then, before he spoke again, he regarded me. The malignance in his eyes had a quality to it immaculate, as if his hatred of me was so precisely calibrated to who and what I was it was clean of anything personal. "A word of advice to a medical man, Haslam. If you'd understand the contagion of madness plaguing this nation, you should think of politics as a tell-tale symptom. Book passage sometime to Calais, or Boston, and take a stroll around the town. You'll find the disease there is florid. Has it not been said the Adam and Eve of America were born in Bethlem Hospital? Is anybody in this room surprised your Mr. Norris is a bloody Yank? Thank God, sir, this is England, where we do things another way and a son has the opportunity to remedy his father's error."

My God, he meant the Prime Minister, Liverpool's son. "*Error, my Lord?*" I said.

This time he only shook his head and did get to his feet. "Stick to medicine, Mr. Haslam," was all he muttered as he walked away, leaving me to puzzle what indeed our conversation *had* been about.

The report on us his Lordship had a hand in that day did much to register and advance his principles. Considering, it declared, what a mischievous lunatic Norris is, there could be no conceivable foundation to a charge of repugnance to humanity in the manner he'd been kept. His mode of securement, while risking offence to sheltered sensibilities, was on the whole merciful and humane, and no insupportable imposition, especially when you considered that no better restraint could be devised for a criminal at once so dangerous and of so curious a physiology. As for restraint more generally at Bethlem, all custodial energy there was dedicated to the cleanliness, health, and comfort of the patients—consistent, that is, with their security and the safety of the keepers. Little wonder, therefore, that Bethlem was equal if not superior to any asylum in the country, and all in all a shining credit to its governors, medical officers, and anybody else who was ever concerned in its administration.

Though this report was thought by some to err a little on the side of complacency, I don't think anything less than so authoritative a conflation of clean bill of health and ringing endorsement could have silenced our critics in this reform-mad age, even for the hour it did. If only the truth struck so thrilling a chord. Wakefield was already, all on his own, insinuating himself with George Rose, the justice Crowther once fagged for, who was a keen advocate of reform for lunatics and by the way a good friend to the King. That spring Rose had attempted to secure passage of legislation for the tighter regulation of madhouses, and not just the private kind. When the legislation was struck down in the House, Lord Eldon as secretary of lunatics nastily observing, "There could not be a more false humanity than over-humanity with regard to persons afflicted with insanity," Rose, with Wakefield, engineered the setting up of a House of Commons Select Committee on Madhouses, chaired by himself. A *select* committee it certainly was. Many on it had already been to see us in Wakefield's tow, which should indicate which hospital they mainly had their guns trained on.

A PLAN

Meanwhile that winter, the Inquiry not until May, we set about preparations for removal to the new place. With responsibility for a smooth transition falling square on me, Matthews was not always the first lunatic on my mind, though I had every intention, as soon as I could make the time, to see what he'd say to Shaftesbury's disturbing words about Liverpool. I was finding it hard to believe the great man who once invited me into his home could have been involved in underhand republican dealings. But what nonparticipant knows a tenth of what goes on in upper-echelon politics? Perhaps in those days it was the best, or only, way to keep the French conflagration under control. And if true, it was conceivably enough to explain why Matthews was with us, as one who knew that the father of our Prime Minister had been a collaborator with revolutionists.

Before I could see Matthews again, another matter arose to do with him. One day early in January, who should show his grizzled boat at my door but Bryan Crowther. By the look of him it was a medical emergency, and mechanically I groped for my bag. Yet, despite Crowther's sheet-white pallor and shaking hands, it wasn't his own health he'd come about. After coughing up a good deal of phlegm, which occupied his mouth until he located his handkerchief, he informed me that as Matthews' surgeon he thought I should be apprised of plans now in motion to transfer him to a private madhouse.

I sat down at my desk, to learn that in Christmas week, Monro, happening to be seated at a state dinner next to a government under-secretary named Becket, had mentioned to him we had care of a lunatic who would benefit from a purer atmosphere.

While it's possible this remark, which might be thought to run counter to what for eighteen years had been our physician's impregnable position on Matthews, was only one more disheartening bubble from the Monro brain during a meal poor Becket must have found the longest he ate in his life, it was as likely the upshot of systematic wheedling by Crowther. Still, it was interesting Monro should be playing a role in a scheme to get Matthews out. I remember seven years ago when Matthews' wife and friends were engaged in their final effort to free him—before she sailed for Jamaica—I commented to him that in some ways it would be a relief to see the last of our Omni Imperias Emperor.

Monro's response was instructive. After sketching awhile in theatrical absorption, he murmured as if musingly, "And how would we do that, John?"

"Why, by letting him go."

"And carry his Bethlem journal with him, I suppose, so he can recover his fortune as he takes his revenge on us by selling it piece-by-piece to the papers?"

This response astonished me, and I don't know what implication of it the more: that Monro should know Matthews' journal even existed or that he should imagine the charges of a committed lunatic could ever touch us. I don't think it was only the bias of an author that had me also asking why any man, insane or not, should be held against his will for writing down what he considers the truth.

And there was something else I remember thinking at the time: *Monro may be more dangerous than I assume. Thank Christ we're on the same team.* What I didn't think was, *Why am I relieved to be teamed with a dangerous fool?*

Crowther was now informing me Lord Sidmouth, the Home Secretary, was willing to send Matthews wherever in the countryside we wanted.

"He needs to be with his family—" were my first words, no alternative having ever occurred to me.

"Sidmouth's been clear it must be a secure house."

"Has he been as clear about where the money's to come from?"

"Poynder tells me Bethlem's authorized to pay half what it would cost to keep him here. Sidmouth's office will match that amount. The rest must be found. On the basis of what Matthews' friends offered before, our hope is they can—"

"That was six years ago."

Crowther shrugged. "Six years to resent us the more and prosper enough the better to afford him."

"When would he go?"

"Not before the Inquiry. But the Inquiry could be assured he will."

"What the devil has the Inquiry to do with this?"

"A transfer before it starts might have them not so curious why he's been here so long."

"He's been here so long because the Government's wanted him here so long. Not us. They can be told that."

"Good. You do it."

"Where?"

"We're looking in Hackney."

"Don't tell me this is all to create a sponsored resident for Monro's private madhouse—"

"No, Matthews refused even a trip out to look at Monro's. But a Mr. Fox's seems—"

"You've already spoke to Matthews."

Crowther coloured. With his toad-belly pallor, the flush made a shocking motley. "Now that the Government's in on it," he continued, almost pleadingly, "and we've a decent, secure destination for him, it does look like everybody could come out of this happy."

"It's good of you, Bryan, to have set about my happiness so discreetly."

"Your desire," he answered, twitching, "to be rid of Matthews in some way or other has long been known." Hotter, he added, "Don't now tell me you want him kept here, because it would be his death sentence."

"Well? Haven't you just implied I'd seek his release with no regard for how it was attained—?" This was juvenile petulance, but I didn't like his knowing insinuation about the Inquiry. In a complacent tone I added, "New Bethlem should serve him well enough."

"They're building it in reeking unsalubrious swampland," he answered hoarsely, "as you've often enough said yourself."

"Oh, I think we can count on the governors to know what's best for our patients—"

That I meant the opposite yet did not intend, either, what *that* implied would have been clear to anyone who didn't fear I'd crush his backstairs initiative. But the man before me had by this time dissolved to a welter of twitches and tremblings.

"Now, Bryan—" I said, looking him in the eye as with any lunatic, but pulled away when he exploded from his chair and fell across my desk braced on shaking arms, blasting me with his foul breath, yet was at first too overcome with emotion to speak, it was all he could do to continue rasping for breath. Before he half-uttered his heartfelt curse on me—"God damn you to Hell, Haslam"—his eyes fluttered and rolled back in his head. He then pushed clear of my desk and reeled for the door, where he stretched out a hand to steady himself against the jamb but missed it and went staggering into the hall, where he fell with a thud and a grunt and seemed to lie still. Yet when I went to him, he convulsed at my touch, and when I spoke in his ear, he erupted in a gnashing paroxysm.

I called out for keepers. In the end it took four men to cinch him in a straitwaistcoat and place him in a cell. There he spent the night bellowing and sobbing and crying out for his mother. Within forty-eight hours, though still a little shaky, he was calm enough to pick up a scalpel. But he never truly recovered, and over the next several weeks, with the Inquiry winging ever closer, hints began arriving from Poynder that the plans for Matthews' conveyance were beginning to unravel. It was just like our surgeon to set delicate machinery in motion and then disappear into a bottle, as it was just like Monro to come out with something utterly contrary to his stated policy.

Though by this time I had long since felt Matthews had done his duty by Bethlem, I was too enmeshed in my own obligations and worries to glimpse a way to salvage Crowther's initiative without the appearance of condoning it. Our surgeon was in need of no more humiliation (by being picked up after by his nemesis) than he'd already brought on himself. More practically, with the Home Office refusing to do more than match Bethlem's share, if Matthews was to be moved, we were short of money. Staveley had disappeared. Although as he'd stood up to damn me with his question he had every appearance of a small shopkeeper, half a dozen like him might be counted on to chip in. But to find the other six we needed Staveley. They hound you for years to do something, then when *they* could, they vanish into the suburbs. As clear as I can reconstruct my muddy thinking, it was this: If Monro, Crowther, and Staveley can't find it in themselves to see their initiative through, why should I, when they set about it behind my back?

Meanwhile, I was prey to glimpses of myself through the eyes of men motivated to seek my destruction. Crowther had known as well as I did I was the one whose reputation would pay for our incarceration of Matthews. Perhaps it was the overwork, but by winter I was bolting up from the covers in a sweat of dread. Besides everything about Norris, the Inquiry would want to know everything about Matthews, and sooner or later someone would ask me why we'd kept him so long. With Liverpool's predecessor to the Prime Ministership, Mr. Perceval, lately felled by the mad assassin Bellingham, the question was easy if asked of Hadfield or Nicholson. If asked of Matthews it was not.

Of course, I could always assure them Matthews was on his way to Mr. Fox's, with a few details to be worked out, but that might too much resemble our lengthening Norris's neck chain: too little, too timely. Or I could bare-faced lie again and so at least be consistent. But could I? Exhausted or not, would I really be bolting up in the night if I still enjoyed the illusion necessary to utter a convincing lie? My only motive for denying my rhetorical outburst that night in The Sow and Sausage, or saying nothing when Monro called Matthews a menace to the public, was defence of Bethlem when assaults were being made on our integrity. Integrity? My God, it was the Government that wanted him in, not us. Had my behaviour really been no worse than a mad-doctor's negotiating the survival of his madhouse? A strategy of honour, reputation, and fortune? In an age of show, those three do tend to conflate. But where was Bethlem now? And where was I? After eighteen years of blindly carrying out the Government's dirty work and calling it good medicine, I was waking in the night in a state of unease befitting a castaway in far deeper seas than your quack next door. Not only had my first priority not been the health of my patient, but I had stood up in public and lied about it. A puppet on strings played by he-didn't-know-what hands, who if he didn't soon find out what was what, was at risk of answering the Inquiry's question the way he did Staveley's: with dumb, hot-eared paralysis.

THE LETTERS

In the lengthening days of that winter, a number of long-time employees of old Bethlem, as if reluctant to undergo so jarring a change in levels of light, warmth, and general salubriousness as New Bethlem threatened, chose to retire to what they knew: dank, dark, and decay, with Death's added benefits of eternal privacy and silence. First to lumber off was Alf Bulteel, without whom, all considered, the world is none the worse. Next was Bryan Crowther. Him I do regret, as I do my treatment of him. It was the tragic waste of a good intelligence. The next time I saw him after his seizure was only six weeks later, to surreptitiously examine his brain before sewing him up for burial. Dropsical insanity, the usual conformations, nothing otherwise remarkable. These brain descriptors can make too-fitting epitaphs.

After Crowther it was Peter Alavoine. On February 17, 1815, he celebrated his eighty-first birthday and three days later was stricken with a paralysis of the right side. Matthews, though hardly well himself, begging access to see to him, I granted it, and he and I were separately with him a good deal. One morning the codger, his skull a wizened birdling's against his pillow, beckoned me close to whisper there was something he wanted me to have. Conscious of the beady ancient gaze, I extracted a greasy manilla envelope from the East India Company fruit crate, with a hank of robin's-egg chenille tacked round it, that served as his night-table.

T-hoh t-hinghs . . . Ch-hahn, he said. As a consequence of immobility and lack of appetite, he'd contracted pneumonia, by which he'd grown daily more breathless and exhausted. *Whuhn, yho mhuhst nhaht hohp-hehn hit t-hihl hayhm g-hahn. T-hoh, yho mhuhst nehfhayhr show th-hem, t-hoh—*

"Never show who what, Sir Archy?" Matthews said behind me.

With a frantic look at me, Alavoine gasped, *Theh gohvehrnhers!*

"Evidence, is it?" Matthews asked, peering round my shoulder at the envelope. "Mum's the word with Jack on evidence! He's the new kind of recorder!"

Back in my office, it was to be only a peek, but once I saw what I had I dove in.

At noon I spelled Matthews. When he left for lunch I leaned in close to Alavoine. "You old bastard. To serve your friend this way—"

In his affected dialect he whined, "To ignore a dying man's last request—"

"Peter, you love James and have always assured me his letters went out. Why such cruelty? Read them, since the rules say you must, but why for God's sake not send them on?"

These questions inspired a speech of raving self-justification, in which the self being justified figured in the third person. The speaker was not Alavoine but his inhabitant, the one Matthews called Sir Archy. The letters, Sir Archy told me, had been held as "scraps for the dog Alavoine." The plan was, with none of Matthews' letters leaving Bethlem, there'd be no answer from Jamaica. When, out of despair, Matthews stopped writing, Sir Archy would not tell himself this, which is to say would not tell *Alavoine,* but instead that Matthews' more recent productions were being sold direct to Poynder. "A pretty way to twist his feed-tube, don't you think?" he asked me.

"*Whose* feed-tube?"

"Alavoine's! But—" the old head gave a rueful shake—"Matthews never stopped writing—"

"Sell them to Poynder—?" I said, confused.

"Damn Poynder! *He's keeping hers and wants the set!*"

"Margaret Matthews has been writing letters? How many does Poynder have?"

"A good hundred. All the Jamaica ones."

"She's alive!?"

"As of three months ago, which is the time it takes a Jamaica letter to arrive, she was, but must be mad as he is, to write a hundred letters with no reply."

"Does Matthews know she's alive?"

"Only in his heart."

I left him begging me not to tell Matthews he'd so callously betrayed him.

Poynder was at his desk doing his accounts. I told him Alavoine had given me 223 letters from Matthews to his wife. I also told him of Alavoine's charge against himself.

He seemed perturbed by the first piece of information, consternated by the second. "Why would I do that?" he wondered.

"A guilty delusion," I assured him. "He said he kept Matthews' as scraps for the dog Alavoine."

"This is delirium."

"I'm writing her today."

He regarded me with alarm. "You have her address—?"

"If the one on Matthews' letters isn't a fantasy, I do—"

I'm drawn to that other place Poynder watches people from, its lone re-

move. Conversations with him so throw me that once I found myself describing
to him the Methodist minister in his rumpled coat who presided at Sarah's funeral, how he fell on her eulogy in a slavering caress, the object of which bore
no relation to the woman I knew and loved. I can only think telling Poynder
this was my attempt to convey to him how alien and cruel the world has seemed
to me since Sarah's death, and that was a way to let him know how profoundly
I miss her. A probe, in other words, an oblique one, for that other capacity in
which he himself always seemed to operate. But no, even disguised, my anec-
dote was too intimate and frightened him. The abyss yawned. He temporized,
fumbled out a brow-smoothing sentiment the equivalent of *You'll be fine*, then
rapidly discoursed on the shocking rise in the price of coal and whether we
might ask the governors' permission to fire the stoves five days in the week instead of seven. I was never in my life at the same time humiliated and abandoned by a man so familiar to me and yet so alien. The same treatment, come to
think of it, I was trying to tell him I was suffering from the world.

"So no letters have ever come from her that you're aware of?" I now inquired.

"John, you've asked me this before. My answer's the same: none."

"But you did know she's in Jamaica?"

"Isn't that what was said when she disappeared?"

"My letter will by-pass Alavoine."

"Yes, drop it direct to me."

Now, why would he say that?

A few minutes later I ran into Matthews in the upper hall, making his way
back from lunch to sit with Alavoine. When I told him what the old Satan had
been up to, he nodded as at old news.

"You've known this?" I said in amazement.

"Yes, by the fact I've never received a Jamaica answer from her."

"Alavoine tells me Poynder's kept her letters."

"That would further explain it."

"But why?"

"Because she's alive and writing me."

"No, why would Poynder keep them?"

He looked at me startled. "Jack, have you never considered what Poynder's
days must be like? A bachelor whose entire adult life has been lived on these
and Bridewell's premises? Don't you think a little private transgression would
go a long way in an existence like that? Or a woman's genuine loving voice,
though only on paper, not be rare music in it?"

"A transgression not private enough, James, and not little. Far from only between a man and his conscience, it would be criminal interference in others'
lives."

"But don't forget what this place is dedicated to, or how unsignificant those
other lives are. Now imagine a constant aching absence in your heart—"

"I have no need to imagine."

"They incarcerate heroes, do they?"

"Only when the achievement explodes the categories it would enhance their power to congratulate you inside of. That's when they slip the Garter back in their pocket and call the police."

"Tell me the story."

"Is this to be my deathbed confession, a little early but not by much?"

"What? No. Of course not—"

"Jack, if you can't tell your own patient the medical truth, how will you be able to hear what you're wanting from me? I promise you it will do you far less good than admitting to me, who already know it, how sick I am."

"Then it must do me very little good. You know I was never a devotee of the bliss of ignorance."

"Not ignorance. Ambition. The insensibility of that."

"You told Butterclerk and Cluckbeck, I assume, now tell me."

"No, I never told them why I was in. Such innocents would have lost all heart for getting me out."

"Getting you out is a separate concern."

"The one before us being to assist you in outfoxing the hunt. I'm saying my secret can only hobble you."

"I feel hobbled now, not knowing it."

"Not knowing it and pretending you did."

"I've pretended nothing, only defended—sometimes explicitly, sometimes by silence—a decision it has not been in my power to challenge."

"Or understand. Your fear is not appearing in charge, when you never were. Why not act direct on what you already know is true, I mean your knowledge of what kind of man I am?"

I took a breath. "James, the other day I was told Liverpool once collaborated with the republican government in France—"

"Who said that?" he shot back, with a look of surprise.

"Lord Shaftesbury."

He nodded, taking this in.

"So it's true?" I said. "Liverpool, the great assailant of all things republican? And it's through your sometime connexion with him you're in here? You know the details, and now his son is Prime Minister?"

"It's no accident his son's Prime Minister," came the dark reply.

"So it does go high."

"To the very top."

"That's it, then?" I persisted. "Is that the story?"

"Not a fraction of it."

"No? Is it that he's Prime Minister to address an error of his father's?"

"If Shaftesbury said that too, then he has only hints. You should ask, 'The failure of what paternal plan has left him disappointed?'"

"All right, James. What plan?"

He smiled and shook his head.

Now I stepped toward the bed and looked down at him, and when I spoke, though my words came out quiet, it was with so palpable a commotion among the nerves of my lower face that I could only think my failure to defend him before the Grand Committee, coming as it has after a decade of doing nothing to get him out, has not left me unaffected. "James," I said. "You told me I should act on what kind of man you are. I don't know what kind of man you are. All I know is it's past time, if you're to remain in my care, I did you some good."

"You have done some. You brought in Mr. Logan from Bridewell to teach me the engraving art. You've provided the necessary materials ever since, including a table to work on. As well as ink and paper, you supply me with pencils and pens, even though you know perfectly well I'm using them to keep a daily record of the abuses I witness in here. Against house rules, you allow me extra candles to work at night. You haven't put a chain on me in fifteen years. I can go anywhere on the men's side I please. You even let me keep a garden plot. Aside from ensuring I receive my wife's letters, the only good you haven't done is freed me."

"James, because I couldn't."

"Couldn't you? Then why not do like most people in your position?"

"What? Say I only did what I was told?"

"Haven't you always? Do they prosecute lackeys? Despise, yes, but prosecute?"

"What if this is a matter of conscience?"

"And how long did it take to become that? No, Jack, this smells more like fear of a House committee. And since eighteen years of not knowing why I'm in here never moved you to resign, you won't after you know it. Nothing will change."

Saying this, he turned back to his table.

And so I took my leave.

Dear Mags,

After not showing his face in my corner for two months, The Schoolmaster has just been by to beg me to tell him why I'm in. He's quaking in
his boots for fear of going before the House Committee with no idea why
he's had me for eighteen years. Though he's stumbled onto something of
what old Liverpool was up to, I refused to tell him more. Yet I admit his request has put me in mind of the pleasure I derived from telling my story to
the good doctors Birkbeck and Clutterbuck (though for them I omitted that
part), I mean the satisfaction of speaking out about matters otherwise rele-
gated to a wretched morass of pain and confusion in my head. Jack's request also reminded me how disappointed I was when they suddenly
announced they had no need to hear more. In short, now I thought of it, I
was positively itching to tell Jack exactly what the story is and why I'm in
and would do it in a flash if only I could think of one good reason why I
should.

The question was, What would he do with it? Nothing—there was nothing he could do with it. The trouble was neither would he be moved to
try—not Jack. Well what of Haslam, then? Well, what of him? Whatever
else, wasn't this Truth? And double-barrelled too, boom! boom! And
wasn't Truth what Haslam needed if he was to wax mighty enough to burst
the shackles of Jack?

Why, there it was, like a beating heart, my reason.

Why didn't I think of this before? Was it not the fear I'd not emerge un-
powder-blackened? Was that not the real reason I didn't tell Birkbeck and
Clutterbuck? They were not too-innocent lambs, I was too corrupted.

But what of sheepish qualms now? It's crucial times! I'm telling Jack the very next time I see him!

Yours in a sudden state of scarce-containable excitement at the prospect of dealing The Schoolmaster a double death-blast of Truth, with hope of Redemption in Jim's eyes for too many unmanly showings before too many committees,

James

Dearest Father,

    I write you Father on this my eighteenth birthday first of all to assure you that Mother and I are doing very well, though we miss you dearly. Since I have met you only once, your absence is the air I grew up breathing, but Mother finds her distance from you very hard and constantly berates herself that she isn't doing more. I know we're in Jamaica principally for safety's sake and I do like it here, but I promise you Father once I have secured a post and put aside a little money, I shall bring Mum back to London, so she can find out first hand how you are getting along. Otherwise we have no way to know, as your letters never reach us. I can always return here once we have the knowledge you are safe and well.

    Lately Mr. Scrubbs the book-keeper has been putting me in charge of the sugar mill, and even sometimes the boiling house, so he can sneak off to town. I do like the Negroes, they have exuberant souls, but they need to be watched. Faced with a lifetime of overwork, a person will naturally seek every opportunity to shirk that obligation. And yet production must go on; Mr. Lewis expects it. How I hate it when Mr. Scrubbs cart-whips a Negro. He scoffs when I tell him he shouldn't. If it's good enough for our soldiers and sailors, he assures me, it's good enough for our niggers. When I observe that no creature, human or otherwise, deserves to be whipped, he looks at me as if I am mad.

    The only other news I can think of is I have a new tutor. Mr. Puller has decamped for Ireland, blaming the heat. As of this week I'm taught by a Mr. Noble, who is not. But at Christmas (by a long negotiation with

Mother) my schooling comes to an end. I am a man now Father and hope one day to achieve as great things in the world as you have done, and this hope of mine and your achievements I celebrate by writing to you on this my majority day—

Your devoted son

Jim

INQUIRY

At Kitchiner's on the Sunday night of the first week the parliamentary Inquiry into madhouses began, before the bell rang us in to dinner, I took my friend Jerdan aside. (Kitchiner had long since forgiven him and allowed him back on the Committee of Taste. Being of a generous mind, Kitchiner needed little persuading, and Jerdan's alibi that he was out of town at the time helped smooth his reinstatement.) I took Jerdan aside to tell him I thought I'd discovered sufficient reason Matthews was still in Bethlem: his knowing too much about the 1st Earl of Liverpool's republican connexions.

This piece of intelligence elevated the eyebrows of my journalist friend. When he recovered from his bemusement, he peppered me with questions to elicit every detail of my conversation with Shaftesbury, and subsequently Matthews. He then thought a moment and concluded, "As your lunatic assures you, John, there's more to the story. Shaftesbury's right: Nobody gives a tinker's curse what the Prime Minister's father did twenty-five years ago. They're not going to rig a habeas corpus decision without good reason. The question is, What plan or error of his father's is he concealing?"

"Could the answer not be simply he wanted him Prime Minister to have a paw kept on Matthews and others like him?"

"Why?"

"Republicanism—?"

"From what you've told me of Matthews over the years, John, he graduated from republicanism a long time ago."

"Do they know that?"

"Even if they didn't, they're not going to interfere with every habeas corpus hearing of every lunatic republican. It must be something else. Do you know, John, I've spent twelve years listening to you agonize about this lunatic and now you finally have me interested?"

Later, dinner finished, too much of Kitchiner's good wine consumed, as we put on our coats, I confessed to my friend how vulnerable I felt going before the parliamentary Inquiry with no real idea why Matthews was in.

"You've known from early days it was a Bow Street political decision, John," he replied. "Isn't that enough?"

"But why have I stood for it all these years?"

"I don't know. Why have you?"

"What could I have done?"

"Resigned, if it bothered you so much."

"Would that have got him out?"

"I shouldn't think so. Perhaps these hearings will do it."

"They're not about that."

"No, but you seem to think they're about why you've kept him. Do you truly believe anybody cares? Any more than they care what a dead earl nobody liked once did? Isn't this only Conscience, up to her tricks?"

"I should have done more for Matthews," I said glumly.

"They used you, John. Just as they did Matthews. Try to understand it that way. You'll experience a whole new range of emotions. Meanwhile, let me see what I can find out—"

Here his carriage arrived, and we said our goodnights.

Next morning, on May 1st, in a gritty chamber of Westminster Palace, the hearings got off to a sweating start with testimony from a brand new Hercules on the scene, a Yorkshire magistrate named Godfrey Higgins, who'd just arrived from shovelling a fresh steaming load of torture, murder, and arson out of the York Asylum stables. An atmosphere of huffing indignation thus established, Edward Wakefield rose to make his indictment of Bethlem, to illustrate which he passed round the picture of the late James Norris, consumption having in late February laid his enervated demons to rest. Wakefield's performance proceeded pretty much as you'd expect—with two surprises. First was the enthusiasm the committee brought to his every word. To hear their gasps, you'd think their Bethlem suspicions so disturbing that if Wakefield didn't confirm them quick, they must face the fact the only possible source of such depravity was the vulgar ferment of their own imaginations.

A second surprise: From the nature and order of their questions and also certain peculiar expressions on everybody's lips, it was evident they were intimately acquainted with Matthews' journal of Bethlem abuses. (Over the years, he'd crowingly read out favourite passages to me, pluming himself on the retaliation he'd make, so I knew the language.) For their convenience, the committee kept that seminal document on a little table behind and off to one side, for consultation at their leisure. A common sight became an honourable member squeezing out of his seat to refresh his memory.

So much for my satisfaction the charges of a madman could never touch us.

But you have to wonder if the extraordinary precision, beauty, and uniqueness of Matthews' penmanship didn't itself promise truth to a degree the spawn of a mere printing press can only feign. What's a product of mechanical duplication against a perfect original creation from a human hand?

Strange times. Seven years ago that spring we were tilted at by Butterclerk and Cluckbeck, the Quixote and Panza of modern medicine. Their delusions, though dangerous, were also ludicrous, and by a concerted effort we sent them packing. Now our assailants were Wakefield and Rose, a republican who'd linked arms with a close friend to the King, and those two had hoisted themselves on the shoulders of a pair of incarcerated madmen, one incorrigibly violent who in his last days sat for a pathetic memorial, the other who like God in Heaven has kept a record of universal suffering, and this pathetic memorial our accusers gazed at in awe and pity, and this record they pored over like Methodists consulting a missal.

What chance sanity against enemies so devoted?

First called to the stand were our new steward Mr. Wallet and our new matron Mrs. Forbes. Both fresh to their posts, neither hesitated to condemn everything ever done at Bethlem before their own merciful arrival. So enthusiastic a scourge was Wallet that he swore Monro is absent three months at a time and the subcommittee has never toured the place in its entire history, let alone every thirty days, as the rules state they must. This from a man who hadn't been on the premises three months. On the positive side, we heard about his own enlightened initiatives, such as getting patients out of bed in the morning and to the stove room, until you thought, *This fellow will go far.*

Mrs. Forbes began by asserting she was hired because we wanted somebody "humane" (a word that as a member of the committee that hired her I don't recall needing to be spoken). She then claimed she'd found patients lying abed four days in the week, clean patients confined as dirty, calm patients chained to walls, recalcitrant patients answered with violence from the keepers (who enchain, according to her, left and right without consulting anybody), and the apothecary—looking straight at me—giving nothing but powders, and then with a baffling reluctance.

In all it was a churlish, ungrateful day of testimony by tireless self-promoters, and I trudged out pretty besmirched.

Next morning first thing I went to see Matthews, to congratulate him on his journal having reached the committee.

He brightened. "That was my doing, Jack. Wallet was pleased to deliver it direct from my hand to Rose's. Have they grilled you on it yet?"

"No."

"It's a rack they'll split you on."

"A Procrustean bed, you mean."

He didn't hear this, having an announcement to make. "I've decided to tell you why I'm in."

"Good," I said, my voice thin with calm.

"But the day after I do, you must do something for me: A personal tour of New Bethlem, leaving here at two in the afternoon."

"Happily, James. Once you see for yourself what your improving suggestions have wrought, you'll be grateful to live there. It'll be your own Imperias Palace on earth."

"Once I tell you why I'm in, Jack," he said, ignoring this, "you'll be still more vulnerable to destruction than now."

"You mean the truth won't set me free?"

"Not this truth, before this crowd."

"Why sceptical of so virtuous a man as Wakefield, James? Surely your welfare's at the top of his list."

"I don't like his presumption to know what my welfare is. There's a new breed of tyranny on its way, Jack. The coercion I'm used to is the fruit of corruption. Mushrooms on the dungheap. Nobody intends it except the brutes, but that's their nature. What's coming is coercion organized behind bland eyes, with all the good rational folk staunch in support."

"Hear, hear."

"They will destroy you, Jack. Listen—" He meant to the workmen, who were starting that week to demolish the main building, beginning at the far end of the women's wing, now almost empty, and moving inexorably in our direction. "They're tearing down your old haunt."

"They're only tearing down my old haunt because my new haunt's almost ready. James, you sound like an old man, to be suspicious of what's coming, when what you've had here is—" There was no need to say more, only indicate our surroundings. "Let me remind you what awaits you in St. George's Fields— with no small thanks to your unstinting advice to Architect Lewis—"

"I'm used to it here, Jack. I'd rather be up against you than a Wakefield any day. In your abstracted care than his willed."

This statement I found shocking. I had no idea what answer to make to it. "You mean Blue-Mantle—" I attempted to correct him.

"No, I mean Wakefield. There's a reason Blue-Mantle chose him."

"And what is it?"

"What do you think?"

"James, this is sentiment. You must not prefer what I've done to you to anything in this world or any other. It would be unnatural."

"I only prefer it to what's coming."

"You don't know what's coming."

"I know one thing: the end of you as apothecary to Bethlem. It's too evident, Jack, and it must be glaring in the new building, that you no longer belong. So the question now is, how easiest to effect your removal? I know. We'll hobble you against their questions."

"That's why I'm here, James. To be further hobbled."

"Very well. You shall be."

"Proceed. I'm every inch ears."

Matthews opened his mouth, then closed it. He put a hand to his head. I told him I could come back another time, when he felt stronger. He nodded. I took my leave.

TESTIMONY

Almost a week passed in which I was overwhelmed by duties arising from the transfer of patients to New Bethlem (in fours, in hackney carriages). But I did find an hour Thursday morning to drink coffee at the Baltic in Threadneedle Street with Jerdan, whose investigations had confirmed old Liverpool's dealings with revolutionists in the days before things went to the dogs over there and like Pitt he turned vociferously anti-French.

"Which is only to be expected," I said. "Politicians leg it from failure."

"They soon actively wanted war, to install an English ruler in France."

"That was ambitious—"

"Guess who."

"David Williams."

"Very amusing. The Duke of York."

"What? The King's ox of a second son? The soldier's friend, who loves nothing more than a filthy joke? The one who struts about with his shoulders pinned so far back his centre of gravity drags behind him like a train?"

"What better puppet?"

"But this is bizarre, fantasy King-pleasing, not treason."

"No, but true enough and not widely known—not a rumour. And there was something else, something so outrageous, unbelievable, or otherwise shocking that nobody I have access to has more than intimations."

"Then how do you know?"

"By my infallible journalist's secret sense. By the curiously dense space of uneasy silence that surrounds the name of the 1st Earl of Liverpool like a dirty fog."

"That's not much to know. He made everybody uneasy. He was an uneasy man."

"I assure you, John," Jerdan answered, looking at his watch, "it's more than that. Liverpool intended to live forever. But how? Was it by raising a scrupulous yet somehow undemurring son to do his posthumous bidding? One thing I do know, John. No more in those days than now was love lost between our gentlefolk and the monarchy—"

"What are you saying? Everybody knows the 1st Earl was a loyal friend to the King, his most vocal defender."

"Yes, but why so emphatically? And what's easier for a politician than words, any words? John, I'm saying a treasonous scheme wouldn't surprise me. I'm saying your lunatic has knowledge of more than the usual sculduddery of war-time politics, and it has made him a danger to men still alive and still in power. Unfortunately, my sources are now dry as mummied quims. If you'd know more, I suggest you pay a call on our Prime Minister to express your delirious gratitude for his gift of a new hospital, and while you're at it sound him for what error of his father's he's still mopping up after. You don't need to walk in making accusations. Just sound him."

Finding this an over-daunting task and not liking the presumption of treason, I told Jerdan I'd think about it but with the transfer to the new place was lately up to my ears in work.

"Not evasion, this, John, eh?" he replied, eyeing me. "You do still want to know why your man's in, don't you?"

"Assuredly. But do you know how much effort it is to move a hospital single-handed?"

He only shook his head and reached for his coat, saying, "A great deal, no doubt. And you'll get round to the Prime Minister in your spare time—"

That was Thursday.

On Monday it was Monro's turn to climb up on the stand—the only one he got, which was a good thing, because his first impulse was to blame everything on me: abuses of patients by keepers, errors in the administration of medicine, deaths of patients nobody told him were sick (because he wasn't there to tell), and of course the imposition of restraints, viz., "I mentioned to Mr. Haslam that I thought there might be a diminution of the restraints, but he always mentioned to me that there would be mischief, and that I should be responsible for any accident." When not blaming or contradicting me, my colleague showed himself wonderfully incapable of the sort of answer expected in a reforming age. For example, when asked if there might not be thought something indiscriminate about a universal spring regimen of bleeding, purging, and vomiting, his response was that this had been the invariable practice at Bethlem since long before his time, having been handed down to him by his father and his father before him, and to be honest, for himself, he'd never been able to think of anything better to do.

No sooner was this remarkable admission abroad in the room than he confided, "You know, I really don't depend a vast deal upon medicine. I don't think it's the sheet anchor, though it may be necessary to give it at particular times. The disease is not cured by it, in my opinion, and if I'm obliged to make that public, then I must do so."

It's true, Tom. The medicines don't work as cures and never did. Yet if now and then certain over-sanguine, or too-ambitious, elements in the profession must be reminded of this stark fact, it don't mean the head of a public hospital needs to stand up and announce it to a parliamentary committee.

The irony, of course, was that our inquisitors, being already thoroughly sold by Tuke and his disciples on the genteel treatment of lunatics as the only authentic means of cure, were more deadset against medicines than Monro ever was, nay, against any *medical* treatment of madness at all. What shocked them was not the sentiment but the contradiction of his position it betrayed. Monro behaved like a simpleton, but that didn't mean he could have saved himself if he didn't.

Now I was braced for anything at all to come out of his mouth, and it was a good thing I was, because when they asked him why he sanctioned irons at Bethlem but not at his own private madhouse in Hackney, Monro, looking poleaxed, exclaimed, "Why, if a gentleman was put into irons, he wouldn't like it!" When invited to expand upon this might-be-thought archaic response, he confessed, "I am not at all accustomed to gentlemen in irons. It's a thing totally abhorrent to my feelings."

Universal silence.

Finally, to conclude his testimony, just to make sure everybody went away knowing that the brain of a third-generation-at-the-helm can lack a grasp of elementary historical facts just as easily as it can contemporary expectations of one in a high position of public trust, he graced us with two staggeringly candid answers:

Q: Do you know anything, Dr. Monro, of the age of Bethlem Hospital? Was there any establishment for lunatics previous to the present one?

A: I really cannot tell.

Q: Do you know whether there are any records of this hospital existing?

A: I do not know.

Few collegial experiences can strike dismay in the heart like watching a man you've worked with so long he's familiar to you as your own prick exhibit himself in public as the perfect numbskull you knew he was within the first minute you met him. When spurning is not on the cards, familiarity breeds contempt, yes, but also a sort of connivance, to muffle the irritation. But then one day you see exposed to unforgiving daylight the viperish nincompoop you've been in bed with all these years and think, But I knew this. How could I have chose to forget it? And then you think: Good God, what else have I chose to forget?

Next morning I saw Matthews. Though I hadn't told him when I'd come, he seemed to have a monarch's privileged access to knowing. When I entered his cell, he was regally sprawled on his Omni Imperias Throne, like one ready to tell his story. I told him of Monro's performance. He smiled. "They're going to get you too, Jack."

I smiled back. "You think so?"

He nodded, still smiling. "But just to be sure, you need to be told why I'm in."

"Yes, I do."

By this time it was the second week of May, with the city grown unseasonably sweltering. Owing to the stench of the drains (which, now that they approached the end of their use, hadn't so completely stopped being bearable that you didn't suspect the only reason they'd ever been was they had to be) and the crises and overwork and broken sleep that went with evacuating the residents of an entire hospital amidst the uproar of its demolition during a government inquiry against everything it ever stood for, Matthews' narrative jigged through my mind like a Punch and Judy show through a mobbed fairgrounds in a failing twilight.

Having followed his friend and tutor in radicalism, David Williams, to Paris in the autumn of 1792 to accomplish what he could in the way of preventing war between England and France, Matthews returned alone to London at the beginning of January to arrange a meeting between Lord Grenville, the British foreign secretary, and his friend Williams, when he would return in February. To do this, Matthews met on the ninth with our Prime Minister, Mr. Pitt. And none too soon, because the next time Matthews sought an interview with him, only a week later, the belaced tea-drinker (as he called him) was already in the clutches of the gang—a circumstance proved to Matthews' satisfaction when Pitt's secretary refused to see him again. Which also (Matthews assured me) explained the mystery of how Pitt came to make his famous *volte-face* from gracious friend of liberty to heartless despot.

"James, I should think our Prime Minister's change of views on liberty had more to do with French predations on the Continent. For example, their advance on Antwerp."

"No, Jack. The other way around. War was only the second of two fatal consequences of Pitt's refusal to see me again. The first consequence preceded the war by eleven days, not five after Pitt's refusal. Do you remember what happened on January 21st, 1793, and what you were doing when you heard?"

"Doesn't everybody? I was living with Sarah in Shoreditch. Young John was not long born. I'd just come out of a public lecture, by Dr. Hunter. It was the buzz in the foyer. The French had executed their King."

"And ten days later declared war on Holland and Britain."

"You're telling me the execution of Louis XVI and our subsequent war with France were both consequences of Pitt's refusal to see you in January of 1793."

"That's right."

"What was it you wanted to say to the Prime Minister?"

"It was hardly a matter of 'say,' Jack."

"What, then? Ask? Deliver? Do?"

"I had already delivered. Though I didn't know it at the time, the gang had been *kiteing* him ever since. Kiteing is when they employ their magnetic impregnations to lift into the brain some particular idea—here, war with France—so it floats and undulates in the intellect for hours together, fixing the victim's attention to the exclusion of all other thoughts. Pitt was not himself. *He* would have tried harder to prevent the war."

"What, James, had you delivered?"

"Money and royal jewels from the French, against an Allied advance."

"You delivered a French bribe not to press the war?"

He nodded. "I'd set it up in September with Liverpool, before I first went to France."

"An odd sort of diplomacy, don't you think?"

Instead of answering, he told me a story of Williams' refusing to present Grenville with a letter from the French foreign secretary Lebrun, in fact, washing his hands of the entire business, and I begun to see why he felt so abandoned and betrayed by his former mentor. When he next told me his response to this impasse was to return quick to Paris, I said, "Without papers? What did your wife think of all this heading off to the Continent in war time?"

"Margaret didn't like it any more than I did. It always pained me to leave her, which she knew. She worried for my safety."

"Did she agree with your politics?"

"She's my wife, Jack, and stands by me. I'm seeing her soon."

I answered nothing to this. What I thought was, *For your sake, my friend, I hope so.* It had been only two months since I wrote her myself, not enough time for my letter to reach Jamaica, let alone an answer back. Then I said, "James, you don't know that."

"But I do."

"The next letter that comes from her, I promise you, you'll see it."

"No, Jack. This is not about letters getting through. You can't be both arbitrary and just. You can't act like a caring fellow all on a whim. That style of governance may feel natural to the one in power, but the name for it is tyranny, and tyranny's the reason it makes no difference whether Margaret's in Savannah la Mar or London, because either way when she writes a loving word to me she has no way to know if I will ever read it."

"Is that where she still is? Savannah la Mar?"

He shook his head, more in exasperation I would say than denial—I hoped it meant he'd received something from her, something lately—and seemed ready to return to his story, but talk of Margaret had upset him, and that was all for today.

Dearest Jamie,

You arrive in a new place and getting used to everything keeps you so busy it never occurs to you it's not always been the way it is now and won't always be. With everything a new encounter, who thinks of novelty or change? What a surprise therefore when last week Cornwall turned topsy-turvy. No sooner did we receive, just before Christmas, word from London Mr. Lewis had died, than who should arrive in a curricle and pair with a gig for his fierce-looking servant, two black boys we never saw before riding mules, and eight oxen to haul his baggage, but Mr. Lewis's son Matt, to view his inheritance. Such an uproar his arrival threw us into! The news travelling as if by mindsight, all work was immediately dropped, and every white, black, goose, and dog went pelting to greet his new master.

Such a schoolboyish little man Matt Lewis is! Almost a dwarf, with big flat watery buggish eyes, supercilious nostrils, crooked teeth, dire breath, and an exceeding languid manner, and yet he's tremendously witty (in four or five languages, as far as I can tell) and seems awfully kind as he goes about what he calls "making the agreeable" with everybody on the place. And what an adept he is at it. After an interview, you stagger off glazed, yet though he's spent the entire time talking about himself, you somehow feel singled out by his regard, as if he's immediately spied your strengths and holds them in special, loving esteem. He's a strange man, Matt Lewis, but what a fresh breeze of wit and intelligence he's been for us here!

I'm looking forward to the changes he threatens. Already to our amazement we've learned Mr. Wilkinson is not our true overseer but a surrogate for a Mr. Cronshaw, whom Mr. Lewis, Sr., appointed to the post. But Cronshaw's been residing on his own estate ten miles away while pretending in his letters to Mr. Lewis, Sr., he's been all these years here at Cornwall, where everything goes swimmingly with the Negroes (except it doesn't). So it looks like Jamaica has two overseers tossed from their posts. Like John Haslam, Wilkinson was not cruel but supine (though not as supine as Cronshaw!), which left the Negroes at the mercy of everybody under him, a situation worse for them than if he'd been only one cruel man with everybody else scrambling to mitigate his influence.

In any case, Wilkinson is on his way out, while Mr. Wilson and Mr. Scrubbs—the agent and book-keeper—are grovelling madly. But they don't fool Mr. Lewis, as you can tell by his silences, which are otherwise far between. As for Mr. Lewis's safety here, while it's true he was not bred to so rough-and-tumble a place, you need only watch the eyes of his servant Tita—who's been with him since fatally stabbing two banditti who tried to kidnap him in Italy, a tale his master loves to play every part of—you watch Tita's eyes as they watch Wilson and Scrubbs, and you know Mr. Lewis has nothing to fear from enemies of the human kind.

But his bell rings, and as his hostess, or is it second-servant? I must make haste—

Your loving
Margaret

PRICKS

Before I myself first took the stand or saw Matthews again, a lucky chance befell me to approach the Prime Minister when, to everybody's surprise, he briefly showed at a levee held in the lobby of New Bethlem to celebrate how much the Government was doing for poor unfortunates. Liverpool's son is as tall, clumsy, and disordered in appearance as himself, but the younger man's ignoble face on its long neck is not as ugly and creates a livelier impression, owing to a tic douloureux. I was uneasy as he was, and when uneasy my behaviour makes me uneasier. But, as a principal medical officer of the new hospital, I knew I must at least introduce myself, and as long as I was doing that, well, we would see. So I waited my turn, admiring how our Prime Minister withstood with noble, albeit grim fortitude a fawning assault by Monro. As I did, I thought again of Jerdan's suspicions of the Liverpools and resolved to approach with an open mind, or the best I could summon. Otherwise who knew what I was liable to say?

The moment our physician was pried off and sent on his way, I quick-stepped over.

I regret to report it was not a brilliant interview. Though not unintelligent, the Prime Minister seemed vague on who I was, even after I detailed my credentials. When I went on to express delight with the new hospital we stood inside, if he noticed a forced or hollow quality to my exuberance, he didn't let on, only watched me, half his face twitching away. Now I'd thanked him, it was evident if I didn't keep talking he'd turn from me and all would be lost. But in my eagerness to hold him, what came out was, "I have heard your Lordship was eye-witness to the fall of the Bastille. An experience, I daresay, to tell one's grandchildren."

"Sir," he replied, "it was no fairy tale. It was savages loosing savages from a cage. The French king should have shot Bonaparte in '92 and saved Europe two decades and more of misery."

"And you needing to finish what your father begun—"

"What did you say?"

"I refer to your Lordship's uncompromising approach to all things mobbish and republican, which would seem an excellent making good of your father's legacy."

"Legacy, Mr. Haslam? I don't understand."

"Forgive me, your Lordship—" *Damn Jerdan for pushing me to this.* "What I have in mind is—" *What fumbled plan of your father's are you concealing?* "We have a patient in our care named James Tilly Matthews. Seven years ago now, as home secretary, you signed a request we continue to keep him. It was your father, I believe, who first wanted him in. Having always wondered what his crime was, I can't help but ask if you might let us know, so we—"

"A lunatic republican? Why shouldn't he still be in?"

"You do know his case, then?"

"I must have, once. Seven years ago this was?"

"Your Lordship, Matthews is neither a republican nor dangerous, only the sufferer of some curious ideas, which for years now he seems well aware are—"

But this having an appearance of special pleading, he was glancing round for his aide, to get him out of there. Before I could finish, he turned back to me, saying coolly, "You might, Mr. Haslam, want to have a word with Lord Eldon, who as you know, as Lord Chancellor, is our secretary of lunatics. I saw him a minute ago, standing right over there—" Now his aide was pushing toward him, but he turned and walked in another direction, while the Lord Chancellor, being even quicker on his feet than the Prime Minister, was no longer standing anywhere.

That night, insomnious as usual, I worked to place in perspective the unavoidable fact I had been batted off by the son as surely—if less bloodily—as twenty years ago by the father. Yet while his Lordship's behaviour was construable as guilty impatience, it was more likely obliviousness to a matter than implication in it—obliviousness combined with the annoyance of a man held accountable by somebody he never heard of for a triviality he couldn't remember. While his professed ignorance of Matthews' existence amazed me, our lunatic's fame in the street having rivalled Peg Nicholson's for nearly two decades, perhaps it only confirmed his Lordship's distance from any realm that was not politics. For God's sake, he hadn't even heard of me, and I'm known medically halfway to China. No, I had to conclude that if at some point the father had stooped to dishonour, you wouldn't know it from meeting the son, who like him was only a little rough at the edges. It must, I thought, be frequent in politics that by rough edges you gain a negative charge, by which all manner of idle rumours adhere and drag you down through history notorious for crimes as alien to your nature as a smiling mien. Lunatics and journalists are, after all, inveterately suspicious individuals. How much can they know for certain of what they invariably suspect?

Or was this only me fighting aspersions against men I was still dead set on thinking well of?

Thus till dawn's pale fingers, etc., did I toss on my thorny bed of pain.

Two days later was my first time on the stand.

Sarah used to say, Never do battle with mad people, they're crazier than you are. This advice resolved me not to fight my accusers, who though they might not be madmen, their questions did betray a certain lunatic hypocrisy offering constant temptation to return squibs instead of sober accounts. But I never did, acted instead their most pawky, obedient servant—yet never quite giving them what they wanted to hear, either for better or for worse.

It wasn't easy. Standing up there and gazing equably out upon that pack of yip-yapping jackals, who assumed superior doubting looks when I pointed out that a certain amount of restraint is necessary in any madhouse, feigned astonishment when I revealed that a violent lunatic has the strength of three or four sane men, and indicated by their scowls they knew I was only defending my own vicious practice when I observed that, right or wrong, the discipline of restraint has been medically accepted for hundreds of years, not only in the treatment but in the cure of madness.

The Battle of Waterloo has come and gone. Napoleon Bonaparte was a tyrant who centred all power in himself while calling it the French people's, yet still the age dreams of freedom. At our Inquiry, the bone that stuck in every craw was restraint. Spectres of madmen in bondage loomed so dreadful in the room that all anybody could talk about was chains. And who was John Haslam but the Great Enchainer? My God, look what he did to that poor wasted American. Calmly I informed them I could give no reason for Norris's contrivance, not having contrived it, reminding them that my own preference in his case had been a method involving no chains whatsoever; that the extravagance of iron was a governors' subcommittee decision, and yet all considered not a bad one, for unlike a strait-waistcoat, iron doesn't grow hot, chafe, prevent the scratching of itches, militate against personal cleanliness, or get cinched too tight by an inadvertent (I nearly said *drunk or vicious*) keeper; that in all the years we'd had Norris, no governor ever once complained of our manner of securing him, while the madman himself was unstinting with professions of gratitude for our ingeniousness. But in every word of this I was heard as disclaiming my role in what had been done, while seeking to excuse the horror of it.

But when I tried to direct the committee's attention to the flaws in the administrative structure at Bethlem—viz., nobody talked to anybody, except me to Alavoine and Poynder, who were responsible to Monro—they imagined I was blaming my legitimately absent superior (a brainless figurehead, as was evident from his recent performance before them), when who was the one mainly there? Yet if I attempted to speak with the authority of nineteen years of *having been there,* I was considered as therefore obligated to have done more. Much was made of my move of residence to Islington twelve years before, because in their minds it was then I surrendered any control I once might have had of the steward, matron, keepers, and gallery maids. So again I was simultaneously responsible for everything yet not in the least in control. Despite the fact that in nineteen years I was never absent from Bethlem more than three days at a time without the express permission of the governors, the reason patients lost toes was I was never there. But of course if I was there, then why didn't everybody have all their toes? Because there was not enough money even to wrap every lunatic foot in flannel? Oh no, not that. It must be the apothecary's fault.

When I next visited Matthews, he was keen to know how it went.

Badly, I confessed, reminding him that such ritual inquisitions are by their nature unfair: calculated to paint the witness as fool, knave, or some compelling blend of the two. But I had known this and played my part so well that several individuals—governors who'd never previously deigned to meet my eyes—came up afterwards to thank me for *not letting the bastards push us around.*

At first Matthews only looked at me. Then he said, "It's for the best, Jack. Don't prolong it." He seemed exhausted, and from the awkward way he sat on his bed you could tell the pain he was in from the ulceration in his back. By the look of him it was interfering with his sleep. I offered to examine it, but he waved me off, preferring to conclude what he'd started. He now told me a wild tale of his hand-lettered impositions on the credulity of the French and his frustration when the British government twice refused their overtures.

"James," I said. "With a hand, pluck, and guesswork like this, a man could rule the world."

"That's the idea."

Later, summing up, he said, "Jack, I was only ever on the side of peace, but Liverpool and his demoniac associates were intent on assassinating both nations, by which they'd as good as assassinate me too. Their refusal to pay me was only a symptom of their obliviousness. At every opportunity I struggled to explain to them the implications of their actions, but selfish men like to think their lies are containable. They don't want to know a man is not an island but a delicate play of connexion, and it takes very little to close down the game. But once that happens, he's a monster in human disguise, and the rest comes easy as pissing the bed."

"They were politicians, that's all, James. Advancing the narrow interests of their country."

"No, Jack, that's what they weren't doing." Here he leaned so far out of his Omni Imperias Throne that his nose almost touched mine and whispered, *"Where'd the money go, Jack? Where'd the jewels go?"*

I looked at him blank a moment, but only for a moment.

"Ah, Jesus Christ," I said.

He sat back looking grim. "You're hardly the most trusting fellow, Jack. So the question is, Why have you been assuming halfway honourable intentions of the bastards? Is it because once dead, their hated authority ceases to operate and the names of venal brutes assume a grateful sheen? Or could it be some other reason, closer to home?"

The demolishers that day were practically in the next room. Their dust hung in veils of grey haze.

"You see, Jack, David Williams was right about that much: England was as intent on war as France was."

"I thought your money-delivering, wherever it ended up, had taken care of that."

"So did I. But how can a child understand that Lust for Power, War, and Avarice are old bedmates who stay immortal by buggering each other all night long?"

"Surely, James, freedom must ever be fought for."

"No, Jack. Freedom is only fought for in a world where it's considered as a right. Calling freedom a right puts a whine in the voice and a clench in the fist for the simple reason it's gang talk. But if you call freedom what it is—an obligation—then you open the door to knowing that whatever's in it you need, another needs as surely. Only when that's been understood can anything change. Bringing down kings and ministers because they're kings and ministers only leads to more kings and ministers with amended titles. Everybody has obligations, both to himself and to the world, but he has only one right."

"Only one, James? What sort of revolutionary would ask for only one right?"

"A sadder but wiser."

"What is it? The right to destroy?"

"No. To breathe."

"Aah—"

"Is this mockery?"

"Not at all—James, you're not saying, are you, I have an obligation to free you?"

"I'm saying we have one to free each other."

This I let go as an empty parry. What will a goat not eat, or the mad not say? A goat under terrific pressure of mind.

"So that's it, James?" I said next, surprised by a note of pleading in my voice. I would say I had heard enough. "That's why you're in? Private bribes?"

"No. I'm in because the motive of the 1st Earl of Liverpool and his secret Cabinet when dealing with the French revolutionists was only on the face of it, or perhaps only at first, peace in Europe. Their real or subsequent intention was to provoke the French to invade England and in the panic and alarm of that, themselves overthrow our King—perhaps by means of an assassination they could blame on the French—and thereby install Liverpool's son at the helm of affairs, and once the war with France was won, put the Duke of York in charge over there."

"The Duke of York—" I said, wiping the sweat from my face and gazing at the dirt on the trembling handkerchief, for this confirmed Jerdan's information, and what better way than his son head of Britain for Liverpool to live forever? "The Duke of York," I said again, not knowing what I said. "The soldier's idiot friend—Let me, James—" I can't tell you how sick I was of his tale. "Let me—" I took a deep breath and let it out. "You've been in here for eighteen years, first, because Liverpool and his associates had secret dealings with the republican government in France; second, because the money and jewels you carried from France were used to line the private pockets of Liverpool, Pitt, Grenville—"

"Liverpool, yes. Possibly Grenville, as the one in charge of secret funds. Pitt never thought of money and for that reason was never out of debt, but constantly surrounded by those with an interest in bailing him out. All the better with French money. There were also their particular friends and who knows what other of their cronies in Cabinet, who got whatever they could where they could, not to mention the royal family, to keep them mollified—That was one and two, Jack, but mainly there was Liverpool's plot to overthrow the monarchy and put his son in charge. And the only question now remaining is why have I told you?"

"To hobble me before the committee."

"How?"

I was finding it an effort to breathe. "By giving me old news as difficult to prove as to believe concerning politicians in a government nobody remembers. Information I can't usefully or credibly reveal."

"No, that's not it. The idea was never to destroy you by having you know too much and stand up and announce a truth you can't prove and nobody will believe. It wouldn't be like you, Jack, and won't happen. No, like our excursion to New Bethlem tomorrow, this is for John Haslam."

I know now I should have listened to what he was telling me. For one thing it was the first time I ever heard him speak my name. For another, I find it hard to believe the reason I was soon afterward staggering from his room to vomit out my guts in the gallery was shock at treason in government.

NEW BETHLEM

Politicians betray their country all the time. It's one of the things they do. If lawyers are despised because lawyering puts the law above human decency, politicians are distrusted because everybody knows the game of power requires them to put their own professional survival before that of the people they've been elevated to serve. What difference really between underhanded practice in politics and private corruption—even treason? If one, why not the other? But if it wasn't evil in politics I needed to learn, it also wasn't the fact that guilty parties will seek to silence an accessory once he grows a threat. As a revelation, that too was one I had guessed a long time ago, only failed to act on, having too much invested. It wasn't what Matthews' revelation said about government, or how guilty parties behave, that was now affecting me, it was what it said about my career, two decades of compromised principles and injustice to a patient who deserved better, two decades of toad-eating to build a reputation now on the brink of ruin because the powerful had played me as casually as they'd sit around a tea-table dripping honey on the nose of a cat.

But of course this too I had known all along, or could believe I had, once the retching stopped. And now purged of my error, I could move on to the next order of business: accompany my madman—as I had promised him I'd do on the day after he told me why he was in—on a tour of the world paragon of asylums he was on the list to enter. So it was, next day, just after two o'clock, he and I left Old Bethlem for New, in a hackney coach, me regretting I'd gave my word, for I was either still a-tremble from the previous day's bomb-shell or had a touch of the grippe. I couldn't keep breakfast down.

As Matthews preceded me climbing up into the carriage, it struck me that in his jacket, waistcoat, and boots, he could have passed for someone from the street.

"Were your room ready," I told him as we settled into our seats, "this could be your ultimate departure from the old place."

"I can wait."

It wasn't his first trip out since the time he escaped. Only a few years before, an honour guard of six governors had escorted him to the new site, so he could advise on construction. Now he was watching out his window, eager to know what the world had been up to since then. Gazing past his shoulder, I reflected that London ain't the town it was twenty years ago, when you could believe you lived in a city built for people, not commerce, and the streets weren't overrun with rabble from every corner of Britain and the world, all starving for a piece of the pie. What Matthews was thinking I don't know. Peering at the side of his face as he watched, I saw the absorpt look of a gawker at a raree-show.

Once we put Blackfriars Bridge behind us, the streets were quieter because of fewer shops. The Southwark poor are more hid away, in buildings more ramshackle and crowded than in town. One area of open ground is St. George's Fields, like Moorfields but swampier, and faster being swallowed up by houses. New Bethlem has been erected at that southwest juncture of roads through the fields where the old Dog and Duck tavern, more recently a breadmill, once stood. The new building is a conflation of Old Bethlem and St. Luke's, though behind its intimidating walls, grander and severer than either.

After the fellow on the gate (not yet our new porter Mr. Hunnicut, who was still at the old place) had satisfied himself it was really me, he opened the gates, and we rolled up to the entrance. "Do you see how handsome, James," I said as we climbed down. "And how quiet—" Indeed, as we mounted the steps to the great doors, an unholy hush seemed to emanate from the building.

"Jack, let's not play games. We both know how much you hate this place."

"I only hate what its proponents would pretend it stands for. Otherwise I'm grateful to have an opportunity to show you the real effects of your architectural work. They listened to you, James. It's more than they did for me."

After a wondering welcome from an underling to Mr. Wallet, the man sidled away to leave us standing in the vast, cold foyer. For something to interest Matthews before we went up, I drew aside velvet curtains to reveal Cibber's statues of Melancholy and Raving Madness. Seeing that Melancholy in the furbishment had been given a loincloth, I pointed it out to Matthews, who only shook his head, saying, "The new propriety, Jack. But no more absurd than old Cibber last century doing no monument to Nuisance, as the principal qualifier for residence in here."

Next we ascended marble stairs to the first floor, where I noticed with bitter satisfaction how truly chill the air was, even up there. Bitter because, though I'd spared no pains gathering information on modern heating systems to inform the governors' decision, they held their meeting without telling me. Satisfaction because the steam method they chose—the cheapest tendered—confined its benefits to the basement, where the boilers were.

"What time is it, Jack?"

"Nearly four."

"And mealtime four-thirty here too?"

"Yes, same here—"

"What say we break bread with Peg Nicholson?"

"James," I teased him, "you know as well as I do bread's precisely what Peg won't eat, on principle, until the King hands over his crown."

"*Cake* does she eat?"

"When she can get it—"

"Oh, she can get it—" And he held up a small, greasy, newspaper-wrapped oblong, tied with a string.

After I located a female keeper to inform her we'd need an extra meal tray to Peg's room, we toured the women's wing, the only one as yet fully occupied. While we walked through the upper gallery inhaling fresh plaster, I provided a positive commentary. "Notice, James, as you made it clear to the committee were needed, not only many more windows for admitting much glorious light but several that reach low enough to the floor so inmates can enjoy the view without climbing up on these chairs, which instead can be used for the purpose they were designed for: sitting in and looking out." Here I indicated three female lunatics slumped on wood chairs before the windows, one dozing, one sunk in a fixed stare, the third eyeing us with alarm while nasally mutilating a Bach air.

"And glazed windows throughout—" I heard myself say as I pushed open a cell door to reveal Alice James crouched shivering naked on the floor by her bed beneath an unglazed window—"by springtime, at the latest—See, James? Iron bedsteads—"

He was helping Alice onto her bed. When he next drew a small blanket from a high shelf near where we stood and draped it over her scabby shoulders, she whispered, "Thank'ee, Jimmy— You're here now—?"

"Not yet, Alice—"

After goodbyes to Alice, we proceeded on our way, I assuring Matthews of warm rooms (once all the glazing was in), warm baths (once the steam-heating system was working, or replaced), communal dining (once the dining room was completed), ". . . with a keeper, James, at your elbow to cut your meat—"

At *meat* we reached the open doorway of Peg Nicholson, whom, from the look on her face when she lifted it from her needlework to see who said it, the word revolted. Though I'd heard she was as much a favourite here as at the old place (except now the general belief was it was the Prince Regent she once attacked, and most wished she'd succeeded), from the shocking appearance of her that day, she was wasting away. Gaunt and pale, except, her face being turned away, visible at the back of her jaw was a great yellow-black contusion, like a spider bite that had nipped a blood vessel.

"Peg," I said, fearing the drastic loss of weight meant a cancer. "Are you ailing?"

"Not a bit of it," she tartly responded, turning back round as if to face me, but it was Matthews her eyes went to. "I am only pining. Royalty does pine, you know. I understand that now."

"Like anybody else, I should think—?" I murmured, reaching for her pulse.

Her eyes remaining on Matthews, she did not resist. As I counted the beats, I glanced over my shoulder in time to see him pull the string and unfold the greasy newspaper to reveal two crumbled pieces of short-cake, crying, "Happy Birthday, Peg!"

"Why, Jim!" she said, going all shy. "You remembered the Queen's birthday!"

"Peg's eighty-two today, Jack," he muttered, swooping the short-cake in under her nose.

"Happy Birthday, Peg," I said.

She was shaking her head smilingly at the gift.

"Are you refusing shortbread now too, Peg," I asked, "in your pining?"

Already rewrapping it, Matthews said at my ear, "Tell us the time, Jack."

"Twenty-five to five—Why?"

My answer was the peremptory entrance of a female keeper I never saw before, a beetle-browed young woman with a pimply complexion, carrying in each hand a tray containing meat and bread and a bowl of carrot broth. Greeting Peg with brusque endearments, she deposited one of the trays on the bed next to her. Holding the second, she hesitated between me and Matthews as the lunatic to receive it. To spare her embarrassment, I pointed at him. She duly set it down near the foot of Peg's bed, where he sat. A curtsy and she was gone, but in the gallery as she left she said something to a male, who responded obscenely, and when I looked round, the keeper Davies was filling the doorway in his usual insolent manner.

I glanced at Matthews, who looked at me soberly before he looked to Peg. Following his eyes, I saw that hers were fixed in fright on Davies. "You're not needed yet, Mr. Davies," I let him know. "We're old friends here. I'll inform you when we're ready to leave."

"She must eat," Davies replied with a sullen look.

"That's correct. Now leave us till she's finished her meal."

"By your pardon, sir, I'll only need to come back. Because she won't eat."

Now the ugliness of the situation was revealed. "Let me help you, Peg," I murmured and hardly knowing what I did, spooned up a little broth with a trembling hand and raised it to her mouth, which she pressed firmly shut, her head slowly shaking *No,* her eyes once again on Matthews.

I set the spoon in the bowl a moment and flexed my fingers, as if they were stiff. "Why not?" I said.

"His Majesty's cooks are preparing a state feast at the Palace for the day of my investiture," she explained, seeming to address Matthews. "I'm loath to spoil my appetite."

"But stopping eating," I said, "will cause it to fade away altogether—And so will you."

"Because I can't trust his Majesty's cooks I must only pretend to eat. What good are tasters if the effects of the poison are slow?"

"Better eat, in that case, before he arrives, to stay robust and alert and that way foil his schemes."

Once more I lifted the spoon to her mouth. Once more it clamped shut. Really, what was the use? Why was I yet again in the position of trying to reason with a lunatic? I looked at Matthews, and he was watching me. I lowered the spoon. Sighing, I said, "Peg, you must eat. If you don't eat, you'll die."

"This nation will die," she replied, with a meaning look at me, "if I don't soon get my crown."

Davies was still in the doorway. The menace of his energy seemed to flood the room. "By your leave, sir—" Again I looked round at him, at his beefy, brutal face. "Your key does work, sir," he cajoled me. "She'd be dead two weeks ago without it, or long since have all her teeth smashed out. She'll take the broth no trouble if we use the key. Before it's cold—"

I looked at Peg and seemed to see a beseeching expression in her eyes. She must, I reflected, be used to it by now.

"If you would, sir—" Davies said.

When I nodded, he was immediately in the room, followed hard by the keeper Hester, who must have been out there waiting too, and slipped the spoon from my unresisting hand. Being for my eyes, their performance was a professional display. Already Davies was nestled next to Peg, on the side opposite her tray. As she sat paralysed by terror, her needlework fallen to the floor, he, like some dreadful nephew, put his arm around her neck and pulled her to him with his left arm while with the sausage fingers of his meaty right he reached up before her to squeeze her jaws at their hinges, a pressure you'd think would cause them to yield immediately, for by her expression those bruises—no spider's doing—were extremely tender to the touch. But she wouldn't open her teeth, or wouldn't open them far enough, though from her whimpering and writhing you could hear and see too clearly the pain she was in. That's when the mouth-key materialized in Hester's free hand, and Davies giving the anguished Peg's jaw a harder squeeze still, one so painful she cried out, the key was slipped between her teeth and turned, the steel disk neatly opening her mouth—neatly, that is, except for the obvious excruciating agony of it. Now Hester stood over her, tipping in spoonfuls of broth, and each time Peg refused to swallow, Davies pressed her nose shut with the hand no longer required to squeeze open her jaw, affording her no choice. Choke, gag, splutter, but often enough gulp the liquid down.

In five minutes, though it seemed as many hours, the bowl was empty and Davies and Hester were gone from the room. The whole time they'd been upon her, whenever her eyes weren't pressed shut in anguish she held mine, as if to say, *How can you let them do this to me?* But as soon as they were gone, she refused, or was unable, to look at me, as if I had betrayed her beyond the limits of her comprehension. Her distress was obvious and extreme, her hands fluttering helplessly in her lap, trembling and turning as she mumbled a mad litany of royal deliverance.

"Jack—" It was Matthews. I would say I had forgot he was there had I not just watched Peg's ordeal in large part through his eyes.

"What, James?"

"You don't make people talismans."

"Lunatics need to eat," I said quietly. I couldn't look at him.

"You've fed her force."

My gaze was lowered to my lap, where my hands were trembling as wildly almost as Peg's. Sometimes I have thought I'd go mad with not knowing what to do for these people.

"Jack?"

"What?"

"We're men and women in a condition of mental torment. You must treat us humanely or not at all."

When I made no answer to this, he kept on. "Jack, what was it Sir Archy used to say to The Middleman after they would do their worst with me?"

I looked at him.

"Jack, you do know, because it's in the book you wrote about me."

" 'He is the talisman,' " I dully answered.

"Yes, that's it. And he knew what he spoke of. I am your talisman, just as Peg is. *By your use of us you defend your power.* That's the other reason I'm in that you and I have come here to learn. In your own scrabble after immortality, you have done to us exactly as Liverpool and Co. have done to you, no matter what the sugar-candied medical terms you might put it in for your own consumption."

"James," I said, needing to take a deep breath to continue, "I've only ever tried to do my professional best—"

"Your professional best," he jeeringly retorted. "And to be seen by the world to be doing it. But do you know what my life has taught me, Jack? A man's best is not always the right thing, or enough, if it ever was. And sooner or later there comes a time he must walk away."

To have, I suppose, something to occupy my hands, I had picked up Peg's needlework from the floor. It was a likeness of a coat of arms, a canary yellow crown against a white shield, with round about the crown a charge of dolphins leaping out of green waves, two of the dolphins as yet stitched in outline only. What right did Matthews have to tell me my best was not enough and I should walk away, when he believed his own best had saved two nations and he could never forgive his friend Williams for doing just that: walking away? I was thinking this as, my God, he went on talking. I was being hectored by a lunatic I had done everything for I could do, short of ruin myself.

"Your best, Jack, has too long done us all an injustice. As soon as it sinks in how great, that's when the genuine suffering will start for you—"

What happened next I don't know. I guess I threw myself at him. I can still hear Peg's cries, which passed into my skull like knives into cheese. I remember the curious mixture of satisfaction, shock, and terror on Matthews' face as my hands closed upon his throat. I remember I had every intention to kill him if I could. But Davies must have been loitering nearby if not directly outside the door, for he it was who quickly dragged me off. I suppose I fought him too, because next thing I remember I was in a strait-waistcoat, alone in a brand-new cell, rocking and weeping.

Dearest Jamie,

Mr. Lewis has lost no time making changes and doesn't care a jot they're spectacularly failing to recommend him to the white planters. Mr. Scrubbs the book-keeper is already gone, dismissed for his mistreatment of our slaves. This is a consequence of the fact Mr. Lewis, as examining magistrate, has accepted the word of five Negroes against that of one white man (namely the agent, Mr. Wilson, who's still grumbling about the affront to his honour). It's a decision unheard of on this island, where the word of one white man is normally good against that of a dozen blacks.

Among other reforms initiated at Cornwall by Mr. Lewis: The use of the cart-whip is absolutely forbidden. No Negro is otherwise to be struck or punished except by express order of the new overseer Mr. Sorley and then only after a cooling-down period of twenty-four hours. Records are to be kept of all punishments. A white man who has sexual relations with the wife of a slave faces instant dismissal. In addition, though Jamaica law provides the Negroes every second Saturday off work and here at Cornwall they already have every Saturday off, Mr. Lewis has doubled their holidays by adding to the legislated three days at Christmas, three more days: Good Friday and the second Fridays in July and October. July 9th is his own birthday. October is the month of the Duchess of York's (a particular favourite with him). In honour of her, each Cornwall pickaninny-mother will receive a scarlet girdle with a silver medal for every child born, which she must wear on feast days.

In light of the fact our Negroes are still slaves, these may seem paltry measures, but in this place at this time to blacks and whites they are, re-spectively, joy- and dread-inducing initiatives. When you add to them Mr. Lewis's orders for the building of a new Negro lying-in hospital, the sum is a uniquely enlightened regime. No wonder the other planters say he's as bad as the Methodists: a radical menace to the peace of the island. Jim, though Mr. Lewis's over-affectionate attentions make him nervous (I can see why), is greatly impressed by our employer's manifest concern for the well-being of the Negroes and now says he wants to be—in that regard—exactly like him.

"He has money," I pointed out. "I'm not saying he's not a good man, Jim, but he can afford to be liberal. Also, remember this: He's just visiting. He won't be here to suffer the consequences of his actions."

"What do you mean—?" Jim cried.

"He's returning to England, at the end of the month—"

"And never coming back?"

"He promises he is but can't be sure when."

"But he only just got here!"

"I know. I'll miss him too."

So will the Negroes, though the uncomfortable fact is (as Mr. Scrubbs never tired of telling everybody as he packed) two weeks after Mr. Lewis's arrival our production of sugar fell from thirty hogsheads per week to twenty-three. Now we're at seventeen. Who knows how little Mr. Lewis's kindnesses will have them producing if he stays longer?

Human nature is more mysterious than all our intentions, isn't it, Jamie? But I think that's something you and I learned pretty well a long time ago.

Your loving
Margaret

LAST TOUR

Aside from precipitating what I shall call my nervous collapse, Matthews' revelations had two effects I could immediately recognize. First, I now knew he must not be transferred with the rest to New Bethlem, that I must do everything in my power to resuscitate Crowther's initiative and smooth his way to a new life in a private madhouse in the country. Second, he had warned me the truth would hobble me, and it did, far more even, I would say, than he intended, because all on my own I took it further, by convincing myself I wasn't hobbled at all. To do this, I thought of Matthews' story of treasonous intentions by dead politicians and of how he was right, it was less a story now likely to do anybody any good than the events of it, whatever they had been, to go on sowing darkness down the generations. When I thought of myself, it was first and foremost as one more victim of such-and-such former evil. But that's what happens when you have too much invested. You say to yourself, *This isn't going to do anybody any good,* when what you mean is, *There's nothing to be done.* You say, *The bastards,* when you mean, *It was never my fault.* And yet at the same time, I knew that in the end it did come back to me. They could not have used me without what Matthews once called the insensibility of my own ambition. This was the deeper understanding of the matter that in order to get to they would first need to grasp the shallower. For me, meanwhile, the deeper remained a pull-back position, and I had not yet pulled back. Not yet.

If this seems strange logic, it is. But it, along with what I construed as the catharsis of my collapse, must be why I approached my last time on the stand so strangely collected. Sometimes you're dreading a public appearance, and then a crisis in another part of your life or some touch of illness (a megrim will do) provides merciful ballast, and lo and behold you sail through with ease. So too when you go in with the right kind of secrets, the overshadowing kind. They give you power, they make you a better actor. This was the sort of advantage I believed I would have on the stand. Even if the reason Matthews was in was not what this investigation was about, the fact was, I now knew enough from what the man himself had told me to know why he was in. They didn't and never would. He thought he'd hobbled me. I thought I knew better.

Matthews had slipped me my trumps on a Friday and Saturday. My last time to testify was on the Monday. On the Sunday between, at that hour when hardly a glow illuminates the eastern horizon, when the air can be almost clear, I made a gift to myself of a ramble round the periphery of my devastated dominion. It began with a stroll out the front door to the front gate, with a wide skirt of the slope of rubble now spreading across the courtyard from westward, the direction there was no longer any building at all.

(The reason I was at Bethlem before dawn on a Sunday was I'd been sleeping on a cot in my office all month while we worked to move out the last of the male patients before the demolishers started on their rooms. I didn't mind. Returning home at the end of a thirteen-hour day to a cold kettle on the hob and a piece of Mrs. Clark's cake in a biscuit tin was become more loneliness than I could bear. All there was at home for me was sporadic letters from my son John, now a surgeon with the Navy in the North Sea, and though they arrived months apart, they were what I lived for.)

The front gate was chained, but I came to it armed with rings of neatly labelled keys pressed upon me by our new porter, Mr. Hunnicut. Like Wallet and Forbes, Hunnicut is a clean, efficient representative of the modern age, but his finicking method of labelling the keys only confusing me, I needed to try them one by one, now and then pausing to crack my neck. That's how I noticed how bereft the old gates seemed without Melancholy and Raving Madness sprawled a-top.

Free at last, I set out on my ramble. To judge from the energy shown by the demolishers—English workingmen taking down the English Bastille—if I didn't do it this morning, the next chance I had there'd be nothing visible above the wall but sky.

My route took me first westward along the front wall toward Moorgate. At each of the open, barred panels, provided to give citizens complimentary views of lunatics being aired in the days when they didn't just wander out unattended, I stopped to peer in at level nothing: a choppy terrain of bricks and splintered boards. What remained of the building was a good distance to my left, looking like a ship torn in half by its own weight on its plunge to the bottom. The half visible to me had landed upright on the ocean floor, its interior compartments rising in ragged terraces, all in shadow now that the sun (to confound the metaphor) was rising behind it. But if I concentrated, I could determine pretty well which roofless, ragged compartment had been which in that former reality.

At ground level there jutted a row of tiny ceilingless compartments with doorways like notches in the wall that faced the lower gallery, now ceilingless too. These had been the rooms of the female patients. At the edge of the second-level terrace, by counting along, I determined the one that for three decades had served as home to Peg Nicholson. East of Peg's room on that level, farther back, I could see half the upper central hall. From where I stood, it appeared one could take the main staircase from the hall outside my still-extant office and, were the barred door at the top of the west side not chained shut with padlocks that not even Mr. Hunnicut had keys for, step out onto what was now a rubble-strewed open balcony, to a prospect of the City and Westminster to rival—or so it looked from here—the one from the dome of St. Paul's.

It's interesting to stand before a part-demolished building of any kind—not just a prison or madhouse—and look up at its drab or garish-painted or -papered compartments exposed in cross-section to merciless daylight and know that the only way its residents could have tolerated such vile, cramped spaces was they were already dwelling deeper, inside the compartments of their own thoughts. And know that only the human animal, that is blessed and cursed with a brain strong enough to discover freedom in phantasms of hope, dream, and memory, can find comfort in such narrow miserable pens as most people in cities must spend the majority of their lives inside.

I rounded the corner and continued south. No Bethlem to see from Moorgate: No building remained at that end, and if it did, no barred panels entertained pedestrians along there, only a tattered chaos of flyers and scrawled desecrations of a higher wall.

At London Wall I turned east and started down the building along its rear side, or what remained of it. At my left hand, once I passed the corner entrance (unused since before my time), was the wall itself of London Wall, which, though in places the rag-stone has crumbled sufficiently to host shrubbery, still rises a good eight feet above the pavement, and being eight feet thick has had erected on top of it at the far side, beyond more bushes growing high-up there, another, tessellated wall, the Bethlem wall proper, and beyond that, across a narrow yard, would be the building itself, except that for half this walk you now saw nothing above the Bethlem wall but northern sky, the building gone, and you saw the Bethlem wall—I mean more than its parti-glazed, stone-coped battlements—only if you walked at sufficient distance from the first to risk being trampled by a gig in the street.

But once you came as far east as the part of the building still standing, there it was, hulking above you the same soot-blackened pile it always was. And yet though objects of human significance (a weathered blanket, a windmill on a stick, a dead bouquet, a glove with the thumb torn out) dangled from the window ledges; though you knew there were still men in there, because the jingling of their chains and their constant coughing had woke you early enough to get you out here before sunrise; and though you'd just passed the window of James Matthews, Emperor of the Universe, which you knew by the shape of its broken glazing and the cant of its shutter—despite all these signs of human habitation, the building emanated pure desolation. This was because public faith in it had been withdrawn months ago, for deposit at St. George's Fields. Also, its former inhabitants, having lived so long inside, departed as its epitomes, and so carted off its existence as they went, leaving behind a gutted shell. But look! Here comes a medical officer of the place now, in final orbit before he follows the rest out, the last epitome of an institution that every single soul that ever knew it, whether in his right mind or out, would sooner had never existed at all.

Now I'd come as far as opposite the convalescents' airing grounds, or so we used to call them. A huddled rubbish-strewn pen without even a bench to sit on. After that I was opposite where the men's airing grounds used to be before they tore down half the east wing along with my house and office, the infirmary, the Dead House, and laundry building. Again I could see the north sky, and my trip was shorter than it once would have been. I made the turn north then left into the Common Passage and so back to the gates.

Another grapple with keys and locks, curse Hunnicut to Hell, and safe inside once more.

OLD CORRUPTION

Monday I suffered my last time on the stand.

The one way I earned the esteem of just about every lunatic I met with in twenty years was the perfect discipline of myself. My assault on Matthews told me what Sarah used to: It was also how I distinguished myself from them. My intention Monday was to float up there the soul of equanimity, but though I could tell myself my collapse was a healing catharsis, it was also a sign of things to come. For soon as I opened my mouth in answer to a perfunctory and-what-are-your-duties-at-Bethlem-again? question, I could feel the clench in my jaw that told me the emotion ran too deep for containment even here.

When the real questions started, no more than on my previous four excursions to the stand did any concern Matthews. But this was too much like readers presuming to know the diarist from his diary, and for me it was easy to go from anxiety about being asked anything about Matthews to outrage at being asked nothing. Now I think—as Jerdan had hinted and Matthews knew it would be—this was my own conscience at work. For though I communicated every outward sign of an amiable attitude, I self-destructingly neglected to provide the sentiments appropriate to it, characterizing Bryan Crowther, for example, as when not drunk so insane as to require a strait-waistcoat, which though true (and who doesn't now and then need a little strait-waistcoat time? ha ha) must have sounded chilling when delivered as a casual comment on a nineteen-year-colleague just lowered into the ground. This impression of icy distance (though inside I was anything but cool) I confirmed by another, not-so-casual statement I made when asked what general agreement there existed among the Bethlem faculty as to the advantage of emetics in cases of insanity.

Having already stated that I never believed in vomits but was obliged to administer them because Monro said I must (though he didn't believe in them either but before this committee pretended he did), and heartily sick and tired of being made to appear negligent in matters I had no say in when I was the only

one who ever did anything, and sick and tired too of a line of questioning designed to bugger me coming and going, for if I admitted I gave medicine then
it must be to punish not cure, but if a patient wasn't drenched in it then he must
be sorely neglected, I replied as follows: "I confess, gentlemen, I am so much
regulated by my own experience that I have not been disposed to listen to
those who have less of it than myself."

This admission was no less true than my unfortunate characterization of
Crowther in his last days, but the collective gawp it received gave me plenty of
time to wonder what in God's name I thought I was doing. Feebly I added, "I
hope, gentlemen, you will excuse the appearance of vanity in that answer."

Would it were only vanity's appearance.

But at least this was their cue to ask me, finally, about Matthews.

Their first question: "How often and for what periods was he shackled?"

Matthews, I wearily acknowledged, was on his arrival handcuffed. Later, after a scuffle with a keeper, he was briefly leg-ironed. In his case, I added, shackling was hardly the issue. Once it achieved its end—to curb his violence and
break the pride that at first had him thinking he was too good to associate with
other patients—he was so far from a violent patient as to be a positive peace-
maker about the place, the one to whom all parties, whether employee or lunatic, made cases for redress.

By this account, I was seen as attempting to draw a veil over my own cruel-
ties. Why was he put in irons at all if he was innately peaceful?

"While shackling a lunatic may at times be essential," I patiently explained,
"the committee must understand there is an absolute difference between that
and severity of ordinary discipline in any hospital devoted to care of the mad."

This answer, whether they understood it or no, they didn't much like.

Several questions then addressed other aspects of Matthews' treatment,
such as the rumour he was not allowed the warmth of a fire during his enchain-
ment, and that's what accounted for the abscess in his back.

To this I replied that someone's facts must be amiss, for the abscess devel-
oped much later, probably as a result of Matthews' constant stooping and digging in all weather in the plot of garden I allowed him. That this too failed to
convince them was confirmed when they didn't bother even to cross-examine.
I then—too insolently, I fear—volunteered the reminder that no matter what
anybody said, even at St. George's Fields a certain amount of restraint would
continue necessary, and if not restraint then depletory medicines and treatments of various kinds, at least until the day a cure for madness is found. But
(just to rub it in) there was no reason whatsoever to assume restraint and de-
pletion incompatible with every kindness and humanity. Meanwhile, my question for them was, "Why this condescension to him as an innocent, helpless,
unwitting victim of an evil establishment when his journal has been your authoritative guide to the place for six weeks?"

By their annoyed looks, they found this presuming. But it inspired one of

them to ask how my *Illustrations of Madness* could be such a sympathetic account of Matthews' delusions, when its purpose was to characterize him as a
senseless lunatic. Why such loving care to so uncaring an end?

I said I didn't understand the question. I didn't see my *Illustrations* as a loving account, only an honest and accurate one.

"But surely, sir, one designed to defend the decision of the examining committee that he was wholly unfit to be released?"

"No, I simply set forth his delusions and said the reader must exercise his
own judgment of them."

Here Rose, chairman of the proceedings, a decent old man who knew the
salient facts of Matthews' case, spoke up. "Sir, you went further. In your book
you explicitly defend the governors' decision not to 'liberate a mischievous lunatic to disturb the good order and peace of society.' That's your conclusion.
Mr. Matthews' illness has resulted in a dangerous loss of agency. I have your
last page open in front of me."

I was sweating now. Could I really have said it so baldly? Could I really have
forgot I had?

"I was only defending the governors' decision, your Honour, as it was my
duty—"

"Yes, yes, but what did you yourself believe, Mr. Haslam?"

"Privately, your Honour?"

"If you wish. Or as apothecary to Bethlem Hospital, the place where you indicate you wrote your preface. I hope he holds the same view as yourself."

This was too close to home. My face was burning with an emotion lately familiar, and more than shame. "Sir, I believed then, and still believe, that
Matthews is a lunatic. My purpose in writing the *Illustrations* was to publish an
answer to those who, by claiming he was not, had cast aspersions upon Bethlem and the judgment of its governors and medical officers."

"To support, in other words, as you say here—" indicating my book—"the
governors in having him kept. I don't need to remind you, Mr. Haslam, the
purpose of a writ of habeas corpus is to seek the release of the one detained."

"The writ had already been rejected, your Honour. It was evident at the time
there was no longer any chance of Matthews' release." Here I thanked God I'd
earlier restrained myself from blurting to this committee the confusing circumstance of my late resolution to support Matthews' transfer to a private madhouse. "My purpose in writing the *Illustrations* was to defend Bethlem against
unfair charges by making the argument that a lunatic remains a lunatic whether
he's declared one or not."

"And this you sought to do by retailing the dangerous delusions of a madman."

"More laughable and pathetic, I would say, your Honour, than
dangerous—"

"Mr. Haslam, your superior, Dr. Monro, is on record as saying he's heard

Mr. Matthews utter too many threats against the royal family for him to say in conscience he should ever be at liberty. Does he still make these threats?"

"When convinced he's unacknowledged sovereign of the universe, he still makes them, your Honour, yes he does."

"Then he does remain incurably insane, in your view?"

"Yes, though perhaps not so dangerous as formerly."

"Unless, it would seem, to the royal family—"

Was Matthews ever dangerous to anyone? I had sat by and said nothing when Monro declared it. I myself had said and writ that he was.

"The example of Mr. Hadfield must come to mind," Rose prompted me, almost kindly, when I was slow to respond.

"Matthews, your Honour, is not like Hadfield."

"No? How not?"

"Matthews is a man of wit and discernment. Hadfield is not."

"But isn't your professional conviction well known, Mr. Haslam, that madness is madness? That lunatics may be quieter at some times than others, but this doesn't mean they're sometimes sane, too many being adept at putting aside, or obscuring, delusional thinking should the situation require it, the lucid interval being, as you have argued so persuasively in your published work, a much misunderstood concept? How predictable can Mr. Matthews' actions be when his sentiments conform at times with Mr. Hadfield's, and Mr. Hadfield is known to have fired a pistol at the King?"

Rose allowed me time to reply to this eminently sensible query, but what could I say that would not be heard as outright self-contradiction? More than this, the question reminded me that my failing Matthews and my betrayal of him were not unrelated to my history of listening to him as a man of sense when he sounded like one and as a lunatic when he didn't or grew obstreperous. And sitting there with the good Justice Mr. Rose awaiting my answer, I considered how you can think of yourself as a certain sort of person yet watch yourself behave as quite another; and how easy it is that disjunction becomes simply how things are with you, and your failure to reconcile that contradiction, whenever it noses its way to awareness, you tell yourself is only the small, private price you must pay awhile longer yet if you would achieve such-and-such worthy end. And so, like everybody else, at the same time as you inwardly congratulate yourself on your goodness and work toward your admirable goal, you silently endure a nagging fissure in your soul and go on wreaking blind havoc in everything you do.

I was thinking this or something like it when an M.P. named McManus rescued me from further hot-eared silence by leaping up to pursue a new line of questioning:

"Do you not think, Mr. Haslam, that Mr. Matthews' delusions of persecution are a direct result of his detention in Bethlem?"

Not being as interested in my humiliation by Rose as I was, the committee had been for some minutes stifling yawns and sneaking peeks at their watches.

Now they shot to attention with gratified looks that said, *Why, that's exactly what I was thinking.*

By their familiarity with Matthews' journal it had dawned on them that the gang was none other than us—his gaolers—under different names. More than this: Though they had no idea what his delusions were before he was with us, they assumed that once his gaolers were taken away, his delusions would follow. In their minds, the fact he was in at all was the alpha and omega of his mental suffering.

"An ingenious speculation," I replied, smiling through gritted teeth, "though it would seem to assume he arrived amongst us sane. But perhaps a more pertinent question in the circumstances, sir, would be why the Government's wanted him in."

Were McManus a dog he'd be a border collie. His head appeared freshly extracted from an instrument designed to foreshorten and depilate canine heads to pass them for human. As his attention readjusted to me, you could almost hear a whirring from the undersized braincase. "The question I already did ask, Mr. Haslam, was why the medical officers haven't let him go."

"We were not allowed to."

"As you've just informed us." Again he looked to his notes.

"And why not?"

Wanly he looked up. "Mr. Haslam, the procedure here is, we ask the questions, you answer 'em."

General laughter.

"Ho, ho, ho," I said. "Why haven't we let Matthews go?"

"Well, sir, I confess the only reason I know of is his habeas corpus undertaking was refused by the Court. Is there something you now wish to add to that information?"

My mouth opened and then it closed. As Matthews would have reminded me, The Schoolmaster couldn't do what he couldn't do.

Here, a little wearily, Justice Rose said, "Mr. Haslam, if you have nothing to add to your statement, would you mind if Mr. McManus went on with his questions?"

Now was my chance to respond that the issue was not whether Matthews should be in but why he was in. What came out instead, at first quietly, was my own anger.

"The human mind, your Honour, is so intriguing unto itself, it's perfectly understandable when unmedical persons believe they can comprehend it in a state of derangement."

"This committee, Mr. Haslam," Rose shot back impatiently, "does not presume to comprehend derangement but only to inquire into the state of the madhouses."

"If you'd improve the madhouses," I answered, suddenly too furious to restrain myself, "then de-license the private ones forthwith as too devoted to hiding madness away. Give the government houses funding sufficient to keep lunatics long enough to win a chance of remission. Let them open their doors so the public can see how the money's spent, and so they never forget the face of madness and with it the fact that medicine, having scant understanding of the brain and none whatsoever how disease affects thinking, has come up with innumerable treatments but as yet no cure, no matter how hopeful religion seeks to make an ignorant public or how soothing the placebos tossed out by mountebank doctors, politicians, senators, magistrates, men of business, and other interested zealots of reformation."

Gasps.

"Surely, sir," said a voice trembling with indignation, "you don't suggest we return to the barbarous days when people flocked to Bethlem as to the animals at the Tower?"

"People are bedlam, sir, and bedlam people, however cleverly you conceal the resemblance. Along with the three great amusements of human life—war, politics, and the vagaries of the human heart—the mad are our living reminders of this elementary fact. When they're not too annoying and terrifying we keep them at home. When they are, we lodge them in hospitals, in private madhouses, in prisons, or let them roam the streets. But let's not build our walls so high against them we forget they're ourselves merely too distressed by their as yet incurable affliction to be sociable. I repeat: *incurable affliction*. Refuse that kinship, sir, and I wouldn't trust you to know your own face in the mirror."

"Mr. Haslam," someone else put in, "surely you're not telling us there's no appreciable difference between a healthy mind and one that's not?"

"Have you ever examined a human brain, sir?"

"Pickled in a jar, yes I have. What of it?"

"Did you notice how convoluted it was? How heterogeneous? If you did, I wonder you're not as astonished as I am when a human being shows the faintest glimmer of rationality."

"Aren't you overstating your case, sir?" someone else ventured.

"Not in the least. Isn't everybody always a little bit sick? I myself have not known any person completely healthy in body and certainly never one perfectly sound in mind. For I must agree with Dr. Johnson that to speak with exactness, no human mind is in its right state."

Silence while they took this in. So did I, for it was the first time I knew I believed anything quite like it. Or was anywhere near saying it. There's a line between what everybody knows and what can be said, and once you cross it, the articulation of things sounds very different from how they looked and felt in the quiet of your own thoughts. Also, it seems, you have no brake.

"There's only one sound mind," I continued, "and that's God's—at least so I'm assured by certain eminent divines. Which only goes to show what a marvel disembodiment is and how little surprised we should be to find Mystery still rules the affairs of flesh and blood."

Another stunned silence, the kind people slip into as they witness a unique and absolute act. A Hindoo could set himself on fire in the street and they would not be more fascinated.

Still, though this one seemed to, no moment lasts forever, and we were some minutes into the lunch hour. Rose asking for a motion of adjournment, it was swiftly provided and seconded, the committee scrabbling up their papers and scooting from the room as quick as any mob of students from a lecture hall. In the breeze of their exodus, The Schoolmaster's trappings streamed and fluttered upon his person like the rags of a man who'd either just been flayed in his clothes or had a lunatic's unfortunate habit of rending them himself, it was difficult to know which.

SUBSEQUENCE

And yet, and yet. At the governors' annual banquet on St. Matthew's Day, held that year for the first time in the open air of St. George's Fields, Monro greeted me as chattily as if he'd never betrayed me, would never dream of slipping a shiv into my back, telling me about his brain-clap to do a painting of the new building and make a gift of it to the governors.

"Better a likeness of the old," I told him. "It's the one disappearing."

This had not occurred to him, but he didn't like it. "I'd wager, Johnny," he replied, speaking ventriloquist-style as he scanned the crowd, "this lot's dead keen to put the old place behind them."

"Then do it for the patients and staff of the new. Keep us in mind who we are and what we come from."

"Now, now, man," he muttered, still scanning. "Play the game." I'd have said something bitter to this had he not immediately stretched out his arms and strode across me with a great false shout of delight at someone who when he saw who it was gave a start of unbridled contempt.

Not long after, a toast was offered to my health by an alderman named Atkins, who I never saw before, congratulating me on the honest rigour I'd showed in my testimony. But this gesture failing to be followed by three cheers or calls for a speech, I could only raise my glass and return a tremulous smile. Fortunately, everybody immediately drank, as if to forget, and I sank down once more invisible. Still, for the record: The only note heard all afternoon from that crowd of clerks and businessmen was sober self-congratulation, with now and then a muffled dirty guffaw of triumph.

In October, a report issued by the Court of Governors of Bridewell and Bethlem roundly declared Monro and me innocent of any wrongdoing. Vindication, it would seem, and clear sailing once more—until this winter past, when the parliamentary committee published their own report, of which, on Wakefield's instruction, a complimentary copy was posted to every Bethlem governor. Though this other report contained not a single item of information the governors didn't already know, its authors were explicit in their advice it be read through with care before the April election of the medical officers. To further assist our employers in their deliberations, Wakefield kept up a barrage against us in the press, declaring in the *Examiner,* for example, that by our testimony Monro and I were bold-faced deceivers who must be toppled from our high perches and stripped of any honours we'd accrued by our inveterate scheming. And just to make sure, Rose himself is said to have wrote to the governors intimating he didn't want us re-elected.

Needless to say, our governor champions cowardly backed down, voting to postpone our re-election until Monro and I could report to them on the testimony we'd already given. In this way they forced us, as in a nightmare, to become our own assassins, as we attempted to defend ourselves against the absence of any specific charge.

In our joint submission we repeated our justifications concerning Norris and Matthews and generally defended our behaviour and practices, with frequent reminders to our readers that they had already absolved us.

My oral version of an answer the committee greeted with considerable applause, which might have promised a prosperous issue. But since I was in the present humiliating situation subsequent to being toasted by these self-same bastards, I was not deluded. This was all rope-jumping to satisfy no one. Even Monro, by his doleful looks, understood we were dead. Being a half-wit, he was half right. At a special meeting on the 15th of May, the Court of Governors cravenly reversed their verdict by voting overwhelmingly not to re-elect us. For Monro this is no great financial setback, since he never made more than a hundred pounds per year from his Bethlem post and still has his thriving Hackney madhouse, plus a few others, to keep him in paintbrushes. Even so, to soften the blow for him at the same time as ensure the dynasty that spawned him sleeps on, last week the governors elected his idiot son Edward co-physician of Bethlem.

Her apothecary has received harsher treatment. Though Poynder (who in his detached way nimbly escaped prosecution) did, as treasurer of the Court of Governors, the decent thing of moving I be granted a pension of two hundred pounds *per annum,* his motion, after it found a reluctant seconder, was grimly defeated. Upon a begging application from me, a subscription list was undertook for the relief of me and my aged father, but to date no fist-fights have broke out to be first in line to sign. A keeper like the idle, skulking scoundrel Rodbird, a casualty of gin and paralysis, basks in the sunshine of a valetudinary pension, while the apothecary, who served the place in a manner that bolstered its reputation worldwide, gets nothing. Finally, to crown my humiliation most exemplarily, at the same time as they awarded Edward Monro the sinecure of co-physician, the man we hired only last year as our new steward, the insufferable Mr. Wallet, was appointed apothecary of Bethlem.

So here I sit in the solitude of my Islington study and write everything down. This house is come into the market, and at the price the agent's asking (for a rapid sale) I won't be sitting here long. Neither will the books on these shelves. First thing Monday fortnight, my entire library goes on the block. The Leigh and Sotheby's buyer tells me catalogues containing more than a thousand items can take three days to get through. And then there's my mahogany bookcase, with drawers and wardrobe and mahogany ladder. A lucrative week? We shall see. "Works of exceptional taste and learning" they're calling them. I don't know why, they're only what any educated man of medicine should have, with here and there something bizarre and unaccountable, viz., *A Parliamentary Inquiry into Mad-houses 1815*, or *A Curious Collection of Books Hand-printed in Black Letter, undated*.

So what now for John Haslam? Rented rooms closer to town, where the opportunities reside. A package to be made up of my books, with a cover letter and résumé of my achievements in the field, for posting to Marischall College, Aberdeen, whence in due course should arrive a medical degree. That way I can practise in London. It's unlikely the College of Physicians will embrace me, but I could scrape by on a dozen patients of modest means if they're sufficiently chronic or hypochondriacal, and for so few there's no need to lick arse-holes in Warwick Lane. At the Medical Society, at least, I have a few friends. If I ever have fifty pounds to rub together, I can stand for the board of St. Bart's, or even St. Luke's. I can always do duty as an expert witness, which I'm told I have a flair for, and the pay, though sporadic, is good. I have more than one book left in me. Somebody needs to clarify the issue of restraint of lunatics, and while they're at it say something on behalf of the keepers. And of course I'll champion public mad-doctors, who are the ones with medical training. After that, if time still weighs heavy on my hands, perhaps I shall take up Jerdan's offer and scribble for his *London Gazette*.

Who says a man can't start over at fifty-two? One door closes, another opens. Isn't that how it works, out in the world? The harder part will be knowing who John Haslam is, now he's been stripped of The Schoolmaster. It's an end James Matthews devoutly wished, but I think he preferred I do it by choice. Perhaps I'd have got around to it, given time enough—wasn't I beginning to feel the pricks? Mad Bess piles on rags as she goes, but Mad Tom strips down till he's begging naked. She knows who she don't want to be; he needs to remember who he is. When he wasn't raving, Matthews knew who Matthews was, and he was in Bethlem. So then will Haslam know Haslam now Haslam's out. Why else go down with the champion of that weird brotherhood?

MARGARET MATTHEWS

1818

JIM

Mr. Matt Lewis had not long returned to England for his first visit when I began to think it was time Jim and I went home too. Though in early adolescence Jim had found it sometimes difficult to conceal his impatience with me and my fears, as he grew in maturity, so he did in compassion. During those months of Mr. Lewis's absence, he behaved as loving with me almost as he used to when a child. Sometimes we'd eat a meal just the two of us, and when clearing the table he'd make a gentle claw of his free hand and scritch my cropt head as he passed. From a slight, fair youth at fourteen and fifteen, by eighteen he was sun-darkened and strapping: the handsomest, kindest, most thoughtful young man I ever knew. But now he was done with what schooling Jamaica could offer and was chafing to see the world. I resolved that as soon as Mr. Lewis got back we would leave.

I should not have waited. Six weeks before Mr. Lewis's return, Jim received a nick on his ankle while overseeing a crew of our Negroes burning cane trash. By next morning the infection was virulent and by the morning after that he didn't know me or where he was. Sometimes the fever abated, and he'd grow calm and seeming lucid and tell me how much he loved me and I must find his father and he'd join us as soon as he was feeling more himself. Holding the compress to his brow, I assured him I would never leave him, while silently I cursed I had ever brought my precious child to a place where a light scratch could reduce hale youth to this. This and worse. In the tropics it's a short step from the sick-chamber to the grave. Three days after Jim received the scratch he died.

With my beloved young man gone, my Jamaica world fell apart. I was now unfamilied in Hell, and but for the kindness of my friends, I might have taken my own life, out of despair for Jamie and to be with Jim. It was Christabelle who prepared the body in the Negro way, the best in those latitudes. By the day of the funeral—which owing to the heat was inside twenty-four hours—I hadn't slept for so long I was in an automaton state, but at the sight of my boy's coffin descending into the dry earth, were it not for black hands restraining me, I would have thrown myself after it. Those same hands guided me to bed, where I was made to drink a potion that put me to sleep for two days. I awoke knowing I must either find my husband or discover what his fate had been.

When Mr. Lewis returned from England, he was devastated to hear of Jim's death. After we wept together, he insisted we pray, in the middle of the floor, side by side, which we did, and when our knees were bruised from praying, we wept some more. I don't know if Jim's death put a pall on the place for him as it did for me, one that wouldn't lift, but before two months passed, he announced his intention of returning to England.

This time I begged him to take me with him. At first he said he couldn't possibly. With himself not there he needed me on the place to ensure the new book-keeper didn't revert to the cart-whip. He vowed he'd personally locate my husband and write me the same day. But seeing my unhappy expression, he immediately reversed himself, adding, but if I truly felt I must speak to my husband in person, then I could come with him, but I must promise to return to Jamaica the next time he did. And bring Jamie with me, if I wanted; he would enter him on the payroll. And if it happened while in Jamaica my husband required time in an asylum, since the island had no madhouses, either because everybody was so sedate or so crazy, then he would build one at Cornwall.

Yet though before Jim's death I by no means hated our Jamaica life and loved, I think, the Negroes as much as he and Mr. Lewis did, I realized I could promise my employer nothing until I had either laid eyes on my poor dear husband or knew for certain I never would again. The fact, I assured him, I'd had no answers to my letters did not mean he'd not received them or not written. And since Jim's death I had not written him, for fear of the desolating effect of the news. But now I knew I must tell him soon and in person, before my very silence—assuming, that is, he'd been receiving my letters—had a desolating effect.

"In that case, my dear," Mr. Lewis said, sighing but smiling too, "and seeing you're already hard at work growing out your hair, I absolutely insist you come with me."

And so on the first of May—all Cornwall lining the driveway to wave bandannas and kerchiefs, my three friends joking and weeping and godspeeding us half the way—following twelve oxen straining at a train of four baggage carts accompanied by six Negroes walking two on each side and two behind, and after it Tita in a covered gig to keep his gimlet-eye on things, we rode together in Mr. Lewis's curricle the five miles to Savannah la Mar. On the way, he said he only hoped his future dealings with white people would bring him half so much gratitude, affection, and good will as he'd experienced from his Cornwall Negroes. Their kindness had operated on him, he said, like sunshine. Later that same afternoon we boarded the cutter for Black River Bay, a choppy ride of several hours east along that dreary mangrove coast. Two days after, on board the *Sir Godfrey Webster,* a vessel already six hundred tons before it took on Mr. Lewis's baggage, we weighed anchor for England.

On his previous trip home the year before, Mr. Lewis had made inquiries after Jamie but got only far enough to understand that the whereabouts, or fate, of my husband would take time to determine. Old Bethlem was gone, razed, vanished; level ground, camped in by Gipsies. No one he spoke to at New Bethlem had heard of my husband. None of the old staff I'd told him of—Haslam, Alavoine, Crowther, Bulteel, White, Rodbird—still held their positions. Haslam had been dismissed in disgrace. (While dismissal was something like what he deserved, I don't know about *disgrace* and must say I felt for him.) Crowther, Alavoine, Bulteel, and White were all dead, Rodbird reportedly a living corpse. There was a Monro but not the same one. A son, by the sound of it: He was expected at any moment but never appeared. To Mr. Lewis's annoyance, the apothecary, a beggar-on-horseback named Wallet, refused him access to the incurable wing, though just about any of the older, lucid residents there would have known if Jamie was among them, and if he wasn't, where he had gone.

"Did you speak to the clerk, Mr. Poynder?" I had asked Mr. Lewis one morning at Cornwall when he kindly invited me to join him for coffee on the piazza.

"No. He was another one Mr. Wallet didn't want disturbed. I never got past the servants' hall, where a divine service was underway—on a Friday, if you can believe it. The experience was too bizarre: conferring in whispers with the insufferable Wallet in the corner of a room full of lunatic-custodians on their knees in prayer. It told me I've been away from London too much. A new age has dawned in my absence and needs me there to disorganize it."

"As clerk of the place, Poynder would know if Jamie was at New Bethlem or what happened to him. I'm surprised Mr. Wallet didn't—"

"Next time I'll have Tita strangle Mr. Wallet and we'll proceed from there."

Mr. Lewis left New Bethlem in a fury. But his father had worked under the 1st Earl of Liverpool when his Lordship was secretary of war and had been a friend of his, and Mr. Lewis himself had served six years as M.P. for Hindon, so he was well positioned to make inquiries in government. But the only person who seemed to recognize Jamie's name was Liverpool's son, the 2nd Earl, already (and still, for that matter) Prime Minister, and he assured him he had no distinct knowledge of the case. But then, strangely, his Lordship added, "These republican lunatics were thick on the ground—"

"Oh—" Mr. Lewis said, acting the innocent. "Was he a republican? I didn't know that."

It seemed Liverpool knew something he wasn't admitting to.

As he sipped at his coffee, Mr. Lewis regretted having told me all this only to aggravate my fears. To console me, he offered a paean of praise of the glorious modern hospital Jamie was probably ensconced in, adding it must be the extraordinary increase of madness in recent years that would preclude so vast a place keeping track of every last resident.

But I knew that if the apothecary didn't recognize the name, then Jamie was gone before that one's tenure began (whenever that was). And I knew that if the Prime Minister had something to hide about Jamie, then his life had not ceased to be in danger. So the question was, If not dead then gone where?

How dearly I longed to see my dear husband. Acquaintance with the mind of Mr. Lewis had me pining afresh for that quality in Jamie that I constantly missed in missing him, a quality that before Mr. Lewis burst on our Jamaica life, I'd been watching in wonder shine brighter and brighter in Jim as he grew to be a man. I mean the lucid sympathy of intelligence that emanated from these people like rays from the sun. But with the unbearable loss of Jim combining so soon with renewed sight of a comparable intelligence in Matt Lewis, I all of a sudden missed Jamie so much that when my employer said he was returning once more to England, I absolutely must go with him.

Like Jamie's, Matt Lewis's intelligence was prone to eclipses, for he was apt to grow tedious on the subject of himself, and though a true-hearted man and genuinely brilliant, he could be as alarming a bore sane as Jamie was raving. Perhaps there was madness in Matt Lewis too. Perhaps in an imperfect world you don't find intelligence at its keenest pitch without some touch of it. Perhaps there needs a certain pressure, heating the thoughts until they glow, and glowing ignite yours and by that sympathy show you more than you could ever see on your own, but then the brilliance grows too hot, fever sets in, all *common* sense is lost, and that connexion is betrayed.

It might indeed be thought a taste for intelligence so pure and fierce as to resemble mindsight has itself something foolhardy if not mad in it, and when you mix madness with that intelligence, then an ordinary mortal might seem an Icarus, venturing too near the burning brightness. But for myself, I've too often seen to the bottom of the vessel to answer to such pride. But I flatter myself I possess imagination, for I have talent for putting myself in others' shoes. And I do have an eye for intelligence. Jamie, Jim, and Matt Lewis: those (with my dear mother's) are the best faces humanity has ever showed me, and theirs the best eyes I ever looked at humanity through.

HOME

The winds not being in our favour, we headed first for what's called the Gulf of Florida passage, which though not the shortest route, is said the most dependable. Those early days of the voyage, Mr. Lewis appeared in excellent spirits. If, as he liked to say, people claimed he'd gone out to Jamaica because he'd exhausted his welcome in England, Scotland, and on the Continent, he showed no apprehension to be returning home. Tita set up his master's battered piano (bound with brass straps for travel) in a widening of the passageway outside his cabin, and Mr. Lewis sat at it for hours, pounding out impromptu melodies. At meals he insisted I sit on his right hand, joking we were husband and wife, but though he was more familiar than was decent with the two ladies at our table, it was the young sailors who received the more rigorous discernment of his eye. Altogether though, it surprised me how untalkative he was at meals for so generally vivacious a chatterbox. But when he did speak it was in a drawling voice that won every heart it didn't grate on. With his pop-eyes, slouching posture, and habit of licking his little finger and drawing it slowly across his eyebrow as he delivered his sallies, he was the sort of gargoyle a person tends to glance at expectantly, ready to laugh, even if he went whole meals only ogling you.

In light of what came next, those silences now seem dreadful portents. In the second week of the voyage Mr. Lewis began to hæmorrhage from the nose and to complain of stabbing pains in his eye sockets. About the same time, he stopped taking nourishment. Mealtimes found him pacing the deck, shrilly declaiming German and Italian poetry with violent chopping motions of his stubby arms. On the 10th of May, against Tita's and my objections, he gave himself an emetic, which weakened him at the very time he needed all his strength. By then poor Tita was as beside himself as I was. Upon his return in April from Hordley, his other Jamaica estate, Mr. Lewis had suffered what was likely a bout of yellow fever. While Tita and I feared this could be a recurrence,

Mr. Lewis knew it was. One day he called me to him to tell me not to worry, he'd seen to it I'd be well provided for.

This was not what I needed to hear.

"Now, now, Margaret. No blubbering. You must convert each of those pagan little tears into a prayer for me."

But as losing Jim had taught me, prayers, if they work at all, work as comforts not destiny-contrivers. And on the 16th, while propped against pillows reading his beloved Goethe, after taking a minute to write on Tita's hat a memorandum ensuring Tita received his wages, the hat still on Tita's head, Tita sobbing at his breast, he died.

Having told the captain what he'd often told me, "that it was a matter of perfect indifference to him what became of his ugly little husk," Mr. Lewis would have been amused to see so celebrated a life tipped overboard in a hasty coffin wrapped in a sheet loaded with weights, and would have clapped his hands in delight when, on impact with the water, the weights slipped free of the sheet and the bare coffin bobbed to the surface, so the last we saw of his little box it was floating back to Jamaica.

The remainder of the voyage we passed either becalmed in stifling heat or tossed about so violently there was no good reason we didn't founder a thousand times. As for me, I would not have struggled long. Unsonned, unemployered, and by all evidence unhusbanded, what was left for me in this world? But in the third week of July we did reach Gravesend, a fog-world of shouts and splashes and clanks and creaks of ghost-ships, of which there must have been a good hundred in that grey obscurity. There, leaving Tita with letters of condolence for Mr. Lewis's sisters, I descended planking to the wharf to arrange conveyance of my luggage to town. I then boarded a carriage for New Bethlem.

Was the Greenwich Road that morning as unusually busy as it seemed? Were seven years of rural Jamaica enough to make an English port road seem perfectly mobbed when it wasn't? Yet truly everybody really was on the go, exchanging quips and looks, porters and servants weaving in and out— But going whither? Come whence? Not all fresh off boats, surely? How to explain such energy? What drove these people? Sheer life-force? English liberty? Or were these only wide-eyed Jamaica questions, where life is easy-does-it and you have two kinds of inhabitants: lumbering, sun-burned whites and bone-thin, slow-moving blacks?

How different a world Jamaica is from England! I don't mean the people, who are who they are, or the countryside, which in its own way is as green and lovely, I mean the towns. Savannah la Mar is shabby and dirty, yes, but more than that, fugitive, a one-street-to-the-water settlement of booths and lean-to's, not one of them older than the sunny morning forty years ago an earthquake off-shore brought the sea a mile inland to a depth of ten feet. And that was it for then for Savannah la Mar. Today the residents of the island (the Spanish having bid farewell to the native Indians as warmly as they could hack them down) are mainly Europeans and Africans, conquerors and slaves and their multicoloured descendants. With a population entirely from elsewhere and the governor a military puppet on strings pulled from Westminster, the place itself counts for less with its inhabitants than the world they've left behind. Whole-hearted history doesn't happen there.

But newly back in England (so my reflections continued as we came into the more brick-built outskirts of London), you catch a glimpse of what it means to live not in the shadow of exile or cataclysm but of Time. Which is to say, you live in an old country, where it's not disaster or dislocation around the next cor-ner but History, not here to sweep everything away but to say, *You are what you are and will dwell forever in the shadow of this.* And you find yourself thinking perhaps more than you should about that queer fellow Robinson Crusoe and those like him, who escaped to become hollow-eyed, lank-haired kings of their own remote and solitary destinies.

Now I remembered it was not so far from here I had caught sight of my can-nibal sailor, whom John Haslam later reminded me of. And though that was now nearly half a century ago, I still think of my cannibal (if that's what he was) when I think of solitary kings. I suppose if Crusoe, Selkirk, or another ship-wrecked hermit ever ate human flesh, he'd think twice before he told his gentle reader. That he prevailed is the main thing and what most people want to hear about: You can never tell when knowing how he did it could come in handy. Which isn't to say a recourse so extreme as eating humans would fail to catch their interest or they'd not insert a cannibal element if it seemed missing, only that they'd have no solace to offer a prodigal who'd strayed so far from every-thing civilized. All he'd have on his return would be a feeling of specialness in society's eyes, a feeling not likely unmixed if he'd fed on humans. But what if he could know there was someone here who had sympathy enough to under-stand and understanding forgive and not only forgive but forgiving let him know it? What for our cannibal then?

At last we came out of Great Surrey Street into the Lambeth Road, and where it meets St. George's Road, under a solar disk the colour of soot-streaked copper, I saw it: the massive columns of its portico rising above towering brick walls: New Bethlem. As it loomed before me, I experienced, instead of relief to imagine my husband a resident of such a fine modern accommodation, the re-turn of every sensation of doom from twenty years before when approaching Moorfields with the knowledge he was inside.

And I remembered my seven years in Jamaica, especially those last months with Jim gone, waking in the sweltering animal-cry dark from a nightmare of diminishing means, my skiff on the infinite seas for home now child-sized and rudderless, the oars mismatched and shrinking. And as I fell back panting in a rope of bedclothes, I knew that whatever else it was, my absence from my husband's side (or as near to it as I could get) was a setback to my greatest hope. I did not those nights blame John Haslam. I had known at the time what I was doing and would have left England without the obstacle of him. There was no question I needed to get away. I could not risk being in the same city with Justina Latimer after what she told me and fearing what she might do. I wasn't fleeing, only doing what was necessary to preserve my child and myself for the sake of my child, and it never occurred to me I'd not return one day to fight again for my husband. But as I peered through the iron gates of New Bethlem, all I could think was, *So here I am, back at this again. And here's the measure of how much ground I have lost by going away: The child I was pregnant with then and took from this country to protect is in the grave, and the good news now will be that my husband's still in there.*

A clean methodical fellow, the porter, a Mr. Hunnicut, was no Bulteel—those days at least were over—but he was no more prepared to let me in. For one thing, it was not a visiting day. For another, he had no Matthews on his list. When I said in that case I must speak direct to Dr. Monro, he informed me I would need an appointment. And how to arrange that? By writing to The Physician, c/o Bethlem Hospital. And he stepped into his porter's lodge for a scrap of paper to write down the address for me. Waiting, I stood gazing through the gates as I'd done so many times before, through different gates, wondering (as ever) what to do now, when who should I see emerge from the great doors and come, stifling a yawn, down the front steps in his old bag-wig and rusty black coat and worsted stockings, but Mr. Poynder.

After handing me the address, the porter turned to unlatch for him. Closer up, the clerk was older, greyer, transformed somehow about the mouth.

As soon as he stepped through, I stepped in front of him. "If you please, Mr. Poynder, the whereabouts of my husband James Matthews—"

A consternating request, it seemed, the way surprise will consternate age. Then he saw who it was and seemed almost to grow frightened, as if I was a ghost. "Margaret Matthews?" he whispered in amazement, a trembling hand at his heart. "Not dead in Jamaica—?"

So he knew my letters had stopped? "Not since May."

"Thank God! I feared— Never mind what I feared!" And he broke into a smile that revealed, in place of the snaggly old velvet chompers, a snow-white palisade.

"Mr. Poynder, your teeth!"

"Boys' teeth." He rapped them with a fingernail. "Battle of Waterloo teeth. English or French, what does it matter once they're all mixed together in shipping barrels?" And he gazed at me as if they'd turned him a boy again, one who'd undressed me too many times in his mind not to be confounded to find me standing so immediately before him, an entire living person. Coming out of it, he said, "You have a friend here—"

"*Jamie—!*"

"—a Mrs. Latimer."

"Justina Latimer? A gallery maid?"

"Oh, heavens no. But perhaps less mad than too beautiful to be hanged, though she did murder a senior minister in government—and even, I have heard, made an attempt on the life of the Duke of York. Last year when she strangled one of our keepers, we moved her to the incurable wing. But what was he doing in the women's quarters at four in the morning? She speaks of you with fondness though now and then seems of the opinion your leaving London without her was a grievous betrayal. A word of advice: If you visit her, watch your back. And The Monk? How's he?"

"The Monk" was the name Mr. Lewis was generally known by in England, from the title of an obscene novel he once wrote. As I told Mr. Poynder of Mr. Lewis's fate, I imagined he must have spoken to Jamie to know about my connexion to Mr. Lewis. So Jamie had received my letters after all and Alavoine kept only his back?

When Mr. Poynder was done his condolences, I said, "Pray sir, is my husband here?"

Holding up a hand, he glanced round to see if Mr. Hunnicut listened, before he edged closer. "A retirement dream of the Poynder complexion, Mrs. Matthews: a stationer's shop in the warm south. As one who's been and knows trade, any advice?"

"Go with a good range of stock. If it's Jamaica you want, set up in Montego Bay (and only there) with cash enough to see you through the first year. The wharf and best houses burned a few years ago, but they're rebuilding. That same year and the one following, the town was struck by two hurricanes and four earthquakes, but all has been calm since. Don't be stubborn about sticking to pens and paper if it turns out nobody can write or be bothered to, and you'll scrape a living well enough. Is my husband here?"

"Montego Bay! Could a man not die in bliss to the music of such a name, even if it be in a hurricane or earthquake?"

I waited.

"Your husband? Not any more." He patted his breast. "As a matter of fact I have here his August cheque—"

"*Alive!*"

"I should think alive—" and he explained how two years before, Jamie'd been removed to a private madhouse. "Bethlem splits his expenses three ways with the government and his family—"

"I'm his family."

He frowned. "Why then, I don't know. Here I've been thinking the third part was Jamaica sugar money—"

"Where is this house?"

"Hackney, by Hoxton—"

"Not Monro's—?"

"No, no. But the only one who knows, though I don't think he's been, and who ensures all three cheques are—"

"Haslam."

"How'd you know? The removal of your husband to Mr. Fox's was the only Crowther initiative he supported in twenty years. Poor Bryan—"

"Where's Haslam now?"

"Lamb's Conduit Street, Number 56—toward the Foundling Hospital end. He's a widower now, I guess you know—"

"No, I don't—only that his wife was ill. I'm going there now and will say my regrets. I can take him the cheque—"

An astonishing offer, from the response. But the Poynder brain was nothing if not limber. From an inside pocket of his coat jacket appeared a narrow yellow envelope on which was written, in the familiar clerkish hand, the precious words, "James Tilly Matthews, c/o Mr. Fox's, London House Private Hospital, Hackney."

"Very kind of you, madam—" he said, bowing. He then encouraged me to visit my friend Mrs. Latimer and while I was at it to feel free to drop in on himself, any time. When I said I would, he seemed to grow teary-eyed, before bidding me farewell with such feverish warmth I almost imagined myself a long-lost Poynder paramour.

Now it was over the river in a soot-flake soup to Lamb's Conduit Street, thinking Jamie's mysterious benefactors must be his friends. But who? Love, time, and a mattress was all any I ever knew could afford to give. Did somebody grow rich in my absence?

My route took me over Blackfriars Bridge and thence north and west, but on an impulse I ordered us first east, to see if No. 84 Leadenhall Street was still standing, or what condition it was in. Our passage was along The Strand through Temple Bar into darker Fleet Street with its ancient timbered houses, then up Ludgate Hill past St. Paul's into the markets of Cheapside, through a city I knew but scarcely recognized. First, it was smokier than ever. Second, it was teeming—Cheapside was one heaving mob—and I had thought the Greenwich Road was busy. Third, every tenth building was draped in scaffolding. The year before we left for Jamaica, Drury Lane burned down, and the year before that, Covent Garden, though it was all but back up by the time we departed. It seemed the reconstruction fever had got out of hand. Everything was undergoing too drastic changes to justify my Jamaica hope that the fears I suffered there, that exactly this kind of runaway transformation must mean Jamie could not but be overlooked or destroyed in my absence, were only the natural anxiety of exile, and really things change slower at home than you imagine when away. Well, not London. Not these days.

Our progress was a crawl. Carriage traffic and all other in Cheapside, Cornhill, and Leadenhall was like nothing I ever experienced. But we did eventually reach No. 84, and there it was, a quiet shabby pocket of familiar time, with Hodge the Bespoke still doing business on the ground floor, thus confirming the assurances of my agent Mr. Samuel. The only difference was new, sky-blue drapes on the first floor and lace curtains on the second, but whether what Mr. Samuel in his letters invariably referred to as the "respectable family of three" who dwelt behind them would soon be slicing open a notice from me depended on whether I would ever live there again with my husband. For one thing I knew: I could not live there again without him. With Jim I could have, but not alone.

When at last we'd completed our arc—a ride that cost me half a week's Jamaica pay—and came to a halt in Lamb's Conduit Street, my coachman seemed to have the wrong address: ground-floor rooms at the rear, reached by a reeking open passageway. But the exhausted young woman who answered my knock I knew was Haslam's daughter by the way her father's features in becoming hers, managed despite those odds to evoke her mother's beauty.

"Yes?" she said, and I might have been back at Haslam's Old Bethlem door twenty years ago, trying to talk my way past his wife (with this very woman a little girl clutching her skirts). Except this time from behind my gatekeeper there wafted on a warm draft out of ammoniac darkness a demented keening.

"I must give John Haslam this," I said. Not knowing what else to do, I held up the envelope. "Is he here?"

From inside, a querulous moan, overlaid by an infant's wail. In the girl's posture, tremendous weariness. But when she saw the name on the envelope her eyes brightened. "Would you be Margaret, then—?"

Amazed she'd know, or remember, I nodded. "How do you—"

Close by, a male voice said, "Henrietta, who is it?"

The eyes held mine a meaning moment before she stepped back into the gloom, her place taken by John Haslam, slighter than I remembered him, certainly leaner, with no hair on top, the face less masklike, more sunk on the skull but handsomer somehow, perhaps more defined, or only less baffled about the eyes. "Mrs. Matthews," he said, with remarkable emotion. "That was my daughter, Henrietta— Thank Christ you got my letter. Come in, come in—"

As soon as the door closed behind me, we were plunged in darkness. Guiding me four or five steps into a cramped office where a six-to-a-penny candle guttered, he sat me down on a wood chair jammed at an angle to a small writing table and took another. We sat knee-to-knee, so close that were it not for the general fetid ambience and a taste in the air of hot tallow, I think I would have smelled him. Judging from the food stains on his shirt and his ragged dirty cuffs, he no longer much concerned himself with the cleanliness of his linen.

I told him I was sorry to hear about his wife.

As he nodded, his eyes went to the envelope in my hand. "That's not my letter—"

I told him I'd received no letter from him, and what this one was. Heart pounding, I asked him what his had said.

"Now that you're here," he answered, plucking the one I brought and dropping it on the table, "it don't matter."

"Assure me, Mr. Haslam, my husband will see that money."

A low groan from the other room. An old man's, I think. To judge from other sounds, apparently from the same room, his daughter was pacing with a fretful infant.

"I can't do that, Mrs. Matthews, because he won't. But Mr. Fox will, and that's good, because he's the one paid to look after him."

"By whom? The Government, Bethlem, and what friends?"

He shook his head. "A stipulation of your husband's sponsor has been anonymity."

"Mr. Poynder said it's my husband's family."

"Mr. Poynder doesn't know. The arrangements were initiated by Mr. Crowther."

"With your support."

"I only pursued what he begun."

"Is it Crowther, then?"

"Crowther died penniless. He drank his wages."

"Who, then? The Quaker David Williams? He was early my husband's devoted champion—"

At the mention of Williams' name, Haslam looked away. Turning back with a sigh, he said, "Yes, Williams would seem an excellent candidate, as one who owed your husband a great deal. Unfortunately, he departed this world for a better before the opportunity presented itself."

From the next room, muttering laughter, followed by a growl of curses.

I was looking at Jamie's envelope on Haslam's table. "Mr. Haslam, my husband did receive my Jamaica letters—?"

He looked at me. "He received some. Whether Jamaica ones, I can't say—"

"But Mr. Poynder knew—" I stopped.

"Yes. It would seem your letters are how he did." Saying this, he drew from a shelf a bulging packet, which he placed between us. "Your husband's to you. I assumed Alavoine would be reading them, I had no idea he was keeping them. That Poynder was keeping yours I discovered too late. Now nothing can be done, I'm afraid. I have no more power over him. As the one daily about the premises and world expert on the place, my responsibility was to know what my secretary did, but I was too busy with words, and when it comes to words, even the right ones, it seems, can be a blinkered response."

"Or none at all. Mr. Haslam— Have you changed?"

He laughed. "Mrs. Matthews, does this look to you like the residence of a man who'd sooner drown than swim dog-paddle?"

"Let me take my husband his cheques."

"If you'll allow me the honour to accompany you—"

"Mr. Poynder says you've never been."

"Mr. Poynder is a fountain-head of misinformation. I'm active on the London House board. I'm there all the time. Sometimes I take the whole family. My daughter's a good friend to your husband—"

"I prefer to go alone."

"Then you must find yourself a coachman who knows the way."

"That—" I stood up—"sounds more like the bully I remember."

He sighed. "Mrs. Matthews, you've come at an odd time. Please—"

Groans again, louder this time.

"Odd, yes— Mr. Haslam, what are those sounds?"

He was scanning my appearance. "Tomorrow," he said, "I want you looking smart as a carrot."

Now I laughed. "Are you sure you're the one—"

"Fix your hair and wear the best thing you own. Where are you staying?"

"Is my husband well?"

"Well and cared for, that's not it."

"*It?*"

Another groan.

"Mr. Haslam, do you keep patients here?"

"Am I running a house for lunatics, you're asking me? Yes, with this difference from the others: My lunatic stays free."

Suddenly I had no strength for the old struggle. I reached for my husband's letters.

He placed a hand on my arm. "Only my father, Mrs. Matthews. Another I owe a debt to. He always told me, 'Rise, boy! Rise!' but it was never enough— and d'you know what? He was right. A man throws off the shackles of rank and authority and learns to think for himself. This raises him up, and lo and behold the world sees him raised up, which raises him still higher. But it turns out that rise is only the perfection of his humiliation, when he realizes the folk he now and then moves among have never stopped, and never will stop, assuming he has a servant's heart—" He lifted his hand from my arm. "Mrs. Matthews, where are you staying?"

Promptly at one o'clock the next day a carriage pulled up beneath my hotel window. Not at all ready, I watched it in the hope it wasn't Haslam. But he it was who climbed out and stood a moment looking round. He was cleanly if old-fashionedly dressed. He glanced up, in my direction, but there must have been a reflection off the pane, for I don't think he saw me before he strode inside.

When the maid knocked, I was not half dressed. I'd stayed up reading my husband's letters, then couldn't sleep for the commotion of love, horror, and dread they threw me in, then overslept. When at last I came downstairs in my riding-habit, Haslam, who was standing in the centre of the lobby facing the street, wheeled round and boomed, "Can you do no better than that?" at which Mrs. Doherty (whose establishment it was), the young couple she was in conversation with at the desk, and a traveller seated on a divan at the window reading a newspaper all looked at me. As I continued my descent, a foolish grin splitting my burning face as if nothing could be more amusing than this gentleman's teasing, he added, just as loud, "I mean it. Have you nothing finer?"

Reaching him, I told him in a low, furious voice that the only thing finer I owned was a ball gown and did he expect me to wear that? (When Mr. Lewis discovered all the English ever do in Jamaica no matter how hot it gets is eat and dance, he made a gift of one for me in blue silk, for when he needed a woman on his arm.)

"Yes," Haslam said, looking at his watch. "I do. Go put it on."

I stared at him. Had the double catastrophe of disgrace and ruin cracked him another way?

"Quickly!" he cried. "We go nowhere until you change."

Back in my room, Betty fastened me into my silk gown and helped make something of my hair. When I came down again, Haslam, this time the only one in the lobby, instead of showing himself pleased by my efforts (as I should never have expected), muttered, "What took you so long?" before hurrying me out the door with a shout to the coachman: "Reading Lane, Hackney!" We practically galloped off.

Now I demanded to know what this was all about, but only handing me an envelope containing Jamie's cheques for Mr. Fox, he spent most of the ride talking about his daughter, Henrietta. Two years before, she'd eloped with a brute named Felpice, living with him in Manchester a year before he sauntered drunk into a canal. Widowed penniless, she worked as a gallery maid in a private Manchester madhouse until, her condition grown unmistakable, she returned home at last, to give birth to a healthy girl, delivered by Haslam himself.

To hear him tell the story, things could not have turned out better. His dream was his daughter would one day ascend to Matron of Bethlem. In other words, the unhappy girl, her dash for freedom ending where it started, except with a fatherless infant to rear and a senile relative to nurse, now bore the burden of her parent's devastated ambition. But when I implied as much by asking wasn't Matron of Bethlem a dreary fate to wish on your own child, Haslam assured me Henrietta wished it too, and he only wanted her happy doing what she had the will and talent to do. He added that taking her back, and holding her to his bosom, was the best thing he ever did in his life. Just now their circumstances were hard, but there was a new life in the house, and new love, which gave them strength, and that was enough.

This causing me to remember he also had a son, I inquired after him. Quietly Haslam spoke the terrible words, "Lost at sea." It had happened the previous winter and by the emotion in his face remained a crushing loss. Before I knew what I did I touched his hand and told him I too had lost my son. At this news he couldn't speak, but only directed at me a sorrowing gaze, then looked away, biting his lip. The rest of the trip we passed in silence.

We were now in open country. Cattle grazed in the fields, and once we stopped for a river of sheep to flow round us. We must have travelled a good three miles. When a low paling swept in close on the right, our pace slowed un-til, by a massive dusty willow, we came to a halt before the front gate of a hand-some three-story brick house set in a good acre of lawn and garden. The air out here was clean and fresh, and altogether the establishment had the open airy look of a country house with its windows flung open on a Sunday morning. And festive too, for patriotic streamers flapped on wires strung from the willow-twig arch over the lawn-gate all the way to the front door. These, how-ever, for some reason Haslam cursed our entire march up the flagstone walk. My own attention was on something else: an excited hubbub of sound that from inside the carriage had sounded like a convocation of herring gulls on a distant pond. But climbing down, I realized it was human: the excited timbre of a garden party in back of this very house.

Haslam rang the bell. As we waited, he directed scowls at the streamers.

"What is it?" I said.

He shook his head.

The door was opened by a shock-haired, well-tanned little gentleman who when Haslam greeted him with *Fine day, Mr. Garwood,* replied haughtily, "You think I don't know that, as one who enjoys complete direction and regulation of the sun?"

"One day," Haslam replied, "we must get to the bottom of that."

With a look indicating such investigation could prove dangerous, Mr. Gar-wood asked me, "Are you the Queen?"

"The Queen's recently died, sir," Haslam said, "as you well know."

"Yes I do," Mr. Garwood shot back, still staring at me, "but she lives on in my heart. Did you know I greet all royal personages in my capacity as pillar of fire? But I need to be sure who they are. Would you, in that case, be the sadly missed Princess Caroline?"

"Mr. Garwood," Haslam interrupted him, "whose idea was the streamers?"

The little man's attention returned to Haslam. "Mr. Fox's, I believe, sir." Now he grew confidential. "I wonder, sir, if you've noticed, as they flap away, they snap and tap and whap away, but by God—" twisting his hands—*"is there a reason?"* He moved closer. "You need only say the word, sir. Nothing's sim-pler for a pillar of fire—"

"Than what?" Haslam wanted to know. "Ignition? And if Fox should need them for another occasion—?"

"You mean only not this one?"

"Exactly. Where is he?"

"In back. I'm loath to take you through indoors only to burn down the house—"

"You came to us just now from indoors," Haslam reminded him.

"What, *this?*" Mr. Garwood replied, looking down at himself. "This was nothing. A mad dash—"

Haslam was glancing to the side. "We'll go round—" he murmured.

"Keep to the path!" Mr. Garwood cried as we left him. "Watch those rose thorns don't thrash, slash, and gash you!"

The south wall was indeed roses to the eaves. The voices grew steadily louder until the sights and sounds of a sizable gathering of lunatics and their families and friends burst upon us, with everybody so finely dressed and chattering away so animatedly it was difficult to distinguish which were truly mad. It was like a royal garden party, with numbers of poets and painters in attendance, and every host and guest charmingly insane. White wicker lawn-chairs stood in casual arrangements. Tables were set about containing bouquets and punch bowls and plates piled with delicacies. It was the cheerfullest, sunniest get-together I ever saw, excepting only a Negro John-Canoe Day that Mr. Lewis once took me to in Black River, Jamaica. At Fox's a string quartet was poking around in their instrument cases with the pasty-faced, dishevelled look universal with musicians who find themselves abroad in daylight.

I was scanning for Jamie. "Where's my husband?" I called to Haslam, but he was too busy storming ahead with bellows of "Fox!"

Suddenly a snow-haired, flush-faced gentleman wheeled from a confab with a Methodist-looking family, the parents gazing in alarm at their daughter as she spoke with mad force yet was so emaciated she looked ready to clatter to the grass in a heap of bones. "Why, John!" the snow-haired man cried, riveting me with a quick-study glance. "How delightful—"

"Shears and a ladder, Fox!" Haslam barked. "All streamers down forthwith. It was made perfectly clear: *No bloody show!*"

Fox's surprising response to this outburst was to indicate with one arm the blue sky and the sunny gathering, while the other he folded across his belly in a dramatic bow—which caused the frail girl to emit shrill peals of laughter but Haslam to veer off, ferociously annoyed.

"Where's Rankin?" he shouted over his shoulder, heading toward double doors standing open at the back of the house. Like a pet on a rope, I followed but soon fell behind, slowing to a halt in a large parlour with the sun warm on my back.

"Rankin!" Haslam continued roaring from deeper inside the house. At one point he must have descended to the cellar, for several *Rankins* boomed beneath my feet.

I had just turned to go back outside, thinking I had missed Jamie in the crowd, when a familiar voice called from an upper floor, "John! He's up here! Hanging one of my engravings!"

"Jamie!" I cried, but as in a dream it came out a piteous mew. I gathered my skirts and raced to a central hall, where Haslam stood gazing upward. *"Tell him to get the deuce down here now!"* he bellowed. I couldn't see at whom or what. The space was a flood of light. At last, balusters emerged from the glare of a

sky-light, bordering galleries on the first and second floors, yet nothing could be seen to break the line of them until a head poked out over the upper one, and whose was it but my dear beloved husband's and who was he looking straight at but me?

A ROYAL VISIT

"Mags!" Jamie cried. "You're back, at last! Where's Jim? Wait there!"

I glanced at Haslam, who was grimacing at the second floor. *"Rankin!"* he shouted. *"Get the bloody hell down here, now!"*

From the sound of it, Jamie was taking the stairs two at a time. *"Please don't fall,"* I whispered.

"He could," Haslam said, still looking up. "Sometimes does. *Rankin, goddammit!"*

Now an ancient head showed itself over the top balustrade. "Guv'nor?"

Jamie descended the last flight carrying under his arm an enormous portfolio in mustard-coloured pasteboard, which, the felt slippers he wore causing him to slide on the polish of the second stair, caught on the banister, flipping from his grasp and skidding across the floor, its contents fanning over the polished surface, some piling in a drift against Haslam's leg—and then Jamie was in my arms.

How insubstantial he felt, how unfleshed.

"Where's Jim?" he asked again, looking worried, when we separated.

I drew a deep breath, but Mr. Rankin, a tall, taciturn old fellow with a touch, I would say, of Negro blood in him, was already with us, and Jamie turned to introduce him, even as Haslam stepped up to order Rankin away to fetch shears and a foot-stool. For a moment we all three stood and watched him laboriously go, until Haslam, thinking better of it, hurried after to move him along. Jamie then stooped to begin gathering up his drawings, every one of which, I noticed as I helped him, was architectural: omni imperias asylums and mad palaces. Once he'd tucked all back safe into the portfolio, he drew me into the sunshine of the parlour. There we sat on a brown canvas sofa in a bower of ferns, squeezing hands and drinking each other in.

How like Jim he was! How amazing to see the father again after seven years of seeing him only in the son: the intelligence in the eyes, the stubborn line of the mouth—yet so very old, his hair now grown out pure white. It was like seeing Jim, half a century later. When I tried to say this another way, I sobbed.

"Don't cry, Mags. Crowther was right. The country air's done me good. That ulcerous growth in my back has remitted to nothing. Next to nothing. We all must go sometime. Fox and I talk every day. I help Mrs. Fox with the domestic arrangements, see to the books, make out the bills, compose the correspondence, and letter everything. I must show you the vegetable garden, which last winter I entirely rethought. Greenhouse cabbages and turnips is next. I've reduced our butter consumption by half: too bile-conducing. Also, knowing as I do each of the fourteen other patients and their histories—think of it! only fifteen of us!—Fox invites me along when he shows visitors through. I'm his best advertisement for how we do things here. With a private madhouse, half the work's fundraising. I do my best to place a positive, forward-thinking cast on my commentary—Say, Mags! I know! You could work here too! I can put in a word—"

"Jamie, my work is getting you out—"

This pulled him up short. His eyes went to his hands then returned to me. "This is my home, Mags. It's important work I do here. Everybody here is a citizen."

"And what am I?"

"The bride of my life and mother to my son. A woman who knows this: Outside it's the modern age, where every day the truth is buried deeper and legions of honest men and women go mad with delving. What we offer here at London House is sanctuary from the burying and the delving both." He looked about him then tipped his head closer. "Here's something else: Haslam's broke free of The Schoolmaster. Here the gang has no agents and no Air Loom inside a mile. To put it plain, I've slipped their clutches. But this could change any time—"

"Jamie— We lost Jim."

As he stared at me, more sober than stunned, only no longer talking, I recounted the unremarkable, horrific sequence from first scratch to last breath.

He was quiet a moment before he said, "So they made their move—"

"Not the gang, Jamie—"

He nodded. "From what you've just told me, Mags, Jim died not three weeks after I first came here. You don't escape without consequences. The matter is simple: Jim died so I might live. Until now, even I wouldn't have thought they could be so heartless, but it happens I know their energy has lately been going into the study and spread of infectious diseases—"

Someone was standing so close he was pressing against us.

"William—" Jamie said, not needing to look to know it was Mr. Garwood, "my wife, Margaret."

The sun coming through the doors made a blazing nimbus of Mr. Garwood's hair. "The King's here," he said. "I greeted him in my capacity as pillar of fire, but he showed no interest." He turned to me. "Margaret, what's happened? You look devastated."

"She is," Jamie said. "William, pray inform Mr. Fox the King's arrived."

As we watched Mr. Garwood pass out the doors to the garden, Jamie said, "Jim was the hero of my dreams, Mags, but that don't mean I can't understand it's a thousand times worse for you. I'm sorry. I never in my worst nightmares dreamed they'd go this far."

"Jamie, our son died of an infection."

Grimly knowing, he shook his head. "There are infections, Mags, and infections." He was reaching for his portfolio. "He wants to see these."

"Not the King, Jamie. Nobody's laid eyes on the King in seven years. Even I know that, and I've been out of the country that long."

"Well, it looks like eyes are to be laid on him today," he replied, stretching one arm long to achieve a grip on the portfolio and taking my hand with his free one. "Come on!"

Mr. Garwood having left the front door standing wide open, it framed an interesting scene. Immediately to the left, just outside the entrance, old Rankin stood at full attention on a foot-stool, gripping a pair of shears, apparently for snipping the streamer wire (which he hadn't yet done). Farther down the walk a short distance, on the other side, John Haslam stood with his hands clasped behind his back. At the foot of the walk, making his way slowly through the gate, followed by four men who even at that distance had the look of doctors, the group of them visible against the shining black, gold-trimmed, eight-horse carriage they all must have just climbed out of, was a tall old gentleman leaning on a walking stick. With his long white hair and flowing beard, he might have been King Lear fresh off the heath, except he was outfitted in fine black leather riding boots and a glorious military-style outfit of midnight blue and gold turned up with scarlet, like a Hussar.

"Come," Jamie whispered. "We'll sneak up close as we can before he sees us. Once he does, protocol says we can only stand still or back away."

By the time we took up places as far down the walk as we dared, the King had reached Haslam, who was on the other side of the walk from us, closer to the gate. Though stooped, his Majesty was taller than Haslam and stood very close to him, peering near-sightedly into his face. The doctors had halted several paces behind. Like Haslam's, their hands were clasped behind their backs. "Don't we know you, sir?" the King demanded of Haslam in a loud voice.

"John Haslam, your Majesty. Your Majesty may remember I was for some years apothecary to Bethlem Hospital. I now—"

"What? Bethlem? What? *What?*" Abruptly the King turned and walked back to his doctors. Haslam's eyes followed him. "He says he's apothecary to Bethlem."

One of the doctors coughed into his hand and said, "Was, your Majesty. That's John Haslam."

"He told me who he is!" the King shouted, and then looked about him in the silence, seeming quite lost until, spotting Haslam, he headed back to him. "Was it not on your watch, sir, Bethlem at Moorfields grew a stinking Hell-pit?"

"We all did our best, your Majesty, in conditions a consequence of government neglect."

"What? What? *What?*" The King returned to the doctors. "He says the problem at Moorfields was government neglect."

This information caused the superior sniffs and lowered lids of fastidious sufferance. Briefly, the King studied these responses before he returned to Haslam with another question. "Ever much call at Moorfields, sir, for strait-waistcoats?"

"No, your Majesty. I never believed in them."

"What?—*what?*" the King cried. "What, sir, if I told you a strait-waistcoat was the best friend I ever had?"

"Then I would say his Majesty has been in the care of Mr. Willis."

Here one of the doctors seemed to receive a sharp stab in the arse.

The King too felt the prick. "How now, sir!" he exclaimed with an eye-popping glare. "Is this insolence?"

"I don't intend it as such, your Majesty."

"You don't intend it as such," the King replied sarcastically, eyeing Haslam darkly a few moments before seeming to forgive, or forget, and waxing conversational once more. "So what's your opinion, sir, of New Bethlem?"

"An ostentatious blazon of national degradation, your Majesty. More of the same as the old, only by policy and more out of sight."

"He says New Bethlem's a blazon of national degradation!" the King shouted over his shoulder to the doctors. "He says it's more of the same, only more out of sight!" To Haslam he said, "Is this, sir, how you brought universal ruin on yourself? By saying things nobody wants to hear?"

"It was less anything I said, your Majesty, than the need of a parliamentary committee to discover someone to blame."

"Scape-goated, what?"

"In a word, your Majesty."

"And not just the one you say over and over to yourself, so you can sleep at night?"

"As to my conscience, your Majesty, there was one patient I might have done more for."

The King looked grimly at this. "Not Peg Nicholson, I hope. It was my particular instruction she be well cared for."

At the mention of Peg Nicholson, Haslam's expression went a little grim too. "No, not her, your Majesty. Though she'd thrive better at the new place if your Majesty paid her the visit she's been expecting now over thirty years."

"Good God! It's high time we visited—" And over his shoulder the King shouted, "Next week, gentleman, New Bethlem! A lunatic has too long awaited an audience with her beloved sovereign!" Returning to Haslam he said in a confidential voice, "And Hadfield—? There was a low creature, sir. He tried to shoot me, you know."

"An evil business, your Majesty. The man is very mad. But likely to outlive us all."

"At least he'll have that," the King replied before adding, with satisfaction, "and then the flames. And yourself, sir? I suppose they packed you off with a fat pension."

"No, your Majesty, with nothing."

"You must be very bitter, sir."

"Not bitter, your Majesty. But it would have been only fair, when—"

"Fair," the King said, cutting him off. He returned to his doctors. "He says a pension would have been only fair."

The doctors' response to this assertion was noncommittal. "Winthrup!" the King cried at the youngest. "What d'you think? No pension for Haslam. Fair? Not fair? What? What?"

Winthrup cleared his throat. "I think, your Majesty, the Committee made the decision it did based on the evidence before it."

"That passes for thinking with you, does it, Winthrup? One of you, an opinion! Has this man received justice or has he not?"

But no doctor being willing to venture out on that particular ice, the King swung away in annoyance from them all. Ignoring Haslam, he continued down the walk, followed by the doctors. Fox had by this time taken up a proprietary stance in his doorway, close by Rankin, still at attention on his stool. But it was us next on the royal route, and when the King came even with Jamie, than whom he stood more than a head taller, he leaned down and peered at him very close. "And who are you, sir?"

"James Tilly Matthews, your Majesty."

"Look at this!" the King called round to the doctors. "The very fellow I'm here to see!" But when he turned back, it was me he peered at. "And who's this?"

"My wife, Margaret, your Majesty."

"Is it, now?" and the great florid face swept in so close to mine that to this day I don't know whether to say it was the noblest or most grotesque I ever saw. I do know the teeth were in good repair, the breath passable, the eyes protuberant in the Hanover way, the nose large, the lips fleshy, and the forehead somewhat receded. But the royal visage was too close, too famous, too insistent with its own abrupt and hectoring energy, for any judgment to be renderable then or now by this cowering witness to it. "You're a dear little one," the King was saying, "aren't you? Do you stay here at Mr. Fox's to look after your husband?"

"No, your Majesty. I've just come from Jamaica."

"Jamaica!" he cried in astonishment. "Truly? So what's your view? Do we free our slaves or not?"

"I think it must be done, your Majesty."

"What? What? *Must?* What?—what?"

"Nothing could be more barbaric," I said in a shaking voice, "than for human beings to buy and sell one another."

"Not buy and sell, madam," the King reminded me gravely. "The *trade* is no longer permitted."

"To own, then."

"Ah, yes, yes, yes." He turned away looking disappointed and walked back to his doctors. "She says people should not own one another." Returning to me, he confided in a lowered voice, "Let me tell you, my dear, why I hate the abolitionists. First, they're in league with the French, and look what happened there. Second, they spout the vulgarest rhetoric you ever heard outside a military jakes. Third, they once counted among their allies not only my former Prime Minister, Mr. Pitt, a blade-nosed milksop and (though I loved him once) the closest thing to a weasel on two legs, but also the Leader of the Opposition, Mr. Fox, who once declared the storming of the Bastille by far the best and greatest thing that ever happened in the history of the world and would have sent me to the guillotine if we had one. Like attracts like, and those two together with the abolitionists made the traitor John Wilkes, who would have enjoyed nothing better than to see me skewered on a stake and pecked at by vultures, appear a demigod. Such men are low creatures when you compare our Prime Minister today or his father my good friend of beloved memory Lord Liverpool, both staunch (by the way) against abolition." When I replied nothing to this—what could I?—he continued to gaze at me with an inclination of his head, like a man mentally reviewing what he's just said, before at last returning his attention to Jamie.

"So, sir, should Bethlem have given Mr. Haslam a pension or not?"

"Not, your Majesty," Jamie replied shortly. "In those days everything he touched he harmed, and he never deserved reward for a period of his life when he was too thoroughly a puppet of the gang."

"Gang?—gang?" the King cried. "What?—what gang? What?"

Which was Jamie's cue to launch into a detailed description of the Air Loom.

At first his Majesty listened intently. But when Jamie attempted to proceed from an account of the engine itself to a history of its destructive effects upon the nation, with particular emphasis on the corn shortages that followed the miserable summer of '94 and the insurrection that spread like wildfire through the Navy in '96 and seven, his Majesty, whose mind was of a practical bent—and besides, to him all this was old news—came back to the engine, saying, "I always wondered, Mr. Matthews, how the operation at a distance of magnets could fail to keep us all daily in mind of the narrowness of our assumptions concerning the true nature of the physical universe."

Jamie blinked at this.

"Mr. Priestley, Mr. Beddoes, Mr. Davy, and M. Lavoisier, with their ingenious work on these new invisible elements they call gases, have laid you staunch foundations," the King continued. "And Herr Mesmer—lately, as you must know, gone to his rest—was admirably concerned to discover in the etherial fluid a therapeutic principle that might improve people's physical and psychical health. Since then, as you'll also know, M. Puységur and his colleagues have been doing scouting work on somnambulism, hypnosis, clairvoyance, etc. But tell me. Did you never think of designing a counter-instrument? Instead of building on Mesmeric principles (which nobody's ever remotely understood), why don't you invert those of this modern Air Loom device—which though you say it's been commandeered by villains, you obviously enjoy a wonderful understanding of—and so fight its baleful influence that way, by doubling its own force against deducible aspects of its own vincibility?"

By this date, being entirely out of public view, the King was a figure as beloved as his too-visible son the Prince Regent was hated, which isn't to say our old monarch wasn't widely assumed to have degenerated to a bloated gibbering idiot. Perhaps he had his bad days, but I must say I never heard anybody speak with more genius to Jamie about the Air Loom. You could see the gratitude in my husband's eyes for his Majesty's immediate grasp, for example, of the distinction between the physical and psychical effects of the machine, while appreciating how the two can never be wholly distinguished. "Look at me," the King candidly invited him at one point in a conversation that must have lasted half an hour. "To what extent are these dreadful torments of mind I sometimes suffer the effect of an ailment as yet undiscovered by medical science? Disease unknown, cure unknown!"

This conversation continued so long I feared Mr. Rankin's knees would give out and he'd fall and break his crown on the flagstones. But suddenly the King exclaimed, "Now I will let you go!" and broke from Jamie to continue his progress up the walk.

When I stole a glance at Jamie, I was amazed to see an expression unbefitting a man who'd just enjoyed a half-hour of undivided attention from his Royal Majesty.

"He never asked to see my architectural plans," he complained in a whisper.

I was trying to think of something to say that was not *Why should he?* when the King, puffing out his chest, shouted at Rankin, "Cut'em down, sir? Go ahead! But why stop with flags in my honour? As long as you're up there, why not slaughter me like an animal? That's right! Don't hesitate, sir! Plunge 'em in!" He meant the shears, into his breast. "Or are you no less wretched a coward than your murderous associates?"

When Mr. Rankin proved too alarmed by this royal challenge to plunge in or say anything, his Majesty, indicating the streamers, cried, "So let the damn things fly, man!" and passed on to Mr. Fox. To him, once he'd stepped close enough to see who it was, he cried, "Is this *Fox*?" and when Fox acknowledged it was, shouted, "No Antichrist of Mendacity this Fox, what?" a greeting an astonished Fox, who'd not been standing close enough to hear what the King confided to me concerning his political namesake, could be seen struggling through the rest of his interview to recover from.

NO KINGS

At last the King disappeared inside the house, and we could all breathe again. Old Rankin climbed down off his stool and sat slumped against it. The next time I looked over he was stretched out flat on the grass like a dead man. I don't think he'll soon forget his audience with the King. Jamie picked up his portfolio, which had been leaning the whole time against the back of his leg, and we walked over to the willow tree, where Haslam was sitting on a bench, mopping at his brow.

"I'm sorry I had no choice but to tell his Majesty the truth about your Bethlem days, John," Jamie said with a look of apology.

"And I'm sorry, James," Haslam replied as he shifted over to make room for us, "it was you he asked."

I was sitting down between them when it occurred to me to ask Jamie who was paying for his keep here.

"Bethlem, the government, and John, equally between them," he answered, as readily as he'd assured the King that Haslam deserved no pension. "It's how John has begged, and received, my unqualified forgiveness."

When I looked to Haslam, he said, with a smile, "A pension, James, would have made the expense of you easier."

"But rewarded with a pension," Jamie replied, "The Schoolmaster might show, to assure me he owed me nothing."

"No risk of that now. Here's your error to avoid: believing the less I can afford it, the more good it's doing me."

Jamie laughed. "But I do think something like that!"

"I know. You're still deluded."

At this, Jamie crowed, "Used to be, John! Used to be! And you too! Yet how much either of us even then if you had it in you to believe my Liverpool information?"

"I fought hard not to, James—" Haslam smilingly reminded him. "With everything I had."

"No," Jamie replied. "You had more."

When we first sat down, Winthrup, the junior doctor, had left the house and walked out to the royal carriage, not deigning to notice us. Now an equerry in a handsome uniform, blue with gold braiding, approached from that direction. Under his arm he carried a folder bound in wine-coloured leather. "His Majesty," he announced, with a low bow to Jamie, "wishes to compare designs with Mr. Matthews, privately, inside."

"Not forgot!" Jamie cried, leaping up.

"The King has architectural talent," Haslam explained as we watched Jamie struggle to keep a grip on his portfolio while following the equerry toward the house. "Lately he's been working on plans for a Corinthian temple in Kew Gardens. He's here for inspiration from your husband's designs."

"Mr. Haslam," I said. "Thank you for taking care of my husband."

"Mrs. Matthews, he deserves nothing less from me."

No reply being encouraged by this, we sat for several minutes in silence. For a time after news of the King's arrival had reached the party on the back lawn, their chatter was muted. But as soon as he entered the house, their noise resumed and seemed to grow. Now the musicians were tuning their instruments. I pictured Jamie and his Majesty in the parlour, studying each other's plans. I hoped the sun was still shining bright enough inside to enable his Majesty, despite his myopia, to relish every detail of Jamie's work.

From the look on his face, Haslam was chafing from the King's peremptory treatment of him. When at last he spoke, it was in a self-justifying vein. "Two principles I always followed, Mrs. Matthews, when dealing with lunatics: First, never deceive them. Second, always show yourself a superior person."

"And if you aren't?"

"Then make it your duty to appear so."

"And that's not deception?"

"No," he replied irritably. "It's self-management. *Decus et tutamen.* Dignity and defence. Any doctor who lays aside dignity and defence will find himself despised and nothing achieved."

"If you ask me, the dignity of doctors consists in looking grave and saying nothing, to mask their own ignorance. I suggest your own method's closer to candour, as the King seemed to recognize."

Frowning at this, Haslam lapsed into gloomy silence. When at last he spoke he said, "Candour's a weapon too, and has a double edge. I became a casualty at Bethlem of my own power, and all the more for feeling I had so little."

"But not so abused as your patients."

He sighed, though as much with sorrow, I would say, as impatience. "Two terrible truths of human nature, Mrs. Matthews: One, victims love their oppressors, just a little. Two, oppressors hate their victims a little more with each injury they do them."

"Why are you telling me these horrid things?"

"Because Bethlem taught me them, and for that reason they seem necessary to any apology I could make for failing your husband so long."

"You don't need to recite depraved conundrums to do that. You were more concerned for your own career and reputation than the welfare of hundreds of wretched sufferers dependent on your care. That's all. That's enough. You could have acted; you didn't."

"The situation was impossible. It broke me. You should know that in a moment of rage I assaulted your husband."

"Does that surprise me? Was his entire Bethlem tenure not one prolonged assault?"

"After that I did act."

"Sporadically and at last. For him, at least."

"I would say I should have acted sooner but don't know how I could have, as the man I was then. All I know is what I know now: a weight on me that feels very like remorse. I wish I didn't feel it, but I do, every hour of the day and every waking hour of the night."

"Because your brain knows if you don't."

"Brains are prone to certain kinds of error. One is assuming they were capable then of what they are only now."

"So are people prone to certain kinds of error."

"And conversations to grow senseless."

For several minutes there was only birdsong, the nickering of the King's horses, the flapping streamers, the rising commotion from behind the house.

To bring us back to something we might agree on, I said, "Mr. Haslam, you can't afford to keep my husband in this place, and I want him with me. Perhaps we could—"

"What could we do? Work together to get him out? Does he want out? Did you ask him?"

"I'm only thinking, once it's sunk in that I'm—"

"Mrs. Matthews, your husband has never not loved you, but he does understand that if there's any place he might continue untormented by the gang, it's here. The upset of change from a place he's continued such a long time so relatively steady and well, in a society where he can serve a useful function, could very well exacerbate his condition. As I'm sure you can see, his general health is not the best, but here, I would say, it's the best it can be. He's a social creature, your husband—"

"So he should stay here so the gang keeps away? Is this the counsel of a mad-doctor who always railed against private madhouses and considered all delusions the effects of diseased brain tissue?"

"Have we been talking about delusions?"

"The gang is one."

He smiled. "Are you sure?"

Now Fox stepped out his front door, but seeing Rankin had failed to remove the foot-stool, he went back inside. "Mrs. Matthews," Haslam said, "I only mean, if you love him—"

"Mr. Haslam, I think the question is, do you?"

But Fox had already come out again and was walking in our direction, and this circumstance Haslam took advantage of not to answer me, though he had plenty of time. He now introduced me to Fox and told a story about him. It seems Fox once took a furious, suicidal maniac to the third floor of this house to calm him with the view. On the way back down, the lunatic pushed him against the balustrade crying, *Now I'll cast you down and leap after!*

Bah! Fox calmly replied. *Any child could do that. Come downstairs with me, and I'll throw you back up here.*

You cannot . . . the lunatic replied irresolutely, following Fox down the stairs.

"Is that not how it happened, Charles?" Haslam now asked.

"Something like that, John," Fox replied, smiling, "something like that—" Turning to me, he said, "I hope, Mrs. Matthews, you won't seek to whisk your husband away from us too soon. He's our guiding light."

"He doesn't want to leave," I admitted.

"No?" Mr. Fox looked pleased at this. Then thinking perhaps of my feelings, with an anxious glance at Haslam, he added more soberly, "He's been happy with us, I assure you."

I now passed Fox the envelope containing Jamie's cheques. After he ascertained what it was, he bowed and tucked it into his coat.

Meanwhile I watched Mr. Rankin, moving slow as a man underwater, emerge from the house and set about picking up the foot-stool.

"I do apologize about the streamers, John," Fox said, watching Rankin in the idle way people have of looking to the object of another's gaze. "Still," and he gave a mischievous great yawn, "his Majesty seemed to like them."

Haslam's response was a grunt.

When Fox turned back to us, he wore a worried expression. "John, why the devil would his Majesty say I'm not an Antichrist of Mendacity?"

"Perhaps he could tell."

"But why should it ever occur to him I could be?"

I might have explained, but Fox had turned away again, to watch Mr. Rankin re-enter the house carrying the foot-stool. "The doctors tell me his Majesty has little stamina," he said, still looking toward the house. "We can't assume he'll stay many minutes in the garden—"

And so we made our way back there, and exactly as we came round the corner his Majesty appeared from inside and the orchestra struck up "God Save the King."

At first his Majesty looked about him squinting and unsteady, but the strains of the anthem and the lifted voices of so fine a gathering soon erected him to full magnificence, and you knew as soon as the singing stopped he'd wade into the crowd and closely question each quaking individual. But not many steps from the house, he stumbled, causing all four doctors to rush forward to help him to a chair. And though, to judge from his querulous response to their solicitude, his Majesty did not appreciate the assistance, it was sitting down that he received our Three Cheers. After that, the orchestra switched to a tune they called "Who Wants a Wife?" by a Mr. Bishop, though it sounded like Mozart to me, and Jamie came breathlessly out of the house to organize everybody for a quadrille-dance, a new step so much the rage it already reached Jamaica before I left.

As people were taking their places, the woman next to me, a genteel soul, confided, "Let me tell you, my dear, I've been in Heaven, and the tunes they play there are better than this." When I asked her what sort of music they have in Heaven, she considered a moment before she replied, "Why, common sense, to be sure."

The next minute everybody was looking to their feet, everybody except the doctors, who had their patient to watch over; the Methodist couple, for whom any sort of dance floor, even a greensward, was a trap door to Hell; their daughter, who by her fidgeting clearly wanted to but whom they would not allow; and the King, who conducted the orchestra from his chair with spirited curlicues of his walking stick while shouting out encouragement to the dancers.

Such a memorable afternoon it was. What providence to find oneself in that place at that time, to dance that dance, now on Haslam's arm and now Jamie's, now on Fox's and now a madman's, now on the madman's father's and now his brother's. Few of us were much practised at quadrilles, but weren't we watching our feet and weren't our hearts in it? Weren't we being moved by the music on this summer's day under the generous eye of his Royal Majesty? Wasn't this the sort of moment life sometimes, somehow, despite everything, throws up, that remains so shining in the mind that you never forget it as long as you live? And don't such memories help keep in view how wondrous it is to be afforded any opportunity at all, even this one—and why not this one, when it's everything it is and nothing it isn't—to live and breathe on this green earth?

The King's stick faltering, the doctors closed in once more, to help him out of his chair. And so, as the orchestra struck up "Rule Britannia," which we all gave hearty voice to, his Majesty was led back into the house, calling to us over and over, "Now I will let you go! Now I will let you go!" and though it took a long time for him to be helped through and out the front door after the music ended and we stopped singing, we didn't speak or move, only closed our eyes in the light of the setting sun until we heard the slams of the doors of the royal carriage and the coachman's cry, and the horses stamp and whinny and take it all away.

And then I was telling Jamie how perfectly ridiculous it was to be sobbing on each other's shoulder this way when we'd see each other again in a few days. He agreed, wiping his eyes, and was there to help me into the carriage that soon arrived to fetch Haslam and me back to London.

Haslam and I spoke little on that trip. Whether it was because we now understood each other perfectly, having said everything that needed to be said between us, or were too exhausted by the day's events for conversation, I hardly knew at the time. But riding in silence with your sometime worst enemy is not always the excruciating uncomfortable experience you anticipate when you first awake on the morning of the day.

And then, as we were coming into town, he suddenly said, "Mrs. Matthews, this afternoon you asked me if I could love a madman—"

"No, I asked you if you love my husband."

"Either way you shall have your answer."

"When?"

"Now. I had to think about it. Yes."

And when we reached Mrs. Doherty's and he was helping me down and said, *Friday, one o'clock, Mrs. Matthews, I'll come by? No kings this time?* I was still too surprised not to answer him, "Friday, Mr. Haslam. No kings."

ACKNOWLEDGMENTS

This novel owes a great deal to the brilliant work of the late Roy Porter, without whose encouragement it would not have been written.

The best accounts of James Tilly Matthews are by Roy Porter and Mike Jay. My own primary source has been Roy Porter's edition of John Haslam's *Illustrations of Madness* (1810; London and New York 1988). Mike Jay has kindly let me see proofs of his nonfiction study of Matthews, *The Air Loom Gang* (London 2003). Among other twentieth-century sources, the richest have been Jonathan Andrews *et al., The History of Bethlem* (London 1997) on Bethlem Hospital; Erving Goffman, *Asylums* (New York 1961) on psychiatric institutions; Roy Porter, *Mind-Forg'd Manacles* (Cambridge 1987) on eighteenth-century madness; and Andrew Scull *et al., Masters of Bedlam* (Princeton 1996) on John Haslam.

As well as his *Illustrations of Madness,* works by Haslam I have used, now and then for his own words and phrases, include his *Observations on Insanity* (London 1798), *Observations on Madness and Melancholy* (London 1809), *Observations of the Physician and Apothecary of Bethlem Hospital* (London 1816), *Considerations on the Moral Management of Insane Persons* (London 1817), *A Letter to the Governors of Bethlem Hospital* (London 1818), *Sound Mind* (London 1819), and *On the Nature of Thought* (London 1835). I have also drawn, again at times verbatim, from Britain's Parliamentary Papers (1815), *Report (4) from the Committee on Madhouses in England,* House of Commons; Anon., *Sketches in Bedlam* (London 1824); John Perceval, *A Narrative of the Treatment Received by a Gentleman, During a State of Mental Derangement,* 2 vols. (London 1838, 1840); Anon., *The Mysteries of the Madhouse* (London 1847); and M.G. Lewis, *Journal of a West India Proprietor, 1815–1817* (London 1929).

The artist Rod Dickinson has constructed an Air Loom based on Matthews' engravings. It may be seen at www.theairloom.org.

For their generous assistance, I thank the staffs of the Wellcome Institute Library, Bethlem Royal Hospital Archive, British Library, Archives des Affaires Étrangères, and Public Record Office. Jonathan Andrews has been extraordinarily helpful with details pertaining to Bethlem and its staff and residents. Any omissions, errors, and conflations and broadenings of historical figures are my doing, not his. For their warmth and hospitality on my several research trips to London, I owe more than a Bethlem Archive souvenir coffee mug to my friends Doug and Judy Vickers. For her clerical support, I thank Marcie Whitecotton-Carroll. For advice on, and contributions to, the work in progress, I am grateful to Jonathan Andrews, Siobhan Blessing, Pamela Erlichman, John Glenday, Mike Jay, Terry Karten, Nicole Langlois, Anne McDermid, Mark Morris, Rosa Spricer, Bruce Stovel, and my wise and tireless editor and champion, Phyllis Bruce.